TATTOO
My Love

VANISHED BOOK TWO

Rainmaker Publishing

First published by Rainmaker Publishing 2023

Copyright © 2023 by Stacey Lynn Hafner

First edition
ISBN: 979-8-9874300-9-5
Cover Design by Lauria
Author photograph by Stacey Lynn Hafner

TATTOO

My Love

VANISHED BOOK TWO

STACEY LYNN HAFNER

To my very own Girl Squad. You all are the best cheerleaders, sounding boards, support system and playmates I could ever ask for. I can't wait to sit on a beach together when we are all thoroughly gray and delightfully old.

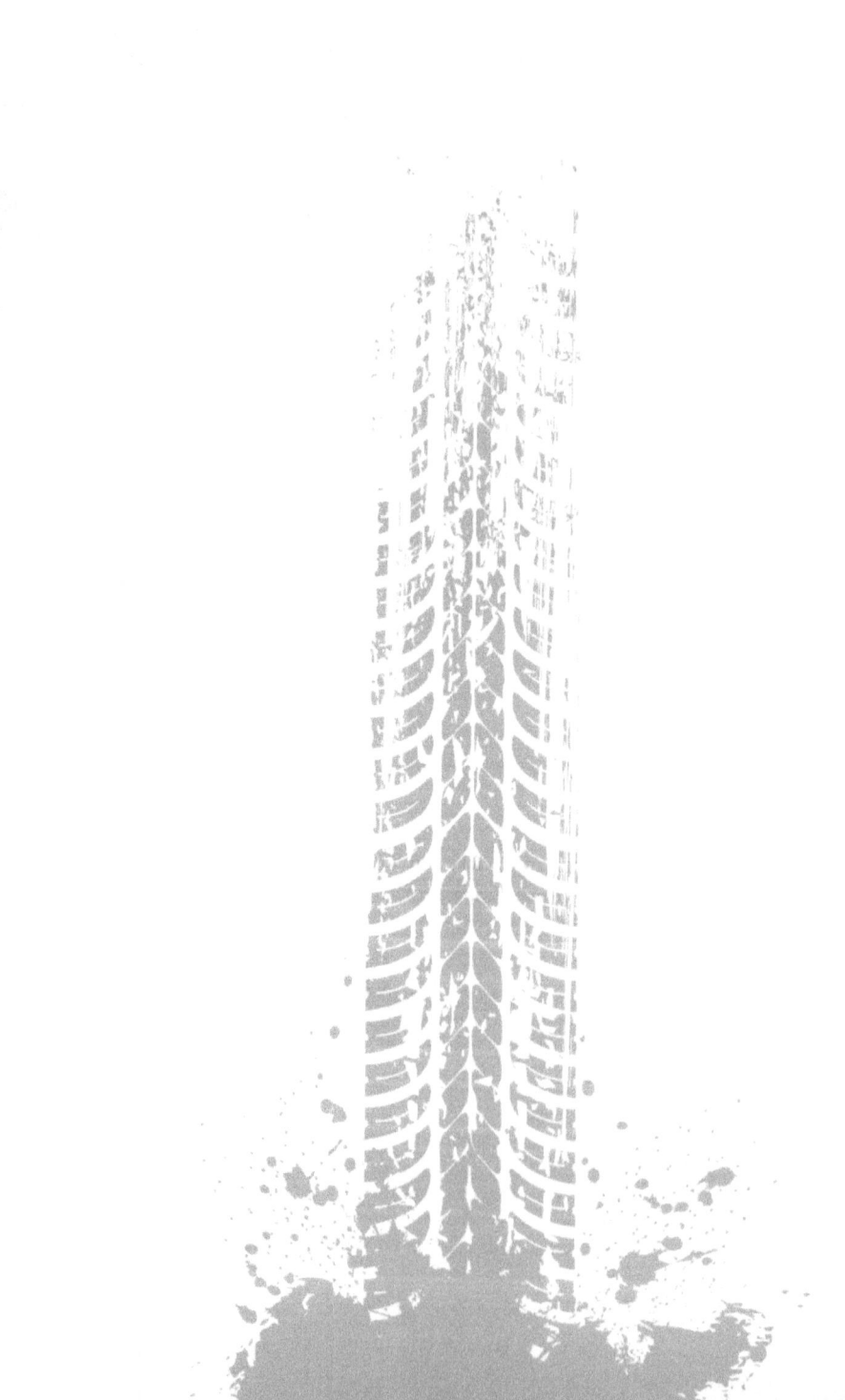

Being deeply loved by someone gives you strength, while loving someone deeply gives you courage.

—Lao Tzu

PROLOGUE

Jax

Sixteen years ago

Five, ten, eleven, twelve...sixteen.

Shit.

I finish counting the money in my pocket. It's not enough. Cliff, my current dickhead foster 'dad', is going to be pissed it's not more. Apparently, the money he gets from the state for fostering kids isn't enough. Once you hit fourteen, he expects you to contribute.

I'm fifteen, like Luke, so I've got no excuses. We've been here, placed with Cliff and his wife, for eight months now. Lori just got here last month, and she's only eleven, so she's safe for a few years yet, although I think Cliff is dangerous to her in other ways. She

1

says she'll be able to go back home soon, and I hope she's right. I don't like the way Cliff looks at her.

But Luke and I are stuck unless we get moved for some reason. He's got no folks, and after the last time my mom got busted for drugs, I doubt the court will ever let me go back there.

I tried to point out there aren't many jobs out there for orphaned fifteen-year-olds, but all that did was get me backhanded for backtalk. When he's sober, he usually only hits once to make his point. It's the days he's been drinking you've got to be careful.

Mr. Turner needed someone to restock his shelves and sweep up each night, but he only had enough work for one, so I told Luke he should take it. He also told Luke he'd pay him to do a mural on the side of his store. We're not telling Cliff about that money.

Sixteen dollars.

My stomach lurches.

I'm going to have to go see Rock for a job.

Luke will be pissed if he finds out. He hates Rock. He knows Rock is into all kinds of shady shit. But I can't go home with only sixteen bucks. I'm still sore from Cliff's last drinking binge.

Crap.

I head to Rock's usual corner and ask around until one of his guys points me in the right direction.

Rock is older, but probably not much older. You don't live long doing the shit he does, not in our neighborhood. But he's managed to build a small power base for himself. People around here know what he does, but they're either too scared or too invested to report him to the cops. No one sees Rock do anything. He's leaning against the back wall of his apartment building, half a dozen followers lingering around.

"Hey, Jacky. What's up?" he calls out when he sees me.

I shrug, my stomach uneasy. "Got any jobs you need done?"

He studies me thoughtfully. I've run 'errands' for him before. I don't ask questions, but I'm smart enough to know not to get caught.

"Where's your friend?"

Assuming he means Luke, I tell him he's working at Mr. Turner's. "Just me," I say.

He shrugs. "Not today, kid. Come by tomorrow. I got something."

I nod and walk away. I wonder if I can avoid Cliff until tomorrow.

"BRING THIS BOX TO THE ADDRESS LISTED. ABE WILL GIVE YOU AN envelope, you bring that right back to me. Got it? No extra stops."

The next day, I'm back at Rock's corner. I still need the money, after all. I'd stayed out until we were required to be home and inside, and luckily Cliff was already passed out. Avoiding Luke had been harder. But I told him I was meeting a girl after school, and he backed off.

I nod at Rock. I've got it. I still have a pit in my stomach. This is such bullshit. But I don't know what else to do.

I zip the box into my backpack and hoof it to the address Rock gave me. But then I'm stuck. No one answers my knock, and I don't hear any noise inside. *Shit.*

Now what?

I wait a couple minutes, but when I hear someone coming up the stairs, I duck out of sight. Something tells me I don't want to be seen here. Whoever it is keeps climbing, not stopping on this floor, and when I'm sure they're gone, I slip back down the stairs and try to hide in the alley across the street. I wait and watch, see if anyone else comes back. Hopefully, this Abe guy I'm supposed to give this delivery to. But no one else comes.

I wait for an hour. My feet are starting to freeze in my cheap sneakers. Rock's going to be pissed it's taking me so long. Maybe I missed him, this Abe guy? But I know that's not true; I haven't taken my eyes off the front door. I straighten, shit, of course. Maybe there's a back door.

Stupid.

I run across the street and up to Abe's apartment building, knocking again.

Still no answer.

Desperate now, I try the doorknob, my stomach lurching when it turns easily, and the door opens.

I call out, but there isn't an answer. I move slowly into the apartment, looking around.

This is all wrong. It sounds wrong, it smells wrong, it feels wrong.

Shit, what did Rock get me into?

I take two more tentative steps inside, and then I see it.

Him.

There's a man laying on the floor, staring unblinkingly at the ceiling, his arms and legs twisted at weird angles. There's so much blood. Too much blood. I don't need to get any closer to know he's dead. I stumble backward and bump into a table, knocking over a lamp that crashes to the floor.

I run.

I run all the way back to Rock's spot. For once, he's alone. I'm out of breath, my heart is beating hard. I feel like I'm going to hurl. I try to put on a tough mask and take the box out of my bag.

"Rock, that guy. He was dead. Someone killed him."

He laughs at me. "What are you talking about? Who's dead?"

"That Abe guy. When I got to the address you gave me-"

"Abe's not dead." He looks over my shoulder and yells, "Hey, Abe! Get over here."

A guy around Rock's age, I've seen him around the neighborhood a couple times, walks over. He's wearing a giant puffer jacket and has a buzz cut. "'Sup?"

"This kid says you're dead."

He smirks at me. "That so? No one told me."

I look between the two of them, my stomach sinking. Shit.

Rock stares at me until it takes everything I've got to keep from shaking. Show no fear. Not to assholes like Rock. Like Cliff.

"You still got the box?"

I hold it up, showing him.

He nods. "Open it."

Knowing I'm going to regret this, I tear into the box.

There's a bloody knife inside.

I can't help it. I turn away and puke against the side of the building.

When I stand back up, Rock is paging through a notebook. I recognize it right away. He has one of Luke's sketchbooks. I start to move forward without thinking and scream, "Why do you have that?"

Abe gets between us, so of course, I don't get anywhere close to Rock. He shoves me back roughly, and I slip in the snow, falling hard on my ass. Rock is calm. He takes the knife and wipes it off on Luke's sketchbook.

He wipes a murder victim's blood on my best friend's sketchbook.

Then he puts the knife back in the box. Turning back to Abe, he says, "You got the envelope?" Abe hands him a fat envelope. "Get lost," he tells him, and Abe walks away.

I'm still on the ground, and Rock squats next to me. "Here's the thing, Jacky. You're smart. I can see that you're smart. But that friend of yours, Luke? I can tell he doesn't like me. And I can't have that kind of... dissension in the neighborhood. So, here's what's going to happen. You're going to take that box and get rid

5

of the knife. Somewhere no one will ever find it. And you're going to take this," he hands me the envelope, showing me the dozens of bills inside, "for a job well done."

He straightens and holds his hand out to me to help me up. I ignore it and scramble to my feet.

"Keep your mouth shut and keep Luke out of my way, and everything will be fine. But if not…, "he shrugs. "I've got a dozen guys that saw me twenty blocks away from that apartment. And I've got three that saw you and Luke right there. You didn't touch anything, did you? Fingerprints and shit. Wouldn't be good. Maybe the police find this notebook… but maybe not. Up to you."

I stare at my feet for countless minutes, thinking about all the possible ways this can go.

None of them look good.

Eventually, I shove the box and the envelope into my backpack and walk away without a word.

"Smart, Jacky. You're smart!" Rock yells after me, laughter in his voice.

CHAPTER

One

Jax

Almost dying has a way of changing your priorities. At least, it seems to have had that effect on me. It's the only explanation I've got for why I'm currently hustling Monique out the front door of *Vanished*, the tattoo shop where I work, and not taking her up on her offer of an after-hours blow job. The really sad part is that I wasn't even tempted, despite knowing firsthand that it would be spectacular. This isn't the first tattoo I've given Monique.

But no. The equipment in my pants didn't even twitch. Not interested. At all.

It probably doesn't help that the last woman I slept with on a brief but semi-regular basis was secretly obsessed with my best friend and tried to kill his girlfriend. To say that it ended badly would be a severe understatement.

It's been months. I haven't gone this long without sex since I was a virgin. And then, at least, I *wanted* to.

Pathetic.

I sigh when the door finally closes behind Monique and flip the 'Open' sign off, locking the door.

"Still riding the celibacy train, huh, big guy?" Logan snarks. She's sitting on a stool behind the counter, sketching while she waits for me to finish up this last appointment.

"Stuff it," I mutter.

She smirks at me but starts working on the deposit. I start the rest of our nightly routine, cleaning up for the morning. I'm interrupted by my phone ringing.

TV Star calling.

"Yo! You're home!" I shout into my cell. My best friend and boss-turned-partner, Lucas Abbott, has been out-of-town doing some promotional stuff in Los Angeles for the reality show based on our tattoo shop and our lives. The new season won't air for several months yet, we're still shooting, but after the whole kidnapping and attempted murder, our producer thought it would be good to get some positive publicity. She even got Luke to agree to bring Ash out.

My life is fucking ridiculous, mainly in a good way, especially considering where I came from. Except for the almost dying from a gunshot and then sleeping with a crazy stalker/murderer thing. And the current state of disinterest that has infected my dick. Other than that, life is great. Really.

"I wish. Flight's canceled."

I hear Ash yelling hello to me in the background and can't help but grin. Doc's quickly becoming like a little sister to me, but more importantly, she makes Luke happy.

"That sucks. So when are you getting back?"

"I don't know. Ash is on hold with the airline. But it may not be until sometime Tuesday or Wednesday."

I shrug even though he can't see me. "So go to the beach for a couple of days. We've got things under control. Freaking cold here right now, anyway." I don't really mind winter, but January in Chicago isn't exactly pleasant outdoor weather. It's been days since we've even seen the sun, fucking gray everywhere.

"Yeah, about that... ."

"What?" I stiffen, annoyed he may actually be worried about us running the shop a couple more days without him. Last month he asked me to step up as a full partner. Does he really not think I can handle this?

He clears his throat, which I know is a tell when he's uncomfortable about something.

"So, I, uh, I kind of promised I'd do this thing Monday afternoon. And now I'm worried I won't be back in time. I was thinking," I hear Ash yelling something again in the background, and Lucas muffles the phone murmuring to her.

"Um. Hello? Want to tell me what's going on?" At least now, I'm pretty sure it's not related to *Vanished*, so I can relax.

Luke comes back on the line. "Yeah, sorry. *We*," he stresses for emphasis, I can practically see Ash grinning at him, "were thinking you might be able to cover it for me."

Immediately I'm suspicious. Luke knows I've got his back. He's being weird and shifty, though, so for some reason, he either thinks this is a bad idea, or he thinks I'm not going to like it. "Want to provide me a little more info, bro?"

"I agreed to speak at this after-school program at one of the high schools. They're trying to bring in local artists, musicians, writers to talk to kids about different careers in the arts. Somebody different every week or maybe month. I can't remember. I think the idea is to provide some kind of outlet since so many schools are having to cut their arts programs. Anyway, they're just starting it. I don't want to leave them hanging the first week, you know? I'm sure they could try to find someone else, but I thought if you could-."

"Sure, yeah." Lucas and I do a lot of volunteer work with local schools and foster programs. Growing up in the system, we know how fucked up that life can be. Not always. But enough. I'm not sure why he'd think I wouldn't be into this idea. "So I just go and talk about tattooing as a job?"

"That's the idea. And then let the kids ask you questions. I think it's only like 30 kids. Some after-school group. 'High-Risk Youth'. You know the drill."

I grunt. Yeah, I know how kids get labeled early on into 'promising' or 'troubled' despite the fact they have very little control over their reality. It's all bullshit. Kids are just fucking kids, you know?

"No problem. I'll cover it. Send me the details?"

"Yeah, I'll text you what I've got. Thanks, Jax. Appreciate it. And I'll, uh, send you Riley's number."

There it is. That's why he's acting shady. Personally, I have very mixed emotions about this information. It's complicated. But I'm glad that Luke seems to be making progress with his bio family. At least some members of it.

"You're such an asshole," I laugh. "It's Riley's class? I thought Riley taught middle school?"

"Yeah, she started at this high school in the fall, I guess. She seems pretty excited about this after-school idea. Thanks for covering for me."

"No problem. Keep us posted when you get a flight out."

"Will do."

We hang up, and I think about what I just committed to. An afternoon with Riley.

Riley Abbott is one of Luke's cousins. Although he only discovered that a few years ago when another one of his cousins tracked him down and told him they were blood. Luke grew up with me in foster care. Poor. Forgotten. Shuffled around. Sometimes hungry. Sometimes beaten. 'High-Risk' some might even call it. Turns out the family his mother ran away from before abandoning Luke was loaded. Family money. Political connections. Fundraisers, fancy parties, mansions... all that shit. It's been a rough adjustment. Until recently, Lucas had firmly put every one of them into a box labeled 'Fuck You All'. Most of them are still trapped in that box, but Riley's managed to sneak out. She's kind of in her own box now. 'I Don't Want To Like You, But I Do.'

Which, unfortunately, is true for me too. Riley is fucking impossible not to like. That's why it's complicated.

She's an open book, sweet and kind and smart. With red hair and ivory skin, and wide gray eyes. And a great smile. Her laugh fucking tinkles. It's impossible to keep a straight face when she laughs. She's a good listener too. She *likes* to listen. She's curious about people.

She's my best friend's family, and she's an Abbott.

And I can't help but like her.

So, yeah. Complicated.

Shit.

Riley

I REALLY CAN'T BELIEVE I'M DOING THIS. BUT TEAGAN INSISTED. AND my cousin is very difficult to say no to.

She's a force. Unlike me. I'm perfectly happy to blend in, non-forcefully. It's been that way since we were kids. We were never as close as I wanted while we were growing up, despite the fact we're the same age. But she had her best friend, Ilyssa, and I had my books. And then, I guess I had Daniel.

She's kind of taken me under her wing since Daniel and I broke up, which I appreciate. She seems to think if she keeps me busy enough and distracted, I won't feel as heartbroken.

The truth is... I'm not heartbroken. Far from it. Which makes me feel bad in some ways. I should feel this loss more than I do. Daniel and I were together for over ten years.

But Daniel and I were also together for over ten years. We were a habit. We weren't in love. And I'm beginning to realize that staying with him as long as I did kept me... on pause, somehow. I didn't grow or experience the world the way I should have, the way I want to.

The way Teagan is bound and determined to make me.

That sounds harsh. She's not *making* me exactly. I want to do this. I'd just... ease in more if left to my own devices.

Teagan cannonballs into everything.

Which is why the two of us, along with Ilyssa, are currently wandering the aisles of a very... prolific sex shop in Chicago.

I mentioned at Happy Hour last week I'd never been to a sex shop. Well, actually, I'd confessed I'd never had a vibrator when Teagan seemed concerned about how I was managing since I haven't been interested in dating since The Incident.

The Incident, of course, being when I walked in on Daniel screwing some other woman three months ago.

"Are you serious? How is that even possible?" Teagan demanded. "Was Daniel that good in the sack?"

No. That's definitely not why.

I have a pang of guilt at my thoughts. He wasn't... bad. But we'd started dating at sixteen, neither of us really knew what we were doing. And we weren't very... adventurous. At least together. Daniel seemed to have plenty of adventures with other women.

Anyway.

So now, here we are. Just three single girls exploring a sex shop.

"This one. You need one of these." Teagan hands me a box with a purple vibrator. "On me. I can't in good conscience let you live another day without experiencing a battery-powered O. You can thank me tomorrow."

"Teagan! Shh!"

"Relax. We're nowhere near your apartment or your school. No one here knows you shape young minds."

Ilyssa smiles, she's used to Teagan's antics. The two of them have been inseparable since we were all six years old.

Teagan crosses the store floor to look through the lingerie. It's... not like what I usually wear. She's flicking through hangers, going rack to rack. Looking for what I'm not sure.

"Ilyssa, this would look freaking amazing on you." Teagan holds up a red lacy bra with a matching garter belt. Ilyssa grabs the hanger and holds it to her body, looking at herself in the mirror. She makes a 'maybe' face and hands it back to her. A few minutes later, Teagan finds something else, holding it out to me.

I make a face. "I don't think I have the cleavage for that," I joke.

She snaps her fingers and points at me. "Hey. Small boobs are still boobs, and boobs are awesome. Take it."

I shrug and grab the hanger from her, studying it. I'll admit it's pretty. Much more coverage than some of the pieces here. It's a royal blue babydoll cut that stops at upper thigh with a matching thong.

I don't do thongs. I'm typically a full-coverage tush kind of girl.

But it is pretty.

Indecisive, I study the sheer fabric and lace. Eventually, I'll date again. And I'm determined this time to be more adventurous. I'm a healthy sexual woman. I'm allowed to have a sexy nightie.

I'm getting it. A rush of thrilling freedom washes over me. I can do whatever I want. I'm an independent, intelligent, single woman.

I'm embracing my 'muliebrity'.

MULIEBRITY
Definition: The condition of being a woman, femininity

I'm an English teacher. I like words. I'm also kind of a nerd. And a Scrabble fiend. I've learned people sometimes think it's weird when I use them in conversation, so I tend to just use them in my head. It's like a game. Except I'm the only player.

And it helps me calm down when I'm stressed or nervous. I find words very soothing.

"Is Lucas really coming to help in your class this week?" Teagan asks, back to her browsing.

I nod, my heart speeding up in happy excitement. "It's not my class, really. We're doing this after-school program. Any of the kids can choose to stay, and the administration has agreed to let students in detention opt-in to this as an alternative. On a trial basis, of course. For the semester. Luke is going to be the first speaker."

"That's so great! I'm kind of surprised he agreed to do it. He still acts like he doesn't want anything to do with most of us Abbotts."

I shrug. She's not wrong. Which is why I'm so thrilled he actually agreed. I've been trying to win over Lucas Abbott for months now. I thought the fact that we were cousins, that we'd both lost our parents, that we were both part of and separate from our large extended family of Abbotts would mean something. That we could be... I don't know, allies or something. But he's been pretty determined to hate us all. He's been more mellow since his girlfriend Ash returned from Nigeria, though. When I called and asked him to come speak, he agreed right away, shocking me. I'm really hoping this means he's willing to give us all a chance.

At least give me a chance.

Ilyssa smiles softly. "Are you going to have any of the others come?"

Teagan rolls her eyes while studying some bondage-inspired lingerie. "Ilyssa has a lady boner for Macy."

"Teagan!"

14

"What? You do."

I giggle. "I mean, he is pretty hot."

The other two murmur their agreement. They're all hot. The staff of Lucas's tattoo shop, *Vanished*. They're all insanely attractive. So I get why Ilyssa would be into Macy.

But Macy isn't the one that unleashes dancing butterflies in my stomach. That honor belongs solely to Jax, Lucas's best friend.

Thinking about Jax when I'm in a store dedicated to everything S E X does odd things to my equilibrium. My head isn't quite sure what to make of him. He's a jovial flirt. Some may even say man whore. His loyalty to Lucas is unmatched. He's talented but seems totally content to stay as Luke's number two. I know from my visits while he was in the hospital that he's funny. And I suspect smarter than he lets on. He studies people; he notices things. I felt like he saw me, which was a heady feeling and one I'm not used to. But that may be my wishful thinking. Because he's also seemed a bit reluctant every time we've hung out. I suspect, well, hope, it's because of that loyalty thing to Luke and not something about me. Because while my head isn't sure what to make of him, my body has no problem labeling it.

He's freaking gorgeous and has become a frequent star in my fantasy life. Who am I kidding? He's gradually become the sole headliner of my fantasy life.

My body is super into Jax.

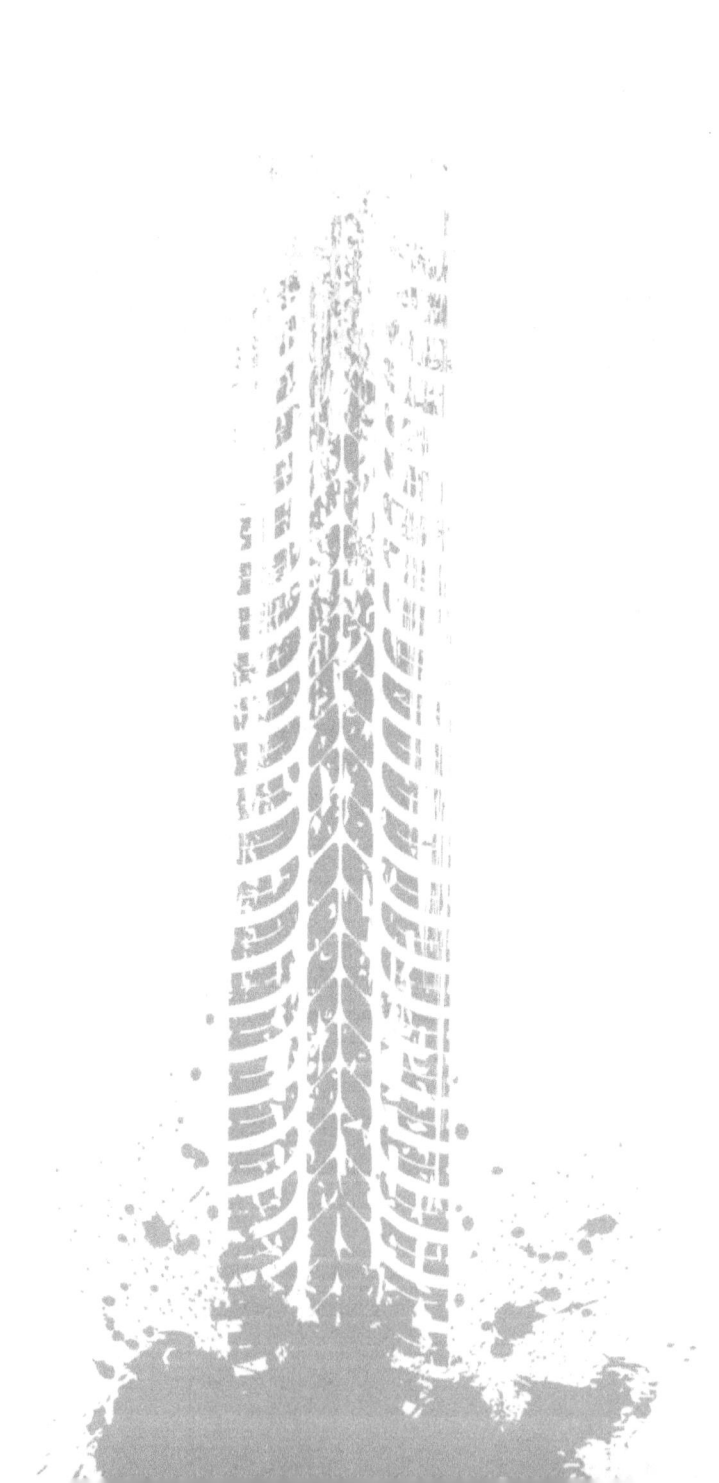

CHAPTER
Two

Jax

Monday afternoon, I jog up to the school's front entrance, barely making it on time. But I am on time. It's freezing outside, and my breath forms little puffs of clouds as I exhale. Riley's at the door, ready to let me in. She has a friendly but confused expression on her face and I'm hit with a sudden realization. Shit, Luke.

"Hey, Teach," I smile down at her. And I do have to look down. Riley's a tiny one. I've got nearly a foot on her. "I'm here to corrupt the next generation."

She laughs briefly, but then her face falls with disappointment. "I, uh, I thought that Lucas was going to come."

I suspect she's taking this as some sort of rejection, which is the last thing I want. And isn't true. Luke would be here if he could. He likes her, he just isn't sure he wants to like her. But I'm more and more convinced he'll come around. Ash has mellowed him out. Not to mention the heart-to-heart he finally had with his uncle a few months back. He's just processing. Taking some time.

I rush to explain the facts. "He and Ash got stuck in LA. Their flight was canceled, and with the holidays, getting re-booked was a nightmare. So, he called in reinforcements. Don't worry about a thing, Teach. I'll be on my best behavior. I won't use any of the bad words." I grin at her.

Her gray eyes widen at my joke. This woman has the most revealing eyes of anyone I've ever met. You can read all her emotions right there. She has no poker face. None. I'm equal parts fascinated and disturbed by it.

"Oh, it's not that," she rushes to explain.

I hold up my hand, stopping what I'm sure will be a rambling and unnecessary apology. "I got this."

She smiles, and my gut tightens. She's got a sweet smile. I've missed it since I got out of the hospital. She came to visit periodically the weeks I was stuck there recovering. Smuggled me hot dogs and KitKats. And I need to stop noticing her smile. I should probably stop noticing a lot of things about Riley.

I clear my throat to break the moment. "Lead the way," I gesture into the hallway.

Riley nods and swishes by me in her jeans and a cranberry-colored sweater. This is the first time I've ever seen her in jeans. When she came to visit me at the hospital during the summer, she was always in these fifties-style dresses or skirts.

She's got a great ass.

Shit.

I force my eyes off her butt and follow her down one hallway and right into another one. It's the twenty-minute period between the last class getting out and when detention and other more legitimate after school activities start. There are enough students around, and I can tell some of them are recognizing me. Conversations pause and start again with an excited rush and loud whispers. I pretend not to notice and stay focused on where Riley is leading me.

Finally, we reach the classroom we're looking for. Riley opens the door and steps inside. There's already a handful of kids in the room, sitting on desktops, chatting with their friends. The bell rings, and several others rush into the room. I see a few more standing outside, looking in, debating. Riley sticks her head out.

"In or out, ladies. Let's go."

The students in the hall look at each other, and then one of them shrugs and walks in, the others following. The room is full at this point, all the desks occupied and even a few kids standing at the back. I feel a quick pang of nerves, but it fades almost as soon as I notice it. At this point, I'm used to the attention, but teenagers can be fucking brutal.

Don't use the bad words, Jax. You promised Riley.

"Settle! People, quiet down!"

The various conversations start to peter out until, eventually, Riley and I have all their attention. "I'm excited to see so many of you here for our first Afternoon with Art. Today I'm pleased to introduce our first guest speaker, Jackson Hall, to tell you a little about his background and what it's like to be a tattoo artist. I expect you all to give Mr. Hall your attention and respect. And I encourage you to take advantage of this time to ask him about his art and what advice he has for any of you who may be interested in pursuing this as a career."

She pauses briefly. "I'm sure many of you recognize Mr. Hall from the reality show he is on, *Vanished Tattoos*, but we are *not* here to talk about reality TV, got it?" I smirk when I see several faces in the room grimace or roll their eyes. But I'm kind of enjoying this side of Riley. The no-nonsense teacher side.

When she feels her words have registered, she steps aside, smiling encouragingly at me.

I step forward. "Hey, everybody, I'm Jax. I don't really go by Mr. Hall, Jax is fine. I'm a tattoo artist. I specialize in New School style tattooing. I've been tattooing since right out of high school. I actually started apprenticing with a shop my Senior year.

"Before I get too far into it, I'd like to know who you are, you know, why you're here, what you're interested in art-wise." I turn to the front row of desks and smile at the girl sitting there. "Can you start us off? What's your name?"

She looks from me to Riley and back again, her eyes wide. "Um. I'm Layla. I'm a sophomore."

"Hi, Layla." She's flustered. I'm used to this reaction, especially from teenage fans, I've learned it's best to just ignore it. "What kind of art are you into?"

"I, uh, I like to draw. And sometimes use watercolor."

"Nice. What do you draw?"

She moves around self-consciously in her seat. "Um. People mostly. Like portraits."

I whistle. "Portraits are tough. Logan is great at them, though, that's her thing."

Layla nods, her eyes wide. I shift gears and point to a kid sitting in the back row. Slouching in the back row. "What about you?"

He looks up at me, then briefly around the room. "Cory."

"You do any art?"

"Nah, man. This just sounded better than doing homework in detention." There are nervous giggles and snorts around the room. I wander down the aisle until I'm standing next to him. I look down at where he's been drawing on the desk. "You tag?" I ask him. He just shrugs and shifts in his seat. I tap my finger on the image he's created. "Not bad. Clean it off before you leave." Cory makes a face at me, but I ignore it and turn back to the rest of the class.

"You?"

I keep moving through the room, getting stories, learning the tiniest bit about each of them. Most of them are actually interested in some kind of art although some are definitely here because they saw me walking the hallways and were curious. Whatever. I'm cool with that. If they're here they're safe, they're not getting into trouble, and maybe they'll be inspired by something.

And then I start telling my story.

At least the public part of it.

Riley

SEEING JAX APPEAR AT MY DOOR, EVEN JUST THE DOOR OF THE SCHOOL I work at, was a surprise. Not an unpleasant one, although I had been hoping this would be a chance for Lucas and me to get to know each other better. Maybe I can get him to come another day, Lucas. If it really is because of a canceled flight and not ... other things.

Leading Jax through the school hallways had been an experience. All the kids and their clishmaclaver would fall silent briefly and then restart with a vengeance focused on the same singular topic. Jax Hall was in the building.

CLISHMACLAVER
Definition: idle talk, gossip

He wears his dark blond hair shorter now than he used to. Before he was shot, I mean. They had to shave a bunch of his hair off when he was in the hospital and when he finally woke up, he just chopped it all. It's cropped pretty short but is longer and spiky on top, which basically means he constantly looks like he's just had sex, and some lucky woman has been running her fingers through his hair. It's also pretty common for him to be sporting some blond scruff on his face. He only shaves when he feels like it, I guess. It's also very sexy.

Riley, I scold myself, *do NOT think about sex when you are on school property.* Pull it together.

I get the attention of the class. There are even more students here than I was hoping for. So my celebrity guest idea seems to have worked, even if it's a different one than originally planned. I'd been very hush-hush about who it was going to be. Trying to build some intrigue around something most students had yet to be interested in.

I turn it over to Jax, grab a seat off to the side, and focus on what he's saying.

He was, is,...brilliant. He is funny and charming and talks to the students at their level. Treats them like equals but calls them out when he needs to. He makes sure they stay respectful. He was encouraging but he was honest.

He was perfect.

At one point, during questions, Cory raises his hand. Cory is in one of my morning English classes. He's bright but not motivated, usually comes without his homework, often doesn't even bother with his textbook. His older brother was in my class several years ago but dropped out before he even got to high school. Cory's already made it farther than Mick, but I'm worried he'll eventually follow that same path.

"Yeah, you said you did New School? I mean, isn't that just like... doodles? How is that art? It's not like Layla or Logan drawing portraits. Seems lame."

I see Layla glaring at him, not at all happy to be dragged into this dig.

Jax laughs, which I suspect is not the reaction Cory was expecting. "I guess some people might think that. But New School is about bold lines and vivid colors. I take things people recognize and make them something new and exaggerated."

"So, what, you're saying you're better than Logan?"

"Nah, man." Jax rolls his eyes. "I'm saying it's different. And different is cool. I'm lucky to work with crazy talented artists, and we've each got our thing."

He takes in the whole class, not just Cory. "You all know Picasso, right? Show of hands?" Most of the room raises their hands. "He was a rebel in his day, and he said this thing once, 'The world doesn't make sense, so why should I paint pictures that do?' That's kind of how I think of my tattoos. I like to make things that have weirdness and joy, you know? Logan, she likes to help people hold a beautiful moment or memory, so she does realism. It's not better or worse; it's just whatever people need. Whatever they love."

There are a few more questions from students around the room, but our time is up unbelievably quickly.

Most of the students bolt as soon as it hits 4 o'clock, but a few linger, casting nervous or curious glances at Jax, who is leaning against the blackboard.

Despite his attitude during the presentation, Cory is one of the ones sticking around. He walks to the front of the room, grabs some kleenex from my desk, and then returns to his seat, scrubbing at something. Some of Jax's fans have finally approached and are thanking him, asking him to sign their notebooks. Cory returns to the front of the room and throws his wad of tissues away. He eyes Jax and then lifts his chin in some testosterone-fueled language. Jax responds by nodding, and Cory leaves. Most of the others do as well soon after.

I smile at him, thrilled with how the afternoon went. "That was great. Thank you so much."

He returns my smile and shrugs. "No problem. It was fun."

"Pulling out the Picasso quote, that was surprising. I bet half of them google him tonight."

Jax shrugs. "I'm full of surprises, Teach." He helps me stack the chairs on the desks, starting on the opposite side of the room.

"He's one of my favorite artists. So you're going to do this every week? Bring in a speaker?"

"Well, we're doing this Afternoon with Art twice a week on Mondays and Wednesdays, although we probably won't have guest speakers every time," I explain.

"How come?" He reaches the end of his row and starts on the next one. We're slowly working our way toward each other and the center of the room. "There's a shit-ton of artists in Chicago. All kinds, too."

I shrug. I know. I'd love to have someone different each week, highlight different types of art, different kinds of careers, but it's a lot of work to get started. I share some of the larger challenges I'm having, most would be solved with just more hours in the day, and then into some of the more minor logistical headaches. "And there's just a lot of hoops with public schools and minors, you know. Everyone has to have a background check on file before they can come in. Lucas was easy because he already had one with the school district because of all his volunteer work with foster kids. I assumed you must as well." I straighten abruptly, a knot of panic congealing in my stomach. "Oh my gosh, you do, right?"

He laughs, turning the last chair over and setting it on the desk. "Yeah, Teach. I do. Don't worry, you didn't endanger any students under your care this afternoon."

"Oh, that's not what I meant!" I protest, worried I've offended him.

He laughs again, turning to face me. "I know. I just like giving you a hard time."

Oh. I can't help my reluctant smile, and I lift my face up to him, meeting his eyes.

My stomach jolts with a different kind of tension, one much more pleasant than panic, and a gentle warmth spreads through me as our gaze holds. He's got great eyes. Seriously gorgeous. They're like a faded blue color with a tiny ring of gold around his pupils. They crinkle when he smiles, especially his swoony crooked smile. He's not smiling right now, though, he's just staring back at me intently.

Despite my earlier promise not to think about sex on school property, all I can think about is him closing the distance and kissing me. What would Jax's kisses be like? I haven't kissed anyone other than Daniel since I was sixteen. A lifetime ago. Something tells me Jax's kisses would be nothing like Daniel's. Could I kiss him? Could I just boldly reach up and kiss him? I own a sexy blue babydoll nightie, after all. I'm capable of all kinds of things.

"I'd like to help."

His words startle me for a second, terrified I'd voiced some of my thoughts out loud. But before I reach full panic and mortification mode, he clarifies.

"I mean, it's easy for me to arrange my schedule at the shop. I could come in and help on Mondays. Find some speakers."

I'm flooded with gratitude at the offer, my school-property-inappropriate thoughts almost forgotten. I'm sure I'll pick them up later.

"Really? You'd be interested in doing that?"

He shrugs. "Yeah, sure. Something like this might have kept me from some bad choices when I was a kid."

"Oh my gosh!" Impulsively, I throw my arms around him and give him a quick hug. He's wearing a confused expression on his face when I pull away. "That would be so amazing. I would love that."

His crooked smile appears, making my pulse skyrocket. "No problem, Teach. This is going to be fun."

I swallow.

Fun.

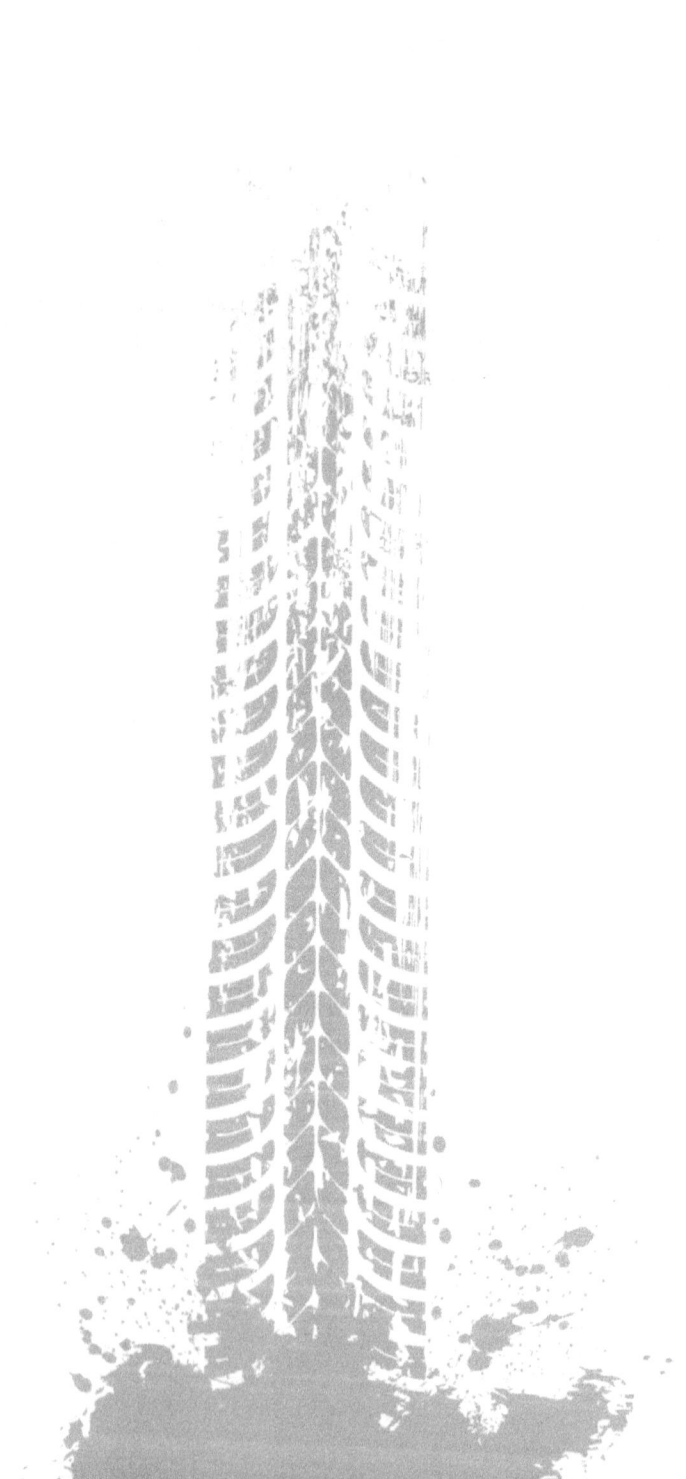

CHAPTER
Three

Jax

"Hey! You made it back." Luke is already at *Vanished* when I show up at the shop on Wednesday morning.

"We did. Finally. I hate LA," he grumbles.

"Poor little TV star," I needle him, laughing.

He grins. "I'll deal with it, I guess. It's easier with Ash there."

I roll my eyes. "You're so whipped." Really though, I kind of love it. This is a life neither of us would have dared dream about when we were kids. Back then, Lucas was just trying to make sure I stayed out of jail, and we were both scrambling just to survive day to day. Sometimes it's still hard to believe where we are. That something won't come along and rip it away. But every day it's a little easier to relax into it. Maybe this actually can be our life.

"She going to be on the show this year?"

He makes a face like he's not sure how he feels about it. "Yeah. Krista finally got her way."

"You cool with it?"

Luke shrugs. "I guess. I mean, she's okay with it. I just… worry about it, you know? I mean, most of our fans have been great on social media. They love her. But there's always someone with something bitchy to say. And I don't really want her to have to deal with all that bullshit. She's been through enough because of me."

"You gotta let that shit go, Luke."

I know what he went through when Ash was kidnapped by his stalker. I was right there, by his side. And I thank the fucking universe every day that we found her and Logan before it was too late. But none of that is on him. None of us saw who Tanya really was.

And if anyone should have, it was me. I was the one she was fucking for months before it happened. It's not like we were having many deep conversations or anything. We were both clear on what it was, and it wasn't ever an actual relationship. But if anyone should have realized there was something off, it was me.

"I'm working on it, brother," he tells me. "So, how did the school thing go?"

"Cool. I'm pretty into it. I told Riley I'd help out for the semester."

He raises his eyebrows in surprise. "Oh, yeah? What's that mean?"

I lift my shoulder, grabbing a seat on one of our tattoo stools. "I told her I'd help out on Monday afternoons. We're kinda dead around here then anyway."

"No, that's cool. You work your own schedule, you know that." We fall silent for a second, then without looking at me, he says, "She doing okay? Riley?"

"You could ask her that, you know."

He sighs, rubbing a hand over his head. "Yeah. I should. Call her."

He wasn't here the night Riley showed up drunk and heartbroken after walking in on her then-fiancé screwing some other woman. Just Mace and I. We took her out and made sure she got home okay.

Well, not home, exactly. She ended up passed out at my place. I slept on the couch.

"Doesn't have to be that deep, Luke. Sign up for another afternoon. Start there."

Luke nods. "I texted her this morning I was back."

"Good. That's good."

He still has a hard time trusting his bio family. But I think he's at least open to the idea of getting to know them now, which is leaps ahead of where he'd been even four months ago. My parents are long gone. Dad disappeared and up and got himself killed when I was a kid before I'd even met Luke. I lost track of my mom around fifteen. But she was a drug addict and always cared more about taking care of her next score than taking care of her kid. Last I heard, she was in Indianapolis, but that was nearly sixteen years ago.

I'm not interested in finding out. She's been dead to me a long time.

Logan shows up an hour later; she and Mace are closing tonight.

"Welcome back. Pick up any stalkers while you were in LA?"

I shoot her a look. *Too soon, Streaks.*

But Luke seems to roll with it okay. "Just one for you. Should arrive next week."

She laughs and gives him a half, sideways hug. "Did you see the message from Connor Thomas? He's ready to schedule."

Luke lights up, "Yeah? When did he call?"

"Last Friday, I think. Before your flight was canceled."

29

Connor Thomas is the second baseman for the Chicago Cubs. And he's a damn good one. MVP last season and just had his contract renewed. He and Luke have been talking for months now about him and some of the guys on the team coming in for a team tattoo. The publicity would be massive.

"Shit. I'll call him now. Thanks, Streaks."

I grab him quick before he can. "Also, the landlord contacted me. The space upstairs is available if we want it. Bonus, it gives us roof access."

We'd been talking about trying to purchase or rent one of the additional spaces in our complex here to use as storage and shipping for the merchandise line I've been building out. We can't keep the shit in the back rooms if we want to both expand the line and hire new artists.

"Awesome. Can we take a look in the next couple of days?"

I nod. "I'll call and set it up."

I love working at *Vanished*. Working with my best friends, tattooing, making my own hours, my own art. It's a pretty sweet deal. And Luke winning the *Top Ink* competition, us having our own reality show, means we're making more money than most. I have no interest in starting my own shop, managing staff, dealing with all that bullshit. But I like having done this, pitched a merch line to Luke. Launching it. Making it successful. It feels like I'm contributing on equal footing, not just riding Luke's coattails.

I owe Luke more than I can ever repay him. But this at least feels like a start.

Riley

WHEN I FINISH UP DAY TWO OF AFTERNOON WITH ART, I'M EXHAUSTED. And seeing the benefit of having a guest speaker. Maybe Jax is right. Maybe I should try harder to get someone in every Monday. I just don't know when I will find the time. I should talk to Jax about the plan for next week and make sure he's still willing to come back and help.

My stomach flips at the idea of contacting Jax. I've never actually called or texted him, I've just shown up unannounced at his door, but he gave me his number before he left on Monday.

I pull out my phone before I lose my nerve and shoot off a message. **Hi Jax, it's Riley. Do you have some time we could connect about Afternoon with Art and the plan for next week?**

My phone buzzes with a response almost immediately.

Hey, Teach. I got some time now if you're free. Just finished up work.

Now would work, although I need to eat. My borborygmus was so loud toward the end there that I was worried all the kids could hear it.

> BORBORYGMUS
> Definition: the noisy rumbling and gurgling that comes from your midsection.

Is it okay if we grab dinner while we chat? I'm starving.

Works for me. You still at school? I'll come pick you up.

I try to squelch the giddy rush I feel at his words, at the fact that I'm going to see him soon, but I'm not entirely successful. **Yes, still at school.**

You dressed warm?

I look down at what I'm wearing, confused by his question. I'm wearing jeans with black knee-high boots and a blue button-down under a black sweater. **I guess so. I live in Chicago, after all.**

I'll be there in 15.

When he pulls up, I see why he was asking about what I'm wearing.

Jax has a motorcycle. As if he wasn't dangerously sexy before, now he's on a motorcycle. My stomach is doing backflips. He pulls off his helmet and gives me that crooked smile of his. Gah. Why does he have to be so attractive? It's very distracting.

Pull it together, Riley. This is not a date after all.

I really should start dating again. Maybe then this…crush…I seem to have formed on Jax will go away. If I had something other than just an active fantasy life to think about right now.

"Hey, Teach. You ready?"

I nod, eying his, now my, ride a little uneasily.

"I've never been on a motorcycle before," I tell him.

His eyes widen in surprise, his smile getting bigger. "Really? I don't get her out much in the winter, but on the warmer days, I try."

I laugh. It's not exactly warm out. But the roads are dry; we haven't had any fresh snow for a few weeks now, and temps were in the low thirties today.

"You up for it?"

"As long as there's food on the other side, I'm in."

He laughs. "Hungry, huh? I'll get you fed." He hands me an extra helmet. "Climb on."

I shove my hat in my bag and put the helmet on. My gloved fingers are clumsy, and I struggle to get it clipped on. He grabs my coat and tugs gently, urging me closer to him so he can help. My breath catches at his nearness, and I focus my gaze down to avoid his eyes. Except there are his lips. That isn't any better. I feel the clasp catch, and he pats me on the head, on my helmet.

"All set. Hop on."

I eye the bike again. It seems huge. And a little daunting.

"Feet go here," He points to the pegs on the bottom. "Grab my shoulders and swing your leg over." I do as he says, taking a minute to bounce around and get balanced on the seat. "Arms around my waist. When I turn right, look over my right shoulder. When I turn left, look left. But don't lean, okay?"

"Okay," I call, hoping he can hear me.

"Hold on," he says, easing us away from the curb.

Jax is big. He's tall and built, and I'm...not. Sitting behind him on his motorcycle only emphasizes the difference in our size. My thighs bracket his, my arms wrapped around his waist. I can feel the muscles in his back flex, and he maneuvers us through the city. The first few minutes, I'm too nervous and distracted to really take it in, but then I start to relax into it. And I love it.

I love the fresh air. The cold is bracing, but it's also invigorating after being inside all day. It feels like I'm more a part of the city, not insulated behind the glass of bus windows or underground in the subway. And the traffic hardly phases Jax; he's able to navigate between cars to get us to our destination faster.

Holding onto Jax for fifteen minutes doesn't hurt, either.

When we stop, he backs us into the curb and has me hop off first. I'm a little clumsy getting back to my feet, but I'm pulsing with adrenaline, a broad grin on my face.

"That was fun!"

Jax laughs, dismounting from his bike and taking his helmet off. He runs a hand through his hair, leaving it spiky and mussed up. "Glad you liked it."

I notice where we are and laugh at his choice. "Duk's?"

He grins at me. "On me. Consider it a thank you for all the ones you smuggled into the hospital for me."

I'd learned that this was his favorite place for Chicago-style hot dogs from watching the show, and I brought him one a couple times when I came to visit him while he recovered.

He slings his arm casually around my shoulders and leads me into the small shop. My stomach jumps at the familiarity, but I tell myself not to read too much into it. Jax is a flirt. He's always been a flirt. That's how he's known on the show. That's how the tabloids talk about him. It's just part of who he is.

And I'm just Riley. An introverted book nerd who likes to play Scrabble, do puzzles and watch cheesy horror movies. Not the gory ones.

Duk's is so small there's barely room for a counter and half a dozen stools. He smiles at the older woman behind the counter and orders two dogs with fries. "Everything on it?" she asks. He looks at me, and I nod.

"Of course."

He grins his approval. That look has the power to convince smart women to do dumb things, I'm sure of it.

We grab two of the stools and wait for our food.

"How'd it go today?" he asks.

I play with my straw absently, thinking about this afternoon. "Pretty good. We had about the same number of students, although I think a couple were disappointed you weren't there." I laugh. "I think you were right, though. It'd be ideal to have someone there every week."

He nods.

The woman behind the counter delivers our order, dropping the trays off in front of us. Without hesitating, I dig in, taking a giant bit of my Chicago dog. I'm starving.

So good.

I think I might groan softly in appreciation. I notice Jax eying me with a small, crooked grin, but I'm too focused on my food to care.

But I'm still me, so with my next bite, a drop of mustard plops onto my jean-covered thigh. I sigh inwardly. Grabbing a napkin, I dip it in water and start scrubbing my thigh. Jax makes a sound next to me and shifts in his seat.

I glance up, prepared to make some self-deprecating joke about my clumsiness, but the look in his eyes stops me.

I don't think a man has ever looked at me with that kind of heat in his eyes.

My stomach clenches, and my thighs tingle, my breathing speeds up.

My mustard is forgotten.

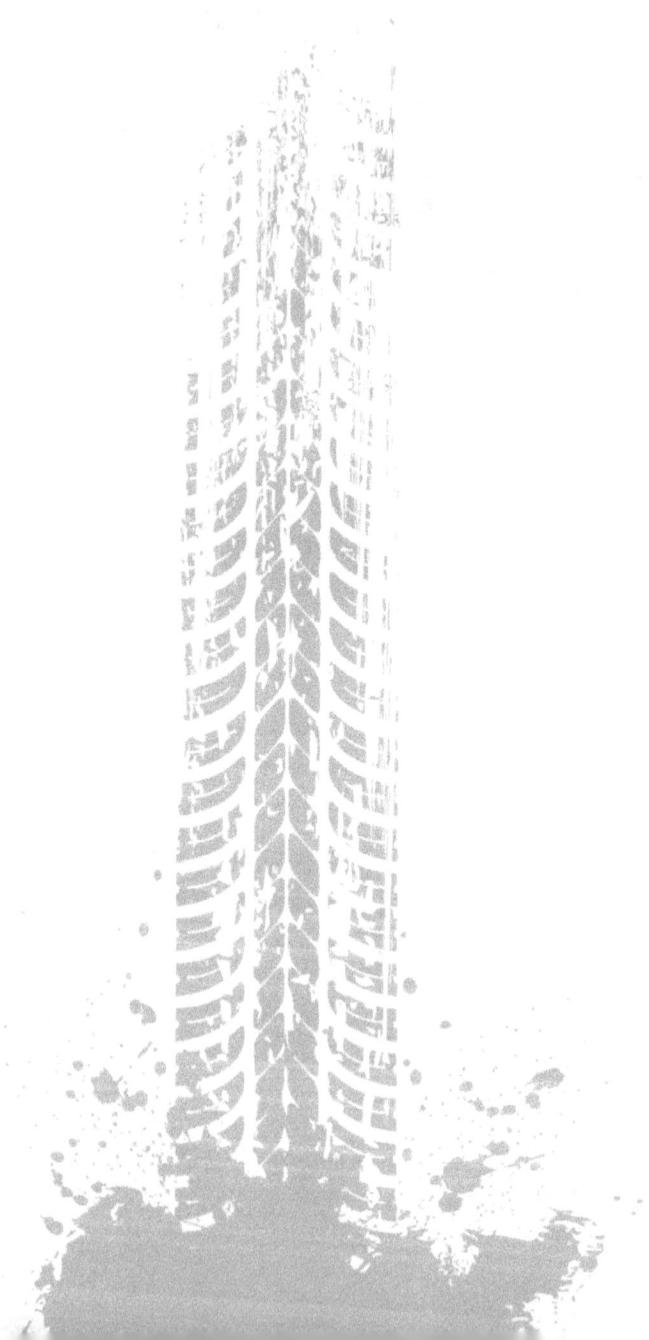

CHAPTER
Four

Jax

All of a sudden, my dick is working again.

Just like that.

Which is both inconvenient and annoying.

And incredibly inappropriate, considering its inspiration seems to be Riley with her expressive gray eyes and wide smile and earnest honesty, and slender thighs.

Riley, Luke's cousin. So off limits.

Riley, an Abbott. So out of my league.

This shouldn't even be sexy. I mean, it's not. It's not sexy. She spilled mustard and is trying to clean it off.

But all my dick can seem to process is that Riley, after already making me suffer through her tight little body wrapped around me, sweet laughter in my ear, on my bike for fifteen minutes, now has her hand between her thighs. Also, she smells fucking incredible. Something light and subtle and vanilla.

Shit. I've got to lock this down, *now*. Before I do something stupid and end up betraying my best friend.

I shift on my stool and focus on my food. I shovel a handful of french fries in my face, ignoring Riley, pretending she didn't just catch me lusting after her.

But she did. I didn't miss the way her eyes widened, her lips forming a silent O. So sweet.

From just a look. What would happen if I actually gave in to the temptation and kissed her? Touched her for real? I get harder just thinking about it.

My stupid fucking dick. Couldn't have gotten excited like this when Monique shoved her bare breasts in my face? What the hell?

I swallow my fries down and take a sip of my soda.

Without looking at her, I try to get our conversation back on track. "So, what's your whole vision for this thing? What did you want to see happen?"

It takes a moment for her to respond as she finishes the giant bite of hot dog she'd taken. I like that she likes Duk's. It's cute.

"Well, the idea was to provide some artistic outlet for students and a safe place after school. Like a lot of schools, we've had to cut a lot of our art and music classes because of funding shortfalls. But for so many students, that's the stuff they love. And there are so many careers out there that require artistic skills or creativity. I wanted them to see that there are ways for them to make a living doing things they love. It doesn't have to be a 'silly hobby' or 'waste of time'. It can be part of their future."

"I get that. I probably wouldn't have graduated if I hadn't had art classes." I shrug, thinking about it.

"Really?"

"Yeah. I mean, Luke was really the one that was determined we were going to prove everyone wrong and get our degrees. But

I doubt he would have been so into it if he hadn't been able to spend a couple hours a day doing art. And I stayed because he stayed."

Riley's silent, but I can feel her eyes on me, listening intently.

"Eventually, he ended up in a school with a good art teacher. She recognized his talent. She was actually the one that helped him get his first apprenticeship. Got him a part-time job working with a tattoo artist that eventually hired us both on. He was a dick, but he taught us about the business. But Ms. Taylor was a good teacher. Like you."

"How do you know I'm a good teacher?"

Riley says stuff like this, I've noticed. Stuff that, if it was someone else, would be annoying. Just fishing for compliments or to make themselves feel good. But Riley really doesn't see herself. And she's genuinely curious about how other people think.

So I give her an honest answer. "It's obvious. You care. And they listen to you."

She gives me a soft smile, liking that. "I do. I loved school. Loved books. Loved learning. I even liked tests! I want my students to have that. To find something they love. It matters so much, especially when things aren't great at home." Her eyes darken, turning a stormy gray.

It's easy to forget Riley had her own rough childhood. Sure, she grew up with the Abbotts and money and privilege and everything that comes with that. But she was in a car accident with her parents when she was a kid, like eight or nine. They both died, and she went to live with Theo and his wife and all their kids.

"So, Afternoon with Art."

"Exactly."

"You said Luke had a good art teacher." I nod, grabbing another bite. "I thought you guys grew up together."

Swallowing, I explain. "We did. But we weren't always placed together. We had a couple homes we were both placed in, which was lucky. And usually, we were in the same district, so attended the same school. But there were a couple years we went to different schools. We still managed to get into trouble together, though." I grin, downplaying how hard those years were.

"I see." Her face clouds as she thinks.

"Luke said he texted you about rescheduling. He still wants to come."

"He did!" Just like that, the sun is back. "He said he could come on Monday, actually, so if you don't want to-"

"I said I would. I meant it."

"Oh. Okay. Good."

"Who else do you have lined up?"

"Well, my cousin Erik knows a guy who illustrates graphic novels, so he's agreed to come. And Luke, obviously. Ilyssa works at an art gallery downtown, and she's lined up one of the female painters they represent to come too."

"Cool. You could do like a theme each month. This month it's visual arts, right? A tattoo artist, an illustrator, a painter, and I don't know, a...."

"Photographer. I'd love to have a photographer."

"Yeah. A photographer."

"And next month we could do music, the month after theater. And the last month, we could do more modern forms of art like graphic design, video game design, animation. I just want to make sure we have a good mix of things that require post-secondary degrees and careers that don't. Some of these kids definitely dream of college, but some of them will be lucky to get through to graduation, and I want them all to find something they can be inspired by. Something they can hope for."

I nod. That makes sense.

"Oh, that's perfect!" she gushes. "I love the theme idea. It will help with recruiting students too. We can do announcements and fliers around the themes so they know what to expect. We should have speakers in on Wednesdays, and then they'd have the weekend to experiment with the art we talked about, and on Mondays, we could have them present and go through other examples of the style."

I can't help but smirk at her a little; she's so excited.

"What?" she demands, a smile on her face. Eyes shining.

I shake my head. "Nothing. You're just such a teacher. Thinking of homework."

She laughs and bumps her shoulder into mine playfully. I nod at her empty tray. "You all set? I'll give you a ride home."

"Thanks. And thanks for the food."

"No problem, Teach."

It hasn't exactly been a hardship. But I keep that thought to myself.

Riley

THE RIDE BACK TO THE SCHOOL IS JUST AS THRILLING AS THE FIRST ride. Turns out I love riding on the back of a motorcycle. Probably good I didn't discover this until I was in my late twenties. Safer.

I'd almost forgotten I'd driven to school this morning, but it was just as easy for Jax to bring me back to my car as for him to take me to my place. And probably less awkward.

He pulls up to my car in the now practically deserted parking lot. My dismount this time isn't any more graceful than when I'd gotten off at Duk's but Jax either doesn't care or pretends not to notice. He's good at that, not noticing the things that make me self-conscious. I like it.

And him.

I like him.

Which I know is stupid. Even if Jax could ever be attracted to someone like me, he would never hook up with me because of Lucas. At least not while Lucas still hates all of us Abbotts.

I manage to unclip the helmet on my own, despite my freezing fingers. The temperature is dropping rapidly, a cold 'arctic blast' is predicted for the next few days. Jax seems to have better gear than me, though, so I think he'll get home okay. He removes his helmet easily, looping it over his handlebars, and turns to me.

"Thanks again. For dinner and helping me bounce around ideas."

He tilts his head and grins crookedly at me. "No problem, Teach. You're a fun dinner date."

He stiffens as if realizing what he said. He's probably worried I'll get the wrong idea.

But would it be the wrong idea? I mean, it's crazy to even think about it, but... I could swear there are times when the heat in his eyes is genuine and not just in my head. But I'm also not super confident in my ability to read these situations. I haven't dated. Not really. Not like a typical late twenty-something woman. Teagan goes through guys like Starbucks to-go cups. And Ilyssa, while not as casual about it, has had several monogamous boyfriends over the years. I never really learned to flirt. I've never sowed any oats. I haven't had any friends with benefits. I haven't experimented much.

Maybe I'm beginning to see why Daniel cheated.

Jax shifts, lowering the kickstand but stays seated on his bike.

I hand him the helmet back, and then, just testing a theory, I give him a hug good-bye.

I feel him tense, but then I feel one of his arms wrap around my waist. He keeps it loose but doesn't seem eager to end the embrace. I feel his nose, freezing cold, nudge the side of my neck. My heart is racing, and I shiver in his arms. Both from the cold and for...other reasons.

Maybe this isn't all in my head. I press my lips together, shift closer to his frame, inhaling his scent. This is nice. Really nice.

He's hard in my arms. Partly because he's still tense but mostly because he's solid muscle. He's just hard everywhere.

Well. I don't know if he's hard *everywhere*, he's just hard everywhere I'm currently touching.

Which makes me think about touching him in other places.

And kissing. I'm overcome with basorexia, standing here shivering in his arms.

> BASOREXIA
> Definition: a strong urge to kiss someone

Geez, Riley. Turn your brain off for a good cause!

No! Wait! Don't turn it off! *School property! School property!*

Reluctantly I pull away.

Jax's eyes are blazing hot, the gold around the pupils brighter than usual.

Oh, wow.

A firetruck drives down the street by the school, its siren breaking the tension between us. I take a step back, digging for my keys. Awkward and embarrassed now. I chance a look at Jax's face. He's still watching the firetruck driving away, disappearing into the red brake lights of the city street. Something else seems to catch his attention, his eyes narrow as he stares at something across the parking lot. I follow his gaze, eventually landing on a lone figure standing at the edge of school property. He doesn't seem familiar, but he's too far away for me to get a good look at him.

Jax is still tense, but not in the same way. Not in an exciting, potentially good way that makes my pulse race and breath hitch. No, now he's tense in a distinctly bad way, obviously unhappy about something.

"Everything okay?" I ask softly, watching Jax as he watches the stranger.

He shakes himself loose and turns his attention back to me.

"All good, Teach." He secures the extra helmet before relaxing into his seat, leaning on the handlebars. "So, I can get started on calling around for next month's speakers if you want. We've got a couple clients that are musicians, and they'd probably have some good contacts."

Back to business. Got it. Message received.

"That would be great, actually. That's the sector I have the least amount of leads. We need both men and women, though. And just a generally diverse list of speakers. I want to make sure all the students are represented. That they have someone they can see themselves in."

"No problem, Teach. I get it."

"Thanks, Jax. Really. I really want this to be successful, but finding the time to do it all…it's hard."

"It's cool. I'm happy to help."

I stand there awkwardly, the cold seeping in, unsure how to say good-bye.

"I'll see you on Monday, right?"

"I'll be here. With Luke. I'll see if he can do Wednesday, but it may be too late for him to rearrange his schedule."

Luke.

Right.

"Yeah, either is great. We can start the Wednesday routine next week. Just let me know. Thanks." I smile and give him a little wave. "Night."

"Bye, Teach."

I can feel his eyes on me while I attempt to unlock my car. Nerves and cold keep my fingers clumsy. I drop my keys once before I can finally make them work. The car beeps as it unlocks, and I slide behind the wheel. I give Jax another wave and start my car. He follows me out of the parking lot, eventually going straight when I turn left.

So, Jax will be there on Monday afternoons to help, and Wednesdays, we'll have guest artists. Perfect. I'll need to reschedule the graphic novelist I'd talked to, but I don't think it will be a problem.

This is going to be great.

And I suspect Mondays will quickly become my favorite day of the week.

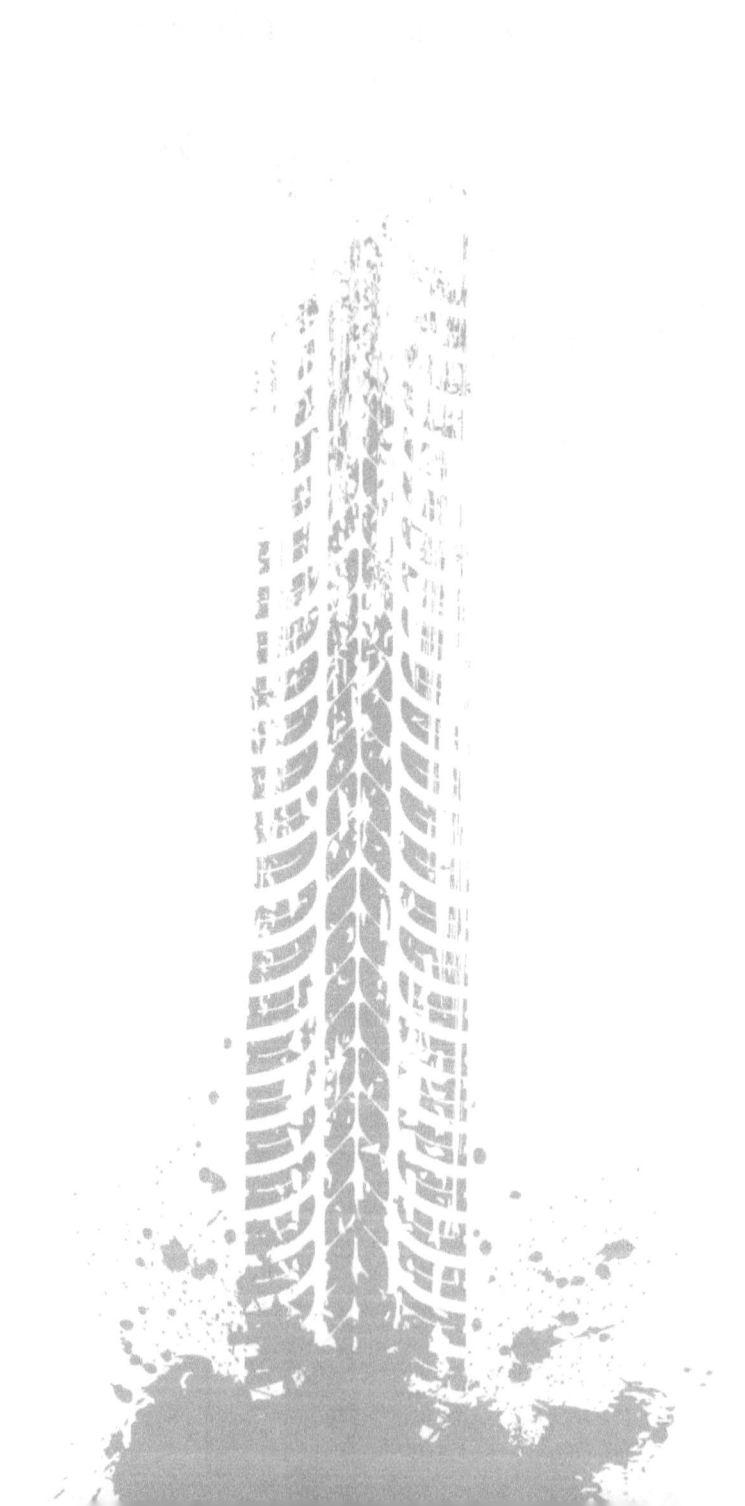

CHAPTER
Five

Riley

Friday night, I meet Teagan and Ilyssa for drinks after we all get off work. Ilyssa and I were too tired to go dancing, but I was seriously bibesy for some reason, so talked Teagan into one of my favorite neighborhood pubs instead. Extensive beer list, decent cocktails, and delicious fries. A plate of which currently sits on the table between us.

> BIBESY
> Definition: a seriously enthusiastic interest in drinking

"I think I've finally convinced Maxwell I'm not interested in sleeping with him," Ilyssa informs us. Maxwell is her eccentric artist boss at the gallery she works at.

"I thought Maxwell was gay?"

Teagan waves her hand dismissively, taking a sip of her gin and tonic. "He doesn't let that stop him from sleeping with women."

Ilyssa laughs. "He's bi. But he's also a giant man whore that I'm not stupid enough to get involved with even if he wasn't my boss. Luckily he hits on everyone, and everything, so he doesn't take rejection very personally."

I can tell I'm probably making a shocked face. "Having him constantly hitting on you sounds stressful. And potentially illegal. I would hate that."

Ilyssa shrugs. "I can handle Maxwell. It's not about him abusing his power. He literally can't help himself. He hits on everyone. Sometimes I use him to screen my dates. See how they respond to getting hit on by a man."

Teagan slams her now empty glass down and raises her hand, signaling for another. "Love that. Homophobes not welcome."

"Bad week, T?" Ilyssa asks wryly, eying the empty drink before us.

She shrugs and quickly changes the subject. "Hey! How was your afternoon project with Lucas?"

"Oh," I start, shifting in my seat. "He actually had to reschedule for this week. Jax came instead."

"Oh." Teagan frowns, I'm sure wondering if he bailed because of the whole Abbott thing.

"His flight was canceled. He and Ash got stuck in LA, so he asked Jax to cover." I rush to explain, defending him. Even though I've worried about the same thing.

"Jax is a nice substitute." Ilyssa smiles encouragingly. "How did it go?"

I'm hit with a rush of excitement and pride. "It was great. He was great. The kids really responded to him. And he's offered to come help every week."

"Oh my god!" The waitress slides up next to us, placing Teagan's replacement G&T on the table, although my cousin is ignoring her, instead, all her attention is focused on me.

I smile a 'thank you' at the waitress and then look from Teagan to Ilyssa, confused. "What?"

Teagan is still studying me, her eyes wide in shock. "You're totally crushing on Jax, aren't you?"

I try to deny it, but I'm an awful liar. "What? Why would you say that?"

"You are! Oh my god! How do you go from *Daniel* to Jax? They have *nothing* in common."

"Maybe that's a good thing," Ilyssa points out sympathetically. "Maybe that's the appeal."

I still haven't responded, and Teagan looks at me, demands, "Riley?"

I bury my face in my hands, embarrassed. "Yes! It's so stupid." I look up to see their reaction.

"Why is it stupid? I don't think it's stupid. Jax is," Teagan lowers her chin and gives me an exaggerated look, "very attractive. I sure wouldn't kick him out of bed."

Ilyssa nods, agreeing. "And he seems nice. Volunteering his time with you."

"I was just surprised. Here I am, thinking through the business suits I know that I could introduce you to, and you're lusting after t-shirts and tattoos. I love it! So much better." Teagan grins at me.

"Yeah, well, I doubt anything will ever happen. He's Lucas's best friend. Even if by some miracle he was attracted to me."

Teagan takes another swallow of her drink. "Stop that. That's just mind-fuckery left over from Daniel. I wouldn't be surprised if Jax gets a little hot for teacher."

We all giggle at that outrageous statement. Ilyssa lifts her glass in a toast, "Hell yeah!" We all clink our drinks together.

Teagan pounds excitedly on the table. "I love this idea! How do we make this happen?"

I shrug, playing with my coaster. "I have no idea. I've never tried to seduce someone before."

"Really?" Ilyssa says, her eyebrows raised in surprise.

"Never had to. I mean, I was with Daniel."

"I've got it!" Teagan snaps her fingers, sitting up straighter. "You need a New Year's Sexual Resolutions list."

"A what now?" Ilyssa asks.

"It's still early in January. Totally acceptable to still be finalizing New Year Resolutions. But your list is about all the sex and experimenting and to-do's you want to accomplish this year now that you are free! Single and Sexy. That's you!"

I laugh, assuming she's joking, but Teagan just watches me with a stubborn expression. Ilyssa, usually my ally against Teagan's more outrageous ideas, has a thoughtful look on her face. Finally, she lifts one shoulder and leans over to pull a notepad out of her purse.

"I'm in. I've been in a dating rut." She rips a page out and hands it to Teagan, then another to me, leaving the opened notebook in front of her. Then she hands out pens.

We're really doing this?

"Yes!" Teagan claps her hands excitedly as if I'd asked the question out loud. "This is awesome. I'm so in."

"I'll go first," Ilyssa taps her pen against her lip. "I want to sketch a male nude model."

"Sketching isn't sex," Teagan protests.

"Foreplay," Ilyssa says with a small, secretive smile.

"Fine. I'll accept it." She turns to me expectantly.

"Uh," I think about this. What do I want to say? What am I willing to say? "I want to have sex blindfolded."

Teagan blinks at me. "You've never done that?"

I shake my head. Nope.

"You should. Write that down."

My cheeks heat. The waitress checks in, and I scramble to cover up my list. Ilyssa orders us another round of drinks. That's good. I'm not opposed to some liquid courage.

"I want to get oral in an elevator." Teagan jots down her resolution.

"Wait. Are you serious?" I interject. "How would that even work?"

"I'll let you know by next December 31st."

I snort, laughing. The beer I'm drinking may be going to my head.

"Naked Twister."

"Oh! I want to play naked, dirty Scrabble!"

"I want to give oral in a public place."

I laugh, "Like an elevator?"

"You're obsessed with oral," Ilyssa says at the same time.

Teagan shakes her head and answers. "No. Outside. And oral is awesome. Both giving and receiving."

"Oh wow. Outside?"

She shrugs, "Oh yeah. You and Daniel never made out outside? Even when you were in high school and had nowhere to make out?"

I shake my head. "We didn't do that much until college."

Teagan snatches my paper away. "Okay. This is fun and all, but I think we really need to focus. Ilyssa? Our girl Riley needs an education."

"Ooooo. Fun! Yes."

"Now, wait. I was just -"

Teagan is scribbling furiously on my paper. "Sex in a public place. Have you ever gone skinny dipping?"

I shake my head. My cheeks are hot, I can tell I'm flushed from alcohol and embarrassment.

She writes that down. "Masturbate with your partner. Oh! How's the new vibe? Do you love it? You should totally use it with a partner. That's going on the list." She writes furiously.

"That's a good one," Ilyssa reassures me.

Really? People do that?

"Sex with clothes on," Ilyssa suggests. She glances at me, "I suspect Daniel wasn't very…" she pauses, then shifts gears. "He doesn't seem like he was ever desperate for you. And I think you deserve to feel that. Sex with clothes ON," she repeats, tapping on the paper while Teagan writes.

"Hands tied. Perform a strip tease," Teagan says.

"Have someone perform a strip tease for *her*," Ilyssa counters.

"Good one! Ooo. Phone or video sex."

"That needs to go on my list, too," Ilyssa mutters.

"Sex in water - bathtub, hot tub, ocean, whatever. Sex in the shower. Stop me if you've done any of these."

Sadly, I can't stop her. Because I haven't. I haven't done any of this.

"Sex in a chair."

I'm starting to get into it a little more. I'm loose and tipsy, and, well, frankly, I'm picturing Jax co-starring in all of these acts, and that makes it even more exciting.

"I want to have sex on a table. Or like a counter or desk. Something where he lifts me up…."

"Love that." Teagan continues to scribble away.

She looks up at me, her lips scrunched, inquisitive. "This is a judgment-free zone. No kink-shaming here. But before I add these next ones, I need to ask if you'd even want to do them. Threesomes? Anal? Again, no judgment."

Oh wow.

I take a minute to consider what she's suggesting. Would I want to do either of those? When I was with Daniel, the answer would have been a swift 'No Way', but now....

"A threesome seems like a lot of work. And... I don't think I'd like that." I try picturing Jax and me with another woman...or another man. "No. Don't put that on the list."

Teagan nods and then looks at Ilyssa with a slight grin. "But... butt stuff seems like it's on the table?"

"I don't know. I'm not sure about that."

"That has to be with someone who knows what they are doing," Teagan says.

"And someone you *trust*," Ilyssa adds.

"We'll revisit when you've made progress on some of the others," Teagan decides.

Ilyssa and Teagan go back to brainstorming items for their own lists, taking the heat off of me. Thank goodness. It was fun and eye-opening, but I'm not used to being the center of attention for that long. Or talking quite so openly about my sex life. Maybe I should have, though. Talked more about my sex life. Maybe then I would have realized sooner how much I was missing.

But that's in the past, I assure myself. I'm not missing out on anything anymore. This year, I'm embracing it all. Trying new things. This is the first step of moving on and leaving all that behind me.

At the end of the night, Teagan folds up my list of 'resolutions' and slips it into my purse, giving me a sloppy hug. "Love you, cousin. This year will be the year of your sexual liberation! I can't wait."

I smile, hugging her back. It feels good to be getting closer to Teagan and Ilyssa. It's sweet the way she's reached out since my break up. "Love you, too," I whisper.

My Uber arrives first, and I slide in, confirming my address. Then I rest my head against the back of the seat and imagine Jax doing a strip tease for me.

I definitely wouldn't say no.

CHAPTER

Jax

Monday afternoon Luke and I head to the school. I talked to Riley about switching it up this week. Me coming Wednesday since Luke couldn't move his appointments, but...I don't know. I'm here.

"Hey, Teach," I call out, bounding up the stairs to the school entrance.

"Jax! Hi!" Her smile slips until she sees Luke walking up behind me. I didn't mean for her to think he'd bailed again. I'd just decided to come along. Just because. It has nothing to do with the adorable pixie in front of me. She's back in one of her skirts today. It's navy with large yellow and white flowers, ending just below her knees, along with a navy top and matching cardigan. I've noticed she never wears heels, just different flats. I wonder if that's because she can be a little clumsy.

"Hi, Luke. Thanks for coming." Riley's voice brings me back to the present.

"Riley. How's it going?" He stops beside me, shoving his hands into his pockets.

"Good. How was your trip to LA?"

"Longer than planned. Sorry about that."

Riley shrugs and turns her smile back to me. "No problem. I got a permanent volunteer out of it."

I can feel Luke studying me, and I try to disguise my thoughts and reactions. "Yeah, I heard about that. Congratulations."

Riley laughs. "Come on back. The students are excited you're here."

The reaction in the halls is even more noticeable now that Luke is here with me. By the time we get to Riley's classroom, there's a small crowd of students behind us, trailing in. The room is packed today. Students are standing along the back wall and sitting on the floor near the front.

I half sit on a table along the wall, leaving Luke to do his thing. Riley settles everyone down and then introduces Luke like she did me last week. And then she comes and stands next to me.

"You're going to need a bigger room," I whisper to her. She turns her head and smiles at me, eyes shining with happiness. I feel like I've been gut-punched. She's so sweet. It's not something I've had much of in my life.

Luke begins, and I force my attention back to him. Our stories are similar, obviously. At least the parts of my story I admit too. Some things Luke doesn't even know.

But he talks about the teacher that encouraged him and how he would practice. How he prepared for *Top Ink*, the reality competition show he won. How he started his own shop.

Eventually, he looks at me, and I push myself off the table and back to my feet.

"So, in two months, we've got a spot at the Chicago Tattoo Expo on Navy Pier. We're opening it up to do flash tattoo sales over the three days, and all the money we make is being donated to charity. Anyone know what flash tattoos are?" he asks.

"Yeah. It means you have drawings people can pick from. They aren't unique," one of the kids in the back of the room pipes up. I don't recognize him from last week. I make myself a note to get his name before he leaves.

"Exactly. We'll have a few dozen images people can choose from. Designs that can be done in an hour or less to maximize the number of people we can do and the money we raise." Luke looks at me.

I step forward and announce, "So we're going to have a little contest. You have four weeks to design images we could use as flash tattoos. I'll be here through the month to help answer questions and give feedback. Luke, Logan, and Macy will choose three designs that we'll include in the Expo options. Whoever creates the design that is chosen the most times over that weekend will win an opportunity to apprentice with us at *Vanished* over the summer. And win $1000."

Screams and murmurs erupt throughout the classroom. It's fucking chaos. At first, Luke and I look at each other, chuckling, but eventually, we've got to get them back under control.

"Alright, alright, alright. Chill." I raise my hand, trying to get their attention back. But it's a lost cause. Students are excitedly talking to their friends around them, already talking about ideas, how they'd spend the money. Shit talking across the room. Smacking their hands together as they shower the room in imaginary cash.

I glance at Luke, who seems just as helpless as I feel.

Suddenly the room is plunged into darkness. Just briefly, a split second, and then the light returns. Riley is standing near the door and light switch.

"Everybody!" her voice fills the room. "Pull it together, people! Back in your seats, quiet down. Quiet!"

Little by little, the scattered voices stop, returning some order to the classroom.

"I can tell you all recognize what an amazing opportunity this is," she continues. "But I'm sure there are still some questions, so let's all let Luke and Jax finish explaining."

We open it up to questions, and Luke's brought some examples of the flash art we already have in the shop so the kids can see what kind of things work. Layla asks a smart question about what kind of designs are typically the most popular - flowers, women, animals? And I see Cory in the back of the room, scribbling away. On paper this time. The kid who answered the question about flash tattoos earlier, his name is Diego. His uncle tattoos in Indianapolis.

The bell rings, and most of the kids bolt, rushing to catch city buses or meet rides. Others group together, talking about the contest, homework, plans for the evening.

Eventually, Layla approaches Luke and shyly thanks him for coming. She's playing nervously with her pen. "Can I ask...I was just wondering, are you and Ms. Abbott related?"

I feel Riley stiffen next to me and glance at her. Shit. This isn't good. Lucas and the Abbotts have made it a point never to publicly acknowledge their relationship. Everyone just silently letting the speculation run wild. I know Luke's reasons for it. We've only gotten brief and unsatisfying answers from the Abbott side about their motivations.

But the Abbotts aren't Riley. And if Luke says something cutting and shitty right now, I'm going to have words with him. And by words, I mean I'm going to pound him.

But my best friend surprises me. He grins at Layla and glances at Riley like they're sharing a secret. "Rumor is she's my cousin."

"Wow. Really? That's so cool," Layla gushes. One of her friends calls to her from the hallway, and she waves at all of us. "Bye. Thanks again!"

Riley is staring at Luke disbelievingly, blinking back tears.

Luke grimaces, "Sorry. Should I not have said that?"

With a watery smile, Riley shakes her head. "No, it's fine. I don't care if people know." Her voice is soft.

I feel a little like an intruder, but I'm also really glad to be here, to see this. Yet another example of how good Ash has been for Luke that he's willing to make even these tiny gestures. I try to lighten the heavy mood.

"Well, that's good. Because it's probably going to be all over school by tomorrow morning."

Luke grabs his phone as it starts buzzing in his pocket. He types a quick response and then looks up, tucking it into his pocket. "Sorry. Ash just pulled into the parking lot. We're supposed to go meet her dad in the suburbs for dinner. You good here?"

"Yeah, no problem. Tell Ash I said hi."

He turns to Riley, standing a little off to the side. She looks nervous. I like that she doesn't get nervous with me anymore. At least not this unsure of her welcome kind of nervous. I know Luke is nervous in his own way too. I wish I could somehow make it easier for the two of them. But I think they've got to navigate this on their own.

"Thanks for the invite, Riley. I hope it's okay we kind of sprung that whole contest thing on you."

She shakes her head and smiles tentatively. "No, I think it's great, really. It's exactly the kind of excitement and possibility I wanted these sessions to be about."

He grins. "Good." He looks at me and back to Riley. "I've got to run, but maybe I could come back at the end of the contest, and after, we could all grab dinner or something? Ash would love to see you again."

Riley's wide smile is blinding. "That would be great! Yes. Absolutely."

See what I mean? This woman has no poker face. I think about her ex cheating on her in their shared bed and get pissed all over again. What a dick. Deliberately hurting her. Cheating is an asshole move no matter what, but to cheat on Riley? Does he like to kick puppies too? Fuck head.

"Cool. I'll figure out a date that works with Jax."

Inwardly, I roll my eyes. Too much to ask for *you* to call her, dude? Come on.

But I keep my mouth shut. He's made enough progress today, I guess.

Luke slaps my back and gives Riley an awkward half-hug before bolting out the door. Well, that's definite progress. We chat while we straighten up the classroom. I ask about some of the students who were new this week. And then we're done, meeting in the center of the desks.

"Did you drive today?" I ask her, not quite ready to leave. Not ready to leave *her*.

"I did. Do you need a ride?"

"No, I've got my car."

"No bike today?"

"Not today. Too cold."

We fall silent.

"Well, I guess I'll see you on Wednesday?" I say, finally moving and pulling my jacket on.

Riley nods. "I'll see you on Wednesday."

"Bye, Teach."

Riley

AFTER JAX LEAVES, I FINISH STRAIGHTENING UP THE CLASSROOM AND grab my stuff, ready to head home. I'm riding high on the success of the day, the excitement of this contest. Lucas calling me his cousin. Spending time with Jax.

To others, Luke's admission may seem small and meaningless, but to me…to me that is huge.

I fold into my jacket, bracing myself against the cold, and hurry across the parking lot to my car. I slide inside and slam the door behind me, shivering. Welcome to mid-January in Chicago. Next month will be even worse. February is always the roughest month of the year for me.

For multiple reasons.

I turn the key, and the engine sputters, attempts to rev, sputters again but refuses to catch. Oh no. I've been planning on getting a new car this spring, but I was hoping I wouldn't have to worry about it for a few months yet. Looks like Blink, my car, has other ideas.

Crap. Crap. Crap.

Noooooo.

Why? The day had been going so well.

Way to keep me balanced, Universe. Ugh.

I try it again but get the same response. It's not going to start.

I really don't want to sit here waiting for a tow truck. The temp is dropping, and it was cold to begin with.

I bang my head against the headrest, closing my eyes in frustration.

Jax!

I grab my phone and call him.

"Hey, Teach. You okay?"

"No, actually. My car won't start. Are you still close, by any chance? Could I still take you up on that ride?"

"No problem. I'm just a couple blocks away. I'll turn around and be right there."

"Thanks, Jax."

"See ya soon, Teach."

Jax is back within five minutes, and I jump from my car into his.

"Brrr. Thank you." I shiver into the seat, loving the blast of heat coming from the car vents.

"You want me to take a look?"

I glance at him sitting behind the wheel. He has some old muscle car that I'm sure is wicked cool, and several of my cousins and students would salivate over it. I don't know anything about cars and generally prefer public transit, but I've decided at least during winter because it's already dark when I leave on Mondays and Wednesdays, I'll drive. Great idea, obviously.

"Do you know about cars?"

He shrugs. "I know a little."

But I shake my head. "No. It's cold, and I don't want to put you out more than I already have. I have Triple A, and my uncle has a mechanic he uses. I'll call and have it dealt with when I'm home."

"You're not 'putting me out'. I don't mind."

"No, really. It's fine."

He shifts gears and heads out. "Where am I headed?"

I give him quick directions to my place and then sit back, enjoying the quiet.

'Enjoying' is the wrong word. I'm keyed up, aware, nervous, excited, filled with anticipation. I'm intoxicated. I feel...*alive*. I'm rhapsodic.

> RHAPSODIC
> Definition: extravagantly emotional

He smells good. And fills the tiny space with his presence. It's impossible not to be fully aware of him. I can't stop myself from stealing quick glances at his profile as he drives. At one point, he catches me and flashes me his crooked smile. Flustered, I look away. I'm guessing he hasn't shaved for a couple of days and is sporting some sexy scruff on his cheeks.

My stomach flips, and I shift self-consciously in my seat.

Sadly, I don't live far from the school, and I'm pointing at my building in less than ten minutes. "That's me. Right up there. The red brick on the corner." Jax pulls into a fire hydrant zone so I can get out.

I feel kind of deflated that our time together is over. "Do you want to come in? I can make us some dinner."

I watch as his jaw tightens. He stares at his thumb as it drums on the steering wheel. My stomach drops. I feel a flush of embarrassment wash over me, and I open my mouth to take the invitation back when he finally responds.

"Sure. Let me park."

I press my lips together, stifling a smile, trying to play it cool. Even though inside my stomach is pin-balling around my torso. Jax drives around the corner and finds an open spot to back into, cutting the engine.

Opening the car door, I move to get out. The strap of my purse gets caught on something. Too late, I realize it's my foot, and I stumble out of the car. I manage to catch myself and stop from hitting the ground, but my bag isn't as lucky. It goes flying, its contents spilling across the snowbank and sidewalk in front of my apartment.

Crap.

Jax climbs out, coming around to help me gather all the pieces of my life.

"I've always wondered what you keep in that monster bag other than hot dogs and candy bars," he jokes, looking at everything I've dumped. I snort an embarrassed half-laugh and bend down to shove things into my bag. The wind is cold under my skirt, making me move faster. Jax is also collecting items. He brings a handful of stuff over to me, places it in my bag, and then he's off, spotting something else in the dirty snow.

I glance around, making sure I haven't missed anything, and then turn back to find Jax frozen in place, a piece of paper in his hand.

Oh my god.

Oh.

My.

God.

Oh my god. He's holding the Sex Resolutions List we made at the bar the other night.

My face is exploding in mortification. Of course, he is. I mean, why wouldn't he be? Why would the Universe allow me the illusion of sophistication and sexiness for at least a sliver of time before revealing my true self?

I sigh. This is my life. Might as well own it.

I walk over and grab the tip of the paper. Jax startles, quickly releasing it as if scorched.

Shrugging, I shove it back in my bag, this time making a mental reminder to take it *out* when I get into my apartment. "Teagan and Ilyssa think I should expand my horizons now that I'm single."

Jax clears his throat before speaking. I force myself to look him in the eye.

Oh.

Oh wow.

The gold in his eyes is glittering again, the faded blue intense as he stares at me. "Do they now?" His voice is husky, and I find myself moving inexorably closer to him. "What do *you* think?" he asks me.

We're practically touching now, we're standing so close. Did I do that? Or did he move too? I can hardly breathe, looking up at him. My heart is pounding through my chest, my stomach rolling with tension.

I'd like him to kiss me. I think that's pretty obvious.

Could I kiss him? I wonder yet again.

"I think," my eyes dip to his mouth, "I think I have a lot to experience. To try. And I want to."

I feel his arm wrap around my waist, pulling me tight against him, and I am thrilled even though we still have dozens of layers between us. "Teach." His voice is rough, and a little tortured and scrapes along my nerves, leaving goosebumps in its wake.

He stares at me, unmoving until my nerves start to overtake my anticipation. Why isn't he doing anything?

Suddenly the wind howls, whipping down the street, the frigid blast of air slamming into my legs, lifting my skirt slightly. I shiver, burrowing into my coat. I'm not dressed to spend an extended period of time outside. Today I'm dressed to go from building to car to building.

Just as suddenly as the wind, Jax steps away from me. "Let's get you inside, Teach."

I nod, knowing that's the right thing to do but still disappointed that's what we're doing.

Darn.

Jax

THIS IS PROBABLY A BAD IDEA. I'VE ALREADY SLIPPED ONCE, AND NOW I'm watching Riley's ass as we walk up the stairs to her apartment. I can't even see her ass. She's covered by a giant, puffy gray coat nearly to her knees. But I know it's *there*. And I know it's tight and a little round and fucking perfect.

And I know one of the items on her list was ANAL???? Underlined several times. I'm assuming the question marks mean she's not sure about adding that particular item to her year of experiences. But there were plenty of other things on that list that *didn't* have question marks to keep my imagination happy.

Did her ex even have a dick? I mean, how do you date a woman like Riley for over a decade and never get her off in the shower? How is that possible? How do you never lift her tight little body onto a table and fuck her until you both come? Or find a quiet corner in the club to tease her to a public orgasm?

How?

I just can't imagine it.

Riley unlocks an apartment door on the third floor. I hear clicks scurrying across the hardwood floor and a soft yip. Riley drops her bags and sinks to her knees, greeting a shaggy white and black dog enthusiastically. "Hi. Hello. Yes, I missed you too," she coos, rubbing his head playfully. She looks up at me from her kneeling position and smiles. "This is Pirate. He's a love but can get a little too friendly sometimes. Just shove him away and tell him to go to his bed." She pushes back up to her feet while Pirate sniffs at me curiously.

I'm not really an animal person. More accurately, I grew up in the city and never had pets; they aren't really a thing for foster kids. But somehow, it doesn't surprise me that Riley does. Have a pet.

Something tickles my nose.

"What smells so good?"

"I started some chili in the crockpot this morning. I can also throw together some garlic bread if that sounds alright?"

"It sounds awesome," I say simply.

"I even have KitKats for dessert." Riley smiles and laughs lightly. She knows those are my favorite.

"Anything I can do to help?"

She smiles and unzips her jacket. "Well, you can keep Pirate company while I get the bread in the oven and change quickly. Then I'll have to take him out for a few minutes while the bread warms up."

"Sure." I shrug out of my coat and hang it over a hook near the door.

Riley walks down the hallway, turning on lights as she goes. "Bathroom's here if you need it. I'll be right back. Make yourself at home."

I look down and see Pirate sitting at my feet, panting happily as he looks up at me. He's actually mostly white with black spots. One is over his left eye, another on his right ear, with tiny black dots across his nose like giant freckles. I wander into the main room, Pirate following along. Her place is cozy and cheerful. She's got a light blue couch buried under blankets and pillows and a bright yellow chair surrounded by bookshelves. There's an in-progress game of Scrabble on her coffee table. I sit on the edge of the couch, and her dog jumps up next to me, turns in three circles, and then plops down with a sigh.

I didn't know dogs sighed. Huh.

He yawns and then just watches me with his brown eyes.

"What?" I ask him. "I'm just here for a little dinner and conversation." He looks at me like he can see right through my lie.

"What? Did you say something?" Riley asks, reappearing in leggings and a baggy hooded sweatshirt.

"Nothing." The fact that Riley returns in some of the least sexy clothes imaginable, and my dick still perks up is…telling.

"Do you want anything to drink? I don't have much, but I've got water, soda, tea. Hot chocolate?"

I smirk, not at all surprised she has no alcohol in her apartment. "Just water is fine, Teach." I stand and follow her into the kitchen, leaning against the counter as she takes down a glass and pours me some water. Then she starts moving around the kitchen, grabbing a cookie sheet and ingredients for garlic bread.

"So, whatever happened with you and the ex-fiance anyway? I didn't really get any details after our night out at O'Neill's." O'Neill's is Macy's parent's bar. It's where we took Riley when she showed up drunk on *Vanished's* doorstep. She stills for a second at my question and then goes back to her task.

"We broke up."

"I get that. But what's the story?"

She glances over her shoulder at me, her eyes revealing a dull pain. "She worked in his office. She wasn't the first. I found out after I ended it." She slathers butter and garlic on a loaf of bread.

"And that's it? He's just…gone?" I'm not sure why I'm pushing this. It's not my business, and I definitely don't make a habit of discussing exes with the women I hang out with. 'Hang out' with.

"Pretty much." She bends over and puts the bread in the oven, reminding me of her perfect ass. Straightening, she wipes her hands on a towel and turns to face me. "We talked a few times after to see if it was worth it to try, you know? But…I knew I didn't want to marry him. I should have ended it ages ago. I should have given him the ring back right away. I should have been honest with everyone, including myself. Daniel's cheating hurt, but ultimately it was a good thing. Me walking in on them." She stirs the chili, which smells heavenly.

"I have to take Pirate out. Do you want to come or stay inside where it's warm?"

"I'll come." No way I'm going to let her go outside by herself while I sit in here. I push off the counter.

We put all our layers back on, Pirate circling and barking happily. Riley clips a leash to Pirate's collar, leading the way out the door. We circle the block in comfortable silence. Which itself is weird for me. It's not like I usually spend a lot of time talking to women, but usually, it's because I'm doing…other things. Things I'm trying very hard to not think about doing to Riley. Mostly unsuccessfully.

Luke's going to kick my ass, and I'm totally going to deserve it.

Pirate stops every few feet, sniffing at something only he cares about. Riley's all bundled up. She looks adorable, buried under all her winter gear.

We get back to her apartment, which now smells like butter and garlic, and Riley starts grabbing bowls and spoons for the chili while I watch, unsure how to help. She dishes us both up, and we sit at her small kitchen table. I take a bite and nearly groan as the spicy flavor explodes on my tongue. Perfect for such a cold day. It's warm and spicy and … cozy. Like the woman sitting across from me. She flashes a small smile seeing my reaction.

"Who are you playing in Scrabble?" I ask, motioning to the game on her coffee table, trying to think about other, safer things.

She looks down in embarrassment. "Oh, ah, I'm just playing against myself. I like word games."

The corner of my mouth quirks up, I can't help it. That's fucking adorable. "Who wins?"

Giggling, she shakes her head, "I'm not that bad. I don't keep score. I just like playing with the letters to make words."

"You're pretty smart, huh?" I ask, both impressed and a little intimidated.

She shrugs. "On some things, sure. But not others. You're smart, too."

I laugh. "I don't spell words in my free time."

Riley studies her chili but sneaks glances up at me while she says, "But you're observant. You watch people and see things. And your art, that's a form of intelligence. And all the stuff you're doing with the merchandise line. You're business smart. And -"

I hold up my hand, cutting her off. "Okay, I get it. We're both brilliant." I grin at her, unable to ignore the warmth in my chest her words cause, even though I try to act like it's not a big deal. As a distraction to my growing attraction to her, this line of conversation did not work. Shit. I'm in trouble. This is so bad.

I sit back in my chair, studying her carefully.

"Riley," I say softly. "This...shouldn't happen."

"Why?" she whispers, and her eyes, damn, those stormy eyes, echo the question. She has no idea how much she reveals with those wide eyes. I appreciate that she doesn't pretend to not know what I'm talking about. But of course, she doesn't. Riley is one of the most upfront and honest people I've ever met. And the sexual tension between us has been steadily building since that first day she popped into my hospital room. Now that we're going to be seeing each other every week....

Why?

I'm bombarded with so many reasons why this is a bad idea, they start canceling each other out until I hear nothing, see nothing, feel nothing but Riley. Her sweetness. Her hidden spine and resilience. Her soft skin and wide eyes, and wider smile. Her goddamn perfect ass.

"I like you," she whispers. "I'm not expecting anything, a commitment or anything if that's what you're worried about. I mean, I just got out of a relationship. But...I like you. Can't we just...see...what happens?"

CHAPTER
Seven

Jax

an't we just see what happens?

I pound the punching bag in front of me, my arms punishing. I'm dripping sweat, enjoying the labored beating of my heart and rough breathing. I'm doing my best to work out some tension. Tension caused by a tiny redhead with giant gray eyes who I should not be imagining naked, although I can't seem to help myself.

I've never had anyone look at me the way she does. I've never had someone tell me all the ways I'm smart. I've never had someone happy to sit and eat a home-cooked meal with me. I've never....

I've never...

I've never...

Fuck! I throw another punch, then several quick jabs, unleashing on the bag in front of me. I've never been so gut-twistingly involved with a woman before. She's got me so conflicted I'm even avoiding my best friend. Opting to use the bag I have in my loft instead of getting in a full workout at the boxing gym. In case Luke was there.

Which is impossible. Avoiding Luke, I mean.

I pause, letting my arms go limp as I drag in a lungful of air.

I'm a fucking coward. Riley, so sweet and brave, just putting it all out there the other night.

I like you.

Can't we just see what happens?

And what do I do? Told her I had to think and basically bolted out the door.

Which isn't true. Thinking is my problem, not the solution. If I wanted to solve my problem, I'd find some willing woman and get laid. Work out the frustration. Keep things friendly but keep my distance from Riley.

But my dick isn't into that idea.

I strip off my sweaty clothes and get in the shower. The lukewarm water feels good on my overheated skin and tense muscles. I picture Monique, then try tapping into some of my tried and true dirty memories…nothing. I growl in frustration, my hand holding my not even semi-hard dick. Nothing.

Then I picture Riley's sweet gray eyes. Remember holding her outside on the sidewalk. How tempted I was to kiss her. The way she looked at me.

I like you.

My dick starts to throb, growing stiff in my hand. I squeeze it, slowly stroking from root to tip. I imagine Riley naked. Her face, her lips forming that little O. I wonder what her tits look like, small and high. Her delicious ass. Squeezing that ass as I thrust into her.

Riley on her knees, looking up at me with those gray eyes as she swallows my dick. I groan, my fist shuttling faster along my length.

Fuck.

Tingles are growing at the base of my spine, and I groan long and low as I chase my orgasm, spreading my feet, thighs tight. What does she look like when she comes? Is she quiet? Or more vocal? Does her skin flush? Does she taste as sweet as her smile?

I brace one hand against the tile, the other still molesting my dick. I growl as my orgasm hits, my body going rigid. I'm still stroking my dick as I erupt, spurting onto the shower wall. I sag in release, trying to catch my breath.

Shit.

That was intense. But unsatisfying.

The release, while needed, does little to improve my mood. What am I doing? Jerking off to fantasies of Riley in my shower? I slam the water off, slightly disgusted with myself, and dry off. I've got to get a handle on this shit.

I've been telling myself that for days. Maybe weeks.

Clearly, it's done little good.

I pull on a pair of jeans and pour a mug of coffee. I collapse onto my couch, burying my head in my hands in frustration.

What am I doing?

I lean back, slouching down so I can rest my head on the back of the couch and stare at the ceiling.

My phone rings, and, not wanting to move, I just flop my hand around next to me until I find it.

Lori calling.

I manage a small smile seeing her name, and accept the call.

"Hey, sweetheart. How are you?"

"Hi! Good! How are you?"

Lori is the closest thing I have to a little sister. Well, until Ash. But I've actually known Lori since she was a little kid. She was placed in one of the same foster homes as Luke and I. Luckily, she wasn't there very long before they 're-homed' her with her mom. Although, based on our conversations over the years, her mom is no prize. But at least she hasn't been in any physical danger. Her mom somehow landed a pretty rich guy, and they moved to the east coast. While Lori hasn't exactly received much parental concern over the years, she hasn't wanted for much as far as material things. We've managed to stay in touch with her infrequent phone calls. She's been checking in more regularly since I got shot. That freaked her out.

"Where are you these days?" Lori travels a lot. I think mainly to stay away from home.

"Guatemala. I love it. I think I'm going to stay through winter and practice my Spanish."

"Nice. It's brutal here right now."

"What's going on with you? Are you dating anyone? I mean, like, for real?"

I roll my eyes, laying my head against the back of the couch again. This is a frequent question or concern of Lori. She thinks I need to settle down. Despite my assurance, I am perfectly fine staying single. I'm not built to be a forever guy. It's probably good she never heard about Tanya. She would flip if she found out I was having regular sex with the woman who tried to kill Ash. She's never met Ash, but she loves her. Lori is a hopeless romantic.

"Are you?" I ask to avoid the question.

"Eh. I've been seeing one of Patrick's lackeys. It wasn't serious. We'll see if we pick it up when I get back. He wasn't thrilled I was leaving the country for two months."

Patrick is the rich step-daddy. "I bet. Text me where you're staying, would you?"

I can practically picture her rolling her eyes at me. "Yes, big brother. I'll send you my whereabouts."

"Do it," I shoot back. "How are you, really? What's going on with you?"

"Can't I just call to say hi?"

"You can. But you don't usually."

She's quiet for a beat, then says softly. "I have to get out of Boston, Jax. Soon or I'll get trapped there."

I stiffen, on high alert. "What's going on, Lori? Are you okay? You know you can come stay here if you need to."

I hear her sigh on the other end and then, "I'm fine. I'm in Guatemala! I'm great. I'm going to hike a volcano tomorrow."

Frowning, I let it drop. But I make a note to check in with her more regularly. And maybe I need a trip to Boston when she gets home.

We chat for a few more minutes about coffee tours and chocolate-making classes, and all the other things she wants to do in Guatemala. When she says good-bye and hangs up, I slouch further into my couch. Luke texted me while I was on the call. He wants to meet at the gym in the morning and grab breakfast before we open *Vanished*. I have no legitimate reason to say no, it's not like I can tell him I don't want to see him because I feel guilty lusting after his sweet but kind of unwanted cousin. So I tell him I'll see him there.

I need to figure my shit out. But I have no idea how.

Riley's dug her way in, and I can't shake her. Or my growing feelings for her.

Which in itself is annoying. I don't catch feelings. Maybe this is some weird near-death-experience thing? Maybe with time, it'll just...go away.

Yeah. Sure. That's going to happen.

Riley

"Wait. I'm sorry. He just *left?*"

I nod at Teagan, just as confused as my cousin. It's Friday night, and we're all at Teagan's, sitting on the floor in front of her fireplace with takeout containers scattered between us. Teagan has a ridiculous condo in River North. It's a massive three-bedroom with a working fireplace, in-unit laundry, a private patio, and roof access. She has to share the roof, but still. Unlike me, Teagan has no issues tapping into her trust fund when she needs or wants to. She's getting her Masters in Business Management with plans to take over the family company from Uncle Eddie someday. She's going to be an executive making a ridiculous salary. I've always wanted to be a teacher. So I have a tiny apartment in Lincoln Park, and she has this palace.

Ilyssa moved into one of the extra bedrooms a month or so ago. I suspect Teagan gives her a good break on the price. But it's walkable to the gallery where she works, and the two of them are always together anyway, so when her last lease was up, it just made sense.

I filled her and Ilyssa in on my non-date with Jax last Monday night. Which was followed by, what I thought, was a very awkward Afternoon with Art on Wednesday. I'd half expected him not to show, Wednesdays aren't his normal day after all, but I should have known better. He told me he'd be there and I'm beginning to see that Jax takes his word seriously. As usual, he'd been great with the students, but he'd left quickly when the session was over. He hadn't stuck around to chat the way he had before. There were no long looks or crooked smiles.

"Okay. Walk me through this step by step."

I take a deep breath and another spring roll. "He gave me a ride home. He found the Sex Resolutions List. He put his arm around me. We went inside. We walked Pirate together. We ate. We talked. He said 'this' shouldn't happen." I use finger quotes and everything. "I asked why. I said I wasn't looking for a commitment. I asked if we could just see what happens. He said he had to think. Then he finished his chili and left."

It's just as depressing the second time through.

"Hmm. Curiouser and curiouser." Teagan flops on her back.

"And then when you saw him on Wednesday?" Ilyssa asks. She's digging into the chicken fried rice, eating with chopsticks right out of the container.

I shrug. "Nothing. I mean, he was great but then he just bolted."

"Lame!" Teagan yells at the ceiling.

"Maybe I read the situation wrong. I'm not very good at all this."

Neither of them responds, I'm sure, not wanting to hurt my feelings. Ilyssa is frowning into her food, Teagan still scowling at the ceiling. Abruptly, she rolls to her side, propping herself up on one elbow. "Well, his loss. And now that I know you're into tatted-up bad boys, I'll reassess my strategy. We should go dancing tomorrow! Meet some guys."

"I am not into bad boys," I feel the need to clarify. I like Jax because he's smart and kind and interesting and strong and loyal and, and, and…gorgeous. He's unbelievably gorgeous. It was weird the first time I snuck into his hospital room, seeing him gorgeous in real life and not on television. And he was not exactly at his best recovering from a shooting and several surgeries.

"Just tattoos?" Teagan questions, her voice teasing.

I lean back against the couch, stretching my feet out in front of me, and accidentally knock over a container of rice. Shoot. I scramble to pick it up and respond, "Believe it or not, I just want someone nice. A nice guy."

"Who will lift you onto a table and ravish you," Ilyssa adds.

I giggle. "And play strip Scrabble."

"Do you think I can find a nice guy to eat me in an elevator?" Teagan asks wistfully.

Ilyssa and I look at each other and burst out laughing. "Doubtful," she tells her friend, throwing a spring roll at her.

She sits up and searches around until she finds the spring roll, popping it into her mouth. "Damn," she sighs dramatically.

"Well, Autumn is very excited to come speak next week. And she's got a ton of examples of jobs she did before her painting could support her. I think you'll love her," Ilyssa tells me.

"Oh! Also, are you still looking for a photographer? You should ask Piper Lockhart. She can probably recommend someone from the paper. And would probably love the chance to do a favor for someone with our last name. You want artistic people in non-artsy jobs, too, right?"

"Non-artsy?" Ilyssa asks her, laughing.

"That's a great idea. Thanks. Do you have her number?"

"I'm sure I've got it somewhere. Remind me, and I'll text it to you."

"Thanks."

"Meanwhile, I have to go testify at yet another parole board hearing next week," Ilyssa shivers. Her stepfather is in prison. For trying to kill her.

It's not great.

Teagan sits up. "Already? It feels like you were just there."

"I know. I wish he'd just die already." She looks at us chagrined. "I'm sorry. That's an awful thing to say."

Teagan gets to her knees and awkwardly knee-walks across the circle so she can put her arm around Ilyssa's shoulders. "You're not awful. Roy tried to kill you. And now you still have to see him. The fact that he still has any control over your life pisses me the fuck off."

"What day is the hearing? We should meet up that night," I offer.

"Monday. So at least, I'll get it out of the way early."

"Okay, text us when you're done. We'll come meet you."

I nod, agreeing to the plan.

"Let's talk about something else," Ilyssa says. "I didn't mean to bring everything down."

"You didn't," I assure her, but Teagan is off and running, telling stories from school, her internship working with Uncle Eddie, and her latest series of dates.

People who don't know her, who don't see how smart she is, acing all her studies, how focused she is, determined to learn every aspect of Uncle Eddie's company so she can take over without whispers of nepotism, how loyal and protective she is of her friends, how she takes care of Ilyssa and now me. People who don't know Teagan probably think she's a blatherskite, but she's not. Even her nonsense is done with purpose. Like now, distracting Ilyssa from her dark thoughts and upcoming hearing with stories of lame dates and ego-driven classmates.

> BLATHERSKITE
> Definition: the kind of person who can't self-edit and cares more about making noise than making sense

Later that night, we all crash at Teagan's, each with our own bedroom, so we can go out to brunch in the morning. Having a Girl Squad is pretty awesome.

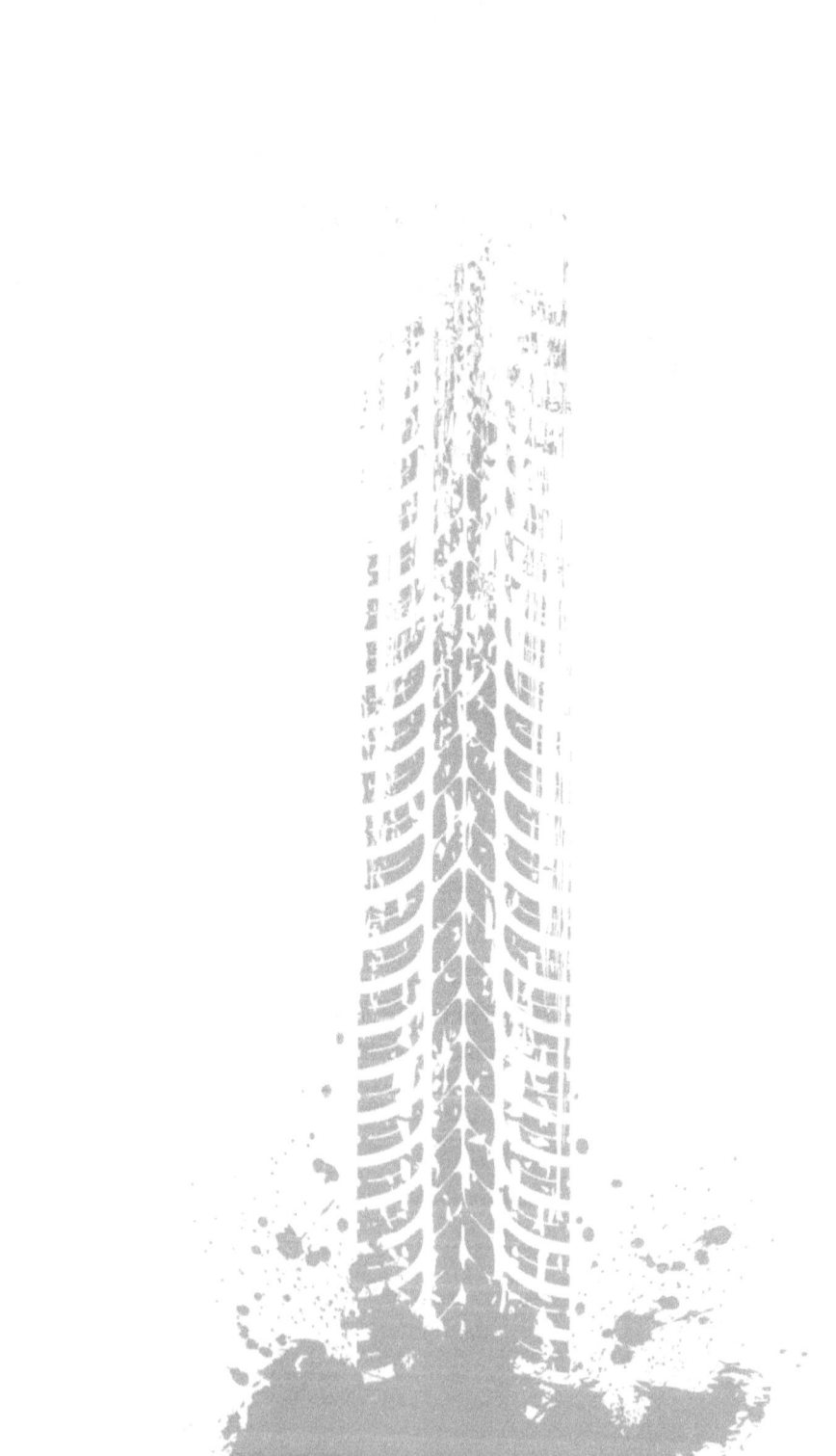

CHAPTER

Eight

Jax

By week three, my presence in the school hallways causes less of a stir. Most of the kids that care are already in the classroom. Others seem to be getting used to me showing up, so it's less noteworthy. Riley gave me an ID last week, so she doesn't have to meet me at the entrance every time. I know my way and step into the classroom a few minutes early, finding Riley.

She's leaning over her desk, jotting notes into a notebook. She's got one of her dresses on today, black with a red and white pattern, cinched at her waist and then flaring out to just below her knees. When I look closer, I see the pattern is actually tiny sea creatures. I grin. She's so cute.

"Hey, Teach. Fancy meeting you here."

She jumps and knocks several pencils off the desk; even that makes me smile. It's not like I snuck up on her. There's a roomful of students in multiple conversations all around her, but clearly, she was focused on something.

"Sorry," I murmur.

She smiles, but it's guarded, not like her genuine smiles. I know I'm being an ass, just pretending that conversation in her apartment never happened, but I don't know how else to deal with it. Last week I did my best to be in and out, avoiding any time alone with her, but…well, I can't keep doing that if I'm going to be volunteering with her every week. And honestly, I don't like it. Avoiding her.

She nervously tucks a piece of hair behind her ear, glancing around the room. "Hi, Jax!" Her voice has a weird fake enthusiasm that annoys me. But before I can say anything else, the bell rings, and an influx of additional students come flooding into the room.

Whatever I might have said is left out there as nothing. Like a blank piece of paper.

Because Luke was the last guest speaker we had, today most of the students are working on sketching potential flash tattoo designs. But the idea with these work sessions is that they can work on whatever they want, whatever style of art, within reason. Sculpture is hard, for example. Then the last hour, they'll be able to present and get critiqued by others in the class. So, Riley and I just wander the aisles between desks, complimenting things, giving suggestions, answering questions. Riley knows less about art, and I hear her mostly asking questions, trying to get her students to think about things from a different perspective. I'm pretty much self-taught, but I've learned a lot from Luke and the judges on *Top Ink*. A lot of my art is instinctual, but that's where a lot of these kids are at, so I can relate.

I end up next to Cory, as usual, slouched in a desk in the back row. He sees me coming and sinks even lower in his chair, tapping his pencil against the side of the desk. He's got a bunch of sheets of paper scattered on the desk, no notebook. I glance at them, then do a double take.

I look up at Cory, surprised. "You did these?"

"Yeah. So?"

I move the sheets around, so I can get a better look. He's got a ton of images and 'doodles' covering the pages, all done in black ink. There's a strong African influence. He's drawn the outline of the continent with images of giraffes and elephants inside the frame. He's also sketched some people, not portraits but images of women with traditional headdresses and hairstyles. They're bold and powerful. Striking.

"These are good. Really good," I tell him.

He shrugs, acting like he couldn't care less. "I know."

I smirk at his response. "You entering the contest?"

Cory just shrugs again. "I don't know. Probably not."

"You should. You got talent."

He shifts in his seat, not looking at me. "These might be too detailed and complicated for flash, but I can help you simplify them. If you want."

"Whatever, man."

"You think about it and let me know next week." I move on to the next aisle and students there. Several have created pieces they want to enter, and several have a lot of potential, but none are nearly as compelling as the ones Cory showed me.

For the last forty-five minutes, Riley opens it up to volunteers who want to have their art critiqued. She stands at the front of the room and lays out the rules, how the critiques will work. Above all, it is meant to help. Honest but kind. Constructive and specific. Coming from a place of support.

And then it's silent. Uncomfortably silent. No one volunteers. Riley seems unfazed by this, and I try to follow her lead, even though I'm itching to take over and force someone up there.

After a few moments, she says, "This is an opportunity for you to improve. Feedback and critique are vital in any profession but especially as artists. But this isn't required. If you don't want to volunteer, that is up to you." She steps back, seemingly uncaring about the tense silence. It's clawing at me. But I hold myself in check.

Eventually, Diego, the kid whose uncle tattoos, stands up and walks to the front of the room. He holds up a drawing he's done in black and red. It's a pretty gruesome image. Blood and gore and a sightless destroyed human figure.

He definitely gets a reaction.

Layla groans. "It's so ugly," she mutters.

"Layla," Riley interrupts softly, "Please use the critique points we discussed. Can you rephrase that in a way it would be more helpful?"

Layla makes a face but appears to be considering how to say it a different way.

I tentatively raise my hand. Yes. Me. Jax Hall, am sitting in a classroom, by choice, at thirty-one, raising my hand to speak. Christ, if Mace and Luke could see me now.

Riley grins when her eyes land on me. A real smile. The first she's given me in days, and it punches me in the gut.

"Jax? Did you want to add something?"

I clear my throat and stand from my perch on the back table. "Yeah, I just think it's important to remember that art doesn't have to be beautiful. It can be interesting, or it can make you think, or make you uncomfortable. It should just say something. I think this says something. What does it say to you?"

Layla tilts her head. "It's angry and violent and...sad."

"It says he's a badass!" Cory yells from the back row. Several other guys woot and cheer.

"Language, Mr. Johnson." Riley frowns at him.

One of the girls that tend to circle around Layla, I think her name is Traci, raises her hand. "I think it's cool that he only used red. That makes it feel more...," she flails, "I don't know. More violent or powerful or something."

"I think that's an interesting point, Traci," Riley says, and I pat myself on the back for getting her name right. "How different would the impact be if he'd used blue or yellow? Color and how you use it matters."

Layla shrugs. "I think it would be interesting to see it in blue. Red is obvious. The color of blood. It would make you look twice if it was in a different color."

"What do you know?" Cory snaps. "You just draw pretty faces. You don't have the imagination to come up with something that sick. It's fucking awesome."

"Cory, this is your second warning. Watch your language. And your tone, please."

Diego, though, just looks thoughtful, like he's considering her words. I'm proud of how he's taking it. I know it's not easy to have people dissect something you've created.

I move to stand behind Cory. A few others have thoughts and suggestions that they offer, and then Diego goes back to his seat. Before the next student can volunteer, I pipe up.

"Nice, Diego. Thanks for being the first to get beat up. It's not easy, I know. How many of you actually watch *Top Ink*? Saw Luke's season? Over half the hands go up, which is a little surprising, considering they were probably only twelve when his season aired. "Those judges were brutal if you remember. Still are. And he just had to take it. Arguing with them wouldn't have changed their minds. It wouldn't have gotten him any farther. He listened, and he took it, and he used it to be better. So he could win.

"He figured out early that winning a fight doesn't matter unless what you win matters. And any fight with a prize that doesn't matter isn't worth the fight." Now I feel like I'm getting annoying and preachy and feel a little overexposed. So I quickly move on. "Anyone else want to stand in front of the firing squad?"

Layla raises her hand and moves to the front of the room.

The critiques continue getting easier as they go until our time is up.

"Just a reminder that artist and painter Autumn Daye will be here on Wednesday! Come with questions. See you then." Riley yells as students scramble out the door.

And then it's just Riley and me.

Riley

I FEEL HIS EYES SETTLE ON ME, AND MY HEART KICKS. LAST WEEK, he'd just bolted after class, obviously avoiding me, and that sucked. But this is a different kind of mild torture. I busy myself stacking chairs, and he does the same. The silence is totally messing with my nerves which always makes me clumsy. One of the chairs slips out of my fingers and clatters to the ground, just missing my toes.

Jax looks up. "You okay?"

I nod, picking up the chair again, this time making it to the top of the desk.

"Riley," he says softly. He's moved, crossing the room to stand next to me. I take a deep breath. Might as well face this, right? I don't want this awkward tension between us for the rest of the semester.

I turn to face him, looking up into his gorgeous eyes. He's studying me, his expression serious. My stomach flips nervously. He's so gorgeous. Why does he have to be so lovely to look at? Why does he have to be so nice, period? Why couldn't he be as curious about me as I am about him? I'm not asking for forever. I just spent over a decade in a ho-hum relationship. I want to get out and experience things!

I'd like to experience some things with Jax.

Is that such a bad idea?

"We should probably talk, huh?" he asks, shoving one hand through his hair, mussing the spiky strands.

No, I think. *We really don't need to do that.*

So I try to end the conversation before it really begins. "I get it. You're not interested. We really don't have to-"

"I never said that, Teach," he interrupts. "I think you know I am. I just think it's a bad idea."

"Because of Luke?"

"Because of a lot of things. But I never said I wasn't interested. And you're smarter than that."

But I'm not. Smart about these things. My phone rings, startling me. Jax takes a step back, and I race to the front of the room, pulling my phone out of my purse.

"Hey, Teagan."

"Hi! I'm in a cab out front. Are you ready?"

My eyes fall to Jax. "Yeah. I'll be right out." I end the call. "I have to go," I tell him. "I'm meeting friends."

He nods, his eyes shuttered. We walk out together, the silence unbearable. I'm going to claw through my skin. The cold air outside is a welcome physical sting.

"I'll see you next week, Teach."

WHEN WE GET TO THE BAR, ILYSSA IS CLEARLY SHAKEN. USUALLY, she's impeccably put together, polished, and poised. But tonight, she's obviously distraught. Her clothes are disheveled, her hair in disarray, her face pale, and eyes dark. For a moment, I'm terrified he actually got released, but Ilyssa informs us his parole request was denied. Unfortunately, he can apply again next year. And he does. Every year. Forcing Ilyssa to go and testify again and again and again.

She grabs her glass of wine and gulps it down as Teagan, and I watch wide-eyed.

"Maybe we should go home," Teagan suggests. "We have wine there…."

"Nope. I'm good right here," Ilyssa says stubbornly. That in itself is a red flag. Ilyssa is not typically stubborn. She pours another glass from the bottle on our table. A heavy pour.

"He just sits there with this stupid look on his face. Trying to convince everyone he's changed. Trying to say he's learned his lesson. Pretending he's not evil. And I'm just so afraid someday they'll believe him."

"You know the DA is on your side. He'll keep fighting it," Teagan reminds her gently.

"I know. But it's so fucked up. I can still feel his eyes on me." She shudders, repulsed.

"I'm so sorry, Ilyssa," I say softly. I can't imagine. I had great parents. I was only nine, barely nine, when they died, but my childhood with them was full of love and laughter, and security. My mom would read me books every night, and my dad would spin the globe, waiting to see what country fell under my tiny finger, and we'd read all about it. They took me to build sand castles on the beach and to do cartwheels in the park. They were exactly the kind of parents I want to be someday. And even though they died way too soon, they made sure I was taken care of. They had Uncle Theo and Aunt Trish there to love me.

When Ilyssa's mom died, all she had was her abusive stepfather And Teagan.

She buries her face in her hands, muffling a screech.

"I just hate having to relive it every fucking time. I hate that it will always be who I am. I hate that he still gets to have any impact on my life. I hate him. I hate him so much. And I hate that he makes me hate. This isn't who I am! Look at me!" She waves her hands along the length of her. "This isn't who I want to be. Who I choose to be. This isn't my life anymore!"

She takes a deep breath, then another healthy drink of her wine, before continuing. "My life is about beauty and order and sophistication and intelligence and style and thoughtfulness and calm. Not this! Not anymore!"

Teagan hops off her stool and embraces her friend, holding her tight and whispering in her ear. I feel a little like an intruder.

I see Ilyssa shake her head, wiping her eyes as she pulls away from Teagan. "No. No, I'm fine, really. Let's just talk about something else, please. Anything. Anything else."

"I learned a new word today," I blurt out, desperate for anything to distract her. Ilyssa blinks at me, and Teagan looks confused. "Tittynope," I offer.

"Tittynope," Ilyssa repeats. I nod, and Teagan slips back onto her stool. "What's it mean?"

"Small amount of something that's left over. Tittynope."

"Tittynope," Ilyssa says again. I'm beginning to feel stupid. I don't have anything else to offer as a distraction? No stories or gossip or drama? Ugh.

But then she starts to giggle. "Tittynope!" she declares, lifting her glass in a toast. Soon we're all laughing hysterically. Ilyssa wipes the tears from her eyes, now a mixture of grief and glee. "Hey, pour me that tittynope of wine. Then we'll get another bottle," Ilyssa declares, and we all burst into laughter again, Teagan doing as she instructed.

"I was kinda hoping it meant something dirty," Teagan jokes.

"Titty-NOPE!" Ilyssa laughs hysterically at her own joke, and we can't help but do the same.

"What else you got?" Teagan asks.

I think for a second. "Cattywampus? It means off-kilter, askew, something that's just not quite right. Most often, it means diagonal. Like catty-corner or kitty-corner."

Ilyssa can't stop laughing. "Cattywampus," she repeats. "That's awesome."

"Ooo! Ooo!" I sit up straight, getting into it now. "Widdershins!"

"Widdershins!" They squeal in delight. Some of the other tables are shooting us looks, trying to figure out what is going on. I ignore them the best I can, focused instead on cheering up Ilyssa, but still a little self-conscious of the attention we're getting.

"What's it mean?" Teagan demands.

"Counterclockwise."

Ilyssa looks at me somewhat blankly, blinking. "Counterclockwise? That's it?"

I shrug. "That's it. Widdershins. Counterclockwise."

She barks out a laugh and shakes her head. Then she grabs both our hands tightly, Teagan with her right and me with her left. "Thanks. Really."

Teagan lifts their joined hands and places a loud smacking kiss on the back of Ilyssa's. "We got you. Forever and Always."

"Forever and Always," Ilyssa repeats. I smile and do the same.

That night I lay in bed, staring at the ceiling, unable to sleep. I replay the day I've had, remembering something Jax said.

Winning a fight doesn't matter unless what you win matters. And any fight with a prize that doesn't matter isn't worth the fight.

Ilyssa has to fight every year to hold on to the life she's made, her security. And she does it, even though it's hard because it *matters*.

What am I willing to fight for? For the life I want? For the woman, I want to be?

I think you know I am.

Is Jax worth a fight?

I'm not entirely sure yet. But I'm pretty sure *I* am.

Now just to pick the fight, I can win.

CHAPTER
Nine

Jax

"What's with you lately?" Mace asks, eying me warily. It's Friday night, and we're closing in thirty minutes. Normally we'd probably just lock up early. All of us are booked for weeks out, so we rarely take walk-ins anymore. But I'm trying to organize some of the merchandise line, and Mace is keeping me company.

"What do you mean?"

"You're overbooking yourself, staying late, not getting any downtime. You're avoiding Luke. He says you haven't been to the boxing gym in days. You haven't filmed any testimonials the last couple weeks. And you haven't shown any interest in getting laid, despite frequent offers. So, what's with you lately?"

I shrug. "Nothing. Just trying to keep on top of everything."

"That right?" Macy says, resting easily on one of the front stools. The look on his face tells me he's not buying it.

"Whatever. I'm going to get back to moving stuff upstairs." I wander down the hall and away from his nosy ass. We finalized the lease for the space above us. I'm psyched we're moving forward, but I'm also distracted and cranky.

I know he's right. Mace. He's right. Somehow I'm so messed up I'm managing to work too much and not enough at the same time. I'm doing everything possible to keep away from Luke without being obvious about it. Which also makes me feel shitty. After some particularly bad choices I managed to keep from him when we were teenagers, I swore I would never lie to Luke again. And I haven't.

I load up the dolly, annoyed by my thoughts as I organize our merchandise.

Mace pokes his head in while I pack more boxes to lug into our new space. "You've got a guest up front."

I stand up, dusting my hands off on my jeans. "Who?"

"I suspect the answer to my question." Mace smirks at me, turning and walking back up front.

I roll my eyes and follow him, easily spotting my visitor. He's not wrong.

"Hey, Teach! What are you doing here?" I try to keep my voice normal and ignore Macy's amused eyes. She's already taken off her coat, holding it folded over her arms. Not planning a quick visit then. I could be in trouble here.

Riley stands awkwardly, shifting from foot to foot. She's wearing jeans and a dark green top with a wide neck. It hangs off her shoulder in this very distracting way. All that creamy ivory skin.

"I want a tattoo," she states.

I tense with surprise and eye her skeptically. "Really. You do? A tattoo?"

She nods, brushing back the hair that falls into her face, tucking it behind her ear.

My eyes follow her fingers, studying her ear and the line of her neck.

This is not a good idea.

My dick disagrees. He likes this idea very much. I was kind of hoping that the other days had been a fluke. Just my dick deciding it was ready to come out of hibernation, but apparently, I'm not that lucky. Because there's been nothing the last several days, and then Riley appears, fully clothed, and he wakes right up again.

Asshole.

"I can check the schedule. I'm sure Lucas would have some time-"

"I don't want Lucas," she interrupts. "I was kind of hoping you might have time. Maybe tonight, even? Now?"

Bad idea.

I glance at the clock, stalling. We're about to close for the night, so it's not like I have another appointment. But I shouldn't. I should limit my exposure to her. Limit it to when we're surrounded by 30 or 40 nosy, needy, borderline obnoxious teenagers.

But I'm not really sure how to turn her down without either hurting her feelings or raising suspicion. The last thing I need is for Riley to know I'm getting hard for her on a regular basis.

"What did you have in mind?" I ask. Both out of curiosity and to buy me some time.

"I'd like something for my parents. My mom loved owls. And my dad liked old maps and books. I thought something for the two of them."

Shit. She pulled the dead parents card. How am I supposed to say no to that? I sigh in resignation, bracing myself for the next couple hours.

"Where do you want it?"

I hear Macy shift on his stool and wonder if I can trick him into sticking around as a buffer.

"I - I'm not sure, either my shoulder or hip."

Really bad idea.

My eyes drift down from that creamy shoulder and eye her jean-clad hips. I can't help imagining those jeans slipping down her hips to get to the skin beneath. I swallow and clear my throat, turning away from her. I move to the counter, where I find Macy behind it.

"What do you think, Mace? Can you stick around a bit longer?" Since the robbery and shooting, we make sure there are always at least two of us for close. Not that that mattered much that night. But it's one of the several safety precautions Lucas implemented.

He smirks at me. Mace was there the night Riley showed up drunk after finding Daniel boinking someone else. He called me on it then, my attraction to her. I'm sure he's loving this. He makes a big show of checking his watch.

"Yeah, sure. I got no plans." He shrugs.

"So…you'll do it?" Riley asks.

Such a bad idea.

"Come on back. We'll work up some sketches."

I guess we're doing this. I'm doing this.

I shoot Macy a look when I hear him chuckle. Well, I guess he's on to my big secret.

Riley follows me into my station and takes a hesitant seat on the tattoo chair. I plop onto my stool and scoot closer to her. But not too close.

"So this is what you want to do on your Friday night, huh?"

She smiles and nods shyly.

"Okay. Tell me more about what you're thinking."

"Oh." Her eyes get wide. "I don't really know. What do you mean?"

I ask her a few questions about style and colors, and size, and what she wants included. Sketching as we talk. This is often how I work, but it has the added benefit of keeping my eyes off her. I work up a few options, and she chooses the one she likes the best. I step out to finish refining it and make a copy on transfer paper so I can stencil it on her skin. I think I've convinced her to do her shoulder.

Safer that way.

Macy smirks at me when he spots me at the printer. "Fuck off," I mutter.

Transfer made, I brace myself to be next to Riley, smelling Riley, touching Riley for the next ninety minutes. Or more.

I'm still studying the image I created when I walk back in. I glance up and see Riley standing next to my chair.

She's wearing nothing but a skimpy beige bra and matching lacy underwear. And my dick stands right up and takes notice.

Riley

I TAKE A SLOW, DEEP INHALE, ATTEMPTING TO CALM MY NERVES.

You can do this, Riley.

Just jump. Fight for the life you want. The woman you want to be.

I slip off my shoes and pull my shirt over my head. I fold it up, setting it gently on the stool Jax just vacated. Then I shimmy out of my jeans, doing the same thing. I shiver. It's cool in the shop, the air teasing my bare skin. Okay. I'm doing this. I can do this.

Not only can I do this, I really need to do this. My attraction to Jax is starting to become problematic. This limerence I have for him is beginning to distract me from everything else.

LIMERENCE
Definition: Intense feelings of obsession or infatuation with another person

I recite the definition in my head, using it to help calm my nerves. I need to scratch this itch, so I can stop obsessing over him so much. This can be my bridge. Moving on from Daniel and my past to my future. Once I'm on the other side, I can start a new season. One where I'm owning my sexuality and not settling for anything. Or anyone. One where I go after what I want.

And right now, I want Jax.

I know he's attracted to me. At least, I'm pretty sure he's attracted to me. And if he's not, well, at least this will force me to move on.

Wow. That will be mortifying, though. So I really hope I'm right. Ilyssa and Teagan seem to think so.

Okay, not thinking about them right now.

I'm not sure what to do with myself, and Jax is taking longer than I thought. Normally I would read something on my phone while I was waiting, but it feels weird to do that in my underwear. It's weird being anywhere other than my apartment wearing nothing but my underwear.

I hear footsteps approaching and stand up straight, presenting a confidence I don't quite feel.

Jax reenters, looking down at his paper. A few steps in, he finally looks up, seeing me. His face mirrors his shock. His eyes travel the length of me, stopping at my toes and moving slowly back up. I force myself to stand still and not fidget even though I still can't read his reaction. When his eyes meet mine again, they are blazing with heat, the gold shimmering in the blue depths. My stomach starts doing backflips.

That seems like a promising response.

He jerks the curtain closed, enclosing us in his little space.

The silence holds us immobile. I'm waiting for something, some sign, some idea, some*thing*. Anything. His eyes slip to my breasts. I'm wearing a new bra and panty set. Purchased with this plan in mind. Just his eyes make my nipples tingle and tighten. I wonder if he can tell that through the lace.

I take a tentative step forward. He clears his throat roughly and watches me but doesn't move. Okay, that's a good sign, I guess? He's not running away. Go for it, Riley. I close the rest of the distance between us until I'm so close my breasts brush against his chest when I take a deep, sustaining breath. And my breasts aren't big. I'm really close.

He's so tall. I won't be able to reach his lips if he doesn't meet me halfway. But I do my best. I place one hand on his shoulder and lift onto my tiptoes, stretching along his frame, reaching for his lips.

"Will you kiss me?" I ask softly.

He groans. Then I watch as his eyes flutter shut, and he lowers his lips to mine.

He does. Jax kisses me. Is kissing me.

Oh my god. Even though I've wanted this, asked for this, fantasized about this, I am not prepared.

His lips are firm and warm and wet against mine. He twists his head, urging my lips apart, and I oblige, thrilled. He deepens the kiss, his tongue teasing mine. Jax's clothes are rough against my skin. My arms lift, wrapping around his neck, and he pulls me tight against him. I can feel my heart pounding in my ears as his kiss goes on and on.

I hear Jax growl before he cups my butt and pulls me roughly against him.

Oh my god. I gasp, tightening my arms around his neck.

He's hard. And my core explodes in aroused tingles. I think my knees went weak, but I can't be positive because he's holding me so tight I'm barely standing as it is.

I feel his fingers digging into my butt and gasp into his kiss. His palms are hot against my bare skin.

"Fuck. Riley," he groans against my lips.

"Will you…kiss my neck?"

He lifts his head and stares deep into my eyes. I press my lips together nervously. Should I not have asked that? I'm trying to be assertive and ask for what I want. But not if it stops him from kissing me somewhere else. So far, I really like Jax's kisses.

"I'm sorry. I -"

His control seems to snap. He grabs me at the waist and lifts me like I weigh nothing, setting me sideways on the tattoo chair. Then he cups my knees and spreads them apart so he can step between them. Oh my god, that's hot. I feel his hands skimming along the outside of my bare thighs, and I shudder with want. I'm already wet and still tingling, just from a few kisses.

Incredibly hot, scorching, sexy kisses.

"Never apologize for asking me to make you feel good." His voice sends shivers down my spine. His eyes still boring into mine.

I want him to really touch me. I want him to do so much more than these hot kisses. I want everything I've done and everything I've never done. With him.

My hands caress his arms, smoothing over the sleeves of his flannel until I can link my fingers behind his neck. I stretch up tall, hyper-aware of his jeans rough against the insides of my knees.

"Are you going to make me ask again?"

His eyes flash and then crinkle as he grins. He presses his lips to the curve of my neck, and I gasp in pleasure, feeling like a live wire has touched my skin. He sucks gently, his breath hot, and then I feel his tongue soothing the spot. I'm trembling. His hot breath moves up my neck until he reaches my ear, and my nerve endings are thrilled. I cry out, gripping fistfuls of his hair and arch against him.

"That feels really good," I whisper. "More."

"Shit. You're killing me," he groans against my skin. His teeth lightly tug on my earlobe. Oh my god. I love that. That feels so good.

"Jax," I say, urging. What I'm not sure. I just want more. Of everything.

His hands squeeze my hips, and his kiss returns to my lips. Teasing, exploring, pleasuring. These are for sure the best kisses of my life. Pleasure starts to fog my brain, silencing all the words, which never happens. I'm not sure I'm ready for it to happen now. I need to think about this seduction, don't I?

I return my hands to his waist, slipping them under his shirt to feel the heat of his skin. I smooth my hands up, admiring his hard abs, the hot skin, and ridges. I let my hands travel back down, my fingertips curl around his waistband, and I move them forward until my hands meet at the front.

I force myself to pull away from his kiss so I can look down. He's hard behind his jeans. The ridge clearly visible. My thighs clench in excitement. He looks huge. I fumble around, my fingers clumsy as I tug at the button and zipper.

"Shit," he mutters, stopping my hands. "Wait. Wait. Let me get rid of Mace."

I freeze, embarrassment washing over me. Right. Macy. Oh my god. How loud were we?

He cups my face, raising it until my eyes meet his. Then he presses a hungry kiss against my lips. "Don't move. I'll be right back."

I nod and watch as he ducks back out.

Now that he's not touching me, my overheated skin feels cold. I shiver on his chair, thinking about what will happen when he returns. What I hope will happen.

The longer he's gone, the colder I get. The more the doubts start to creep in. Am I really doing this?

Crap. Condoms. I didn't even remember to bring condoms. What was I thinking?

Someone more experienced and worldly would have remembered something as basic as condoms when starting a sexual quest. But not me.

My stomach drops.

Oh my god. He's so out of my league. What am I doing?

How many other women have thrown themselves at him in this exact spot? Gorgeous, sexy women who wear thongs on the regular and are far more experienced than me?

I feel gross just thinking about it. All the happy sexy feelings from the last few moments are being quickly erased.

I've got to get out of here. I can't do this.

Stupid to think I could. This isn't me.

I'm scrambling to pull on my clothes before Jax gets back. I can't face him. Not now. Maybe never again.

Okay, that's dramatic. I'm sure I'll be over this mortification in ten years or so.

I shove my arms through my shirt and slip my shoes back on. I grab my jacket, not bothering to put it on just yet. Then I take the coward's way out and sneak through the back door while Jax is up front with Macy.

This was such a mistake.

Jax

Shit. That was hot.

I practically shove Macy out the door. Of course, he's being a dick and dragging his feet. I'm sure he knows exactly why I'm so eager for him to be gone. He's finished most of closing, so I'm more forgiving than I might be otherwise. Finally, the fucker leaves, allowing me to lock up.

I take a deep breath and try to get myself under control. Even now, having a time out from having my hands on her, I know I'm not going to stop. All the reasons I had for not crossing the line with Riley were wiped away the second she touched me wearing nothing but her underwear.

A better man may be able to resist that kind of temptation, but I sure as fuck can't.

Not after the only woman my dick has responded to in the last several months just stripped next to my chair. That's fucking hot. Those slim creamy thighs and hard nipples poking through the lace. And that sweet kiss. So...desperate in the best, sexiest way. Desperate for me. For the pleasure I could give her, we could give each other.

I push the curtain aside, reentering my station, almost pathetically eager.

She's gone.

What the hell?

Poof. Gone.

I'd think it was just an elaborate fantasy, but I can still taste her. And I haven't tasted nearly enough.

No way. No way, Teach.

I finish closing up and then hop on my bike. I'm not going to let her run away from me. Not like this.

I drive through the city streets, heading to Riley's apartment. I should be able to beat her there, even if she drove. Motorcycles can navigate the city faster than cars. But it's also possible she took the el, which means I may be waiting for a while.

I'll wait as long as it takes. I want answers.

I back my bike up to the curb and kick the stand down. The windows in Riley's apartment are still dark, so I make myself comfortable, leaning against my seat, arms, and ankles crossed.

Ten minutes later, she comes walking down the sidewalk, talking to herself. When she gets closer, I see she's actually talking to someone on the phone.

She stumbles to a stop when she spots me.

"I, ah, I have to call you back," she mutters before stepping forward, so she's in front of me.

I eye her up and down, taking in her flushed cheeks and still-swollen lips. Her wide gray eyes reveal all her nerves.

"You okay?" I ask, my voice gruffer than I intended it to be.

She nods jerkily.

I push myself off my cycle and brush away a lock of hair clinging to her bottom lip. I may take advantage of the moment to also smooth my thumb along that lower lip. Her eyes spark with awareness, and despite my annoyance, my body likes her reaction to me.

"Well? Let's go in." I gesture to her apartment.

She walks up the stairs silently, shooting wary looks at me over her shoulder as we go. I don't like that she's so nervous, but I'm sure she can tell I'm not happy with her disappearing act. When we get to her door, she drops her keys, muttering under her breath. I bend down and grab them, taking her hand and placing them into her palm.

"Relax, Teach." And because I can't help myself, I pull her hat off and press my lips to her forehead, breathing her in.

"You're mad," she whispers, gripping my wrist.

I exhale roughly. "Yeah, I'm mad. But I'll get over it."

One corner of her mouth quirks up briefly. "Promise?"

"Riley. Do you want me to leave?" I hope not. We need to talk. But I don't like her like this. She's silent for a second and then shakes her head, unlocking her door. Pirate comes racing, jumping happily at her return. I'm starting to relate.

Once again, she drops to her knees to smother affection on her mutt. I suspect she takes her time, still not excited to face me.

"Do you need to take him out?"

"Yeah, I should. Do you mind?"

"Why don't I take him?" I offer, hoping if she has a few minutes alone, she'll relax a little bit.

She looks up from her spot on the floor, eyes wide with surprise. "You wouldn't mind?"

"Nah. He's cute. I can handle a trip around the block."

I hand her the leash hanging by the door, and she clips it on, then hands it back to me as she stands. I take Pirate around the block, waiting impatiently while he sniffs around and chooses a spot to do his business. When he's done, we head back up to Riley's. She gave me her keys, so I let us in, calling out her name.

She appears in the living room, face still showcasing her nerves. It makes me feel like crap. Part of me wishes I could hold her, make her feel better, but that's kind of why we're here. Last time she was in my arms, she bolted.

I take my coat off and turn to her, diving in. Let's just rip off the band-aid, Teach.

"What the hell, Riley? You just sneak out and disappear? What was that?"

"I'm sorry. I'm not trying to be a tease-"

"Is that what you think?" I interrupt, annoyed. "That I'm pissed because you didn't screw me in one of the tattoo stations at *Vanished*?" I pace away from her, shoving a hand through my hair. I take a deep breath, calming myself down. She doesn't deserve my temper, and that's not why I came. I turn back to her, deliberately gentling my voice. "I'm not pissed at you. I'm... upset that you just took off. You didn't talk to me, Riley."

Her eyes are stormy and wide as she watches me pace. "I'm sorry. I just started thinking, and suddenly I was so overwhelmed, and I've never actually done this before."

"Done what?" I attempt a grin, trying to lighten the mood. "Driven a grown man crazy?"

She grimaces and opens her mouth, but I stop her before she can say anything.

103

"You don't need to apologize. Just tell me what's going on. I mean, one minute you're stripping naked and about to grab my dick, and the next you're slipping out the back door."

Riley sighs and moves to sit on her couch, so I do the same. "Daniel and I started dating when I was sixteen. And we were together until…."

Until she caught the stupid asshole cheating on her.

But I don't know what that has to do with her disappearing act.

She looks away from me, studying her feet. "He's… he's the only one I've ever…."

Oh.

OH.

Shit.

"You mean…."

"Yeah."

I exhale roughly and lean back into her couch. "Wow."

She giggles nervously, and her reaction just makes me like her more. I love how honest she is. No games.

A better man would walk away right now. But I've already established that isn't me.

I shift sideways a little to face her, one leg bent and resting on the couch. "If we're going to do this, I need to talk to Lucas," I tell her.

"Lucas? Why?"

"Because he's my best friend, and you're his family."

"Lucas doesn't care about me," she says softly.

I glance at her sharply, disturbed she still thinks that's true. "He does."

She shrugs, her fingers twisting together. "I am sorry, I just ran. I should have talked to you. It just messed with my head for a second."

"It's cool, Teach. I'm over it. As promised." I grin at her, and she does too. I reach for her, pulling her into my lap so I can start touching her again. "Don't do it again, okay?"

Riley nods, winding her arms around my neck and leaning into me. I run my hand along her thigh, annoyed it's covered by her jeans and not her soft skin beneath my fingers like earlier. But now that my cock isn't in complete control, I know that will have to wait until another night. I've got to talk to Luke.

A few more kisses won't hurt, though.

"I know how you can really make it up to me."

She grins, a glint in her gray eyes. "Oh, yeah? How's that?"

"Will you kiss me?" I repeat her invitation back to her. Her smile kills me. Then she pulls my head to hers, placing gentle teasing kisses against the corners of my mouth. I grip her hips, shifting her in my lap, swallowing my groan.

Finally, she settles her mouth over mine, lips soft and eager. I feel her nails against my scalp, her other hand along my neck where I'm sure she can feel my pulse racing. I sink into her. So sweet. Her kisses somehow both soothe me and work me up. I love the contrast. It turns me on.

She turns me on.

My dick is throbbing against my zipper. Every time she shifts, her ass drags against it. The sweetest fucking pain.

Abruptly I lift her off my lap and set her away from me, breathing heavily.

"I should go."

Her dazed eyes blink and then reflect her confusion.

"But…before…."

"Before you showed me your tits, and I was struck stupid."

She laughs like she thinks I'm kidding. I'm not.

Shrugging, I tell her, "You have really amazing tits."

"They're small."

"They're fucking perfect."

Her eyes sparkle at the compliment.

I press a quick, hungry kiss against her lips and force myself to leave her. "I'll see you soon, Teach. Promise."

CHAPTER

Ten

Riley

"**W**ait. I'm sorry. He just *left?*"

I'm hit with a wave of deja vu at Teagan's disbelief.

But this time, I'm okay with the fact that he just left.

Because he didn't *just* leave. He walked my dog. And he listened to me explain my nerves. And he didn't make fun of me or make me feel stupid. And he kissed me more thoroughly and sweetly and hotly than I've ever been kissed.

And he promised he'd be back. For more. For more of *me*.

I've been wearing a smug little smile all day. I can't help it. Which is sooooo not me. I'm not smug.

But I made out with Jackson Hall on Friday night. Nobody else in the world can say that. So I'm smug. Sue me. Because making out with Jax is awesome.

Seriously awesome.

I still get all hot and tingly when I think about it. I can't imagine what it will be like when I actually get him naked. When we move beyond hot kisses and gentle touches.

I can't imagine. And I can't wait.

Knowing I'm going to see him tomorrow flips my stomach with excitement. I shake my head. I'm like one of my students with a crush.

As if on cue, my phone vibrates with an incoming text.

I can't stop thinking about those pretty nipples covered by lace. Fucking hot, Teach. Can't wait to peel that lace off next time.

Oh my god. My breath catches in my throat. I'm sure my face is flaming. I glance around just to make sure nobody can see the message on my phone, but of course, they can't.

Another message comes in.

I'm going to suck those pretty nipples. I bet they taste so sweet.

STOP. I respond. **I'm in public!**

Interesting. So if you weren't in public, you'd want me to keep going?

I mean, probably? But I'm not going to admit that to him right now.

He sends another. **You should send me a copy of that list. So I can make some plans.**

I exhale an embarrassed giggle snort.

This man is potent. I'm tingling with arousal, desperate for him over miles. From a few texts? Holy cow.

Ilyssa's watching me carefully. She smiles at me. "I know that look," she murmurs. "You're giddy."

I giggle, nodding. "I can't help it! It's so fun!"

"What is?" Teagan asks.

"Flirting. Kissing. Daydreaming. Those first feelings of falling. You know," Ilyssa glances at her friend.

"Oh." Teagan makes a face. "Yeah, I don't do that."

I laugh. I've been laughing a lot for the last thirty-six hours. The three of us met for brunch earlier this morning. Now we're taking advantage of the slightly warmer temperatures to wander the neighborhood, popping in and out of boutiques and other shops. After the bitter cold of the last week, even the slightest spike in temperature fills the city sidewalks. Everyone taking advantage, enjoying the apricity while we can. We all know in Chicago, these days are precious.

APRICITY
Definition: the warmth of the sun in winter

We're currently wandering one of my favorite rare and used bookstores in the city. It's one of those rare zoning miracles where an old house was turned into a shop and somehow hasn't been bought out by a developer. The rooms are cramped, overflowing with books, shelves, and old maps. It smells musty, and my nose constantly itches, but I love it.

"Oh! Daddy would love this," Teagan exclaims, pulling out an ancient atlas depicting maps from the late 1900s. "I'm going to get it. His birthday is coming up."

I stiffen. *Please don't*, I think.

"Speaking of birthdays," Teagan turns her attention to me. Shoot. She's doing it. "What are we doing for your birthday next month?"

I pretend a fascination with the book in front of me. Truthfully though, I have no idea what it is.

"Same as every year," I mutter. "Absolutely nothing."

Teagan sighs, her eyes still on me as I deliberately ignore her. "It's your golden birthday," she points out, gently for Teagan.

"Twenty-eight on the twenty-eighth. Don't you think you should celebrate?"

"Nope," I say. This conversation has effectively destroyed any lingering giddiness from my kissing session with Jax. I'm going to need another fix. Soon.

"But-"

Ilyssa cuts Teagan off before she can complete her argument. "She'll think about it. Right, Riley?"

I nod dismissively because, of course, I won't.

I don't celebrate my birthday.

I haven't since I was nine years old.

CHAPTER
Eleven

Jax

I've got to talk to Luke today. Yesterday was a particular kind of hell, a torture I don't want to have to repeat.

It was Monday, so my afternoon with the art kids. And Riley.

Riley, in her cute little dresses, yesterday it was navy with green and blue dinosaurs. And her no-nonsense teacher's voice. With her wide smile and teasing eyes. We were good until Afternoon with Art was over. But then I gave her a ride home, she decided not to pay for repairs on her old car and is planning on buying a new one soon, and we made out like fucking teenagers. I refused to go inside her apartment. I knew my willpower was not up to that temptation, and instead kissed her in my car until even the heat of our bodies wasn't enough to keep her from shivering. Then I sent her inside. Alone.

And now that I've opened the door to sexting, Riley is surprisingly adept at fucking with me. She's started texting me one item on her 'Sex List' at a time. I never know when one is going to pop up on my screen. I'm a walking hard-on right now. Which, you know, it's nice to have my dick back in working order, but it's also hella awkward in all sorts of day-to-day situations. So, I've got to talk to Luke.

Today.

Because I need Riley in my bed as soon as fucking possible. Naked. Under me. Over me. Full of me.

Christ.

It was hard letting her go last night.

But I'd feel guilty about it. If we'd slept together last night. Feel like I was sneaking around behind my best friend's back. Riley deserves better than that, and surprisingly, I think I do too.

Also, I have a feeling once I start sleeping with Riley, it's not going to be easy to stop, and I really don't want something negative hanging over my head when all I should be thinking about at that point is 1) how often I can get her naked and 2) how to make Riley come as many times as possible.

"Hey, you got time to grab a beer after work tonight?" I try to keep my voice as casual as possible. Like this is not a big deal. Like I don't have something to tell him that may trigger an eruption.

Luke looks up from his phone and eyes me. "Sure. Something on your mind?"

"Just some stuff to talk about," I say with a shrug. I don't want him either stressing about it or bugging me about it, so I try to play it cool.

"I'm in. I'll let Ash know I'm going to be late, and we can head out after my last appointment."

The day passes quickly. I've got back-to-back appointments today, which always makes the time go faster. We head out a little before 5, leaving Macy and Logan to close up at nine.

We grab a table at a pub down the street and order some food and a couple pints.

"So there is something I need to talk to you about." Shit, this is harder than I thought. I've never asked someone's permission to date a girl, and while that's not really what's going on here, it feels pretty damn close. Also, Luke is just starting to make progress with his family, and I don't want to mess that up.

But then I picture Riley's wide gray eyes and wider smile. I remember how fucking hot she was in my arms Friday night. Last night. Luke's going to be okay with this. And if not, we'll work it out.

We may work it out in the boxing gym, but we'll work it out.

I focus on my friend. He's watching me steady and quiet, waiting to hear what's on my mind.

"I'm, uh, I, well…."

I'm off to a great start. Christ.

"I'm interested in Riley." I just blurt it out, leaving it hanging there.

Luke stares at me with a blank expression on his face. "Riley who?"

What the fuck? I roll my eyes and glare at him.

"Are you fucking serious right now? Riley Abbott. Your cousin. Riley."

"I know who she is." His face clouds, eyes snapping. "I just didn't think you'd be that stupid."

I wince. "Guess you were wrong."

"Get *un*interested," Lucas practically growls.

Agitated, I lean back in my seat and run a hand through my hair. "You think I haven't tried that, man? She's just so…." I fade off, unsure how to explain. How to put Riley into words.

"Is this about Tanya?"

I jerk in surprise. "What? No."

"We haven't talked about…that whole thing."

"Fuck. Ash has you so whipped."

Luke laughs, fucker *laughs*, only proving my point. "Why?"

"Wanting to talk about your feelings and shit," I grumble.

He laughs again but isn't ready to drop it. "I just mean… shit. I know she's the last one you…." He waves his hand at me, leaving the rest unspoken.

Jesus Christ, why are all my friends so worried about my dick all of a sudden?

The waitress reappears with our food, giving me a moment to sit back and try to gather my thoughts.

Yes, Tanya is the last woman I fucked. And finding out she was actually stalking my best friend and was slightly homicidal wasn't exactly a pleasant experience. But Riley's got nothing to do with Tanya.

What's going on between me and Riley has nothing to do with all that bullshit.

"If you just need to get back out there-"

"Are you kidding me with this shit?" I cut him off. "Why are you being such an asshole? This isn't about getting laid."

He stares at me for a beat and then sits back, drinking his beer. "Shit. You like her."

"Yes, I like her. What the hell have we been talking about the last five minutes?"

"No, I mean, you're into her. You *like* her."

I don't like him much right now. "Yeah, well, so do you."

He grimaces. "Please do not compare how I feel about her and how you feel about her. That's just nasty."

I roll my eyes at him but relax a bit. I feel like we're getting on the same page. Finally.

"You do though," I accuse. "Admit it."

He shrugs. "Yeah. She's alright." I snort at his weak answer. "Fine. She's a sweetheart. I get it, okay? I like her."

I grin smugly. I'd been working on him to give Riley a chance for months. He's stubborn but slowly she wore him down. We're both silent, digging into our burgers.

"I know I'm not good enough for her. We're just... having some fun. For now."

Luke snorts. "Good enough. Why, because she's an Abbott?" All of a sudden, he's pissed on my behalf. Not what I was going for, but I appreciate the loyalty. He's still overly sensitive when it comes to his bio family and his place in it.

"No, man. Not because she's an Abbott. Because she's Riley."

"And?"

"And she just got out of a ten-year relationship. The last thing she needs is to jump right into another one. And you know, I'm not that guy. Relationship guy."

"So you're...having fun. Keeping it casual. For now." He eyes me skeptically.

I squirm before answering, "Yeah. Besides, our worlds are too different for anything else. She just...wants to have some fun. After the whole Daniel thing."

"I don't know. I mean, Ash and I are making it work." He grins.

It still hits me these moments when I realize how fucking happy he is. How good they are together. They're more than 'making it work'. They're all hashtag relationship goals and shit.

But he seems to have settled into the idea and no longer wants to punch my face in. "Just make sure I don't see any sex tapes on my cameras," he warns me.

Oh shit. Ever since a video of Lucas and Ash was leaked, by Tanya, to the tabloids, Luke has made sure to skim any footage of the shop before handing it over to the show.

I grimace and clear my throat self-consciously. "You, ah, may want to avoid the footage from Friday night."

Luke holds up a hand to stop me from explaining. "No details. Please. I don't want to know." He curses under his breath. "I'll make sure Krista deletes it," he mutters. "Seriously though, I like Riley. But I don't ever want to see the two of you...." he flails his hand, making his point. "Seeing her naked is not something I EVER need to experience. So keep it out of *Vanished*. I beg you."

I smirk at him. "No promises. But I promise to delete the tapes. Or cover the cameras."

"Christ. At least that's something."

I laugh. Relieved that this went much easier than I expected.

And tonight, I'm going inside that apartment.

Fuck yes.

Riley

YOU BUSY?

My heart speeds up seeing the text from Jax. I bite my lip, trying to squelch my smile. I've been doing that a lot the last few days. Smiling.

Not really. You?

Good. Let me up.

My stomach drops. And I run to the window, looking down. I can't see my entryway, but I do see Jax's car parked across the street. Oh my god. He's here?

I look down at myself. I've been home for a couple hours now and have already changed into my comfy clothes for the night. I'm wearing a pair of leggings and an oversized white sweater. Could be worse, I guess.

You're here?

Let me up, Teach.

I hit the buzzer, holding it for a few seconds longer than necessary. And then I walk, stomach in somersaults, to open my apartment door.

In record time, Jax is bounding up the final flight, pausing in my doorway. He's wearing his trademark crooked grin as he looks down at me.

"Hi."

"Hi," I repeat back to him, still having trouble processing the fact that he's standing before me. Unlike me, he looks absolutely delicious in jeans, a leather jacket, and mussy hair. With just a little scruff along his cheeks. I want to run my fingers along his jaw. I realize with a start, I can do that now. If I want to, and I do. Before I can second guess myself, I cup his cheek and lift onto my tiptoes to give him a kiss hello. He meets me halfway, thrilling me. There's still a chill radiating off of him, coming in from the frigid air outside, and I shiver, pulling away so he can enter.

"Nice surprise." I smile at him as he takes his coat off. Pirate comes over sniffing at his feet. He pats the top of Pirate's head absently, his eyes on me.

"Does he need to go out?"

"Not for a few hours yet. I usually take him out again right before I go to bed."

"I'll do that tonight," he says, straightening.

I blink at him, slow to process. "You will?"

"Yep." He moves so he's standing right in front of me. "You're not going to have any clothes on later."

Oh.

Wow.

Okay.

"But you will?" I ask.

"Only long enough to walk your dog."

He picks me up, throwing me over his shoulder, and I yelp in surprise. "Jax! What are you doing? I can walk."

"I know you can. But I'm in a hurry."

I giggle, flushing with pleasure. I feel his hand on the back of my thigh, hot even through my leggings. He moves us down the hallway, kicks my bedroom door shut, and deposits me on my bed. He stares down at me, eyes scorching, and removes the long-sleeved henley shirt he's wearing. My eyes drink him in. My first look at Jax without his shirt on.

And he's like a work of art. Sculpted muscles, hard abs, broad shoulders, just a dusting of hair on his chest. I drink in the sight of him. His chest and arms are covered in tattoos, designs I can't wait to explore with my fingers. And my tongue.

"So, I guess you talked to Lucas?"

"I did." He starts to climb onto the bed, crawling across the mattress up to me.

"And? What did he say?"

He pauses, braced on his arms, bracketing my calves. "Riley. Do you really want to talk about Lucas right now?"

I whisper no, shaking my head.

"Good."

He continues prowling up the bed until he's hovering over me as I lay in the center of my mattress. My heart is pounding so hard I'm afraid it's going to shake the bed. That gold ring in his eyes is shimmering hotly as he stares down at me. My breath catches in my chest, waiting, anticipating.

"I hope you can function on not much sleep, Teach. 'Cause I think it's going to take all night for me to do everything I want to do to you."

His statement makes me giggle. Nerves, excitement, giddiness. "Are you going to kiss me now?" I ask, trailing my hands up his arms, squeezing his massive biceps, then settling them on his shoulders.

"I'm going to do so much more than that."

My insides flip and flutter at his words. I want to exosculate with Jax for hours.

> **EXOSCULATE**
> Definition: to kiss, especially to kiss repeatedly

Starting right now.

I link my fingers behind his neck and gently pull him down. He grins and lowers himself onto me, onto the bed. He shifts and settles, one leg sliding between mine. And then finally, Jax kisses me.

Sighing at the contact, I seem to melt into my mattress. A soft puddle of lazy desire. I love Jax's kisses. He's gentle and sweet one minute, demanding and firm the next. It makes my head hazy with pleasure. I love the weight of him pressing me down. He's hard and solid and I can't get enough of touching him. I'm tugging his hair, caressing his back, squeezing his muscles. I could do this lazy exploring for hours, but Jax seems to have other ideas.

He rolls us, so he's lying on his back with me on top. It takes me a second to find my balance, but he holds me tight, and my legs settle on each side of his hips, hands braced on either side of his head.

"Cute sweater," he mutters, burying his lips into the curve of my neck. I shiver in reaction. I love that. That feels so good. I must have a direct line of sensations from my neck to my core because that lights right up at the contact. I tilt my head, encouraging him to continue exploring my neck.

"Thanks," I squeak out.

"How do you feel about taking that off now?"

I savor our current position for a second before responding. "I feel pretty good about that." I shift until I'm sitting, straddling his lap, which presses the juncture of my thighs into the hard ridge of his erection behind his jeans. He groans, squeezing my hips, and rocks me against him. Oh my god. Sparks. Tingles. Heat. Everywhere.

"Jax," I groan. He's setting me on fire, and we've still got multiple layers of clothing between us.

"Sweater, Riley. Off."

I nod and whip my sweater over my head, tossing it on the floor. I have a white tank top underneath it. It's soft and sheer, and when I glance down, my hard nipples are clearly visible. Something that definitely doesn't escape Jax's notice. His eyes are riveted to my chest. I've always felt a little self-conscious about my breasts, thinking they were far too small to be sexy, but Jax is quickly erasing all those concerns. The expression on his face is hungry as he stares at me. His eyes flick up to mine for a brief second before settling back on my chest. He sits up, bending me back slightly over his arm, my breasts thrusting into the air, and he presses a hot wet kiss to my right nipple. Then he turns his attention to my left, sucking it into his mouth through the skimpy material of my tank.

I gasp, my hands thrusting into his hair, fisting the strands, holding him tightly in place.

"So pretty," he groans. His fingers tickle my bare skin, slipping under the hem of my top. I inhale sharply at the sensations. He moves his attention between my nipples until they're both tight and straining against the wet material. It feels so good. I'm rocking against him, rolling my hips, jolting each time his erection presses against me...right...there. Oh!

Growing desperate, I shift, urging Jax down onto his back. His breathing is harsh, matching mine. "Fucking hot, Teach."

A smile spreads across my face. He makes me feel so good. Free. Empowered. Sexy.

Things I can't remember ever really feeling. Let alone being.

And I want more.

I pull my tank top off, leaving me bare from the waist up. Jax groans, his hips thrust up, nearly unseating me, but he rolls us again until he's leaning over me. My first experience feeling Jax's skin against my own. So good.

"You're killing me, baby."

I cup his cheeks, loving the feel of his sexy scruff against my palms. "Can't have that. How can I make you feel better?" I tease him, pressing soft kisses to his face. He quickly takes control, deepening the kiss, settling into me. One of his thighs moves between mine, pressing against my core, rubbing against me. I cry out at the friction, unable to help myself as sparks shoot through me.

Abruptly, he pulls away, kneeling above me. His fingers curl into the waistband of my leggings, but then he pauses, his eyes meeting mine, questioning. I grin at him, still wanting to play and tease. I've never felt control like this before.

"You first," I tell him.

He smirks. "Whatever you say, Teach. Fucking zipper is strangling my cock anyway."

Should I like it so much when he says stuff like that? I don't know. But I do. And when he quickly strips off his jeans and boxer briefs, leaving him naked next to me, I forget to care.

He's so gorgeous. I want to explore all that skin and muscle and study each tattoo and line. But I also want more. I don't even know everything I want. But everything inside me is straining for Jax. For his eyes, his hands, his body. My eyes slip down his chest and abs, drawn to the erection jutting from the junction of his thighs.

Wow. He fists his cock (oh my god, I said cock), stroking the length. And he's got a healthy amount of length. And thickness. Wow. He puts my new vibrator to shame. If I wasn't wet before... I'm soaked now.

He settles next to me again, his crooked grin in place. "Guess it's your turn."

My stomach lurches with nerves. I'm not sure I can be that brazen; just strip down like he did. Suddenly I'm frozen, acutely aware my overhead light is on. Which I'd appreciated when it gave me a clear view of Jax and all he has to offer, but it seems obscenely bright when shining on me.

My eyes flick to my door, where my light switch lives.

"Um. Do you mind...can we turn the lights off?"

His eyes study my face carefully, making me even more self-conscious.

"You getting shy on me, Teach?"

I nod. "Please?"

I feel him and the bed shift next to me, still unable to meet his eyes. Shoot. I'm ruining everything. But then I see Jax strutting naked across my room, hitting the lights, and plunging us into darkness. He bumps into something coming back to bed and swears under his breath. A nervous giggle escapes me, and he practically dive bombs onto the bed, landing half on top of me. This time I laugh out loud.

"You laughing at me?" he murmurs, pressing kisses to my shoulder and along my collarbone.

"Sorry. Did you hurt yourself?"

He ignores my question, continuing to spread kisses across my skin, humming in pleasure. My eyes are adjusting to the dark. Luckily the street lights outside my window give off enough for me to still appreciate the sight in front of me. But not enough to make me feel quite so vulnerable.

"I'm starting my own sex list," Jax murmurs, his teeth pulling gently at my earlobe. I gasp and grip his shoulders, trying to pull him more fully over me.

"Resolutions," I correct absently.

"Fine. My own list of sex resolutions. Want to know what's on it?"

I nod because I do, but also so he has better access to my neck for his kisses.

"Number One, go down on Riley with all the lights on."

Oh my god. Even though I'd just made that impossible for right now, the idea turns me on even more, flipping my stomach. Stealing my breath.

"Number Two, go down on Riley."

He leans back, curling his fingers once again into the waist of my leggings. This time, when he pauses, I lift my hips, urging him on.

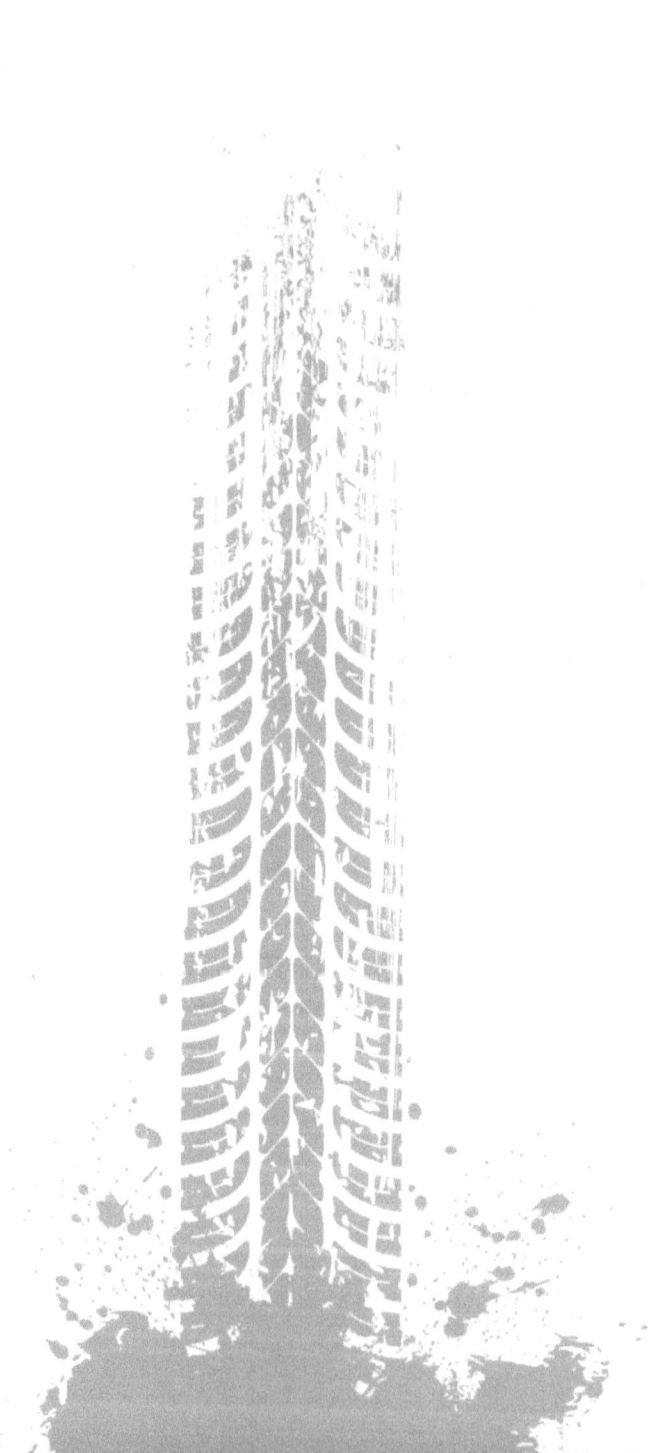

CHAPTER
Twelve

Jax

I peel Riley's leggings down her smooth legs, revealing all of her. Fuck. Naked Riley. So pretty.

She's so sweet and surprisingly sassy. I love watching her eyes spark before she teases me, taunts me with something. My dick is so damn hard.

I kiss her flat stomach, letting my tongue trail over her skin to her mound. I hear her gasp, her back arching into me. The sound goes right to my throbbing cock. My eyes move up her body, I pause briefly at those perky tits, so responsive, before finding her face. She's flushed, lips parted as she exhales in tiny pants, her stormy eyes hazy with pleasure.

I trace my hands along her sides, down her legs, cupping behind her knees. I urge her legs apart, keeping my eyes on hers.

She bites her lip nervously, hesitating only briefly before her knees fall to the sides.

"So pretty, Teach."

"Jax." The way she sighs my name works me up, my entire body tightening in expectation.

I take one finger and trace her slit, grinning when I feel how wet she is. Just as turned on as I am. I suck the finger I used to tease her with, tasting how sweet and tangy she is. Her eyes widen in surprise, her chest rising and falling rapidly.

"You want that, Riley? You want to feel my mouth on you?"

She nods, those wide eyes watching me.

I shift, settling between those slim, soft thighs. My tongue swipes through her folds, teasing her, tasting her. And then I settle in, enjoying her. She moans, so sweet, and I feel her tugging on my hair, keeping me close as if I was going to go anywhere. My face is between Riley's thighs. I'm cool right here. For as long as she wants me.

I take my time, learning what she likes, listening to her body and her response. So sweet. She twists beneath me, gasping, thrusting her hips into my tongue. Eventually, my throbbing cock forces me to move things along. I use my fingers to spread her wetness, slipping a single digit inside her sex. She cries out, back arching. Fuck, I can't wait until it's my cock inside her. So tight and sweet.

"Yes, Jax. Oh god."

"You're so gorgeous like this. All hot and needy. Are you going to come for me?"

Her eyes are wild as they look at me. "More. Please. I need your mouth."

I resist for a second, just to torture us both. Then I slip a second finger inside her, thrusting, curling, and lower my mouth back to her sex and flick my tongue against her clit. She's pulling at my hair again, her other hand gripping my forearms, her nails stinging my skin. She's straining against me. I can feel her tightening around my fingers, her body clasping, begging. Suddenly making Riley come is the most important thing in my world. Her thighs clench, back arching as she starts to shake, finally breaking apart with an ecstatic cry. She trembles against me, and I stay right where I am, tasting her arousal until she finally sighs, going limp.

I surge to my feet, finding the condoms I brought with me. Returning to bed, I move up her body, pressing kisses all along the way. She sighs and smiles at me when I reach her lips, kissing her hotly.

Fuck, I need to get inside her. I need to feel her come apart like that while I'm buried in her tight little body.

"That was fucking hot. You ready for more?" My knees nudge her thighs apart, settling on top of her. Her hand caresses my cheek as she presses a soft kiss to my lips. Damn, she's so sweet.

"Yes. Can we have sex now?"

I chuckle, grinning. "Isn't that what we've been doing?"

She laughs. "I want more. I want you."

"I've got no problem with that, Teach."

I roll to my side, tearing into the first condom wrapper and rolling it down my length, and then return to my place between her thighs. Riley urges me down, silently asking for a kiss which I'm happy to do. I sink into her kiss, using my tongue to explore and tease. My hand smooths along her ribs, moving to cup her breast, plucking the nipple. She gasps into my kiss, and I feel her hands on my lower back, fingers pressing into my skin. I'm dying to get inside her.

I shift my hips, bracing myself. I break our kiss and smile into her eyes. "You have no idea how long I've wanted to do this."

Her eyes spark with curiosity. "How long?" she whispers.

Smirking, I confess, "So long, Teach. Since that first time, you came to the hospital, when you brought me Duk's."

"Really?" Her eyes are wide, and I suspect I should be paying more attention to this conversation, but I'm distracted by her soft touches on my back.

"Yeah. You were so cute and nervous and sweet, and all I wanted to do was mess you up. Just like this." I hum against her neck, moving down, wanting her nipple in my mouth without the cotton between us. She presses her fingers into my skin and shivers.

Fuck. I can't wait anymore. My cock is going to explode.

I grip my dick, lining us up, and ease inside her. So hot and tight and wet. Fuck. So good. I can't take my eyes off where we're joined as she takes me. She's lifting into me, her body begging for more. When I'm as deep as I can go, I drag my eyes up her body to her face. Wanting to watch her expressions. Her mouth forms that delicious little O. I can't wait to see that mouth on my dick.

I groan and flex my hips, pulling out and thrusting back in. Riley bends her knees, squeezing my hips as she meets my thrusts. Giving and taking. Her small breasts jiggle as my control starts to fray. I need her to come again; I'm not going to last much longer.

"So good, Riley. Fuck, you feel so good. Squeeze my dick." My hips slam into her, no longer able to move slowly. But I need to make sure she comes again. I lick up her neck, finding that sensitive spot below her ear and, at the same time, moving my hand between us, finding her clit, strumming, urging her closer.

She gasps again, her breaths ragged and heavy against my cheek.

"Oh! Jax. That's...." Her body strains against me, tightening. "Oh god," she groans.

I'm losing it. I feel my orgasm coming on. "Riley."

She groans in small bursts, shuddering against me as she breaks apart, and with that, I let go, thrusting into her orgasm, chasing my own, losing myself in the pleasure we create.

I'm breathing heavy, mindlessly rolling my hips against her, sucking every good feeling I possibly can from the moment.

"Shit," I groan, collapsing on top of her.

Riley sighs, holding me tight. I can hear her heartbeat, slowing, steady. "Wow," she whispers. I feel her fingers moving through my hair against my scalp. Nice. I don't want to move. I'm not sure I could. I should at least roll off her. I just don't want to. She feels nice beneath me, around me, touching me.

This is a new sensation for me, and if I had more energy, I might be worried. Usually, once I've come, I'm eager to get a little space and breath my own air. But with Riley...I like keeping her close. I like her hands in my hair. I like her body cushioning mine.

She sighs, and I force myself off her, getting up to deal with the condom. I get a glass of water, Pirate dancing around my feet, before returning to her bed. She smiles sleepily and makes room for me next to her. Without hesitation, she curves into my side, resting her head on my chest. I glance at her clock, checking the time. Should probably take Pirate out soon.

"What time do you have to get up in the morning?" I ask her.

She rubs her cheek against my skin. "By six."

I groan. "That's brutal, Teach."

"I know. Life of a teacher." She gives a little shrug against me. Absently, I find myself teasing my hand along her bare spine, cupping her ass. I didn't pay nearly enough attention to that ass. Next time. For now, I just squeeze and caress and enjoy while relaxing.

"Can I stay? Or do you need me to head out?"

She stiffens, levering herself up onto one elbow. "What do you mean? I thought you were going to keep me up all night?" She grins at me, teasing.

A warm feeling spreads through my chest. A feeling I recognize is going to lead to trouble, but I can't find the energy to care right now.

Instead, I tell her, "You should take a twenty-minute nap while I walk Pirate. 'Cause I'm going to be ready for more when I get back."

"Promises, promises." She wiggles her eyebrows at me. I squeeze her ass one more time and give her a swift kiss.

"Twenty minutes, Teach. And then we start on that list of yours."

Riley

I COULDN'T ACTUALLY JUST LAY IN BED WHILE JAX WALKED MY DOG, SO despite his protests, I pull my clothes back on, bundle up, and we take Pirate around the block together. The second we're back inside, he strips me down, leaving my clothes in a pile on my living room floor, and hurries us back to bed. This time he urges me onto my stomach, kneading and caressing, even nibbling, my butt cheeks until I'm a quivering puddle of need.

"Jax. Now, please."

His arm slips beneath my stomach, urging me onto my hands and knees as he presses hot, open-mouthed kisses along my spine. I shiver and brace myself while Jax takes care of protection. And then I feel him, his hands squeezing my butt as he eases inside me. It's just as good, just as hot as the first time. He's so big next to me, I feel completely surrounded by him. His hard chest against my back, thighs between mine, one arm around my waist, the other hand alternating between teasing my nipples and slipping between my thighs to tease my core, his breath is warm and humid against my neck. God. I shiver in his arms, loving all of it. He's desperate for me, something I've never had before, and the feeling is heady.

Jax moves against me, and I feel his erection hot and heavy as he thrusts, his hips starting to slam against my butt, rocking me forward and back on my arms.

"Fuck. That ass," Jax mutters, his fingers plucking my clit. I can't help the cry that escapes. It feels so good. The tingles are already pooling, spreading. I don't think I've ever come this fast before. His mouth latches onto that sensitive spot below my ear, and I clench, crying out again.

"Yes. Riley. Squeeze my cock. Do it again," he orders, groaning. His thrusts are coming faster, more urgent. My arms give out until I'm resting on my elbows, tilting my butt farther in the air. Jax feels so deep inside me, I feel so full.

So good. I want to come. I need to come. It feels so close. I rock back against him, meeting his thrusts, dying for more.

"Jax." Mindlessly I start softly chanting his name. His fingertips press into the skin of my hips, likely leaving bruises as he starts to lose control. His hand cups my sex, devilish fingers circling my clit until, finally, gloriously, his touch sends me over the edge again. I shake as the orgasm washes over me, through my haze of pleasure, I feel Jax pounding into me until he, too, finally shouts, stilling. Then he shudders as I feel him come.

He releases my hips, and I sink into the bed, struggling to keep my eyes open. I feel the heat of him along my back for a moment before he disappears, returning soon after. He pulls me into his arms, situating us on my bed until he's comfortable. I'm limp, letting him rearrange me against him.

I should sleep. But I'm fighting it, wanting to savor every second of this night. I've never experienced such a feeling of eudaemonia, and I want to prolong it as much as possible, even if it means I'm fighting exhaustion all day tomorrow.

EUDAEMONIA
Definition: well-being, happiness

My fingers trace along the ridges of his stomach, fascinated that even relaxed his muscles are visible. Fascinated by the designs covering his skin. I lightly explore his chest, my fingers find the jagged and puckered edges of his scar, the remains of the night he was shot. When he almost died. He grabs my hand, quickly pulling it away and holding it against his abdomen. I roll into him, propping my chin on his chest so I can look into his face.

"Does it still bother you? Your injuries?"

He shrugs, staring at the ceiling. "I'm fine."

I shift, climbing, so I'm straddling his waist. I lean down and press a kiss on his scar. "That's not what I asked. Does it still bother you?"

His hands immediately go to my breasts, covering the mounds, his palms rough against my nipples. I roll my hips against him, my core against his rapidly hardening erection. But I'm not going to let him distract me.

"Jax? Will you talk to me?" my voice is soft, trying to urge, not demand. I know sex can change things, but we were friends. Are friends. At least becoming friends, and I don't want to lose that just because he's also the best sex of my life. I can't do that. Completely separate the two.

He sighs and releases my breasts instead squeezing my hips. "I don't like talking about it."

I lay down, settling on top of him, tucking my head beneath his chin. "Why?"

I feel his shoulder shift beneath me as he attempts to shrug again. "I don't like thinking about it. I don't remember exactly what happened, just bits and pieces. And how fucking long it felt before I was back to normal."

"Are you? Back to normal?"

"Mostly. I guess." He's silent for several moments, and I listen to his heart beating beneath my chest, feel his fingers lightly dragging up and down my spine. "Sometimes I walk to the front in *Vanished*, and all I can think about is what happened. Or I have dreams with these flashes I don't totally recognize, but they freak me out."

I press a kiss to his chest, unsure what to say. I hate that he went through that. I hate that it ever happened.

"But I think it freaks Luke out even more. I think he wants to pretend it never happened. Because then he doesn't have to think about everything that came after, and he blames himself for that."

"You mean…Tanya?"

"Yeah." He goes quiet again. "Which is stupid. It wasn't his fault. If anything…." He fades off.

I don't know everything that happened, but I know enough. I know Jax and Tanya were hooking up. I know Tanya was secretly obsessed and stalking Lucas and Ash. And I know they barely found Ash and Logan in time before they were both killed.

"It wasn't either of your faults. Tanya was mentally ill. And she is the only one responsible."

He doesn't respond, and I know it's not always that easy. That your head and your heart don't always absorb those kinds of facts at the same rate. Jax is very protective of Lucas, part of that loyalty that is so much a part of him. If he can find a way to blame himself for that tragic mess, I'm sure he has.

Instead, to distract him from the dark thoughts I'd unknowingly unleashed, I slide myself up his body until my face hovers over his. I glance at my clock quickly before turning my attention back to him. "I've got six hours before I need to get ready for work. I believe you promised me a sleepless night."

He grins his sexy, crooked grin and rolls me under him, taking my mouth in a heated kiss. When he breaks the kiss, his eyes are serious as they move over my face. "I like you, Teach. But you know I'm not that guy, right?"

I feel a sharp pang in my heart, stomach flipping with nerves instead of arousal. "What guy? What do you mean?"

"I'm not…I'm not a forever guy. I can be right now. I want to be your right now. But we should keep this fun. That's what you're looking for, right?"

I nod. "I'm not asking for any promises, Jax. I meant what I said, I just want to see what happens." Which is true. I'm not looking to go from one engagement right to another. And the next time I get engaged, I'd like to be sure it's right, not just expected. I want some time to explore and experiment and embrace my newfound independence. But I'm quickly becoming addicted to the way I feel when I'm with Jax, and it stings a little that he's already assuming an end.

"But," I take a deep breath, bracing myself to set this boundary. "I don't think I'd be very good at super casual either. I mean, you aren't…sleeping with anyone else, are you?"

He laughs. It starts subtly, just his quirky smile, but then it grows until my bed is shaking, and he collapses onto his back. I hold my sheet against my nakedness and sit up so I can look down at him.

"Why is that funny?"

"It just is." He inhales deeply, still chuckling, but pulls himself together. "No, Teach. I'm not sleeping with anyone else. And I won't. Not if you want this to be just you and me."

I nod. Imagining him with other people makes me feel a little nauseous. I can't do that. I can't be that girl.

"Done."

"Just like that?"

He sits up, cups my cheek, and kisses me sweetly. I feel his hand tug on the sheet until the cool air tickles my bare skin. His fingers tease along the inside of my thighs, reaching my slit, teasing further until I gasp and my thighs fall open. His kiss takes me back to the bed, arousal spreading quickly through my limbs.

"Just like that," he murmurs.

And then he keeps me from sleeping most of the night.

Just like he promised.

CHAPTER
Thirteen

Jax

You **busy tonight?**
Sorry, Stud. Thursday dinner with the girls.

I grin at Riley's new nickname for me. It takes away a little of the disappointment that I'm not going to get to see her tonight. Although it's probably for the best. Two nights in a row can be forgiven, especially at the beginning. I didn't get enough of her on Tuesday night, so I was back in her bed and between her thighs last night. Although I did lay off her enough for her to get a few hours of sleep. But three nights in a row…that might give the wrong idea.

I'm not sure if it would be giving Riley the wrong idea or me, though.

The last two nights have been pretty sweet. And I have months of no sex to make up for, that's all.

I'm debating whether or not I should offer to swing by after her Girls' Night as I wander back up front. I wonder if I'll ever be able to make this walk again without remembering, without worrying I'll meet a gun on the other side. Maybe Riley's right. After I'd dumped so much baggage on her Tuesday night, she'd gently suggested I look into PTSD counseling the next morning. Maybe I should talk to someone. *Vanished* is my home. I want to be comfortable here.

I enter the lobby and stiffen, seeing who has entered the shop. It's not some high kid with a gun and a twitchy trigger finger. No. This is so much worse.

Mother fucker. I knew that was him. The other week at the school, I *knew* it.

"Rock," I acknowledge grimly.

He looks up from his phone with a smirk. It makes me want to punch him.

"Jacky, m'boy. How you been?"

My fists clench, and I force my muscles to relax. I'm not going to let this prick see any reaction from me. "It's Jax now. And I'm not your boy," I tell him. I move behind the counter. Putting something solid between us.

"That's no way to talk to a paying customer. I thought I taught you better than that."

I ignore that crack and respond to his first remark. "I didn't see your name on the appointment list." And I never fucking will if I have anything to say about it.

"What, I need an appointment? Jacky...." He draws out my old nickname like he's hurt, needling me.

"Yeah. You do. And we're booked for months out. So, I guess you'll have to go somewhere else."

He opens his mouth to respond but just then, the door chimes again, and he turns to see who is coming in.

My stomach sinks. Fuck. I was really hoping I could get rid of him without anyone else being exposed to his evil, but my streak of bad luck is continuing.

Rock smiles, turning on all his fake charm, and greets Logan. "Hey, Blondie. You here for a tattoo?"

I smirk, knowing Logan isn't going to tolerate being talked to like that.

She eyes him up and down, a spark of temper in her eyes. "I know you're not talking to me because that's not my name. But let me be clear since you seem easily confused. Anything I choose to do with my body is none of your fucking business."

Logan turns her attention to me, and I subtly jerk my head to the back, indicating she should get out of here. She nods, a frown on her face, and moves down the hall. I hear her mutter 'jackass' as she does, shooting another look at Rock, and despite everything, it makes me grin.

"Bitch," Rock spits out. From the corner of my eye, I see Logan stiffen and spin back around, but before she can do more, I'm over the counter, shoving Rock back. He stumbles but recovers his balance and starts moving forward. I refuse to back down, getting right into his face.

"Get the fuck out," I growl.

"You kicking me out, Jacky? After everything I've done for you?"

My breathing is harsh, I'm barely holding it together. Everything in me wants to unleash and just start pounding on him. But that's not who I am anymore. Riley's big gray eyes appear in my mind, and I step back, putting space between my present and my past. No.

"I don't owe you anything. And I don't want to see you again. Ever. Get out."

Logan appears at my side, cell phone at her ear.

"I'm calling the police," she tells Rock. "You should be gone when they get here."

He glares at the two of us, and I see him debating what he can get away with. But finally, he smiles again and steps back. "Yeah, sure. I'm gone. I'll see you around, Jacky. Tell Luke I stopped by."

Like hell. That's not happening. I watch silently as he walks out. For moments after, I can't move, just watching the door to make sure he doesn't come back.

"Well. He was fun," Logan remarks. Her sarcasm shakes me loose from my paralysis.

I look at her. "Police?"

She shakes her head. "I didn't call. Wasn't sure what you were dealing with."

I nod. "Thanks."

"Want to tell me about it?"

I shake my head. "No. But if you do see him again, call the police. Don't mess with him."

Logan nods. "Got it."

Rock is back. The last time I saw him, comes flooding back. After he'd basically threatened to frame Lucas and me for murder, he'd owned me. And he knew it. I'd always been big for my age, but that summer, I hit a growth spurt and filled out even more. Rock decided he could make some money off of me and kept pushing me into underground fights. It was fucked up in addition to being illegal but it also kept Cliff off my back. I'd won plenty of money. By then, Luke had been placed in another home, so he wasn't around enough to realize the bruises came from more than just Cliff and my own stupid temper.

Then Rock had gotten busted for dealing. He'd gotten caught by an undercover cop, no room for error, and pled out, soon after, he'd been sent to prison. Those few months I spent terrified. Sure he'd offer up two 'murderers' for a lighter sentence. I kept looking over my shoulder, sure any second Luke or I would be arrested. But it never happened, and finally, I started to relax. We finished school, started apprenticing. Eventually, Luke got cast on *Top Ink*. Rock was gone and so was the threat he held over me.

But I guess he's out. And, for some reason, feels the need to seek me out. I don't know what that's about, but I know I don't like it. Shit.

"You good?" Logan asks, studying me carefully.

I pull her into a half hug, arm curling around her neck. "I'm good, Streaks. Thanks."

She pushes me away, rolling her eyes at her nickname.

"Don't mention this to Luke, okay?"

Logan eyes me suspiciously. I've never asked her to keep anything from Luke. I'm sure all her instincts are screaming at her. I raise my hands and shrug. "Just let me tell him, okay? I'll tell him."

"I won't lie to him," she says slowly.

I nod. Hopefully, she won't need to. There's no reason for Luke to ask about Rock after all these years. I'll deal with it before he becomes an issue. Luke will never need to know.

Riley

I'VE BEEN SMILING NONSTOP FOR DAYS.

Even now, as I'm packing up my stuff to leave for the day and meet Teagan and Ilyssa for dinner, I catch myself humming with a ridiculous grin on my face.

I sense I'm not alone, just a feeling of another body moving behind me and I straighten, turning to greet whatever student is coming with questions.

But it's not a student. Not a current student anyway.

"Mick. How are you?" I'm confused but not worried. Not at this point, anyway. Mick had been my student four years ago, my second year as a teacher.

He doesn't respond, just wanders into the classroom, and eventually, the silence starts to make me wary. "Cory isn't here this afternoon."

"I know. You think I don't know where my brother is and what he gets up to?"

His tone has an edge to it that I don't like. I finish putting my jacket on, wanting to get out of here as quickly as possible. "What can I help you with, Mick?"

"So, you're the one giving my brother all kinds of crazy ideas. It took me a second when he said, Ms. Abbott. And then I remembered. And, of course, some rich, white girl teacher is going to think drawing pictures is going to make everything okay."

Where is this animosity coming from? I remember Mick being a surly kid, angry and disinterested, but I'd never sensed this kind of hostility back then.

"Cory is very talented. I just want him to succeed in whatever he decides to do."

"Why don't you mind your own business, bitch? Cory has responsibilities, and I don't need him spending his time on this bullshit."

Okay. This is not a situation I want to be in. I swallow as if that will absorb the fear. Mick looks…dark. He's glaring down at me, standing much too close, with an ugly emotion I've never been on the receiving end of before. Suddenly I'm acutely aware that we are alone and that the school has likely emptied out at this hour. And I am very aware that is not a good scenario.

Despite my unease, I am determined to stay calm and professional. I will not be pusillanimous in front of him.

PUSILLANIMOUS
Definition: afraid or timid.

At least I won't show it. I will not give him that satisfaction. I hate a bully. I hate people who deliberately try to intimidate or create fear. I don't understand why people get pleasure from that. Why wouldn't you just want to be nice? Doesn't that feel better?

"I think you should go, Mick. You're no longer a student here and aren't allowed on school property. I'll have to report you to security."

He steps closer, glowering down at me. Inside, I'm shaking. Terrified he was going to call my bluff.

Layla chooses that moment to appear in the doorway, her arms full of books. She hesitates for a moment, taking in the scene. Mick hovering over me, an angry expression on his face. I step back, using her presence as an excuse to cross the room, still maintaining the illusion that I'm not intimidated.

"Ms. Abbott, did you still want to meet my Uncle Dalvin? He's waiting out front for me."

I scramble to keep up. Clever girl, Layla. I have no idea who her uncle is, and we've never once discussed my meeting him. "Yes, of course. I nearly forgot. Thank you, Layla." I turn away from Mick, grabbing my bag. When I turn back, she's looking at Mick with an expression of disgust on her face.

Stay smart, Layla, I think. I shift so I'm standing between them, not wanting him to get too close to her.

"I'm Layla Barnes," she tells him. "Who are you?"

I expect Mick to come back with some insulting remark, but instead, I see a flicker of recognition, and maybe respect, cross his face. And then he just…leaves. Just like that. Walks passed the two of us and out the door.

I exhale shakily, still trying to mask my uneasiness as I turn to face her.

"You okay, Ms. Abbott?"

I smile, hoping I'm disguising my still-rough nerves. "Yes, I'm fine, Layla. Thank you. What was that exactly?" I ask her.

She shrugs. "The guys in the neighborhood are afraid of my uncle. And I've seen that guy around before. I'm sure he's heard of Uncle Dalvin."

"Is your uncle that scary?"

"Not to me," she chirps. "But I like that he is to other people. It keeps them off my back, you know?"

I hit the lights and close the door behind us, walking toward the main entrance.

"Do you want me to walk out with you? In case he's still hanging around?"

"No, thank you. I'll be fine." Despite my nervous stomach, letting a fifteen-year-old escort me to the bus stop as protection seems ridiculous and wrong. Besides, I can't show Mick that he got to me. That will only make him believe I'm vulnerable.

"Okay. Night, Ms. Abbott!" Layla bounces away. Teenagers. So quick to recover.

"Good night, Layla. I'll see you tomorrow."

Days are short in Chicago during January. The sun has set by the time I walk out the school doors, inhaling the cold, brittle air, still trying to settle my nerves as I head to the nearby bus stop. The bus ride is quick, less than ten minutes, and then I'll transfer to the el. In nice weather, I usually just walk to the subway, but when it's cold and dark, I use the bus.

I stand in the glass enclosure, waiting for my bus to arrive, when I feel the eyes on me. I glance around and finally settle on Mick across the street. Watching me.

Shaking, I pull out my phone. Just keeping it handy. If he makes any move toward me, I'm calling the police. From the corner of my eye, I see the lights of the bus two blocks away, slowly approaching. My stomach is jumping all over the place, waiting for something to happen.

I see a quick flash of flickering orange light and a small glowing circle as Mick lights a cigarette. Eyes still on me.

My bus arrives and I climb on, taking a seat where I can keep my eyes on the figure across the street. It seems to take forever, but finally, the doors close, and the bus pulls away from the curb. I see Mick, still standing there, staring as I ride away.

I exhale heavily, my hands starting to shake now that I'm safe. I'd never felt that vulnerable before, and it was more than a little terrifying. And I know it's likely Mick will be back. He had more to say to me before we got interrupted.

I need to be better prepared next time.

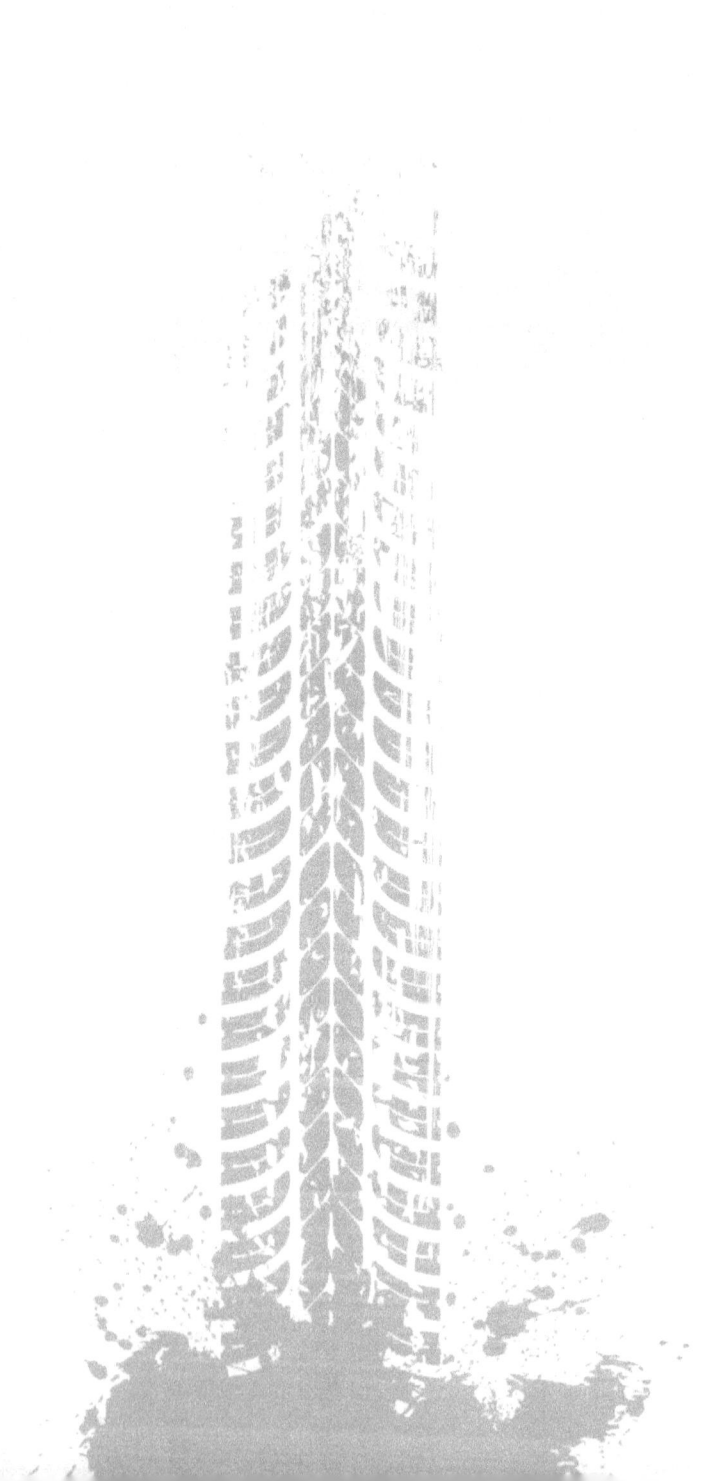

CHAPTER
Fourteen

Riley

Saturday afternoon, I enter the neighborhood community center, trying to fake my way through my nerves. Teagan and Ilyssa are behind me, my backup support squad. We follow the signs to the gymnasium and push open the heavy doors. There are a dozen women, maybe more, in different clusters around a large rectangular mat on the polished floor. The three of us drop our coats and bags on an empty spot on the bleachers, and I scan my eyes across the room until I see her. The beautiful brunette standing alone with a clipboard in her hand off to the side of the rest of the women. I take a deep breath and walk over.

I approach Ash, nerves bouncing around my stomach. "Hi," I say softly.

She glances up, surprise reflected in her eyes, but she flashes a friendly smile. "Riley. Hi!"

I bounce from foot to foot. "We, ah, signed up for your self-defense class." I tilt my head, indicating Teagan and Ilyssa chatting off to the side. Teagan's flexing her arms and grabbing Ilyssa from behind, swinging her in circles. But she's not quite strong enough to lift her, so they both end up stumbling around and laughing at her attempt. "Is it okay? That we're here?"

"Of course! It's good to see you."

"You too." I smile in relief. I'd learned that Ash taught self-defense classes twice a week here, and after my frightening run-in with Mick earlier this week, I decided this would be both a chance to feel more prepared if it ever happens again and get to know Ash better. Teagan and Ilyssa wander over, still laughing breathlessly. "Ash, this is my cousin Teagan. And our friend Ilyssa."

Ash shakes their hands, welcoming them. "Teagan. I've heard about you," she says.

Teagan lights up. "Oh yeah? Only fabulous things, I'm sure."

Ash laughs. "Welcome. We're just about to get started, so grab a spot on the mat." The three of us fall into the loose circle while Ash gets everyone's attention, kicking off the class. This is the first of an eight-week session, so she goes through a lot of basics, things to keep you safe even before you find yourself with a potential attacker. How to stay aware of your surroundings, how to carry yourself, how to respond in situations you feel uncomfortable. We practice yelling NO. Just getting used to taking up space, being loud, creating a scene if you need to.

I'm surprised by how hard it is for me to yell loudly. It seems like such a silly thing to practice, but when I go to yell, it comes out shockingly mild. I raise my voice in school all the time, talking over students, getting their attention. But this is different. In the last thirty minutes of class Ash has us practice getting out of basic holds, if someone were to grab our forearm or shoulders, what are the best ways to respond.

When our time is up, I'm buzzing with endorphins feeling both proud of what I can do and excited to come back next week and learn more. I linger on the side and wait while Ash is approached by other women from the class.

Finally, she's alone, and I approach again. "We were going to grab some food. Do you... want to join us?" I ask.

"Oh! You totally should! That would be so fun," Teagan insists, overhearing my invitation.

Ash hesitates. "Actually, I'm supposed to meet Lucas. Let me see where he's at. Maybe I could come for a few minutes."

I nod and wander back to Teagan and Ilyssa, giving her some space and privacy.

Ilyssa smiles, pulling on her coat. "That was great. I've thought about doing something like this for ages. Thanks for getting us here, Riley."

"Do you think Ash will come? I'd love to get to know her," Teagan whispers.

I shrug and glance back over to where Ash stands. I hope so. But I don't know. Lucas had mentioned all of us getting dinner sometime, but maybe he was just being polite in the moment. Ash is on her phone, talking, I'm assuming, to Lucas. Her eyes flash to me in surprise, and then she laughs. I feel myself heat in embarrassment. Somehow I know she's just found out Jax and I are... Jax and I.

"Where are you going?" she calls out, asking about our next location.

My heart skips in excitement. "Just down the street. To *Feast*." I mention a gastro-pub a couple of blocks away. She murmurs back into her cell, smiles softly, and ends the call. Throwing her bag over her shoulder, she crosses the room to where the three of us have gathered, waiting. "I'm in. It sounds like the full *Vanished* crew may come meet us if that's okay with you guys."

"Great!" Teagan exclaims, bouncing on her toes. My stomach flips in excitement. Ash, Lucas, and Jax. I'm going to get to spend time with all three. I'm thrilled that Lucas is letting us in just a little more, blending his worlds.

The four of us head out, grabbing a giant corner booth at *Feast*, with plenty of room for the others to join us when they can. Teagan peppers Ash with questions about her work, her travels, her story. This is the first time they've officially met, and while I know this is Teagan's style, I hope she's not making Ash uncomfortable. But she seems to be taking it all in stride. After we order, I make a point to steer the conversation away from Ash, getting her out of the hot seat. We're halfway through our lunch when the *Vanished* crew arrives.

My stomach flips, and I smile in excitement as they approach our table. Jax looks fantastic as usual, rumpled and confident, and sexy. Lucas stops next to Ash's chair and bends to kiss her. She smiles at him and says hello. It's sweet. I'm happy he found her. I introduce Macy and Logan to Teagan and Ilyssa, and then we're all shifting, making room, and getting comfortable. Jax slides into the booth next to me, and his presence immediately spreads heat across my skin.

"Hey, Teach," he murmurs, flashing me a lazy grin. His voice is low and gravely turning the heat up. He shifts and stretches his arm along the back of the booth behind me. I feel dangerous tingles along my right side as he presses against me.

I'm self-conscious, feeling like everyone's eyes are on us, like everyone can see his effect on me. But when I glance around the table, no one seems to be paying us that much attention.

"Hi there," I murmur softly, turning slightly into him.

"This is fun," he says, nodding at the people around us. "And unexpected."

I shrug, smiling, pleased with how it worked out.

Macy grins at the waitress, and she comes racing over to help the new arrivals. They all put their orders in, and then Ash and I do our best to introduce topics that can include everyone, despite very few of them having ever met before. It's a little awkward and forced, but eventually, people settle into smaller conversations. Teagan turns her rapid-fire-getting-to-know-you cross-examination on Logan, who seems surprisingly entertained. The little I know of Logan, I was kind of worried she would hate Teagan. Macy turns his flirtatious grin on Ilyssa, who, while I know is swooning inside, stays shockingly together. Ash and Lucas bounce between the two conversations, thrilling Teagan, I'm sure.

I exhale roughly in relief. Jax's fingers trace lightly along the back of my neck, and I can't repress my shiver of awareness. Reaching for my glass of water, I miscalculate and hit the glass, causing it to wobble. Jax quickly snags it before it can tip over and sets it right.

"Relax, Teach. This is a good thing." He gestures again at the group around us. I nod, taking another calming breath.

"Decided to go to a self-defense class today?" His change of subject makes me tense right back up.

"Yep," I say, voice chipper, giving him an innocent smile.

"Anything you want to tell me about, Teach?"

"Nope," I say, not meeting his eyes. "Just decided it would be good for us all to know. Just in case."

"Just in case, huh?"

"Yep," I repeat, pushing my plate of leftover fries in his direction. He watches me suspiciously for a heartbeat and then grabs some fries, digging in.

Luckily, Teagan interrupts us. Unfortunately, she does so by introducing my least favorite topic.

She pulls a wrapped gift out of her bag and sets it on the table in front of me. "Don't get mad. I'm not going to make anyone sing, but your birthday is coming up, and I think this is probably the closest you're going to get to celebrating. So…here. Happy Birthday."

Jax

I'M NOT BUYING IT.

Something's going on with Riley.

She's not a very good liar - I suspect she's had very little practice. Out of the blue, she decides to crash one of Ash's self-defense classes? No way. I know how careful she is to open doors for Lucas but not crowd him. She's never once tried to get to him through Ash. Or wanted it to seem like she was. So I suspect this is more about the content of the class than the teacher. I decide to drop it for now, but I plan to bring it up again later. When we're alone.

Which frankly cannot happen soon enough.

I settle into eating.

And then Teagan drops her gift bomb, announcing Riley's upcoming birthday. Shit.

I glance at Luke, who seems just as surprised by this information, although, of course, he would be. Turning back to Riley, I ask, "It's your birthday?"

She shakes her head, not looking at me. Not looking at anyone, really.

Teagan reaches across the table and squeezes Riley's hand briefly. "It's just a present. Something that made me think of you. On a random Saturday. Because I love you."

Riley's reaction is confusing. Don't most people love their birthdays? I mean, it's not like I have a lot of fond memories of my own birthdays growing up, but Riley….

Oh fuck.

Suddenly I'm sure this has something to do with her parent's death.

She's tense against me. But slowly reaches out and grabs the present with a shaky exhale. Luckily the others are still distracted by food and conversation; I'm sure she'd hate to have everyone's eyes on her. I watch as Riley tears the wrapping paper revealing an aqua-covered book. She studies it for a minute and then starts to giggle.

"Seriously? Where did you find this?"

Teagan's eyes are dancing with laughter as she shrugs. "I thought it would help with that strip, dirty Scrabble idea."

I stiffen hearing that, my eyes going to the book for a closer look. *The Big Book of Filth. 6500 sex slang words and phrases.* I smirk, amused. This actually seems like a perfect gift for Riley.

"Oh, my god. This is hilarious." She's paging through it, eyes scanning the pages.

"What are you finding?" I nudge her, getting her attention.

"Promiscuous Man." She reads some of the terms listed underneath, laughing as Teagan cracks up next to us, and then flips to a new page. Some of the others at the table have tuned in now, curious about what has this side of the table so entertained. "Sex for One. Oh," Riley pauses, blushing. "I can't say those out loud. Teagan!"

Teagan is laughing hysterically. "Let me! Let me!"

"No! People are still eating!" But there's laughter in her voice, and I'm just glad the darkness that had settled over her has fully cleared.

"I just want to see!" Riley hands her the book, and it gets passed around for the next several minutes as everyone takes a turn, laughing at the ridiculous and raunchy slang.

Feeling full and chill, I lean back in the booth taking in the scene around me. Riley turns, eyes smiling, and it punches me in the chest. "You ready to get out of here? Or you want a drink before we go?" As usual, I'm anxious to get her alone and get her naked, but I also recognize this is a good thing, what is happening this afternoon, and am a little reluctant to cut it short.

Her eyes dance as she teases me. "Is that you offering me a ride home? I came with Teagan and Ilyssa."

"I don't think they'll mind. And I wasn't offering to take you home exactly." I smirk, letting the dirty thoughts in my head spill into my expression.

She grins. "No, I don't think they will. But I'd love a doch-an-dorris."

I raise my eyebrow in confusion. "Is that some specialty cocktail?"

She flushes, her eyes slipping away. "No, it, uh, means a last drink. Like a drink for the road."

It makes me chuckle, her getting all shy. I like that she's smart. Her obsession with words. It's cute. Riley's the first woman I've ever been with I describe as cute. It used to be a red flag, waving me off, warning me I shouldn't get too close. But we're passed that now. I know this is temporary. I know she's eventually going to move on, find her next Daniel. Hopefully, one that isn't an asshole. Get that ring and the wedding and the kids. But I like being her right now. I'm discovering I like sweet.

At least Riley's kind of sweet.

We order another round, and there's an awkward moment when Teagan tries to figure out if Riley needs a ride home or not without coming right out and asking. Riley and I haven't really discussed how we're handling these kinds of situations. I mean, it's kind of obvious that everyone here knows, but everyone is also politely pretending nothing has changed.

Even though everything has changed. We've never had an afternoon hang out with Abbotts before, and there are two currently at this table. Three counting Luke.

"…about Pirate?" I tune back in and see a tiny shadow flicker in Riley's eyes.

"Oh shoot. You're right. I wasn't thinking." I hear Riley's voice sounding disappointed. "I guess I do need a ride home."

I stiffen, not liking that idea. At all. I'll take her home if she needs to go, but I hoped to bring her back to my place tonight. I've got a much better shower for shower sex. Which I happen to know is on her list.

"We'll walk Pirate," Teagan offers. "Just give me your key, and I'll drop it in your mail slot so you can get it in the morning."

"Are you sure?" Riley bites her bottom lip, teasing it uncertainly.

"Of course. No big deal. I love dogs, and our apartment doesn't allow them. So Pirate is my fix." She holds out her hand for the key. While Riley twists her key off the key ring, Teagan catches my eye and winks. I huff out a small laugh. I can see why Luke kind of likes this one, too, another cousin. She's ballsy and fun. And I'm currently benefiting from her offer, so automatically like her more.

As Ash stands and gives Riley a hug, Luke holds out his fist for me to pound. "I'll see you at class next week?" I hear Ash ask and see Riley nod, a shy smile on her face.

"Later, brother." I follow Riley out, cupping the back of her neck as we walk. She shivers at my touch, her response already making me hard.

I need to get her home.

Fast.

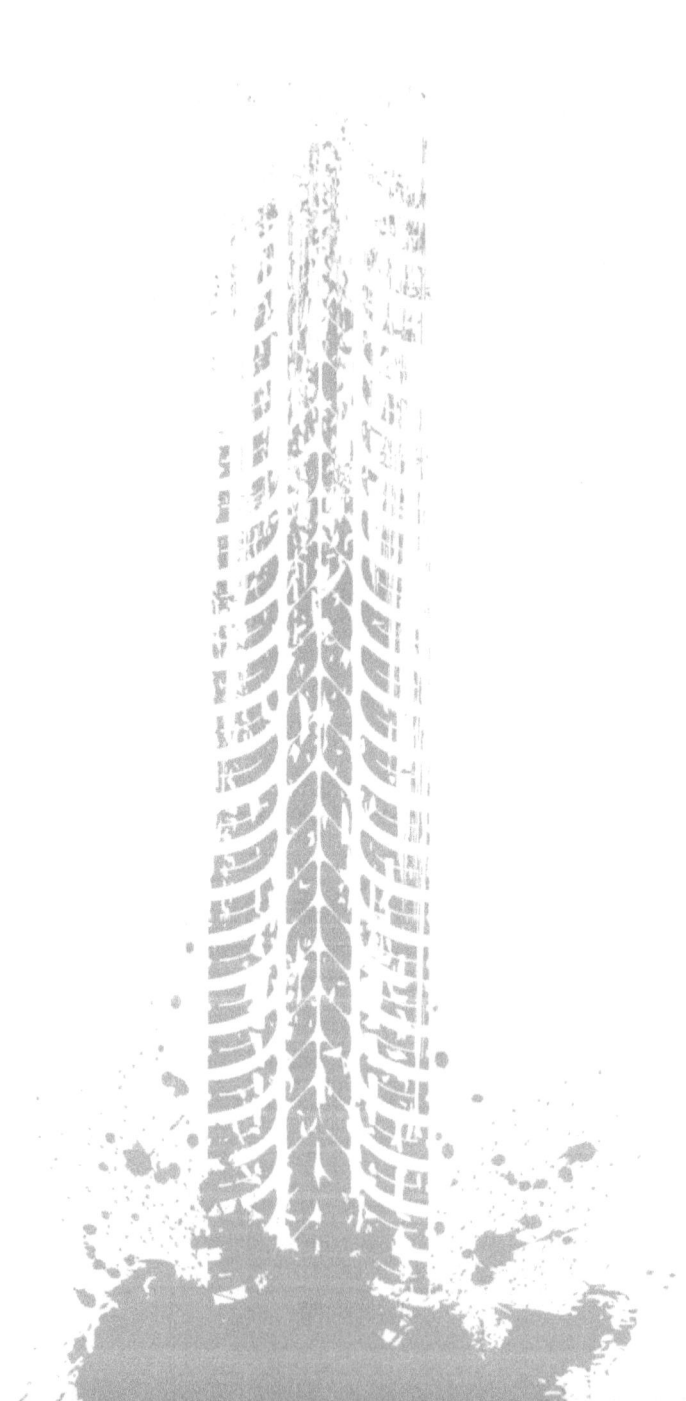

CHAPTER
Fifteen

Riley

My stomach is tense with nerves as Jax lets us into his loft. The last time I was here was the night I found Daniel in bed with someone else, got drunk, crashed *Vanished*, and somehow ended up at Macy's parents' bar with him and Jax. I'd been far too drunk, completely sozzled, to make it anywhere on my own, and Jax had taken me back here and put me to bed. While he slept on the couch.

I'm assuming that isn't his plan tonight.

> SOZZLED
> Definition: hammered, wrecked, drunk

I love his loft. It's got enormous windows along one entire wall, which would let in a lot of light during the day, but the sun has already set as we were having fun with our friends, so now there's just a soft orange glow.

I think I can claim Lucas as a friend now. Almost. Kind of.

I drop my bag on his couch, turning to face him, fighting the nervous tension. Jax stands back, watching me as I reacquaint myself with his home. He throws his keys on the counter, his eyes raking over me, leaving heat in their wake. I love that look. The simmer in his eyes. He takes a step forward, closing the distance between us.

"Riley?" He continues his advance, and my previous nerves turn to excited tremors.

"Yeah?"

He pulls his shirt off, and I'm immediately distracted by his chest and abs. He hasn't even touched me, yet I can feel my body responding to him. A warm glow starting low in my belly. Lower.

"I need to fuck you now. That okay with you?"

A warm glow? Try a raging inferno.

"Very okay," I inform him.

My pulse starts to race as he reaches out and grabs me, yanking me forward until I collide with his bare chest. My lips part in a gasp of surprise, and he swoops in, kissing me, tongue caressing mine. I fall into his kiss, everything inside me reaching for him, for this. His arms wrap around me, just under my butt, lifting me against him, never breaking the kiss. Instinctively my thighs spread, squeezing his hips, anchoring myself against him. He walks us to his bed, every step, his erection grinding into my core until I'm shameless, moaning against his lips, grinding into him.

He finally breaks the kiss when we reach his bed, lowering me to the mattress. His eyes are hot as he looks down at me. "I've got big plans for the next twenty-four hours," he informs me.

A bubble of happiness and excitement escapes me in a breathy laugh. "You do?"

His mouth quirks up, and he strips his jeans off, kicking out of them. "I do."

"Are we going to do the four-legged frolic now? Shake the sheets? Sink the little man in the boat?" I attempt to use my huskiest sexy voice as I articulate these words that seem so foreign and unnatural. But I'm trying new things. That's what this year is for, right?

Jax freezes, staring down at me, a smile tugging at his lips. Raising his eyebrows, he asks me, "What now?"

"They were in the book. Not sexy?" I ask, already knowing the answer. Luckily the massive length of him straining at his boxer briefs assures me I haven't totally blown it.

He shakes his head, a chuckle moving through his chest. "Not sexy." He moves closer, stepping between my thighs, urging them apart. Eyes intent on mine, he says, "*You're* sexy."

My head tilts to the side, a warm flush of surprise and pleasure moving over me. "I am?"

"You are."

"How?" I whisper.

He laughs at me, settling into his crooked smile. "What do you mean how?"

I look down at myself. I'm just me. I'm still in leggings and an oversized hoodie I put on after our class. I'm skinny with no hips and tiny boobs, and a book obsession. I have good skin and pretty hair, and nice eyes, but I've never really thought of myself as particularly 'sexy'. "What about me is sexy?"

He eases one knee onto the mattress between my thighs and urges me back. I scoot farther up onto the bed. I'm getting distracted from my line of questioning, his presence overwhelming me.

"You make me feel incredible."

That gives me pause, my breath sticking in my throat for a second.

I do?

I know he does that for me, but it didn't occur to me that I could do that for him as well.

"I do?"

"You do." He's hovering over me, like he's stalking me, easing me back as he moves us up the bed. Of their own accord, my hands move to his chest, lightly tracing over his skin.

"How?" I whisper, staring up at him, his eyes burning into me.

"You're thinking too much, Teach." I've fully reclined at this point with him braced on his arms above me. He leans down and presses a hot kiss to my neck, just under my jawline. I shiver, wishing I had fewer clothes on.

"But I want to understand. I'm curious."

He makes this sound, like a painful chuckle, and rests his forehead against mine for a brief moment. The silence stretches tight between us until I think he's not going to respond to my silly questions. But then he does. He lifts his head, staring into my eyes.

"You see the good parts of me and reflect them back. Of everyone. You care. You're so honest. Every response, everything you do. You're the kindest person I've ever met."

My stomach is fluttering, heartbeat speeding up. "And that's sexy?"

His voice is low and rough when he answers, "Yeah, Teach. It is." He lowers, settling his frame entirely over mine, sending waves of sensation through my body. My arms twine around his neck as we kiss. I'll never get tired of his kisses, I'm convinced. I part my lips, our tongues tangling, teasing. He's warm and hard, and my mind goes hazy as he deepens the kiss. Immediately tingles spread through my limbs, pooling at my core, making me wet. Just from kisses. I feel the heat of his fingers slipping under my sweatshirt, finding my bare skin. I exhale, my stomach instinctively sucking in, moving away from that heat and arching my back. He leans up and whips my top off, then he's sinking back onto me. And the heat feels so much stronger now with all my bare skin pressed against him.

He rolls us suddenly, his hands grabbing my butt and settling me over his erection. I gasp, moving my hips, feeling his hands squeezing my butt cheeks.

"Also, I love your ass. So perfect. Fuck." His hips thrust up, pressing against my core, setting me on fire. Then his hands smooth up my sides, unhooking my bra, and cup my bare breasts. I moan and curve into his palms.

"And you have fucking gorgeous tits." His hands shift, plucking my nipples. My hands settle on his chest as I move against him, hips pressing into him as I press against the ridge of his erection. Sparks are setting me on fire. I need to get the rest of my clothes off. Feel him for real.

"They're small." For some reason, I feel compelled to point this out.

He pinches my nipples roughly, teasingly, a streak of uncertainty moving through me. But also exciting me.

"Are you trying to piss me off?" he asks roughly. "Or do you just want me to prove you wrong?"

I grin down at him, biting my lip teasingly. He makes me feel sexy. The way he touches me, the hunger in his eyes, the heat in his touch. I've become addicted to the way he can make me feel.

"Prove me wrong, Jax."

Jax

PROVE ME WRONG, JAX.

Shit. She has no idea what that little tease does to me. Her little flashes of shyness and sex and sass ramp me up faster than the most blatant come-on ever has. I sit up, ducking my head to get to her nipples. I flick my tongue and scrape my teeth gently over the tips watching as they tighten and flush before sucking one hotly into my mouth. Her fingers dive into my hair as she arches into me, her cry of pleasure going right to my dick. I smooth my hands along her thighs, pressing my thumbs against her core through the fabric of her leggings. I can already feel the heat and wetness as I move my thumbs, teasing her.

Her hips rock in my lap as she instinctively uses my fingers and throbbing cock to get herself off. I switch my attention to her other breast. I love watching the expressions moving over her face, her mouth making that little O. And still, I can't wait to feel that surrounding my cock. Soon. She's killing me.

I twist my wrist and slide my fingers into her leggings, seeking that heat, that wetness. She tilts her hips, pressing into my palm, and I groan at her response. I fucking love the way she responds to me. I spread her wetness through her folds, teasing her clit with my thumb.

"So wet," I groan against her skin. "Do you like me sucking on these pretty tits?"

Her hand fists my hair as she breaths in soft pants, still moving her hips restlessly. I feel her body start to tighten up as she strains toward her orgasm. I want to feel her come on my fingers.

Then my tongue.

Then my cock.

Then I'm going to make her do it again and again. All night.

I sink two fingers inside her, thrusting, at the same time, working her clit with tight circles. She makes this sound, one I'll forever remember, sure it will instantly make me hard until I'm too old to do anything about it.

"Are you going to come for me, Riley? Come on my fingers?"

I feel her finger nails biting into my skin, her knees squeezing my hips as she grinds into my hand and lap.

"I can feel you tightening up on my fingers. Do you want to come, gorgeous?"

"Jax. *Yes.*"

I latch onto one of her nipples again, sucking deeply, at the same time fluttering my fingers inside her, pressing down on her clit, and she detonates. Riley cries out, the most delicious fucking sound in my ears. Her core squeezes my fingers, a rush of wetness coating the tips.

"Fuck. Riley. You've got me so hard. Can you feel me?"

She smashes her lips to mine, still shaking in my arms as she rides out her orgasm. Her breaths come fast and short until she sighs, going limp and sinking into me. I need to get her naked. I need to feel her on my cock.

I flip us, stripping the rest of our clothing off, and grab a condom. I thrust into her warmth and wetness, too keyed up to be gentle. I hook one arm under her thigh, raising it high against my ribs to sink even deeper into her. My hips slam into her, streaks of pleasure spearing through me.

"Riley...god...fuck....so tight."

Her hands move down my neck, my chest, and abs, finally reaching around and grabbing my ass as I move against her, hungry for her. Starving. I grind my hips into her, knowing I'm hitting her clit. Because as good as she feels, I want more. I want to feel her come apart again while I'm buried inside her. My eyes settle on her chest as I hold myself above her.

"Look at you, so pretty," I breathe. "Those gorgeous tits. Have I convinced you yet?" Her tiny mounds shake with our movements, flushed with arousal.

Her hands are back in my hair, restless, and she looks up at me. "Yes. So good, Jax. I can't...oh god. More. I need...."

I force myself to pause, determined to make her come again before I let go. I shift again, going to my knees, dragging her up my thighs, her body limp. I reenter her, my hands teasing her back to life. I suck the curve of her neck, scrape my teeth along the column, then soothe it with my tongue. Gripping her hips, I move her along my dick, waiting until she catches the rhythm. Then I use my hands and mouth to touch and tease her until I feel her starting to tighten up on me again.

She squeezes my shoulders, eyes closed, head thrown back, as her hips rock against mine. I cup her cheek and trace her lower lip with my thumb, then tease it inside her mouth.

"Suck." My voice is rough and jagged. Her eyes meet mine, wide, hazy, dark with arousal. I see a flash of confusion as she does what I ask, sucking my thumb greedily into her mouth. I take my thumb away, so I can kiss her hungrily. My hand slips between us, and I use that thumb to tease her clit again. Her hips falter, breaking her rhythm, and she cries out, closing her eyes.

"Eyes open, baby. Look at me. I want to watch you come."

Her soft pants spur me on, lifting and lowering her on my dick as I keep my thumb torturing her. Her gray eyes are sweet and soft and sexy. They widen in surprise, and I feel her squeezing my dick as she comes apart. She moans, and I hold her still on my cock while she shakes, never taking my eyes off her. An endless time later, she melts into me again, whispering my name in my ear.

I surge into her, taking her back to the mattress to pound out my release. And she lets me, her hands moving soothingly over my naked skin, streaks of pleasure following wherever she touches, urging me on. Her gaze stays on me as I thrust. She bends her knees higher, squeezing my ribs, this angle allowing me to go even deeper. A few thrusts later, I'm groaning her name, exploding inside her.

My hips jerk as my orgasm goes on and on, and then I collapse on top of her, spent. I burrow into her neck, loving how soft and warm she is, while I catch my breath.

Fuck. That was good.

Eventually, I pull away and flop onto my back, staring at the ceiling. She moves with me, snuggling into my side, one leg slipping between mine.

"Damn, Teach." My hand smooths down her side and cups her ass, squeezing.

She giggles and props her chin on my chest, looking up at me.

"I like having sex with you," she says, a small smile playing on her lips.

I chuckle, which causes her to bounce around on my chest. "That's good. Because I like having sex with you. We should do it as much as possible."

"If you insist." I glance down at her, smiling. All these warm and soft feelings in my chest are dangerous. I know that. Going to lead to trouble. But trying to ignore them the last six months hadn't worked very well either. At least this way, I'm having amazing sex and hanging out with a funny and sweet woman. One who actually seems to like *me*. Not my connection to Luke. Not what my celebrity can do for her. Not just some hot no strings sex.

So yeah. I know in these moments that I'm probably going down a road with a messy dead end, but frankly, I'm too fucking exhausted from that lengthy orgasm to give a shit right now.

She's drawing random images on my skin, her finger light and teasing. My apartment has grown darker during that marathon fuck session.

"What kind of plans?"

"Hmm?" I ask, squeezing her ass cheek again. God. That ass kills me.

"You said you have big plans for the next twenty-four hours. What kind of plans?"

I lightly smack that ass, and she lets out an adorable squeak. "Do you have anything you need to do tomorrow?"

She sucks in her lips, thinking. "I need to be home in time to do some prep for the week, but nothing specific, no."

Grinning, I feel my dick twitch in anticipation. Fucker should be exhausted for hours after that, but I'm finding Riley is excellent for my recovery.

"Good. Because I thought we could make some progress on your resolutions. And I have to finish making mine."

She buries her face against my ribs and giggles. "Are you serious?"

"Hell, yes. I even bought Scrabble."

Riley sits up so she can meet my eyes. "You did not."

"Yeah, I did. Although it seems silly to get dressed just so we can play strip Scrabble. But I'm sure we can figure something out."

She's laughing and looking around, trying to spot the board game.

"It's on the kitchen bar."

She pops up, a massive smile on her face, and pulls on my t-shirt before running across the room. Seconds later, she's back, bouncing onto the mattress beside me, ready to set up the game.

I laugh at her, but don't have it in me to deny her something she's so excited about. We discuss rules, double and triple word scores now involve some kissing, and then pull letters to play. I start us off strong with 'P-E-E-N'. My eyes go wide when she counters with 'C-U-N-T', my dick pulsing to attention.

"New rule. You have to be able to say the word out loud if you're going to play it."

She laughs, her cheeks pink, and avoids my eyes as she replenishes her letters. "Rules have to be established and agreed to before the start of gameplay," she informs me primly. Which only makes me harder.

Damn. Never in a million years would I have believed I could be turned on by a fucking word board game.

We barely have a dozen words on the board before I'm sliding my cock back inside her, throwing the game into disarray with my thrusts. Riley is laughing sweetly in my ear, whispering the words I've now scattered across my bed. Fuck. So hot.

After, we're lying together, tangled in my sheets, when I bring up her gift and Teagan's little bombshell.

"So, not a fan of birthdays, huh, Teach?" She stiffens in my arms, as I expected her too. I try to keep things light despite the heaviness, keep my body relaxed, gently caressing the length of her back. "Will you tell me about it?"

She's quiet long enough I begin to think she's going to ignore my question, and eventually, she rolls onto her back, away from me. I bite back a protest, suspecting she needs a little space.

I hear her sigh, and finally, she decides to share. "It was on my birthday. The accident. We had gone out to eat at my favorite restaurant and played ski ball for hours. On the way home, the weather was bad. The roads were icy, and people lost control, my dad, too. It was a big pile-up. The front of the car was crushed, but I was in the back. I just…remember a lot of screaming. Metal. People. But I found out later it was just me. Screaming."

Damn. That's rough. Tragic, really. My chest is tight, picturing a nine-year-old Riley trapped in a car with her parents dying. On her fucking birthday.

I roll into her, wanting to distract from some of the bad memories I've forced her to bring up. Pressing a kiss to her shoulder, I settle half over her frame.

"I'm sorry. About your folks."

She smiles softly at the ceiling, but her hands move through my hair.

I don't know what else to say to her, so I do what I do know how to do. I kiss her. I nibble at her lips. Press kisses along her neck. Suck lightly at her collarbone. I don't know what to say to make her feel better, so I'm distracting her. Probably someone better for Riley would be able to help her through this, but I'll use the skills I have.

CHAPTER
Sixteen

Riley

Jax and I are dating. I guess. It feels, I feel, giddy and silly and sexy and fun. January blends into February. We settle into a routine, seeing each other Saturday nights and Monday afternoons, which often turn into Monday nights. And while he doesn't come every Wednesday, he drops into Afternoon with Art midweek when he can. Other nights we text and talk and tease. Thursdays, I still do dinner and drinks with the girls. This week Ash and her best friend Gabby are actually going to join us.

Life is good. I'm happy.

If I have moments when that little voice in my head reminds me this isn't supposed to get serious, I shush it back to silence.

Today, we're finding out the *Vanished* contest winners. Lucas is coming with Jax to announce the students whose art will be featured at their booth during the Tattoo Expo next month. My classroom fills up quickly after school, so many anxious and excited teenagers dying to hear the news first. Even my stomach is bouncing with fluttery nerves.

Cory wanders in, hood pulled low over his eyes, and takes his usual seat in the back of the room. His attitude still leaves a lot to be desired, but he's continued to come most days even when he isn't in detention which makes me hopeful. I've seen Mick pick him up after school a couple of nights, but he hasn't bothered me again, staying outside the school walls. His presence still makes me nervous, though.

Jax and Lucas arrive, and I feel a rush of excitement and happiness at seeing them. My eyes meet Jax, and he grins at me. I saw him just yesterday morning, but I'm still hungry for the sight of him. Always. I'm unsure how successful I am in hiding my growing feelings for Jax from my students. We stay professional on school property, but I'm not exactly known for my poker face. Luckily most teenagers have trouble seeing adults as actual people and are far more concerned with their own lives.

"Happy Monday, everyone. Today we're following up on our last session with Lisa and Gary on music in advertising and jingles." I pause, letting that sink in. I see Jax smirking out of the corner of my eye and force myself not to look directly at him, or I know I'll break. The students are looking at each other uncertainly, shifting in their seats.

Layla raises her hand, and I look at her, nodding. "Ms. Abbott? I thought today we were hearing about the contest?" She looks at Jax and Lucas with an uncertain question in her eyes before returning to me. The room fills with susurrus as other students agree, question, fidget in their seats.

SUSURRUS
Definition: whispering, murmuring, or rustling

I widen my eyes in fake surprise. "Oh! You wanted to do that now? You didn't want to wait until the end of the day?"

At this point, the students catch on to my ruse and start yelling, ribbing me, calling me out. I laugh, unable to keep up the pretense any longer.

"Okay, okay. Yes. Today is the Big Announcement! We had thirty-four students enter pieces to be considered for the flash tattoo contest. And I'll turn it over to Lucas Abbott to tell us more. Luke?"

He steps forward, a folder in his hands. "First, I have to say, this was some super impressive work. There's a lot of talent in this room, and after talking to the *Vanished* team, we've decided to do this every year." Jax nods behind him, a smile on his face. He looks…proud, which causes a warm pang in my chest. "Also, I don't know if any of you watch *Top Ink*," several students raise their hands, or clap, or claim they do, interrupting him briefly. "But last month, Derik Vonn won the most recent season." Again there are several statements around the room, acknowledging they know him, like him, a few chiming in someone else should have won. "What you probably don't know is that Derik actually tried out for my season and wasn't selected to compete. And he's applied every other season since then and was turned down. Until this season. And now he's the champion. So, even if you aren't one of the three finalists this year, that doesn't mean anything. It doesn't determine anything about next year or even next month. Or you. Got it?"

I see several students with wide eyes nodding. Some look down, already disappointed, scribbling on notebooks in front of them. I can tell the students who didn't enter and are just here out of support or curiosity.

"Okay, last thing, before I announce the winners. I just want to remind everyone that Jax had no part in the judging, and we didn't know who submitted which designs until the end." He steps up to the whiteboard and pulls the first piece of paper out of his folder, taping the image on the board. "First finalist, Diego Lopez." Diego smiles widely, fist-pounding a few of his friends sitting nearby. Lucas grins, waiting until the fervor dies down a bit. He hangs up the next image. "Second finalist, Traci Huang."

Traci looks shocked, her eyes wide with disbelief. Layla squeals excitedly and leans across her desk to hug her. "I told you!" she yells.

"And finally, number three. Cory Johnson."

A smile bursts across my face. I didn't even know Cory had entered. I knew Jax thought he should, that he'd been working with him on some ideas, but that Cory had been going back and forth, pretending he didn't care. My eyes find him in the back, he's sitting up straight, looking up for the first time, his face stunned.

I'm equally stunned, able to see for the first time today what he's been hiding under that hood. Cory has a nasty black eye and a split lip, clearly remnants of a violent weekend. And that's all I can see, but I suspect there are more bruises hiding under his bulky clothes. I try to stay focused on the positive, knowing now is not the right time to deal with the other.

"Congratulations to the finalists!" I state loudly. The room erupts in applause and cheers for a few minutes, and I let them ride that wave a little longer before calming everyone down again.

"Unfortunately, I have to head back to *Vanished*, but great work, everyone. Finalist should check in with Jax at the end of the day for next steps." Lucas waves, says a quick good-bye, and heads out.

"Before we revisit Wednesday and critique any work people want to show, I want to invite the finalists to come up and discuss their designs and inspiration. Not required, of course, but an opportunity to share with the rest of us and celebrate your win."

Diego shrugs and raises his hand, standing at the same time. I smile and motion for him to come on up.

"Yeah, so I wanted to do something strong and powerful that represented my Mexican heritage. So I did a really basic skull and added a cool, elaborate jaguar headpiece."

My eyes wander to Cory as I listen to Diego's explanation, then meet Jax's gaze. I can tell he's concerned as well by his expression.

And while it's far from ideal, I cross my fingers this is just a stupid teenage fight and not something far worse.

Jax

I KEEP AN EYE ON CORY FOR THE REST OF THE AFTERNOON. I'VE HAD too many of my own bruises not to recognize the after-effects of a beating. The question is, who gave him the beating and why. It pisses me off, and I'm struggling to keep it tamped down where others won't notice. I can read the concern in Riley's eyes as well. When his hood fell back, revealing his injuries, I saw her reaction, like a punch in the chest.

At the end of the afternoon, I call a huddle with the three finalists. I'm feeling weirdly proud of each of them, even though it really has nothing to do with me. But the team at *Vanished* was really impressed with a lot of the entries, and I feel like I called these three as the front runners. That the rest of the crew agreed with me feels good. Luke's even agreed to let them do a little promotion and appear on an episode of our show, assuming they all get parent or guardian sign-off beforehand.

The three of them gather around me. Traci and Diego both with excited grins on their faces. Cory just looks nervous and shifty.

"Congrats, guys. Well done. The crew is really excited to add your work to our options. The expo is the second weekend in March. Friday through Sunday. After school and on the weekend, if you want to work the booth, let me know, and we'll get you set up. You're all welcome to hang out there as much as you want, but it's up to you. So, what other questions do you have?"

Traci asks what sort of things they would do, working the booth, and I explain it would mainly be handing out information, scheduling people into slots, collecting emails from people, and probably doing some running for the team. Grabbing us coffee and lunch, and water. She nods.

Cory is staring at his shoes. "We'd get paid?" he asks.

"Yep. Twenty bucks an hour."

"Cool," Diego says.

"What else?"

The three of them look at each other, shrug, and shake their heads. They're good to go. I let them know about the possibility of shooting testimonials and give them the permission and release forms. Traci and Diego are buzzing with excitement, but Cory's vibe doesn't change.

"Okay, so I guess I'll see you guys next Wednesday. No school Monday, right?" They nod and yell their good-byes.

"Cory, hold back for a second."

I see him stiffen, but he waits near the doorway until the other students have all filed out. Riley, sensing the situation, turns her back to us while she packs up her stuff, giving us at least a little privacy.

"You okay?" I ask him.

"Fine, man. My ride's here. I gotta go."

"Cory." My voice is low and forceful. I'm not fucking around here, kid. "Are you okay?"

He finally looks me in the eye, and the turmoil I see there is like looking back in time. Fuck. This kid is in real trouble. I know it.

"I'm cool."

I start to put my hand on his shoulder and then think better of it, dropping my arm to my side.

"Let me see your phone." He sighs roughly, ready to complain. I just roll my eyes and hold out my hand. "Give it to me."

I ignore the mutters under his breath as he slaps his phone into my palm. I enter my number and then send myself a text, capturing his as well.

"You call me if you need to. If you ever need a safe space to crash."

He snatches his phone back and shoves it into his pocket. "Whatever, man. Can I go?"

I nod, fighting all my instincts to push, knowing that won't work, and he bolts out the door.

Shit.

I sigh, raking one hand through my hair. Suddenly, Riley is at my side, her hand gently rubbing down my back.

"You okay?"

I try to smile at her. "Yeah."

"Is Cory okay, you think?" Her eyes move to the door, where he'd just disappeared.

"I don't think so," I say grimly.

She chews her lip anxiously, a concerned expression on her face.

"Come on. Let's get out of here." I squeeze her tightly before releasing her.

We head back to her place since she has to work so much earlier than I do, grabbing take-out sushi on the way.

She snuggles into my side as we eat and talk about the afternoon session, her ideas, and upcoming speakers. She asks me about the merchandise line and the shop, and the show. It strikes me how domestic and... normal this feels, catching up with Riley over dinner. At least, I think that's what this is, I've never really had it before. But I like it. It's warm and soft, and cozy. I'm relaxed around her.

I feel like I've spent most of my life wearing armor. When I was a kid yanked away from my folks and then back again, never landing somewhere completely safe. Then as a teenager, fighting for money. Even now, with the show, being in the public eye, I'm always...alert when I'm out in public. But here, with her, I can shed all that shit and just relax.

Be me.

We clear our empty containers, and Riley makes some tea, which I'm learning is part of her nightly routine. I snag a KitKat out of her candy bowl. She looks at me, tilting her head with a small smile.

"Movie?" she asks.

"Sure. You pick." I've also discovered Riley has a very broad taste in movies but is particularly fond of cheesy horror flicks. We settle again on the couch, my arm along the back, and she leans into me, her hand on my thigh. She decides on *The Descent* about female cavers and peeks up at me with a sweet smile before turning her attention to the television.

There's a scene right in the beginning with a family in a car accident that makes me tense, worried it's going to upset her. Too close to her own experience. But she seems okay, her body doesn't tense up, there's no major reaction, and I settle back down.

She does jump ten minutes in at a bad dream one of the characters has. Again a few minutes later, at another jump scare. Her hands fly to her face during the predictable cave-in. Another jump, and she cringes at a fall. She buries her face in my side at a broken bone.

An hour in, she jerks against me, letting out a small shriek when the first cave monster appears. It makes me chuckle, and I tighten my arm around her shoulder.

"You good, Teach?"

She smiles and nods with a slight giggle, relaxing into me again. "This is a little more intense than I was expecting it to be."

I laugh and pull her closer.

By the end of the movie, I'm feeling a weird combination of mellow and turned on. But I'm definitely not interested in any more television. I start nuzzling through her hair to her neck while the credits roll, pressing a hot kiss against her skin there. She sighs softly and tilts her head, exposing more of her neck for me.

I grab her hips and pull her over me, so she's straddling my lap. She smiles at me and gently spears her fingers into my hair, lightly scraping against my scalp. I hum appreciatively, closing my eyes. She gives me a soft kiss, her sweetness making my chest tight even as my dick hardens beneath her.

"I think I need something more fun to think about after that," she whispers.

"Oh yeah? I can probably help with that."

The hot and hazy look in her eyes makes my dick twitch, and I pull her more tightly against me. She smiles and wraps her arms around my neck, leaning into me. Our kiss is hot and sweet and keeps me wanting more. I deepen the kiss, parting her lips with my tongue to explore more. It's slow and soft and lazy. She sighs and sinks farther into me. She's still wearing one of her little dresses, blue with gray robots, and I bunch her skirt up so I can get to her slim thighs. I feel her shiver when my fingers finally touch bare skin.

I trace teasing patterns along her thigh and nip at her bottom lip. She twists slightly in my arms and pulls down her side zipper leaving her dress gaping in front. An invitation.

Grinning, I press my lips to her skin just above the neckline, inhaling her warm scent.

"So pretty, Teach. I like the robots."

She laughs softly. "Thanks. Me too."

Her little hands slip under my shirt, lifting it up and off. She pauses and moves her eyes over my chest, a small smile playing at her mouth. I fucking love the way she looks at me. It makes me feel practically invincible. And when she comes with my name on her lips, I feel like a fucking king. No one else gets that. Only me.

Riley grabs a fistful of my hair and kisses me hungrily, rocking in my lap. I grip her hips and thrust against her, teasing us both with what we don't yet have.

I groan. "You have so many clothes on. Let's get them off."

She nods distractedly, which only makes me hotter. She pushes off my shoulders so she can stand between my splayed knees and shimmies her dress off to fall at her feet. So sexy. Even more, because she's shedding her shyness, not even noticing the living room lights on all around us. My eyes travel the length of her, taking it all in, my dick pulsing urgently against my jeans. When my eyes meet hers, I see the trace of nerves and try to reassure her in the only way I know how.

I lean forward, my hands holding her waist, and I press a hot kiss to her chest, just above her bra. "Gorgeous. So sweet." I nuzzle into the valley between her breasts. "Will you take this off for me?"

Her breath hitches, hands smoothing over my shoulders before she reaches behind her and releases the clasp. I groan into her skin and take one nipple into my mouth, sucking gently. I watch as she tilts her head back, mouth forming that little O that makes me so hard.

"Fuck," I groan into her skin. "I want that mouth on my cock so bad."

I feel her stiffen in my arms, her head tilting back down to look at me.

"You want that?" she asks softly, surprise in her voice.

Her surprise makes me chuckle. Doesn't every guy want that? Her eyes slide away, clearly uncomfortable, which cuts off my laughter.

"Teach, if you don't want-"

I watch her eyes go wide as she glances back at me. "No! It's not that. Daniel didn't like it. But I...," she trails off, her eyes going hazy as she looks down at me.

If I ever actually meet that guy.... A streak of annoyance and rage races through me, but I try not to focus on that. I have more important things to focus on right now.

Like Riley.

"First, I think we've established Daniel is a fucking idiot. Second, can we add your ex to the list of things we don't talk about while naked?"

She giggles. The sound washes over me, erasing my annoyance and kicking my desire for her up a notch.

"Teagan loves oral."

"Riley."

She blinks at me.

"Also, on the list of topics we don't talk about naked."

"Right. Sorry." She laughs nervously. "No exes. No family. Check."

Shit, she makes me laugh. I don't think I've ever laughed this much with a woman. Except maybe Logan, which is not at all the same.

Also, really don't want to think about Logan right now.

Instead, I stand, cupping her face in my hands, and kiss her, getting us both back on track. She holds my wrists and kisses me back, sighing happily.

I pull back just enough to tell her, "I never want you, us, to do something you don't want to. But if you're asking me, then yes. I want to feel your mouth on my dick. I've jacked off imaging that dozens of times. Hundreds. But in those fantasies, you're just as into it as me. So I only want, if you want."

Her eyes dilate with arousal, her breathing unsteady. Her grip on my wrists becomes almost frantic. "I want," she breathes.

Fuck, yes.

Riley

MY BREATH CATCHES AT THE SMOLDERING HEAT IN HIS EYES. A WAVE of arousal washes through me, tingles and warmth settling in my core. Jax kisses me again, the urgency in his touch keeping my body humming. His hands grab my butt, squeezing and kneading, feeling so good I can't help the moan that escapes.

I trace my hands along his shoulders and down his chest, finally reaching the waistband of his jeans, and I tug the button open, slipping my hand inside to cup his erection. He groans into our kiss, his hands on my butt pulling, arching me into him, trapping my hand between us. I wiggle away, breaking our kiss, so I can push his jeans down his legs. My stomach is fluttering, my core heavy with arousal, and I glance up at him once again, held captive by the hot glittering of his gaze. He takes a deep breath, his chest expanding, and I move my eyes back down his abs, settling on his erection, straining the fabric of his underwear.

Oh. Wow.

I peek up at him again and then slip my fingers beneath the band, pulling his underwear down and off.

I think I sigh. I hear him exhale roughly, and almost in a daze, a sexy daze, I reach out and grip his length in my palm. He's hard and hot and smooth, and I can hear him groan when I squeeze him firmly. His hips thrust into my touch, his eyes riveted on my hand.

"Fuck," he mutters softly, watching me move my hand along his length.

"Sit," I order softly, relishing my effect on him. I've never felt as sexy and powerful as I do when Jax looks at me. If I can make him feel half as good as he makes me feel, I want to.

His eyes fly up to mine, and I feel his dick pulse in my hand. He quickly does as I ask, his eagerness only ratcheting up my own arousal. I kneel in front of him, between his splayed knees. God, he's gorgeous. My hands move up and down his thighs as I take him in. He's sitting low, slouching on my couch, his head resting on the back cushion. His chest and hard abs laid out for me to enjoy. And his hard length laying against those abs. So hot. I shift, making myself comfortable, using my hands to tease him, touching him everywhere except where I know he most wants my touch.

I watch as his head tilts back even more, his eyes fluttering shut as he enjoys my attention. My touch. Sex with Jax is amazing. I'm not sure I could have even imagined it, how good he can make me feel. Even this. Even now. When he's not even touching me.

But I know he will. Soon.

But first....

I lean forward, one hand gently gripping his erection, tilting it away from his abs so I can get to it. My stomach flutters again wildly, tingles settling in my sex. I lick his tip teasingly back and forth and squeeze. He groans loudly, his hands fisting at his sides. I settle higher on my knees, bracing one hand on his upper thigh, and slowly take him in my mouth.

He groans again, louder, and I feel one of his hands in my hair, fingers caressing my scalp.

"Fuck...so good, Riley. So hot and sweet," he rasps, his voice sending shivers over my skin. "Suck me."

I do, sucking him as deep as I can, using my tongue to caress the underside of his erection. He's large, and there's no way I can fit the entire length of him in my mouth, but I use my hand to caress the rest. His abs and thighs tighten as he thrusts into my mouth. I love it. I pop off and tease the tip again, and Jax's groans make me feel like a freaking goddess. Having this man putty in my hands is a heady and fantastic feeling.

His eyes are slitted and heavy as they watch me touch him.

"More?" I tease, a wide smile on my face.

"Riley," he growls, making me giggle. But my humor is short-lived, overshadowed by arousal and heat as I take his length in my mouth once again. Settling into pleasing him.

It doesn't take long before his breathing is choppy and ragged, his body tightening beneath me before I hear him, voice straining, "Riley. I'm going to come. Do you want that, baby? For me to come in your mouth?"

Oh my god.

Can you come from just a question? Because it kind of feels like I could, right now. I'm so turned on.

I hum and nod, hallowing my cheeks as I suck, determined to make that happen.

"Oh fuuuuuuck," Jax groans, his hands in my hair, realizing what I'm doing. He thrusts into my lips, throwing his head back as he shouts his release, pulsing in my hand and my mouth. I swallow, feeling proud and satisfied and crazy aroused.

He slumps into the couch, breathing heavily as he recovers. Abruptly he sits forward, taking my mouth in a fevered kiss.

"So good, Teach. You fucking wrecked me." He leans his forehead against mine, breathing still unsteady. Then he grabs my waist and pulls me onto his lap. I lean into him, enjoying his soft kisses and caresses. His hands move across my skin, his fingers plucking at my nipples before slipping between my thighs. I sigh, parting my legs to give him more access. He drags my underwear down my legs impatiently so he can get to the soft, wet skin beneath.

He groans into my neck, feeling how wet I am, slipping two fingers into my core, teasing me. His mouth is hot and sends shivers down my spine as he presses hungry kisses along my neck, over my collarbone, finally reaching my nipples and doing some sucking of his own.

I spear my fingers through his hair, just enjoying his attention.

"So wet and sweet. Did you like that, Riley? Making me come?" He murmurs against my skin.

I nod and whisper yes, pulling his mouth back to mine for an anxious kiss. His fingers are teasing over my folds, thrusting into me, flicking over my clit. All the hot and tingly feelings that have been building inside me collide together and settle into my sex, focusing on his touch.

"Jax. That feels so good. Can you…please…." I'm frantic in his arms, chasing that high, spiraling tighter and tighter.

He lifts his head and moves his eyes along the entire length of me, laid out before him. I should be embarrassed, naked, and vulnerable in full light before him, but I feel too good to care. And I know he can make me feel even better.

"Can I…what? Can I make you come? Is that what you want, Riley? Do you want me to make you come?"

"Yes," I cry out, desperate, hips thrusting to meet his teasing, delightfully evil fingers.

He smashes his lips to mine in a heated, frantic kiss. He increases the tempo of his fingers, thrusting inside me, and presses his thumb against my clit. His thumb rotates in tight circles, and I detonate, screaming into his mouth as my orgasm crashes through me, shaking my limbs.

When I come back to myself, feeling languid and very relaxed, I'm curled up on Jax's lap with his arms warm and heavy around me. I lift my chin so I can place a kiss along his jaw. He looks down at me, an equally sated look in his eyes which spreads a gentle contented warmth through my chest.

He squeezes my butt cheek and urges me to my feet.

"C'mon, Teach. Let's go to bed."

Well, I'm not going to argue with that idea.

He twines our fingers together as we walk and snuggles into my back as we settle into bed, spooning me.

I shush the voice in my head, warning me I'm getting too attached, too comfortable for something that's only supposed to be 'right now'. I ignore the voice telling me to be careful and guard my recovering heart.

I like this. I want this. I want him.

I want 'right now' to stretch on as long as possible.

FINIFUGAL
Definition: fear of finishing things, anytime you want to prolong a final moment or prevent a seemingly inevitable ending. The resistance to the ending of things.

Finifugal.

CHAPTER
Seventeen

Jax

I'm getting far too comfortable spending my nights with Riley.

And my mornings.

And my evenings.

Fuck, I want to be with her all the time. I have to fight to stay away.

I'm losing the fight more and more often. Finding myself at Riley's or bringing her to my place more and more frequently. Last night, Friday night, was one of those nights, catching up with her after a few drinks with Luke and the gang. We'd had a hot and fun night, so I'm slightly disappointed to wake up by myself in her bed.

I roll to the side, sitting up, taking a moment to stretch. Pirate comes wandering into the bedroom and sits at my feet, his tongue hanging out.

"Where's your owner, dog?"

He just pants, looking up at me. I groan and stretch, functional enough to pull on my jeans before I go on a hunt to find her. Just in case.

"Riley," I call out, my voice still raspy with sleep.

There's no answer, but I hear sounds coming from the living room, so move down the hallway in that direction.

I find her dancing to music I can't hear, her airpods cranked to some beat she's slowly rolling her hips to. I can't help the grin that spreads across my face watching her. Damn, she's cute. She's pulled on some short sleep shorts and a tank top. The arms are wide enough I get peaks of her breasts as she moves. I lean against the wall, enjoying the show for a few minutes.

"Whatcha doing, Teach?" I finally speak up, loud enough to reach her through her music.

She spins, startled, and lets out a little squeak. Then she laughs at herself, calming down.

"I like to balter in the morning. I don't always have time before school, though." Her smile is sweet and a little shy.

"You like to what?" I push off the wall and start moving across the room toward her.

She grins wider, tracking my progress. "Balter. It means dance gracelessly, without skill but with great enjoyment."

I'm right in front of her now, my hands holding her hips.

"Want to balter with me?"

I laugh, but she starts bouncing around again, spinning and shaking her hips.

It's not sexy. Or very graceful. Not 'skilled', which I guess is the point. But it, she, is fucking adorable. Suddenly I feel like the Grinch in the scene when his heart grows several sizes.

Oh shit.

This isn't good.

This is, in fact, very, very bad.

Time to refocus this on what it's supposed to be. Fun. Sex. Short term.

I check the time, and on her next shimmy in front of me, I wrap my arms just under her butt, lifting her in the air against me. Her face is just above mine, glowing, and she settles against me, her arms around my neck.

"I've got two hours before I need to be at *Vanished*. I want to spend them between your thighs."

She laughs and gives me a slow kiss.

"If you insist. I was going to make breakfast for us."

"I'll grab something on the way to the shop." I'm moving us back to her bedroom while we talk.

She shifts in my arms, wrapping her legs around my waist, and kisses me again. "How late are you working tonight?"

"Four. Mace and Logan are closing, but Luke and I were going to meet up with all of you after class again."

I reach my destination, lowering us both back to her mattress.

"Good. I like that." Her smile is so sweet.

"I like you." It just slips out. Just like that. Without even thinking about it.

I watch her eyes soften and shine, her reaction battling with my uneasy 'should I be freaking out' inner monologue. I do like her. It's okay to say it. It doesn't mean anything is going to change. Needs to change.

Right?

I kiss her, both to shut up my inner voice and to make sure I don't say anything else.

And I spend the next two hours exactly the way I wanted.

BY THE TIME I FINISH MY LAST TATTOO OF THE DAY, I'M ANXIOUS AND glancing at the clock every five minutes.

Fucking pathetic.

And I think Luke is on to me, pretending to drag his feet getting out the door even though I know he's just as anxious to get to Ash. We climb into his car, I've already arranged for Riley to give me a ride back to my place in her new car. Well, used car. New to her. I'm still kind of shocked she decided to go that route, knowing how much money she has access to. But I appreciate that she doesn't…I don't know…show it off, I guess. It's easy for me to forget she has more money sitting in the bank than I could make in three lifetimes, even as well as the shop and the show are doing.

"You took off kind of early last night," Luke mentions.

I hum, neither agreeing or disagreeing, looking out the window.

"You see Riley last night?" he persists.

"Yeah, I swung by."

He nods, turning left and going south. It should only take us fifteen or twenty minutes to get there, depending on traffic. It's become a regular thing, us meeting up with Riley and Ash after their self-defense class. Sometimes Logan or Macy, Teagan, and Ilyssa join us, depending on the day. I like that Lucas and Riley are getting along. That Ash and Riley are becoming friends. Teagan's a lot, but I kinda like her. And she makes Luke laugh.

It's good. It's good he's making roads with his bio family.

"You two are hanging out a lot."

I shrug. "We have fun."

"Fun, huh?"

"Yep."

He snorts, clearly not buying it. "You talk to her about her birthday?"

"Yeah. A little. You're still okay with us closing the shop early that night, right?"

He rolls his eyes. Even while driving. This may not be the first time I've asked him this question.

"Yes. Logan moved her appointments to the next night and swapped them around. You're all set." He mutters something under his breath.

"What was that, asshole?"

"I said, and you call me whipped."

"Riley and I are not you and Ash."

"Oh really? What kind of lotion does Riley wear?"

"Vanilla. Why?"

Luke howls with laughter. "You know what kind of lotion she wears. You're planning a surprise for her birthday. You spend most nights together. You are not just hanging out. Or having fun. You, my friend, are into her."

I shove a hand through my hair, annoyed. With nothing really to say. I've started to suspect he's right, that I am. That this isn't just a casual thing that will run its course and fade away like all my past 'relationships'. At least not for me. But I also know Riley is just figuring things out post-Daniel. Ten *years* with Daniel. She wants to experience things. Experiment. Have some fun. And when she's ready for more, I won't be the guy.

I'm not the guy.

I need to remember that.

"Don't turn into one of those people that thinks everyone should be in love because they are. I'm good."

We drive the rest of the way in silence, finally pulling into a parking spot by the restaurant. We climb out, but he grabs me on the sidewalk before I get to the door.

"Just promise me one thing, and then I'll drop it."

I raise my eyebrow, impatient.

"Don't decide you don't deserve love just because we never had it before. Don't forget what you told me when I was messing things up with Ash. Maybe it's not Riley. Maybe it is. Even I can see this is different. You're different. In a good way."

I give him a half-hearted shove. "Fuck you, trying to make me cry and shit."

He laughs, letting me drop the subject.

We go inside, and my eyes find Riley immediately. She's sitting with the others, laughing, eyes shining. My chest gets tight watching them. Watching her.

I am so screwed.

Riley

I AGREE TO GO BACK TO JAX'S PLACE, AND HE AGREES TO STOP BY MY place first so I can walk Pirate and not feel like a neglectful doggie mom. By the time we get to my apartment, he's offered to let Pirate come with us. Which is sweet and thoughtful and so very Jax.

We're walking him around my block before driving over to Jax's. Pirate sniffs and stops, choosing a spot to do his business. Jax takes advantage of the moment to give me a sweet kiss, which quickly escalates. Until Pirate barks and jumps on us, breaking us apart.

"Ugly mutt. You're lucky you've never successfully cock-blocked me, even though I think you've tried." But he's squatting down, ruffling his fur as he complains, so neither of us, me or Pirate, take him that seriously.

He straightens, and we keep walking, Pirate dancing around Jax's feet, almost tripping him.

I laugh, but something out of the corner of my eye catches my attention, an ugly feeling sliding across my skin. I pause, confusing both Pirate, who is pulling at his leash and Jax, whose long stride takes him a few feet in front of me, before he realizes I've stopped moving. He turns with a questioning look on his face.

Pirate whines and comes to sit next to my feet. I lean down and absently scratch his head, my eyes still scanning the street.

"Riley?" I hear Jax's voice, but I'm still trying to figure out what has my skin prickling. I hear Ash's voice in my head, telling us to trust our instincts. They exist for a reason. And that's when I see it. The tiny orange glow moving through the air in my apartment alley. A car pulls down the street, the headlights glancing quickly into the shadows revealing Mick leaning against the brick wall.

When he realizes I'm staring right at him, he pushes off and saunters in our direction. Jax has noticed what's gained my attention, moving to my side and putting himself between the other man and me.

"Hey, Ms. Abbott. How you doing tonight?"

I don't respond, my voice stuck in my throat. He knows where I live. How does he know where I live? Why does he know where I live? Pirate woofs next to me and starts to growl, ears flattening.

"Can I help you, man?" Jax asks him, his stance ready and protective. Mick is still practically a child, he's not a physical threat to Jax, but I have no idea if he's got a weapon of some kind. I step forward, but Jax puts his arm out, keeping me back.

Mick glares at him. "You must be Jax. Heard about you, too."

"I don't know who you are, but you should go."

Mick takes another drag of his cigarette, his eyes returning to me. "Told you to leave my brother be."

"He a student?" Jax asks me over his shoulder, not taking his eyes off this man-child for even a second.

I shake my head and then realize he can't see me, "No. Related to one. Cory's brother."

"Go inside, Riley."

I shake my head again and place a hand on Jax's tense back. I can feel how tight his muscles are, even through his coat.

"Riley."

"With you," I say quietly. I'm not trying to be difficult, but I'm not letting Jax out of my sight. Not with an unknown threat in front of us. I'll gladly go inside, but I want him with me.

"You should listen to the man, Ms. Abbott. And you should leave my brother alone. He's got responsibilities."

"Let's go," I urge Jax, turning, ready to walk away. At that moment, Mick reaches out as if to make his point, Jax stiff-arms him, preventing him from getting close to me, and Mick jerks, stumbling backward on the icy sidewalk and falls on his butt.

"Get the fuck out of here," Jax growls. "And stay away."

Mick glares at him from the ground. "Rock says to say 'hi'."

Suddenly the furious energy coming off Jax magnifies. I can feel the waves coming off him as his whole body tightens.

"The fuck you say?"

He takes a menacing step forward, and I grip his arm, worried about his response.

Mick stands, brushing himself off. "Rock says hi, Jacky."

Jax surges forward, grabbing Mick's coat in both fists. Face inches apart, he snarls, "Get. The. Fuck. Out. I see you around her again, and you'll need an ambulance escort to leave. Hear me?"

He releases him so forcefully Mick stumbles away. Despite the flash of fear I saw on his face, he laughs now.

"GO! Now." Jax's expression is furious, a rage I've never seen before. Mick laughs before slowly walking away from us.

Tentatively, I reach out and grip his hand, slipping my fingers against his and squeezing. It takes a moment, his breath heaving as he watches Mick disappear down the street.

"Jax?"

Almost reluctantly, he turns his attention back to me, and I swallow a gasp seeing the storm of rage in his eyes.

"That's Cory's brother?" he demands.

I nod. "He was a student of mine a few years ago. He's dropped out since but should have graduated last year."

He shoves a hand through his hair, cursing.

Pirate whines, clearly picking up on the tension around us. "Let's go inside," I offer. He nods, but his head is obviously still somewhere else, which concerns me. Mick has thrown him, and I've never seen Jax spin before.

Once inside, he continues to pace, prowling around my tiny apartment, and I put on a pot of tea, not knowing what else to do. But tea usually soothes me, so I figure it's worth a shot.

"Has he been here before?"

I shake my head, pulling out a box of lavender tea. "No. I didn't know he knew where I lived."

"Fuck. But he's bothered you before?"

I hesitate, pouring the hot water into mugs.

"Riley?"

Turning, I set his tea on my counter. Close to where he paces. "He, uh, came by after school one night."

He's watching me closely. I fidget a little under his stare. "One night like three, four weeks ago? Is he why you signed up for Ash's class?"

I nod.

"Fuck!" he yells again, causing me to jump. Pirate barks and starts to whine from his dog bed.

I set my mug down next to his untouched one and move to intercept his pacing. I knew he'd be pissed if he found out someone had threatened me, subtly or otherwise, which is why I'd avoided telling him about Mick before now. Or why I'd suddenly been inspired to take a self-defense class. Despite outward appearances, Jax is a caretaker. It's in his nature. His protectiveness of Luke. The way he is with the kids. How he is with me. He's always thinking about how to defend his people, how to take care of others in his life, never himself.

But this…this reaction is something else entirely. He's spiraling and freaking out, and I don't know why. He's spinning out in a way that has my stomach in knots.

He stops abruptly, finding me in his path. I look up at him, seeing the wildness in his eyes.

"Jax." I cup his cheeks in my palms. "Stop. Please." I wrap my arms around his waist, placing my ear against his heart. It thumps rapidly against his chest, and I just hold him, waiting for his arms to come around me, for his heart to slow. "Will you kiss me?"

He grunts, but I feel some of the tension release out of him. I tilt my head up, seeking his kiss. He bends his head as I stretch up, meeting me halfway, and presses his lips to mine. But I can tell he's still distracted, still thinking about whatever dark thoughts brought us here.

"Will you talk to me? Please."

He exhales roughly and moves to sit on my couch, resting his head in his hands. I pick up our mugs and go to join him. I sit close to him, my palm resting on his thigh.

"Who is Rock?" I ask quietly.

He looks at me abruptly, his eyes blazing with rage and terror. "Never go near him, Riley. Promise me. If Mick is mixed up with Rock…."

I have no intention of seeking out Mick and will flag him to school staff immediately on Monday. But I still want to know what has Jax so torn up.

Not knowing what else to do, I crawl into his lap, straddling him to press my torso against his and hold him tight. I wrap myself around him, attempting to soothe him.

"I promise. Tell me."

His arms squeeze me tight.

"He's a murderer."

He's a murderer.

Murderer.

My stomach sinks, and my heart starts to pound. I feel sick and completely bumfuzzled.

> BUMFUZZLE
> Definition: confused and flustered, perplexed, bewildered

"What...what are you talking about?"

Jax shakes his head, lifting me off him, and stands, moving away from me. His reaction makes me feel worse. He's pulling away when I want him to do the opposite. I want him to let me in, share with me, let me help.

"Jax?" I follow him across the room, watching helplessly as he puts his coat back on.

"I'm sorry, I have to go. I have to...." He shrugs and shakes his head.

"Wait. Talk to me. Please."

He shakes his head again. "I can't right now. I have to...deal with this."

"Deal with this? What does that mean?"

I'm starting to panic now, imagining him doing all sorts of stupid things. And then I get angry. Angry at the idea that he would do something dangerous, that he's in such a bad head space, he would try to 'deal with this' on his own.

"Jax. Stop." My voice is strong, stronger than I feel, hands on my hips as I block my doorway. Distracted, he looks at me, his body tense and restless. "I'm worried," I tell him honestly.

Jax exhales roughly and pulls me into his arms. "I'm sorry. I just need to think. I'll call you later."

I nod against his chest, squeezing him tight. "Just think?" I ask. "Promise?"

He presses a kiss to the top of my head. "Promise."

"Okay." I take a slow breath and then tilt my head to look up at him. "Will you kiss me first?"

His grin is forced and a little sad as he cups my cheeks and bends to press our lips together. His kiss tastes desperate, tinged with fear. He lifts me against him, deepening our kiss, his tongue caressing mine.

I wrap my legs around his waist, hitching myself higher. I put all my anxiety into the kiss, hiding nothing. His hands cup my butt as our kiss goes on and on. Finally, he breaks away, both of us breathing heavily. He rests his forehead against mine as our hearts slow, returning to normal.

He sets me down, putting a sliver of distance between us.

"Don't worry, Teach." I feel his lips on my forehead. "I'll call you," he promises again, and then he leaves. And I'm left standing in the middle of my apartment, feeling uneasy and suddenly very alone.

CHAPTER

Eighteen

Jax

Fuck.

This is so fucked up.

I can't let Rock anywhere near Riley. Just the idea makes me feel like I'm going to vomit. How did this happen? I haven't seen anything of Rock since I kicked him out of *Vanished* weeks ago. But clearly, he's around, doing what he does. Knowing things he shouldn't. I can't let him anywhere near Riley.

I can't bring that to her door.

What the fuck am I going to do?

I brace myself against the cold, hands shoved deep into my pockets as I head to the el. I feel shitty about freaking Riley out, but I need some time to figure out what the hell I'm going to do. I need to think.

I take a deep breath, trying to calm down. And I need to think about this like I am now. Who I am now. Not who I was when I was sixteen. I have resources now. I'm not as fucking helpless as I was back then.

I'm not.

But I also have so much to lose now. Things I couldn't have even imagined back then. And Luke. Fuck. If this comes back and messes with Luke. With *Vanished*. The show. Ash.

Riley.

I need a plan.

I ride the el to the Loop, pulling my hat out of my pocket and shoving it down on my head. I need to grab a few things and then go to the library. Or a coffee shop.

It takes me an hour to get what I need, and my nerves make me short and pissed off at everything and everyone. Thank god no one has seemed to recognize me. Or at least no one that wants an autograph, a selfie, or a chat.

Finally, I get a coffee and sit down. Just an anonymous coffee drinker at a random cafe in the third-largest city in the country. Nothing special. Nothing anyone should pay attention to.

I should have done this a long time ago. But after that day, I did everything possible to bury every memory as deeply and permanently as possible. And now that I'm choosing to go back to it, everything is coming to me in slow, faded images.

I type what I can remember into the search engine and see what I can find about the dead man in the apartment fifteen years ago. I don't know much about computers, but I know others finding these searches on my devices would be pretty incriminating. At least I'm using public wifi and not the wifi at *Vanished*. If that matters. At least a step removed from Luke. And I bought a cheap new tablet. One I don't intend to use again. I know it's not enough to cover my tracks if the police ever come looking for me, but hopefully, that won't happen.

Hopefully, I can keep it from happening.

It takes forever. And I don't find much. It's still unsolved. It hadn't occurred to me until just now that someone else may have been convicted for this murder. An innocent person. The guilt and relief I feel battle inside me. I find his name. He didn't have any family. Thankfully. But that's probably part of the reason there isn't much information. No one to demand answers. To share stories of him with the press.

I see what I can find of Rock online. Mick. Recent drug busts in the city. See if I recognize any of the names from back then. From Rock's crew. Underground fights. I try to remember some of the other fighters, regular betters, see if any of them are on social media. In jail. Dead. I commit everything to memory.

What are the chances Rock still has that notebook? He'd been in jail for years. Would he have bothered holding on to that? Safeguarding it? Or is it lost to time?

I know I can't take that chance. I need to know. If it still exists, I need to get rid of it.

Fuck.

I crumple my now-empty coffee cup and toss it away. On the walk back to the el, I ditch the tablet.

Back at my place, I'm restless. I can't sit still.

I debate my next move. But eventually, I know it's my best of bad options. I grab my phone.

"Melrose."

"Hey, Detective Dylan. It's Jax. Been a while."

He's silent on the other end. This is risky. Melrose is no idiot. And he has no problem sticking his nose where it doesn't belong. I need to find a balance between him being willing to help but not interested in digging too deep.

"Jax," he finally says. "Please tell me this call isn't going to result in a shit ton of paperwork."

"Hoping to call in a favor."

"I don't owe you any favors."

I roll my eyes. "Consider it an investment in a future favor, then."

He sighs over the line. "Tell me. And I'll consider it."

"I'm doing some volunteer work at one of the local high schools, and there's a couple guys hanging around I'm worried are trouble. Can you check into them and let me know what you find out?"

The silence on the other end stretches forever, annoying me. I don't ask many people for help, and it's never been a cop I've turned to. But Melrose and Lucas have formed an uneasy alliance over the years, and last year when Ash and Logan were in trouble, Melrose showed up for us in a big way.

I'm hoping he'll do the same now. For me.

"Names?"

"Mick Johnson, probably late teens, early twenties. And Rock Ferrangi. Mid to late thirties."

"I'll get back to you."

The line goes dead. I exhale in relief. I hope he gets back to me soon. In the meantime, I need to track down some of the other old names and leads I'd found. Carefully.

But quickly. Because, on top of everything else, I have a twisted suspicion Cory's recent bruises are from the same place I used to get mine.

I'm kicking myself for not putting it together sooner. I'd had no reason to think Rock was connected to Cory. But now I know he is. Cory has a brother named Mick, and Mick is clearly working with Rock. Rock who used to blackmail me into underground, no rules, fights.

Twice a month. That's how often they were organized. Which means I've got less than a week before Cory shows up to school with a fresh round of injuries.

I'd like to keep that from happening.

Somehow.

I glance at my phone, knowing I should call Riley and tell her I'm okay. But I can't answer the questions I know she's going to have, and I don't want to lie to her. Instead, I take the coward's way out and send her a text. I can't believe with everything I've been through in life, it's a tiny redhead with giant gray eyes that unnerves me the most.

Riley

I SHOULD BE GRADING BOOK REPORTS RIGHT NOW, BUT I CAN'T SEEM to focus on anything for very long. Usually, I love this aspect of my job. I like the peek into what my students are thinking, what books they choose, how they relate to different characters. These in-school training days tend to be an excellent opportunity to catch up on things. No students, just teacher training and work time. But this afternoon, I am suffering from full-on aprosexia.

APROSEXIA

Definition: A complete inability to focus or concentrate due to a distracted, wandering mind

He's a murderer.

Jax's words keep reverberating around my brain. What is Mick doing hanging out with a murderer? How does *Jax* know a murderer? How much danger is Cory in? Are all of us in? Are we in danger? What is happening?

Where is Jax?

He's gone radio silent. I'm struggling to give him space. But I also want answers. And I don't think that's unreasonable. I mean, that's quite a bomb to drop and then bail. *Murderer.*

On the other hand, I feel like I'm learning a little about Jax, and I think this is how he processes things. He did the same thing early on when I told him I wanted to see where this could go. He bailed so he could think. And then he came back, ready to talk.

But when I freaked out and ran away, he came after me.

And when I took things into my own hands and went to seduce him at *Vanished*, we moved forward. After I ran away and he came after me.

Gah!

Maybe I should do that again. Seek him out. Go to him.

I check the time. I could probably sneak out a little early. It's not like me, but training is done for the day. No one would really miss me. And I'm not making any progress on these book reports. And I won't. I know that. Not until I talk to Jax.

Decision made, I pack up my stuff, shoving papers into my bag.

I poke my head into the room next door and let my friend and fellow English teacher know I'm leaving. She doesn't even blink, just tells me she'll see me tomorrow.

The bus to subway to bus route to *Vanished* takes forever, ratcheting my nerves up unbearably. A light dusting of snow has started to fall, the gray and heaviness of the sky seeming to echo my depressing thoughts, weighing the city down.

I walk through the front door, hearing the dinging when it opens, and stomp my feet to shake off the snow. Mateo, the high school student who works here part-time, is behind the counter. I've only met him a handful of times, but I know his story. His cousin is the one that shot Jax last spring when he and Mateo tried to rob the store. It's a complicated situation, but Lucas and Jax agreed to give Mateo a chance when all the details of his situation came out, and now he works here as part of his probation. He's a quiet kid but polite and eager and seems to be adjusting well.

He smiles when he sees me.

"Hi, Mateo. Getting in some extra hours on your day off of school?"

He shrugs. "Kinda. I'm just answering the phone. Luke and Logan made me bring my homework to do before worrying about anything else. So not really school free."

I laugh. "Could be worse," I point out with a smile.

"I know. I'm almost done, so tomorrow I can work with Logan." He looks so proud of himself.

Mateo and Logan are collaborating on designs for the merchandise line that Jax launched. Mateo writes poetry, and Logan creates companion artwork.

This group, the family that Lucas and Jax have found and built, awes me sometimes. Growing up, I didn't know Luke existed. None of us did. I hardly knew my aunt, his mother, existed. She was gone long before I was even born, and my dad and uncles never talked about her. I only learned about Luke four years ago, right before he was cast on *Top Ink*. I got to know him the same way most of America did, on television. I don't know what happened between him and Ethan and Uncle Theo, but I know the fallout from those early conversations kept Lucas away from the rest of us. Away from us for years.

And I know this family, his *Vanished* family, is still his 'real' family in his eyes. But it means so much to me that he's starting to make room for us, the Abbotts, in his world too.

Lucas suddenly appears, entering the lobby, interrupting my thoughts.

His welcoming smile makes me feel even better. "Hey, Riley. How's it going?"

"Good. Sorry for barging in. I hope that's okay."

He laughs. "According to Teagan, that's what family does, right?"

Suddenly I'm blinking back tears. Hearing him so easily refer to us as family. Luckily Lucas is giving Mateo a hard time and doesn't notice, not turning back to me until I'm under control again.

"Here to see Jax?"

"Yeah, if that's okay. Is he busy?"

Luke glances at the computer, checking the schedule. "He should be about done. You can go on back and say hi. He's with a regular."

"Thanks." I smile at the two of them and then go to find Jax. Unfortunately, I quickly regret not just waiting up front.

Because I find Jax with a half-naked woman in his arms.

CHAPTER
Nineteen

Jax

Christ, I'm so annoyed right now. Everything about the last 48 hours seems specifically designed to piss me off.

"Monique, it's not going to happen."

I'm even annoyed Monique somehow managed to get on my schedule again so soon. But I had a cancellation, and someone put her on my calendar. And she's once again determined to offer more than just money for my services. I've been dodging her wandering fingers for over an hour now, ignoring the breasts she keeps arching into my face.

She laughs at my rejection. I don't know why, but she seems to think I've decided to play hard to get or something. Why, I have no fucking clue. Her confidence is something I used to find sexy, and she and I had some good times together. It is still sexy; I'm just not interested.

And while I can tell myself it's because I agreed to keep this thing with Riley exclusive while it lasts, and I'm not a cheating asshole, deep down, I know it's more than that. I'm literally not interested. My dick isn't into it, my head isn't into it.

Call me pathetic.

I just want to see Riley. Talk to Riley. Touch Riley. Hear her laugh.

I'm such an asshole. Because I know, I'm still not ready to talk, to answer her questions, but I need her. I need her sweetness and light to counter Rock and all the darkness he brings back into my life.

Finally, I get the last touches done on Monique's newest tattoo. She slides one hand down my arm unnecessarily, fingers lingering on the back of my hand. I shake her off and stand, pushing off the stool. I go through the aftercare instructions, even though Monique probably knows them as well as I do at this point. I turn my back to her, putting my tool and materials away. Unfortunately, she's still not taking the hint, and I feel her come up behind me. Her hands snake around my waist, and she tries to slip them under my shirt.

I whirl around, grabbing her hands in front of me, but she's sneaky and somehow manages to wrap them around my neck, pressing herself against me.

"You should put your shirt back on. I'll meet you out front."

"Jax, you turned me down last time. You do it again, I'm going to think there's something wrong with me." She leans in to kiss me, but I bend back out of her reach.

"Monique, I told you I'm seeing someone. It's not going to happen."

She eyes me skeptically, "You? Dating?"

"Yes. Please put your shirt on." I try to step back, but I'm pinned between her and my tray. Shit. I put my hands on her waist to move her, and she takes that opportunity to move closer and winds her arms around my waist. She plasters herself against me and puts her lips on mine, kissing me.

I jerk away, and a small sound and movement near the door catch my eye. I see Riley standing just inside the curtain.

Fuck. Of course, she walks in right at this exact moment. The worst possible moment. I can only imagine what this looks like to her. And after walking in on Daniel. Damn it.

Her eyes are wide and hurt as she blinks at us. And I feel my gut roll, terrified I've screwed this up. That I've hurt her. When that's the last thing, I want to do. The one thing I was determined not to do.

I growl, dropping my hands as if burned, and nudge Monique away, dodging to the side.

Monique's heavily made-up eyes widen comically as she looks between Riley and me. "Oh! Shit. I should probably go."

"Yeah," I mutter. "You should."

Fuck.

I'm pissed. I'm pissed she didn't back off when I told her to. I'm pissed knowing what this must look like to Riley. I'm pissed, I'm now going to have a fight instead of going home and having sex, with *Riley*, like I'd hoped and, frankly, had been looking forward to all fucking day.

Monique scurries around, finally putting her shirt back on, and rushes out the door.

I study Riley carefully. Of course, this is one of the rare times I can't read her expression. She's wearing a black and white striped skirt today with loafers and a fuzzy mint green sweater. Her hair is down and soft and shiny. She's so pretty. I can feel my adrenaline spiking as she remains silent. Ready for the fight I know is coming. And I'm so annoyed about it.

"It's not what it looked like, Teach." I cringe, hearing the words coming out of my mouth. Isn't that the cry of every cheating asshole? Shit. "I mean, she offered, but I turned her down."

"I heard you."

"I swear, nothing was going to happen. Nothing *did* happen. She just didn't want to take no for an answer."

"Must be hard to be so irresistible," she says, her voice monotone, but a small smile teases her lips.

"You believe me?"

Her giggle releases all my building tension. It just…deflates right out of me. Thank fuck.

"That was mean," I accuse and jerk her into my arms. She stumbles at the sudden move, falling into me.

Her arms wind around my neck. "Oh, was that mean? I kind of thought you disappearing for two days was pretty mean." Her eyes flash with anger.

I grimace. Ouch.

I rest my forehead against hers and breath her in. Fresh air and vanilla. "I'm sorry I ducked out."

She tilts her chin, giving me a quick kiss, her eyes searching mine. "Are you okay?"

Shrugging, I give her a kiss back. "It'll be okay. I just have to figure some things out."

"I'm here, you know."

"Thanks, Teach.

"She kissed you." Her eyes darken as she stares up into mine. "I don't like that she kissed you."

I don't like it either. Despite the promises we made when we started, this isn't just fun for me anymore. She's getting under my skin in ways I didn't anticipate and thought would never happen to me. One day, likely soon, she's going to realize I have nothing to offer her other than orgasms. Someday soon, she'll realize that's not enough, and she deserves so much more. I need to take each day she lets me have.

And night.

"She was my last appointment. Want to get out of here?"

She nods, sliding her palm into mine. "Let's go."

I want to take her home and screw the vision of Monique's kiss out of both our heads.

Riley

IN THE TIME IT TAKES US TO ORDER TAKEOUT AND GET BACK TO JAX'S, he seems to have relaxed. A little, anyway. He's not quite back to his usual self but seems closer. I've already texted Teagan about walking Pirate so I can focus on this. On Jax.

I'm unsure how hard I should push him to talk to me. Or if I should just let him come to it on his own time. It makes me nervous and keeps me on edge, even though I'm trying to be normal and get him to relax and be normal with me. I'm not sure how successful I am. Pretending to be normal. I'm not great at subterfuge.

I went to *Vanished* to confront him about Rock and Mick, but seeing that woman kissing him has added a whole new element to our dynamic. I didn't exactly enjoy seeing another woman all over him. It definitely brought on a brief case of the collywobbles.

COLLYWOBBLES
Definition: stomach pain or queasiness

But it was also obvious the second I saw Jax's face that he wasn't into it. Believe me, I remember how much Daniel was enjoying himself between the legs of another woman. I know the difference.

So while it feels like we should talk about it, I'm not really sure what there is to say. Other than what we've already said. I know he was expecting me to freak out, which I easily could have. He was tense and ready for a fight; it was obvious in his body language. He still seems wound up despite my best efforts.

He lets us into his loft, throws his keys on the kitchen island, and sets our takeout bags down. And then he turns to me.

His eyes are intense as they bore into mine, maybe more intense than I've ever seen him. This has thrown him even more than me, and I'm not really sure why.

"I didn't kiss her."

"I know," I assure him.

"You know I wouldn't do that." He moves to stand right in front of me, still staring hard into my eyes.

I nod, believing him. "I know. I trust you," I say softly.

Those three words seem to unleash something in him. His kiss is almost desperate as he clutches me to him. He twists his head, his tongue parting my lips and slipping inside. I feel his hands cupping my face as he deepens our kiss, my nerves quickly transition to arousal. These kinds of things are fickle, I guess, because embarrassingly quickly, I'm rubbing against him, wanting so much more.

He lifts me effortlessly and sets me on the kitchen island, putting me at eye level with him. He's wasting no time, spreading my thighs and stepping between them as he continues with those ravaging kisses. His hands are hot, squeezing my thighs, skimming along my skin until he reaches my hips and settles there. I lace my hands behind his head, keeping our kiss going on and on. I love his kisses. He groans against my lips, and I feel his fingers flexing against my hips.

It's thrilling knowing he wants me this much. So much intensity and heat. Sometimes I wonder if I can handle it. Will it burn me someday soon?

His fingers curl into the band of my underwear, and he jerks them down and off. I sense him fumbling with his zipper, freeing his erection.

"Are you ready for me, Teach? I need you." His fingers slip between my legs parting my core. I'm aroused, loving his touches, his kisses, but I'm not…ready, yet. Which he quickly figures out.

"Fuck," he mutters softly, a slight hitch in his touch. Then he switches direction, throwing my skirt up and ducking down, and I feel his hot breath against my core.

I gasp, my arms going back to brace myself on the counter. Jax kisses the inside of my knee and lifts my leg until it's resting over his shoulder. Then he presses a kiss to the opposite inner thigh, lifting the other leg to his other shoulder. Oh god. His hot breath fans over my core, and I shiver in reaction. And then he kisses my sex, his tongue teasing through my folds, and I cry out.

I fall back against the counter, no longer able to support my weight. It's so freaking sexy not being able to see him as he moves, breathes, kisses, licks, and explores under my skirt. My back bows as I feel him plunge two fingers inside me, fluttering, his tongue flat, lapping against my core.

"Jax!" I gasp.

He hums against my skin, the vibrations sending shivers down my limbs. He's on a mission, intent to make me come as quickly as possible, and he's succeeding.

My entire body tenses, legs shaking; I'm straining against him, chasing pleasure until it borders on pain. He latches on to my clit and sucks, still moving those devilish fingers, and I splinter into a million pieces, screaming my release. He doesn't let up, continuing to taste and tease until I feel a second orgasm slam into me. It's so intense, waves of pleasure shivering through me, and it goes on and on and on.

"Jax!" I groan and fight to catch my breath, a giant puddle on his countertop. Tears leak from my eyes as I slowly come back to myself. I push against his forehead, needing a break, my sex too sensitive for anymore.

Jax presses one last kiss to my mound and finally emerges from the material of my skirt. He freezes and curses when he sees my tears.

"Shit. Shit, Riley. Did I hurt you?"

A ragged laugh escapes me, and I shake my head, struggling to sit up. His face is tense, worried. "No. Just overwhelmed me." I wind my arms around his neck, pulling him close for a kiss. I can taste my orgasm on his lips, and an erotic shudder moves through me.

"Finish, please. I want you."

I watch as he slides the condom on and shifts me to the counter's edge. I'm at the perfect height, and he thrusts into me so deep. I moan and move my hips against him, he feels so good. He's hot and hard and so strong and solid in my arms.

"Fuck...Riley...god."

I pull him tight and press kisses along the cord of his throat, straining as he moves against me. I grab his face and kiss him desperately. "Hurry. Show me you want me."

He groans, pumping his hips into me as I edge forward, meeting him thrust for thrust. His hips start to move unsteadily, frantically. I stretch against him, so I can whisper into his ear.

"Jax. Show me. Please. I want you to come."

He swears, and his grip on my hips tightens as he slams into me faster and faster. I can see our reflection in his dark windows across the room. Can see how powerful he is as he thrusts, his back muscles flexing, his butt cheeks clenching. It's unbelievably sexy. Finally, I feel him stiffen in my arms, groaning along my throat as he jerks and stills, his breath heavy in my ear.

"Riley."

I feel sated and warm and want nothing more than to melt into him.

But apparently, my stomach has other ideas because it takes this quiet moment to growl loudly, cracking us both up. He shakes with laughter in my arms and slides out of me. I bite back a cry. After two orgasms and that rough ride, I'm a little sensitive.

He chuckles. "Sorry, Teach. I guess I should feed you before I sex you up."

I smile and assure him, "I've got no complaints. But I am hungry. Obviously."

We kiss softly, and he helps me down. My legs are weak, and it takes me a minute to get steady. We eat in the quiet, standing at the other end of his kitchen island. The end he didn't just defile me on.

And then we strip off our clothes and climb into bed. It's still early, but I think we both need to feel this closeness right now. I snuggle into his side, sighing in contentment.

He's lying on his back, hands laced behind his head, relaxed.

There are so many things we need to talk about. So many things I need to know. But what do I ask?

"Do you," I hesitate briefly, then carry on, "do you ever wish I was more like that?"

"Like what?"

I'm sated and sleepy and not careful with my words. "Like her. Like that woman, Monique."

He rears up, surprise and annoyance all over his face. "What? Why would you ask me that?"

I'm a little taken aback by his reaction. I clearly didn't think this through. I open my mouth to try to diffuse what I sense is about to go off the rails.

"Wait," he cuts me off before I can compose my response, "let me be clear. No. I don't wish you were someone else, someone different. And why would you ask me that?" He jerks the sheet off, moving out of bed and angrily pulling on a pair of sweatpants.

Oh crap. He's angry.

And so gorgeous. I'm trying hard not to be distracted by his chest, abs, and tattoos on display before me. Focus, Riley.

"I just meant... I don't know... she's obviously more experienced than me. And more confident. I would never-"

His rough bark of laughter interrupts me. "Riley, our first kiss happened when you stripped to your underwear next to my chair." He grabs a bottle of water and chugs, his throat flexing.

I feel my face flush with embarrassment. "Only because you'd never have kissed me otherwise!" I point out.

He shoots me a look. I'm sitting awkwardly in his bed, his sheet pulled up to cover my nakedness.

"I would have. There's no way I could have ignored this for long. But yeah. You almost naked, standing in front of me, asking me to kiss you? There was no way I could have resisted that. Not when I wanted you so bad."

"You did?"

He rolls his eyes, but at least he doesn't seem angry anymore. "Seriously? You couldn't tell how twisted up I was?"

My heart rate increases. "I...I thought maybe...but I wasn't sure. And I...I mean, for me, this...is amazing. But I know you're probably used to...more."

He settles onto his bed, sitting almost in touching distance, and studies me carefully. "Riley. It's not like I'm making any...I don't know...*allowances* for you or something. Fuck, I practically mauled you over the counter earlier. I ate you until you cried. I'm not bored, Teach. Far from it."

I press my lips together, not sure what to say. Deep down, that had been a concern. That I'm not exciting enough, experienced enough, erotic enough to satisfy him for long.

He shoves a hand through his hair, leaving it spiking out in multiple directions. I love it when his hair is messy. I'm so distracted by how hot he is it takes me a second to process what he says next. "Are you? Is that what this is about? Do you want to have sex with other people?"

"What? No!"

It's on the tip of my tongue to tell him how I feel. That no other man could ever compare to him because even though we agreed this would be just for 'right now' I'm so far past that I can't even see it anymore. That the idea of dating anyone else, kissing anyone else, having sex with anyone else makes me feel hollow inside.

It's on the tip of my tongue to tell him I'm falling in love with him.

But instead, we're interrupted by his entrance buzzer going off. I jerk in surprise and then meet his eyes again. He's staring at me, guarded and intense. I open my mouth about to say... something. I'm not sure what, but his buzzer goes off again.

He curses and stands up, crossing to his front door, and checks the security system. He swears again.

"You better get dressed," he tells me and buzzes whoever it is in.

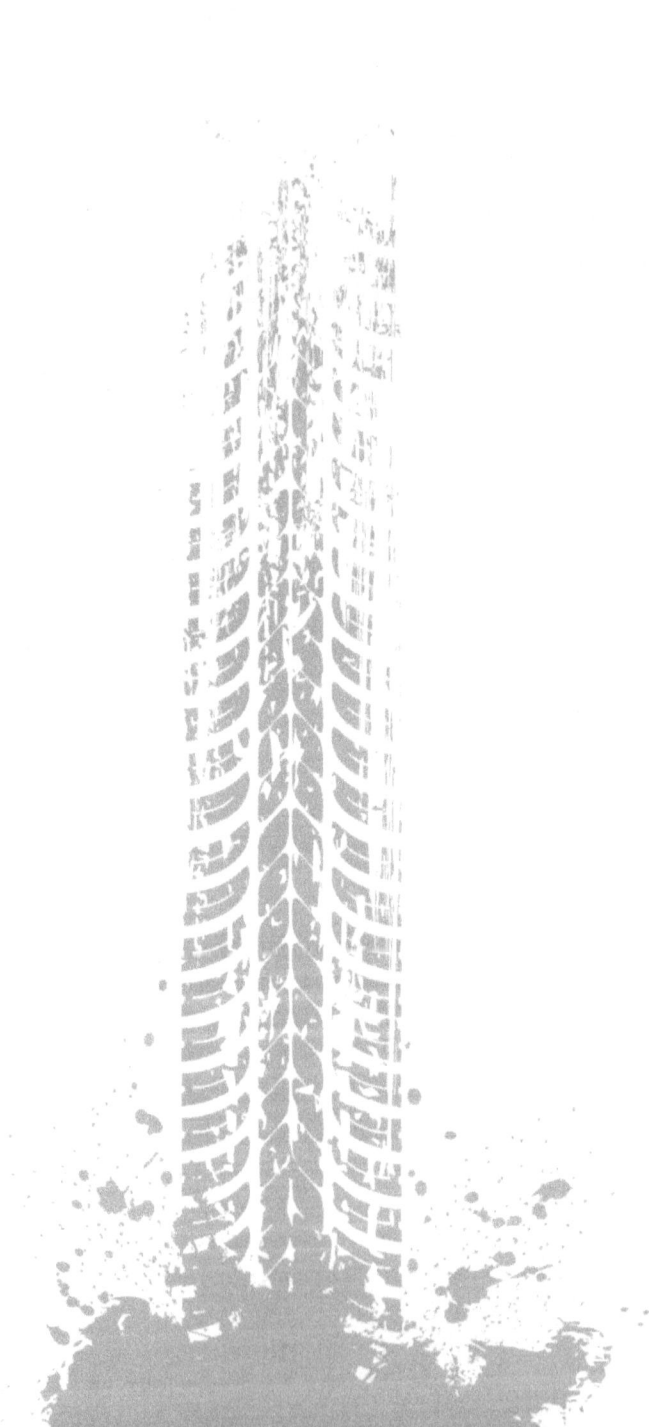

CHAPTER

Twenty

Jax

Christ, I'm losing it.

I feel completely out of control and can't really figure out why or how to fix it. But this whole thing with Rock and Mick has obviously sent me reeling, destabilizing the ground I've built my adult life on. And then being away, staying away from Riley. Only to then have her walk in while Monique was all over me. Then she asks that question. As if she's not enough. Like I would want her to be different. But maybe that's her projecting, and she's the one that wants something different.

I'm feeling raw and exposed and a little ragey.

And now I have to deal with this.

I see Riley scramble out of bed, flailing a bit, a confused look on her face, as she pulls on one of my t-shirts and a pair of leggings she had in her giant purse. I grab a shirt as well, pulling it on over my sweats, and squeeze her hand briefly when I walk by, trying to reassure her.

Then I'm back at my door, opening it to Melrose on the other side.

"Jax." He nods, expression grim. "We need to talk."

I step aside, giving him room to enter.

His eyes land on Riley, standing uncertainly between my bed and the kitchen island. "Sorry. I didn't realize you had company."

I shrug. "Riley, this is Detective Dylan Melrose. Melrose, this is Riley Abbott."

His eyes flash with recognition, but he doesn't otherwise react.

"Is…is everything okay?"

"I called him after our run-in with Mick."

"Oh." Her eyes go wide when I announce this.

Melrose watches me with that steady cop gaze. "You said they were hanging around the school. Not that you had a 'run in'."

"They are."

He frowns, clearly sensing there's more to this than I admitted on our brief call. And I'm definitely not liking the fact he felt the need to come over and discuss whatever it was he found in person on a Monday night.

I wave my arm towards the couch and chairs, silently inviting everyone to sit. Melrose moves farther inside, following my lead. Riley hesitates, and then I see her digging through my cabinets to find some mugs and tea. I don't have the selection she does, but she finds the box of tea bags I have and starts to make three cups.

Melrose grabs a chair, and I sit opposite him on my couch.

"You picked some bad ones, Jax."

I'm sitting forward, my elbows resting on my knees, braced for whatever he has to tell me.

"Tell me."

"Well, Mick is pretty low-level. He's been busted on some petty shit, but nothing major has stuck. And he's starting to associate with some major players. If he's hanging around the school, he's likely dealing to students or has a student doing it for him."

"I haven't seen him dealing. But I'll keep a better eye on it."

Riley walks over, setting tea in front of each of us, and then takes a seat on the couch near me. Close enough, our thighs touch. Likely eliminating any doubt Melrose has about what's happening here. Between me and an Abbott.

"And Rock? You've seen him at the school too?"

"Just once. But Mick mentioned him by name, so I'm guessing they're working together."

"That lines up with what I've heard, yeah."

I run a hand through my hair. "Fuck."

"He's bad news, man. Just got out. He's been busted for dealing and assault multiple times, but we could never get him until he was caught in an undercover operation. He tried to plea it down, but we got lucky with the DA and the judge. They gave him the longest sentence allowed. But he kept a tight reign on his people even from prison, and now that he's out, it looks like he's reclaimed his throne pretty seamlessly. Although there are a few players that have mysteriously disappeared since his release. No one's talking, but there's a lot of speculation by the cops in the neighborhood."

He's a murderer.

Fuck.

Riley stays silent, but I feel her tense next to me, even though I'm sure she has a million questions, and I appreciate the trust and loyalty that has her waiting until we're alone.

"What school are you volunteering at?"

"Mine," Riley offers. She explains she's a high school teacher and gives Melrose the name and address.

He frowns. "That's not Rock's neighborhood. He's expanding."

"Or maybe just teaming up with Mick for some reason," I offer.

"Look, I can't tell you much, but there's multiple cases looking at these two, but witnesses and hard evidence are hard to find. Without that, you know there's nothing we can do. Steer clear of this mess, Jax."

"I get it. Thanks for looking into it for me."

Melrose nods and moves to stand.

I do the same but then hesitate, glancing at Riley. Thinking of Cory.

"What do you know about the underground fight scene? Especially ones that use minors."

Melrose studies me carefully. "I know they exist. I know it's a fucking nightmare to bust any of them. Most of them have shady cops right in the mix, fighting, betting. Fucking bullshit."

I nod. I remember.

"You think these two are involved in that?"

I nod again. I do.

"And there's minors fighting? You sure of that?"

I'm sure. "I can't prove it."

He stares at me silently, waiting.

"I'm sure."

I can practically feel Riley's eyes on me. But I keep my eyes on Melrose, watching his reaction.

"And Rock?"

"He runs a ring."

He waits.

"I'm sure."

"Fuck," Melrose mutters. "You have anything I can act on?"

I think of Cory. But I'd like to keep him out of this as much as possible. If it's possible.

"Not yet."

"Let me know when you do."

I stand, knowing our conversation is over. For now. He follows me across the room, slaps me on the shoulder, and heads out. I look at my closed door for a moment, dreading turning around and facing Riley and her questions.

I inhale deeply and brace to face her. She's still at the couch, standing with her mug of tea in hand, gray eyes soft and thoughtful. She tilts her head to the side.

"Will you come sit with me?"

Feeling heavy and nervous, I move to her side. She takes my hand, and I collapse onto the couch next to her. Setting her mug down, she climbs into my lap, straddling me, wrapping herself around me. Soothing me. I exhale roughly into the curve of her neck, my arms going around her waist and pulling her tight. Letting her.

I need this right now. And I'm not sure she'll want to do it when she knows everything.

Riley

My heart and mind are racing with everything I just learned and everything I suspect because of it. I'm relieved to know that after Jax left me the other night, he called a police officer, but it was pretty obvious he didn't tell his friend Melrose everything. And all that has been left unsaid makes me incredibly nervous. Because it's also pretty apparent that Jax isn't going to leave it to the police.

I know we need to talk, but for now, I just hold him, enjoying the steady beat of his heart against mine. This is quickly becoming my favorite position. He squeezes my butt and presses a kiss to my shoulder. It doesn't feel like the start of anything, just him taking the comfort I'm offering.

I straighten, leaning back far enough to look into his eyes. I kiss him softly and ask, "Will you tell me about Rock?"

He sighs roughly and drops his head back, staring up at the ceiling.

"I knew him when I was a kid. The second foster home Luke and I were both in was pretty shitty. We had to pay 'rent' even though we were just kids. Rock kind of ran the neighborhood, and I got sucked into taking jobs with him to make money for my foster dad."

My heart twists for both of them. I know from some of the volunteer work they do they didn't have a great experience in foster care. They do a lot to highlight good foster families and ensure kids in the system have options if they land somewhere unsafe. I listen quietly as he shares a little of his story, running my hands along his arm and shoulders.

"It was stupid. Luke hated it. Would get pissed at me all the time, but it was the easy option. He always had some package to deliver or pick up. Stupid shit. I'm sure it was illegal, but I felt like I wasn't really doing anything that wrong if I didn't know for sure. I didn't ask questions, and I was big and fast for my age, so Rock used me."

He shifts beneath me, his hands squeezing my hips, tilting his head back up to meet my eyes.

"You sure you want to know all this, Teach?"

I nod. "I want to know whatever you are comfortable telling me."

His eyes are dark. Bleak. The gold ring muted. "I hate talking about it."

I snuggle into his chest, press a kiss to his cheek. "I'm here."

He sighs again and then continues. "Eventually, he decided I could make more money for him by fighting. Every other weekend he'd organize a fight. He had quite the operation set up. Usually, at least four matchups, but sometimes he'd have a whole weekend of fights. Betting. Fuck he even had ring girls for the crowd. I was only sixteen but big for my age, and people didn't ask many questions. Melrose is right; there were definitely cops in the crowd. Some would even take a fight, make some extra money. Working 'security' for Rock. Others just betting.

"Eventually, he got caught in that sting operation Melrose mentioned, and Luke got hired on full-time tattooing, hooked me up with a job there too. And I just…moved on. But now Rock is out, and he's working with Mick, and I'm sure they've got Cory fighting. I just fucking know it. And I'm not sure how to help him."

Oh god. I squeeze him tighter, trying to let him know how sorry I am. How much I admire him. How *good* he is.

"I'm sorry that happened to you."

"Not your fault, Teach."

I lean back and cup his cheeks, kissing him softly. He's stiff in my arms, and it takes a few moments, a few kisses, before he exuviates some of his demons and relaxes enough to kiss me back. It's soft and slow and lazy. I'm just trying to chase some of the dark memories away.

> EXUVIATE
> Definition: sheds, cast off

"How long? Did he have you fighting?"

"Almost three years." His eyes are painfully hollow. Shadows filling the spaces normally so light and teasing.

I caress his cheek, feeling the rough stubble, fingers tracing his lips.

"I'm glad you told me. We'll figure this out."

He stiffens and lifts me off his lap, standing and pacing in front of the couch. "I don't want you anywhere near this, Teach. He's too dangerous."

"You don't get to decide that, Jax. I care about you, and I care about Cory. You don't get to just decide how we deal with this."

"There isn't a 'we' here, Riley. I'll deal with this. I won't put you in danger."

I stand up, hands on my hips, angry for the first time during this conversation. "You don't *put* me anywhere. I make my own choices."

He opens his mouth, prepared to argue more, I'm sure, but I cut him off.

"You said murderer."

Jax freezes.

"You said Rock was a murderer," I remind him.

"Riley."

"Tell me the rest."

He sinks to his chair, burying his face in his hands. "I can't."

I kneel before him, holding his wrists, urging him to look at me.

"I can't, Riley. Please don't ask me. Please just trust me. He's dangerous. You heard Melrose."

My stomach twists. I'm totally conflicted.

"I heard Melrose," I agree. "But you know, don't you? You know it for certain."

He just looks at me with wild eyes, clearly terrified, and swallows. Which terrifies me.

"Are you in danger, Jax?"

He shakes his head but says, "I don't know. I never expected to see him again."

Oh god. I'm shaking inside but trying desperately to be strong for him.

"Look at me. We will figure this out. We will help Cory. And we will work with Melrose to get Rock off the streets and out of your life." My voice is confident and firm despite my inner turmoil. "Don't shut me out, please. Let me be there for you."

He grabs me up, curling me into his lap, and squeezes me so tightly I fight for breath. But I'm holding him just as tight.

I will not lose him. Not this way.

I will not let this take him from me.

CHAPTER
Twenty-One

Jax

I listen to Riley breathe next to me in the dark, feel her softness and warmth. I wish I could sleep, but my head is a mess, trying to figure a way out of this. I can't tell her the whole truth. I can't tell her my stupid choices have put Lucas in danger. That he could lose everything, even his freedom, because of me. She could lose another family, one she's tried so hard to build, because of me.

What the fuck am I going to do?

I've got to figure out if Rock still has that notebook. And I need to get rid of him. Somehow. Not just for me but for Luke, for Riley, for Cory. This is on me. I know Melrose will have my back. That at least seemed clear from our conversation. But I have to give him something to work with. Something I don't have right now.

Riley shifts next to me, rolling away, and I follow her, wrapping my arm around her waist and curving into her back. I'll keep her close as long as I can. I know it can't last much longer. Until then, I just need to make sure she's safe. And once I take care of Rock, she can move on, and I'll have a clear conscious.

He knows about her. Mick's visit proved that. Rock knows about Riley. Knows she's important to me.

She sighs, and I can't resist pressing a kiss to her bare shoulder. I'm such an asshole, dragging her into this shit. But until I know the threat is gone, I'm not letting her out of my sight.

Eventually, her scent and steady breathing relaxes me enough I finally fall into a rocky sleep.

Too early, I hear her alarm go off. She reaches for her phone, silencing the annoying chime, and then turns back into me. She can sleep in a little later this morning since they have another day of meetings and no classes, but it's still hours before I need to start my day. Her breath is hot and moist against my chest, and I groan, pulling her close. We cuddle for a few minutes until her alarm goes off again, and I roll to my back, groaning. She kisses me quickly and slides out of bed, padding across my loft to the bathroom.

While she's in the bathroom, I stare at the ceiling, trying to organize my thoughts. Protect Cory. Keep Riley safe. Get rid of Rock. It's like a chant or mantra that circles in my head.

But how?

How?

I pull myself out of bed, fighting exhaustion, and grab a blue sweater and some jeans. When Riley re-emerges, I'm at the coffee pot pouring mugs for each of us.

"I'll give you a ride home and then to school."

She smiles sweetly. "Are you sure? You can go back to bed."

I pull her close and kiss the side of her neck, loving her little shiver. "Give me five minutes. Drink your coffee."

Riley wraps her arms around my waist. "Are you okay? I mean, last night…."

"I'm okay, Teach."

I'm nowhere near okay. But I need to figure some things out without her, without her worrying. My head's a fucking shit show right now.

After dropping Riley off at school, I head to the old neighborhood. The one where I got sucked into Rock's shadow. I circle for a while and then park my car across from the lot Rock and his crew used to hang out. It's early in the day, the apartment lot is empty. I don't know if this is still his spot, but it's the only lead I have. After thirty minutes, I get out, lock my car, and run down the street for a cup of coffee. Then I'm back, ready to wait. As long as it takes.

I don't really have a plan. Not a full one, anyway. I just know I need to do *something*.

It takes a couple hours, but then I see him. Just like he used to be. Ruling over the yard. His followers slowly assemble as the day moves on. I spot Cory's brother, Mick, hanging around. Around noon, I see Cory.

Fuck.

He talks to his brother for a few minutes, then shoves his hands deep into his coat pockets and wanders away, shoulders slumped. I start my car and pull out, following his path towards the el.

When he's a block away, I pull alongside him and roll my window down.

"Cory!"

He freezes and looks around, spotting me. He scowls. His bruises are healing, turning a green mixed in with the fading purple.

I jerk my head to the side. "Get in."

He doesn't move, just stares at me, and then glances down the street the direction he just came from.

"Come on, get in. I'll buy you lunch."

Shifting from foot to foot, he still hesitates. "I gotta get home."

I just roll my eyes. "What, cause you have someone waiting there for you?" He and I both know that's not true. "I'm hungry. Let's go." *Come on, kid.* I urge silently.

Reluctantly, he finally gives in, opening my passenger door and sliding inside. "Where to? What do you feel like eating?"

He just shrugs, staring at his feet.

"Put your seatbelt on."

He rolls his eyes but does it. I take a chance and head to a nearby diner Luke and I used to hang out. It's been years since I've been to this neighborhood. I've got no idea it's still in business or not.

A few minutes later, I pull into a parking spot. It's still here and open. I climb out, and Cory does the same, following me into the restaurant. I grab a booth and pull out the laminated menus, passing him one as he sits across from me. When the waitress comes over, Cory orders a burger and fries with a coke, and I do the same. He watches as she walks away, but I'm studying him. Taking stock of every bruise and scrape.

I have no idea how to start this conversation. But I need him to know I know. I need him to know I'll do my best to help him.

Does he even want help? I'm assuming he does. No kid wants to be beaten up on a regular basis, even if they are getting paid for it.

"I lived in this neighborhood. For a while. Had a foster placement around here."

His eyes flicker to me and then back to the table as he picks at his fingernails.

"Luke too. We got placed together. Twice."

He shrugs but doesn't otherwise respond.

"My foster dad, this one, he demanded money. Money we didn't have and wasn't easy to come by, you know? Not when you're fifteen."

"Why you telling me this, man?"

The waitress arrives with our food, preventing me from snapping back at him. Instead, I take a deep breath, leaning back, and watch Cory start to devour his burger.

"Because I did some stupid shit back then. I used to run errands for older guys in the neighborhood."

He hesitates for a brief second before taking another bite.

"Like Rock. I used to run for him. And other things."

Cory falters and then shoves some fries into his mouth.

"Cory."

I wait. I can wait all day if I have to.

Finally, he looks up at me, his eyes wary and scared.

"When's the next fight?"

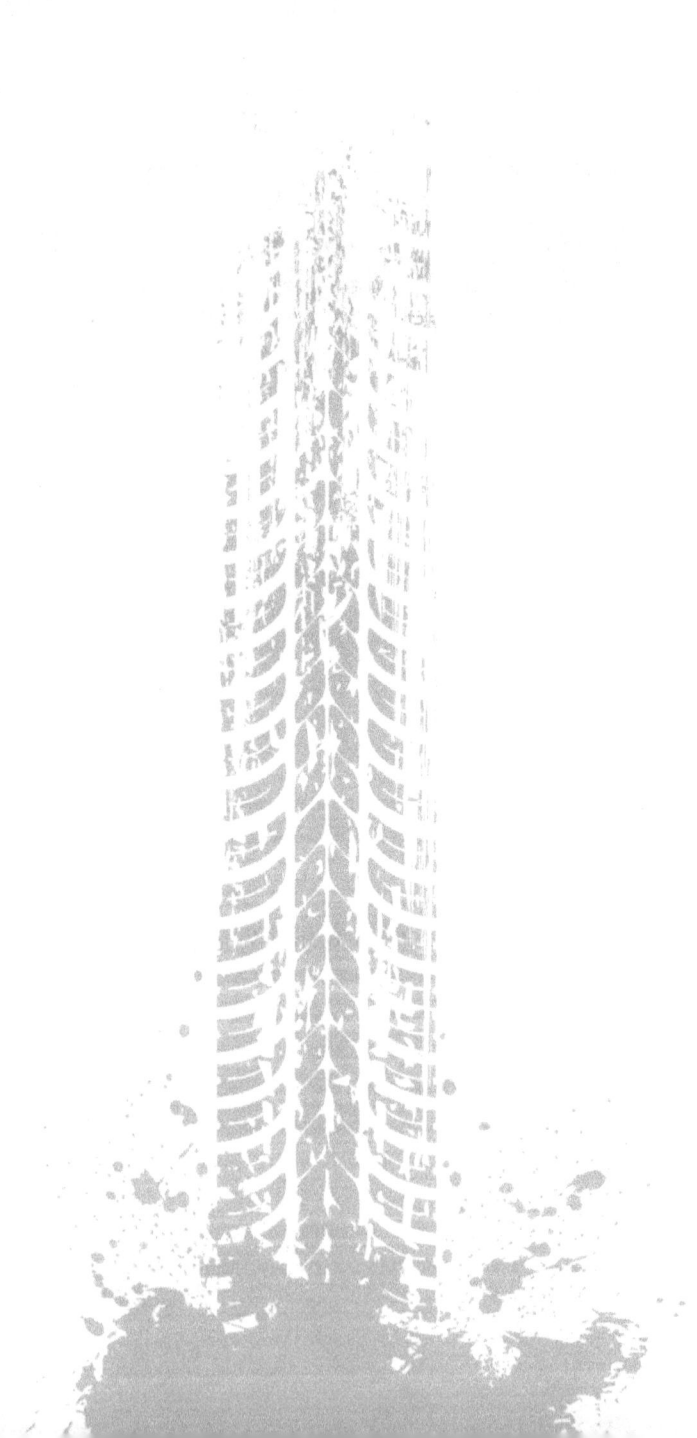

CHAPTER
Twenty-Two

Riley

J ax is...being...not clingy exactly, but he's definitely more needy than usual. For one, when I'm not working, he barely leaves my side. He drives me to school every morning, and if he can't pick me up at the end of the night, he orders an Uber to take me home, to *Vanished*, or back to his place, depending. And we haven't spent a night apart since over a week ago when he finally told me about his past and Rock.

I know he didn't tell me everything. I know there's more. More he feels like he can't admit or I can't handle, and I'm trying not to push, to be patient and understanding, but I also know this isn't sustainable. I won't become inured to living like this. Not when we're so close to something so much better. Something that could be so close to perfect.

INURE

Definition: to accept or grow accustomed to something undesirable

I love him, but I can't do this indefinitely.

I do.

Love him.

That's become clear to me in the midst of all this.

I love his sense of humor. I love his loyalty. I love how his brain works, the art he creates, and the business sense he applies to it. I love how observant he is. How he always knows when I'm awkward or uncomfortable and can so easily make me feel better. I love when he's soft and sweet. And when he's not. I love it when he's wild for me like he can't get enough. I love that he'll play Scrabble with me and cuddle during horror movies. Things Daniel hated and would just roll his eyes at while working on his laptop.

I love how he makes me feel. More confident, sexier, more bold. But still me. He thinks my fixation with words is endearing. And my clumsiness is cute. He doesn't care about my family or our connections. He just likes me. Riley.

I should tell him at some point. Tell him this isn't about having fun, passing the time, or enjoying 'right now' for me anymore. But I know this isn't the time. He's preoccupied and freaked out, worried about keeping everyone safe.

I'm just worried about him. I'm not convinced Rock wants anything from me. And while I know it might be naive, I also feel like having the name Abbott affords me a certain amount of protection. My family has a lot of money and influence in this city. My uncle is a U.S. Senator. Does some local dealer really want to bring all that down on him by messing with me? It seems a little hard to believe.

But Jax's fear and protectiveness are very real. And he knows this man far better than I do.

And Detective Melrose's warning to steer clear keeps coming back to me. And then his acknowledgment that Jax wouldn't coming right after.

This is the never-ending circle my thoughts are stuck in.

Oh no. Crap. I've been spacing out, thankful it's Wednesday afternoon, and I can let our guest presenter take the lead instead of paying attention. With all the expectant faces currently looking at me, I've clearly missed something.

I take a chance. "What questions do you all have?" And breathe a sigh of relief when several hands shoot up. I smile at the singer/songwriter Jax had found for us and call on the students. I force myself to stay focused for the rest of the session. Just as we're finishing up, I see Jax wander into the classroom.

No Uber for me today, then.

Finally, our time is up, and students start to spill out of the room. Several hang around to greet Jax and chat for a bit, always loving it when he pops in on a Wednesday.

I also love it. Love how he is with the kids. I've caught myself daring to daydream, imagine a future where Jax and I have kids. He'd be such a fantastic dad. I always shut these thoughts down quickly, though. We haven't even discussed if he wants kids someday.

We haven't even discussed that I *want* a future with him.

I see Layla's face light up, and she bolts to the door, returning with a giant of a man in tow. She's got his hand, pulling him into the room behind her as he laughs.

"Ms. Abbott! This is my Uncle Dalvin," she grins widely, introducing us.

Dalvin smiles and politely shakes my hand. His hand is massive and dwarfs mine, but he's obviously deliberate and careful with his strength. His hair is cropped tight and close with rich mahogany skin. His nose is crooked like it's been broken more than once, but his smile is wide and friendly, revealing a peek-a-boo dimple in his cheek.

"Dalvin Barnes. Shit, man, how the hell are you?" I hear Jax coming up behind me and scowl at him for swearing in school, but he doesn't notice.

Luckily there aren't that many students around.

Dalvin and Jax do some complicated male handshake and back-slapping, and then Jax is standing right next to me, close enough to touch but keeping his hands to himself. For now.

"Jax. Been a long time," Dalvin drawls. They know each other?

"Years," Jax agrees. "Riley, do you know who this is?"

"I know he's Layla's uncle, but I suspect you mean something else." I grin at him.

"Dalvin Barnes is the MMA cruiserweight champion three years running," he tells me.

I can feel my eyes widen in surprise, and I meet Dalvin's eyes. "Wow. Nice to meet you." I don't entirely understand what that means, but I know MMA is an intense fighting sport, and Jax is clearly excited and impressed. "I'm your niece's English teacher. Layla is a great student."

He smiles and grabs Layla's head, messing her up. She grimaces and ducks away, whining, "Uncle Dalvin." But clearly worships the man.

"Nice to meet you too. Layla talks about the two of you all the time. Made me promise weeks ago I'd stop by."

I look at Layla and tease. "Not that scary, huh?"

Layla shrugs, laughing. "Not to me." She smiles widely, then, spotting Traci, rushes to her friend's side.

Dalvin turns to Jax. "How you been, man? Shop going good?"

"Yeah. You should stop by, get some new ink."

"I just might."

"Anytime. You just let me know."

"Uncle Dalvin?" Layla calls across the room. "Can we give Traci a ride home?"

"Yeah, but we gotta head out. I've got to be at the gym by 6:30."

"Okay, I just have to run to my locker. I'll be right back."

Dalvin rolls his eyes, then mutters to Jax. "I've been up against some of the best fighters in the world, but teenage girls? Terrifying."

Jax laughs, and the two men discuss Dalvin's upcoming fight schedule and training. I excuse myself to chase out the remaining stragglers and pack up my stuff. I spot Cory lurking in the hallway, warily eying Dalvin and Jax back inside.

"Cory? Can I help you with anything?"

He's gotten worse, more withdrawn, and angry since the day he was announced as a finalist, fresh bruises covering his face. But there are moments his armor slips, and I can see he's scared and confused.

"I was… just wanting to talk to Jax, but he's busy."

I smile gently. "You're welcome to wait. He'll be done soon."

I see Layla and Traci returning out of the corner of my eye, and Cory stiffens, glancing at his phone.

"Nah, it's cool. I gotta go anyway."

"Wait, I'll walk you out." Anything to try and get him to open up. Maybe I can stall him long enough for Jax to help him.

Cory's eyes get wide, and he shakes his head. "Nah. You shouldn't do that."

And then I know. I look at him steadily. "Cory, is Mick picking you up?"

He nods. "He's out front. I gotta go." He starts to back away.

I'm torn. I want Mick to know that Cory has people, people who will protect him. But I also don't want to put Cory in a bad position. Mick made it clear he doesn't want me 'sticking my nose in', and it probably takes a lot of courage for Cory to keep coming every Monday and Wednesday when his brother is so obviously against it.

My inner debate takes too long, and Cory disappears around the corner. My heart aching as I watch him go.

Jax

FINALLY, A FUCKING BREAK.

Dalvin was one of the more serious competitors back in the day when Rock had me fighting. Thankfully, we were never paired up because he is a massive bruiser. He's also several years older. He's one of the guys I remember not liking the loose rules and questionable ages of some of the other fighters. I remember him giving me pointers on how to protect myself against some of the other guys I went up against. He used the underground scene to make some quick money and train for the career he really wanted. And was good enough to have. He went pro right before I finally got out.

It's hard enough for me to remember all the kids' first names; I had no idea Layla was related to the Dalvin Barnes. Fucking lucky ass break.

I hope.

The second Riley excuses herself, I lift my chin, signaling we should step aside. He follows me with a serious expression on his face.

"What's up?"

"You still have any connections in the old scene?"

He studies me for a minute before responding. "You looking to catch a fight?"

"The opposite, actually. And I need some information."

"Yeah, I still know people. I scout there sometimes for talent. Try to get some of them to go legit. It's safer but doesn't pay as much. At least not right away."

I remember.

"Can you hook me up with an introduction?" I ask. "Quietly."

"I'll see what I can do, yeah. Anything I can help with?"

"I'm not sure yet. But I'll let you know when I do."

He nods.

Layla rushes in, "We're ready!"

Dalvin gives me one last look and then lifts his chin. "I'll see you around, Jax."

I watch as they walk out, my eyes landing on Riley just outside the door. I can tell immediately she's upset.

"What's wrong?" I ask as I approach.

She glances up at me, her gray eyes worried. "Cory. He said he wanted to talk to you but then rushed out to Mick. I tried to get him to wait."

Shit.

I jog to the front entrance, but he's gone. Everyone is pretty much gone at this time of night. Damn it.

There's a fight this weekend. Last week, during lunch, I promised him I'd find a way out for him. But I still haven't figured out a plan, and the speeding hours until he's forced into the cage again are like a noose around both our necks.

I won't let him get hurt again. I'll kidnap him myself if I need to, keep him out of the ring.

I feel Riley's presence at my side and turn to look down at her. She's got her coat and bag ready to go. I sling my arm around her shoulder and steer her through the parking lot to my car.

"You know, if I'd known you were going to become my personal chauffeur, I wouldn't have bothered to buy another car." She opens the door and climbs inside.

I grunt. I know she thinks I'm being overly protective. Worried about a threat we don't even know for sure is there.

I'm sure. Rock won't hesitate to use her or hurt her if he thinks it will benefit him in some way. But she's more worried about Cory and me. I don't like that she's not taking the threat to herself seriously, but I also don't want to freak her out any more than I already am.

"I talked to the school counselor today. And I reported."

Inhaling slowly, I force myself to relax. I know she had too. We'd talked about it. As a teacher, Riley is required to report any suspicions of abuse. And Cory being forced to fight for money definitely constitutes abuse. But I don't like it. If anything gets back to Rock, it's just going to put a bigger target on Cory. I need time. I need to figure out a plan. But I also don't want Cory hurt again. So even though I don't really like it, don't trust the system to keep him safe; the more potential chances someone gets him out, the better.

I pull in front of her apartment, illegally parked.

"You're not coming in?"

"I can't. I have a late appointment and then some stuff I have to take care of."

She frowns at my vague 'stuff'. I know she's worried but tries not to pry, which I appreciate. I've already told her more than I think I should have. Then I ever wanted her to know.

I told her I wouldn't shut her out, but this world isn't for Riley. I won't drag her into this darkness. I've brought her too close to it as it is.

"I'll be over tomorrow night, though," I promise. I've got plans for tomorrow night. Something to hopefully take her mind off all this. At least for a little while.

Her smile soothes my ragged nerves, and she leans toward me, offering me a soft kiss. When she starts to pull away, I follow her, prolonging our kiss a little more. I feel her smile under my lips as I continue to taste her. Always so sweet. It's selfish of me to keep her in my life, but I need her right now.

When all this is settled, I'll let her go. But it's not safe right now.

Fuck, letting her go is going to suck.

Finally, I end the kiss and rest my forehead against hers while we each catch our breath. "Stay in the inner courtyard, yeah? When you walk Pirate."

She huffs, annoyed, and I'd grin at how adorable she is if I wasn't so freaked out about her outside alone.

"Promise me, Riley."

Pulling away, she grabs her stuff to get out of the car.

"Teach-"

"I promise. I'll stay in the apartment courtyard. But we need to talk about this, Jax."

Terror claws at my chest. I know I'm driving her crazy, but if anything happened to her, I'd never forgive myself.

"We will. I'm working on it."

Still poised to hop out, she looks at me. "I could help, you know. If you'd let me. Talk to me."

I look away, feeling raw and exposed. "I'll see you tomorrow, Teach."

I hear her sigh again and then feel a blast of cold as she finally opens the door and gets out. I watch until she's inside, her secured apartment door closing behind her.

And then I drive away.

I wasn't lying. I'm not telling Riley everything, but I won't lie to her. I do have a late client coming in. And after, I'm doing some scouting.

If it was just about me, I'd call Melrose right now, tell him everything, end Rock. But it's not just about me. I need to keep Riley safe. I need to make sure Cory stays clear of this.

And Luke. Rock could destroy Luke. And it would be my fault. Maybe now, people would find it hard to believe. Lucas is crazy popular, with the city, with the media. But back then? The people that knew us back then would probably have no problems imagining he and I would end up as criminals. I can't let this come back to him.

I can't.

I need to figure out if Rock still has that notebook or not.

CHAPTER
Twenty-Three

Riley

The next night, as promised, Jax is at my door.

"Ready to go?" he grins.

"What? Where are we going?" He's been so paranoid lately I was assuming we'd just be hanging out here at my place. Dinner. Movie. Or strip Scrabble. Some fun, sexy times.

"It's a surprise."

I eye him skeptically. "I don't like surprises." Especially today. My birthday. We haven't discussed it again since that night, but I know he knows. He remembers those things. He pays attention. If Teagan has a surprise party planned…my chest hurts just thinking about it.

He rolls his eyes at me, then uses that crooked grin of his to his advantage. My stomach still jolts every time he turns that look on me. I have gained no immunity through exposure.

"That's not true. You don't like surprises if it means you'll be the center of attention. But you like other kinds of surprises."

I feel a slight pang in my chest that he knows that about me. That he's figured that out.

"This is the good kind of surprise. Promise," he tells me.

Smiling, trusting him, I agree. "Where are we going?"

He rolls his eyes again. "Surprise, Teach. Remember?"

I laugh, feeling lighter than I have in over a week. "Okay, but what should I wear? Am I dressed okay?"

He moves his eyes down my body, and I feel it like a caress, right through my baggy jeans and gray cable knit sweater. When his gaze travels back up, stopping heated and intense on mine, I shiver. No immunity to that look, either. I doubt I ever will. I think I am destined to be forever defenseless, constantly susceptible.

I'm good with that.

"You're perfect, just like that."

A flush of pleasure moves through me at his words and heated look. I grab my coat and follow him out the door. His palm slips against mine, and he tangles our fingers together. He's doing that more and more, I've noticed. He holds my hand as we walk. I'm not even sure he realizes he does it. It makes me think my growing feelings may not be one-sided. That maybe his 'keep it casual' 'keep it fun' rules are fading a bit with time. That his care and attention aren't just about the danger he thinks we're in.

Those thoughts will probably lead me straight into heartbreak, but I can't seem to stop myself. I spot his bike parked in front of my building and do a little skip of excitement. I haven't been on his bike since that first impromptu dinner at Duk's. The weather hasn't been nice enough for him to take it out, but the brutal cold of deep winter is finally starting to break. We've got a ways to go for spring, but the end is finally in sight.

He laughs at my enthusiasm and hands me my helmet.

I mean, his extra helmet. For me to borrow.

I climb on, wrapping my arms around his waist and snuggling into his back. He squeezes my thigh and takes off, driving us through the city. After a few minutes, I realize he's driving aimlessly, just letting me enjoy the ride. He takes us to Lake Shore Drive, so we have the lake on one side and the city on the other. I love it.

Eventually, he turns us back in and pulls into the *Vanished* parking lot, cutting the engine.

"What are we doing here?"

"Teach!" His voice is exasperated, but his eyes dance with that teasing light I love.

I throw my hands in the air, giggling. "Okay, okay! I'm sorry. I'm following. No more questions." I balance myself on his shoulders and swing my leg off his motorcycle. I'm better this time than the first, less unsteady. He grabs my hand as we walk to the back door, letting us in with his keys. It's dark inside, well, darker than it's ever been when I've visited. I wonder where everyone is, they're usually open until nine on Thursdays, but I'm determined not to ask him any more questions. He flips one set of light switches but leaves most of them untouched. Enough that we can see, but not enough that anyone outside would mistake *Vanished* for being open. He leads me to his usual station, and I frown, confused, when I step inside.

There are sketches taped all over the walls. Two or three dozen at least.

I glance at him, his expression actually showing some nervousness. "Wha-" I stop myself before I can finish, and his eyes laugh at me and my inability to not ask questions.

"Take a look," he says softly, tilting his head to the drawings.

I step closer, inspecting the images. Realizing what they are, I gasp in surprise, looking at him over my shoulder.

"You still want that tattoo?" he asks.

Turning back to the images, I try to take it all in. He's drawn different versions of the tattoo I had asked him for weeks ago. An owl for my mom, maps, and books for my dad. Different versions, different styles. Some are hyperrealistic, others more cartoony, and some feminine and cute. Some are in black and white, others in vibrant colors. One looks almost like a watercolor painting. I'm overwhelmed. It all evokes intense desiderium, but for the first time, it's mixed with sweetness and excitement.

> DESIDERIUM
> Definition: an ardent longing for something lost

I move to stand in front of him, wrapping my arms around his waist and rest my cheek against his chest. "This is amazing. Thank you."

He shrugs but holds me close. I feel him press a kiss to the top of my head. "Pick your favorite."

I squeeze him quickly before turning away and studying the drawings again. They're all beautiful, but I immediately know which one I want. His eyes flare when he sees what I've chosen.

Some people may be surprised at my choice, thinking the cuter or softer ones would be more my style. But I know this is what Jax specializes in, the New School style he loves. And I want this to be obviously and wholly from Jax. I want it to represent him too.

He steals a quick kiss and then guides me to his chair. My stomach flutters with excited, nervous energy as he moves around me, setting everything up. Finally, he sits on his stool and scoots up next to me. I've decided to get it on my hip, and my jeans are undone, the waist folded down so he can get to the skin.

"Ready, Teach?" he asks.

I nod. "You should kiss me first," I tell him. He grins and does, then refocuses on his art.

I exhale roughly when the needle starts buzzing against my skin, outlining the image.

His eyes flick up to my face for a brief second. "Breathe, Teach. Try to think about something else."

I inhale slowly and deeply, trying to follow his advice, but it's not easy.

"Tell me about them. Your parents."

Staring at the ceiling, not the needle rapidly moving in and out of my skin, I do. I tell him about the trips we took when I was a kid. The books they read me. The games we played. How they handled my nightmares and scraped knees. My mom, who started my love of words. Her favorite word was vellichor. Both the sound and the meaning. 'The appealing mystique of an old bookstore.' It's been years since I've spent this much time thinking about them, talking about them. And the memories are sweet. The more I talk, the more I remember. The more I can share. Before I know it, hours have passed, and Jax is finishing the final highlights. The last bit of shading.

"Done. Want to take a look?"

I nod eagerly, and Jax helps me to my feet so I can cross over to the full-length mirror.

Tears spring to my eyes as I study my reflection. "It's perfect," I whisper, voice choked with beauty and grief. It's beautiful. He's even incorporated some of the memories I told him, writing the title of some of my favorite childhood books into the spines of the books in the image. Into my tattoo.

"I love it," I tell him, turning to meet his eyes.

He pulls me into his arms and kisses me softly. "Happy Birthday, Teach."

And then he holds me until the silent tears stop.

Jax

HER TEARS KILL ME, BUT I THINK THEY'RE GOOD TEARS. BITTERSWEET. I'm hoping they help her let go of some of the grief a little.

Eventually, she sniffs, shakes her head, and leans back. She wipes her tears and gives me a shaky smile.

"Thank you. This is…a perfect present."

"Good." I grin at her, feeling a wave of satisfaction that I made her happy. And I fucking love having my ink on her. When she chose the image she did, my style, me, I got fucking hard, a rush of possessiveness moving through me. I'm still sporting a semi, but I'm determined to give her the best birthday she's had since she lost her parents, and that means orgasms will have to wait a little longer.

But hopefully not too long.

Because I'm also exhausted. I spent hours last night following Rock. But now I know where he lives and what kind of car he drives. I know where to start looking for that notebook. Am I an idiot for planning to break into Rock's home and car?

Yep. Absolutely. I know that. I know it's a stupid, desperate move. But I am desperate. And I don't know what else to do.

I push those thoughts away. Those aren't for tonight.

Instead, I kiss Riley, teasing my tongue between her lips while she sighs. Tickle my fingers up her rib cage until I can cup her breast, plucking her nipple until she gasps. Moving directions, I cup her ass and lift her against me. She wraps her legs around my waist without hesitation, making me want to fucking pound my chest with pride. I love how she's always so sweet and responsive in my arms.

But orgasms are for later, I remind myself and set her back on her feet.

"So, now you have a choice."

Eyes shining, she smiles up at me. "What kind of choice?"

"Luke and Ash invited us over for birthday cake. If you want to go." I don't want to push her into anything she isn't ready for or doesn't want. I'm just hoping…she's ready to release some of the guilt and celebrate.

Because if anyone in this world deserves to be celebrated, it's Riley.

She steps back, her eyes wide and soft. "They did?"

I nod. "If you want. If not, we can just go back to my place and have some cake there." No pressure. But I hold my breath, waiting for her response.

"Okay," she says softly. "I'd like to go."

"Yeah?" a broad smile spreads across my face. Relieved I didn't push too far.

She bites her lips, a worried expression on her face.

"What's wrong, Teach?"

"Do you think…it would be okay to invite Teagan and Ilyssa? I'd feel bad…after telling them no."

"I'm sure that's fine." If he doesn't want Teagan Abbott in his condo, we'll just move everyone to my place. "I'll message Luke, okay?"

"Macy and Logan, too?" she asks.

I laugh, my chest expanding, and I kiss her again, psyched she's up for it. That she wants to include the people most important to me. She giggles when I get carried away and playfully shoves me away.

"I want cake," she teases. "But no singing Happy Birthday, okay?"

Laughing, I promise no singing, and we both start calling and messaging our friends.

I KNOCK AND THEN LET US INTO LUCAS'S CONDO, YELLING HELLO. I've had keys for a few years since he first got the place, but I've gotten more careful about announcing myself since Ash moved in. I've never caught them naked, but it's been close enough to freak me out, and now... I knock. Even when they're expecting me. Those two get lost in each other and forget everything. Next thing you know, they're having sex.

All the time.

Kind of like me and Riley.

"Hi, guys!" Ash pops into the entryway and gives me a hug before turning to Riley. "Happy birthday, Riley." She hugs her, Riley flushing happily. I could tell on the ride over she was a little anxious, but she and Ash are getting to be close friends.

I think. I know they've hung out a couple times outside of our weekly Saturday hangs. But she's never been here. To Luke's home. And she's already a little off because of her birthday.

When they pull away, Ash keeps her arm around Riley's shoulder and steers her into the dining room slash kitchen area where Luke's cutting a cake buried in chocolate frosting. I follow behind.

"Hey!" he calls out, seeing us. Setting the knife down, he comes around the counter and hugs Riley, lifting her slightly off her feet as he squeezes her. She laughs, and I feel myself relaxing, just now realizing how tense I'd been about this going well.

Logan and Macy are already here, drinks in hand.

"Finally!" Macy jumps up to also hug Riley, slapping me on the back. "I was ready to eat the cake without you, but Ash kept threatening to stab me with a fork."

Riley laughs again and playfully jabs him in the side with her elbow. "You'd eat my cake without me? Mace, I'm hurt!"

"You can't trust Macy with baked goods. He's a scavenger," Logan pipes in. She stays seated on her stool. Logan's not a hugger. But she smiles and waves when Riley says hi to her.

So far, so good.

The doorbell rings. Teagan and Ilyssa are here. I shoot a glance at Luke, he frowns slightly but quickly shakes it off. I know it's not about Riley and Teagan. He likes them as people. The problem is more that he wants to keep punishing his uncle and his cousin Ethan. And he worries letting other Abbotts into his life, like these two, will give them the impression he's over everything that's happened.

And he's not. Even though I think Ash is helping him work through it.

It means a lot that he agreed to this just to make Riley more comfortable. It means a lot to me. More because I know it's fucking hard for him.

"I'll get it," I offer and head back to the front door.

Teagan and Ilyssa smile when they see me and walk in. I grab their coats and throw them on top of mine and Riley's over the back of one of the couches.

"Okay," Teagan starts, her hands on her hips, reminding me a little of Riley when she's…riled up. "How'd you do it? How'd you get her to agree to this? She hates her birthday."

I shrug, about to brush it off as no big deal, but all of a sudden, Riley is standing at my side, slipping an arm around my waist. "He muddled my mind with orgasms. I couldn't say no."

My eyes widen in surprise, and I have to fight not to bust out laughing. I fight hard to show no reaction.

"What!?" Teagan stares at her for a beat and then shrieks with laughter. She pulls Riley into a hug, and I relax enough to smirk. When Teagan finally releases her, she's pulled into yet another hug by Ilyssa and more birthday wishes. The two of them head back to join the others, but Teagan grabs my wrist, stopping me.

"Seriously, thank you. This is huge."

I smile and nod, not sure what to say.

"And I'm glad she's finally getting some quality O's. But if you break her heart, I will castrate you." She taps my cheek lightly and then walks away, following the others.

Okay. I guess it's time for cake.

CHAPTER
Twenty-Four

Jax

Friday afternoon, I texted Cory and told him to meet me after school. There's supposed to be another fight this weekend, and I still haven't figured out how to stop it. But if I can't stop Rock yet, I can still help Cory. If he'll let me.

After the final bell, I spot him dragging his feet across the parking lot. But he heads my way to where I'm leaning against my car door, so at least he's willing to hear me out.

"What?"

Surly little bastard.

"Checking in. Rock got you fighting again tonight?"

Cory shrugs, eying me sideways. "I guess."

I exhale in frustration. "Dangerous. I know."

"He pays. I need the money."

"Why? What's the money for?"

"Why do you care? Ain't no cameras around here."

"Because I've been there. Told you. Why do you need the money?"

"My mom. She's been sick. Can't work much right now."

Fuck.

"And Mick?"

He shrugs again. "Bad knee. He's too slow."

Yeah, right. I'm sure that's it. I push off my car and stretch to my full height. "Do you want to fight? Or is he making you?"

He won't look at me. Instead, staring off into the neighborhood behind the school. "He's my brother."

"Does your mom know? What he's making you do?"

Cory shakes his head.

Well, that's a relief, at least.

Kind of.

"Look, I have reasons for wanting to end Rock's little fight club. But if he's organized a fight for this weekend, it's gonna happen. Do you want my help? Do you want an out?"

He doesn't answer. But he doesn't leave either.

"Can't get hit if you're not there. I can help you lay low for the weekend. You can stay with me. Or I've got a friend that works with a place. A home for kids in trouble. I already called, and they have a bed if you want it."

He snorts. "And then what? My brother will just kick my ass on Monday. And he won't pay me for it."

I shove a hand through my hair in frustration. "I know it's not perfect. I know it's just a bunch of shitty options. But I'll do what I can."

"Whatever, man. Thanks for nothing." He starts to walk away.

"Cory-"

"See you Monday, I guess," he calls out, heading toward a violent weekend.

Fucking damn it.

Riley finds me ten minutes later, still in the same spot. I'm so lost in my head and trying to figure this out she's right in front of me before I even notice her.

"Hey, you." She smiles and lays her hand on my coat, over my stomach. She won't kiss me here, not on school property, but just having her near helps me feel better.

"Cory's got a fight this weekend," I tell her.

Her gray eyes darken with worry, and she takes my hand, squeezing. "What can I do?"

"I don't fucking know," I admit, jamming my hand through my hair again in frustration. "I don't know."

She tugs on my hand. "Come on. Take me home, and I'll make dinner. Then I'll let you pick something from my resolutions list."

I give her a half smile, knowing she's trying to cheer me up. Although, I should take another look at that list. I'm sure we've done most of them by now, but just in case. I open my passenger door before walking around and getting behind the wheel. Back at my place, Riley takes stock of my cupboards and the contents of my fridge before giving up and ordering us a pizza. Haven't been to the grocery store in too long, obviously.

"Thanks, Teach."

She smiles at me, so fucking pretty she literally takes my breath away for a second. Needing her, I pull her into my arms, rubbing my hands up and down her back. On my next pass, I pinch the tab of her zipper and take it down with my caress.

"I need you," my voice is hoarse, strangled. I'm feeling particularly ragged tonight, and even though I know it's an asshole move, I want to lose myself in her softness. I want to pretend for a little while that I deserve her, deserve this. That I could actually be more than a temporary fuck.

"Jax." Her gentle hands cup my cheeks, scratching softly. "Do you need a distraction?"

I don't answer, just pull her closer and bury my lips in the curve of her neck.

And she lets me. Lets me take this way. Lets me be selfish. Lets me lose myself in her for a little while.

My phone rings, vibrating across my bed stand, pulling me abruptly and confusingly from sleep. Riley is tangled up in me and my sheets. She groans and rolls to the side while I'm flailing around, trying to grab my phone. I blink against the glaring light of my screen. It's three in the morning. Unknown number. While I'm still struggling to wake up and take stock, the call ends. I sit up, waking Riley in the process. She mumbles, asking me what's going on.

The phone screen lights up again, and I'm fast enough to grab it this time.

"Yeah?"

There's silence on the other end, but I hear city noises and harsh breathing.

"Someone there?" I ask. "Hello?" I feel the mattress shift as Riley moves next to me, offering silent support.

I hear a groan and then a raspy voice. "Jax?"

It takes me a second to place it, but then I realize. "Cory?" Fuck, he sounds awful. I surge out of bed, frantically looking around for my jeans and shoving them on.

"Yeah." He's quiet again, just his ragged breathing on the other end.

"Are you okay? Do you need me to come get you?" I pull on a shirt, searching for my keys.

"Hurt. Rock paired me up...."

Fuck. Fuck.

"Where are you?"

"By that diner, you took me to."

"Stay put. I'm on my way."

I turn and see Riley, also fully dressed in jeans and one of my sweatshirts. I shake my head. "No way, Teach-"

Her fists hit her hips, and she glares at me. "I am going. You can't stop me."

Still shaking my head, I shove my arms into my coat.

"Jax, I'm going. With or without you."

"You don't know where he is."

"I'll follow you."

"You don't have a car here."

She screeches in frustration. "Stop being a jerk. I'm going."

I open my mouth to argue, and she stops me cold with, "You are *not* going alone. Either I come, or Lucas does."

Fuck.

"Fine. But you're staying at my side or in the car. Got it?"

We're silent on the drive, tense and worried. I knew I should have stopped him. I should never have let him walk away this afternoon. I knew it was dangerous.

I *knew.*

And I still did nothing.

Riley sets her hand on my thigh, and like she can read my mind, she says, "This isn't your fault, Jax."

I grab her hand and squeeze but don't respond.

Because she's wrong. And I know it.

It is my fault.

Riley

JAX PULLS INTO A PARKING SPOT IN FRONT OF A NONDESCRIPT restaurant just a few miles from my apartment. He's quiet and tense, and I can tell he's beating himself up for failing Cory. But he didn't. We all did. Everyone in that kids life let him down. Sometimes it's so hard to believe in the system when I've seen how slow it is to act. And I get it. Taking kids away from their homes shouldn't be something that is done lightly. Investigations take time. To be sure.

But sometimes, time is up, and we're just finding out.

"Stay put," he orders and slams out of the car.

I scramble out behind him. I don't want him to be alone right now. Even for a few minutes.

He storms into the diner, and I race to catch up. I practically plow into his back when he stops abruptly just inside. His eyes flicker to me briefly but then quickly return to scanning the booths and tables. It's open twenty-four hours but doesn't have much of a crowd at this time of night. It takes seconds for us to see Cory isn't here.

Jax crosses over to the counter and asks the waitress working if she's seen anyone matching Cory's description, but she just shrugs and shakes her head. I turn, and my eyes pass over the windows into the dark outside.

"She hasn't seen him." Jax is practically vibrating next to me, his tension radiating off him.

I point to the corner and the gas station next door. "You said it was an unknown number, right? There's a pay phone."

"Those still work?"

I shrug. "Sometimes. Maybe."

Jax is out the door before I even finish the word.

"Cory!" he bellows, rapidly crossing the lot. I see movement in the shadows, just out of the circle of light near the pay phone. As we get closer, I can make out a human figure sitting, leaning, against the outer wall of the gas station. The figure focuses into Cory as we approach. Jax crouches down in front of him, gently calling his name.

Cory blinks his eyes open, and my heart wrenches getting a better look at his injuries. Even in the dark, I can see how battered he is, still covered in blood.

"Can you stand up?"

He can't. Not without Jax's help. As Jax helps him to his feet, I notice Cory's shoulder hanging at a weird angle. Oh god. This is really bad.

"Jax," I say softly, Cory's head is lolling to the side; he's practically passed out on his feet. Jax has his arm around Cory's waist, acting as a human crutch. "He needs to go to the hospital."

"No cops," Cory mutters.

I watch Jax's face, his jaw clenches before he turns his eyes to me. "Call Ash. We'll go there first. If she thinks he needs more, we'll…figure it out."

I nod, relieved. Ash is a brilliant trauma surgeon. She'll be able to help him.

Pulling out my cell phone, I call Ash while we move back to the car, Jax practically carrying Cory back across the street. She doesn't answer at first, and I hang up, redialing when I get her voice mail. Jax lays Cory down on the back seat, and I get back in the passenger seat when it's finally picked up.

"Riley?" I hear Luke on the other end. "Is Jax okay? What's going on? It's like four in the morning." His voice is rough with sleep, but I can hear the panic in it.

"Sorry. Jax is fine. We're both fine, but one of my students, Cory, he's…he's hurt. Bad." I realize I'm crying, tears splashing onto my jeans.

"Where are you?"

"In the car. We're on our way. Can Ash….?"

"Shit. Yeah. Yeah, we'll be waiting for you."

"Thanks, Luke."

It's an endless drive even though at this time of night, with no traffic, it takes us no time at all. Cory groans every time we hit the smallest pothole. I'm turned around in my seat, urging him to drink some water while Jax drives. Lucas is clearly watching for us because he's practically opening the car door before Jax has even finished parking.

I hear him cursing under his breath when he gets a look at Cory in the back seat.

"What the fuck happened?" he asks.

"Later. Help me get him inside." Between the two of them, they manage to get Cory on his feet and move quickly inside the warm condo. Ash is inside, ready for us. She's got towels laid out and directs the guys to lift him onto the dining room table. She cuts his shirt off, and my breath is knocked out, seeing the bruises already forming on his torso.

While Ash does her assessment, Jax is patiently using a wet rag to clean the blood off Cory's face and skin.

"His shoulder is dislocated. Lucas, can you help me?" She instructs Lucas on how to hold and brace Cory while she not so gently pops his shoulder back into place. Cory makes an awful sound, and I have to bite my lip, trying to stifle my tears.

She moves with efficiency and confidence, inspecting all his injuries, mumbling to herself as she goes. Time moves painfully slowly while I stand on the side, unable to be helpful. Finally, she has Jax and Lucas carefully carry Cory to the guest room, and then the four of us huddle back in the living room.

"He will be sore for several days, but I think he'll be okay. I'm worried about a concussion, and one of those bruises looked like it could be pretty deep. I think he should stay here so I can keep an eye on him."

"Thanks, Ash."

She smiles sadly at Jax, squeezes Lucas's hand, and then returns to Cory's side.

"What the hell happened?"

Jax's eyes are haunted as he looks between Lucas and me. I slip my hand into his, offering my support, my comfort, whatever he needs right now. Luke's eyes slide between us and flicker, taking in my mussy hair and the fact I'm wearing Jax's sweatshirt, I'm sure.

I know Jax has talked to him about the fact that we are…whatever we are. But it's never been quite so in his face as it is right now.

"Rock," Jax finally admits.

Luke's face hardens. "Rock is out?"

"Unfortunately, yeah."

"How the fuck did Cory get mixed up with him?" he demands.

"Short story? His brother."

Luke starts pacing back and forth the length of the living room, cursing the whole time. He stops abruptly. "I can call Melrose. See if he can do anything."

My stomach is in a knot of nervous energy, realizing Jax hasn't told Lucas about any of this. I don't know why it didn't occur to me he was keeping this from Luke. I guess because I assumed he told Lucas everything. The fact that he obviously hasn't told Luke this gives me a sinking feeling there's more he hasn't told Luke. Hasn't told either of us.

Jax is tense next to me when he admits, "Melrose knows."

Oh no.

I don't want to be in the middle of Jax and Lucas fighting. I don't want Jax and Lucas to fight, period. But Lucas is clearly furious when Jax drops that bomb.

"Melrose knows. How long has this been going on, brother?" I've heard the men in *Vanished* refer to each other as 'brother' often, but not like this. Lucas's voice is icy.

Jax jams a hand through his hair and exhales roughly, a look of defeat settling over his face. "Rock came by the shop. About a month ago."

"A month."

"I was handling it."

"Oh, this is handling it? What the fuck, Jax?"

I interject, stepping slightly between them, positioning myself in front of Jax and facing Lucas. "Let's all take a breath. We're exhausted and worried. Let's just try to get some rest and figure it out tomorrow. Then we can call Melrose and find a safe place for Cory to stay." For a heartbeat, I'm worried neither of them is going to back down, but then I see Lucas nod, and I exhale in relief.

"You can stay here. Jax has a room downstairs."

"Thanks."

"We'll talk in the morning, yeah?" Despite the words he says, it's clearly not a question. But he slaps Jax on the shoulder as he passes by, his face softening. "Get some sleep. We'll figure things out."

Jax's shoulders are heavy as he leads me to his 'room'. I pull off my jeans and Jax's sweatshirt, and he tosses me a t-shirt from the dresser, which I gratefully slip on and climb into bed. He strips to his underwear and does the same.

He's stiff and quiet, and despite the small space we're sharing, he's never felt farther away.

He's taking this all on his own, owning it in his soul. I'm terrified he won't be able to let anyone truly help, even Luke. My chest is a dull ache as I pretend to get a few hours of sleep. Painfully aware of Jax lying next to me doing the same.

TOSKA
Definition: a dull ache of the soul, a spiritual anguish

CHAPTER

Twenty-Five

Riley

I sneak out of bed the next morning, letting Jax sleep. I know he, like me, didn't get much of it. All I'd spent most of the night doing was uhtceare. And I could practically feel him brooding next to me in the early hours when we finally got settled.

> **UHTCEARE**
> Definition: Lying awake and worrying about the day ahead

Walking upstairs, I run into Ash coming out of Cory's room. She looks far more rested than I feel, which makes no sense considering she's spent the night checking on Cory. But maybe she's more used to crazy hours and lack of sleep being a surgeon.

"Hi. How is he?" I whisper.

She starts a little, my voice surprising her. Smiling, she slips her arm through mine and leads me into the kitchen. "He'll be okay. He's going to be sore and should spend a few days just resting and letting his body heal."

Ash opens a kitchen cabinet and pulls out some mugs. "Sit," she points me to the kitchen table. "Do you want some coffee?"

"Yes, please."

"We have tea, too, if you want that."

I shake my head, "Coffee is good. Thanks. I think I need the extra caffeine today."

"You got it."

"Lucas still asleep?"

"He got up a few minutes ago. In the shower." She sets a full mug in front of me. "Sugar? Cream?"

"Some sugar if you have it. Thanks."

She turns and opens another cabinet and then hands me a container of sugar. I doctor up my coffee and take a sip, letting my chin rest in my hand.

"How are you?" Ash asks me softly, taking a seat next to me.

All of a sudden, tears flood my eyes. Feeling silly, I shake my head and stare into my coffee.

"Oh, Riley." She reaches across the table and takes my hand, squeezing sympathetically.

"Sorry," I choke, clearing my throat.

"You don't have to be sorry. You've had a couple rough days, that's obvious."

"I'm just so worried about both of them. And I don't know how to help."

She doesn't respond immediately, but her calm presence and hand on mine feel reassuring.

"I think you do help, even if you don't see it. Cory's here. He's safe. And Jax-"

"What about Jax?" Lucas asks, walking into the kitchen. Ash lights up at the sight of him, and he immediately bends down to give her a quick kiss.

"There's coffee in the pot."

"Thanks, beautiful."

I quickly wipe my tears, putting a smile on my face. "Morning."

And then Jax is also there, stretching and rolling his neck to wake up. "Can I get some of that?" he asks Luke, nodding to the coffee. Luke pours him a mug and slides it in front of him as Jax takes a seat next to me. Luke stays standing, leaning his hip against the counter.

"So, want to tell me what the hell is going on?"

Jax rubs his face. "Christ, I just woke up."

"Let's focus on Cory first," Ash suggests. "He doesn't have any life-threatening injuries, but he will need time to recover. He'll need a safe place to do that. What's his home situation like?"

"His brother is bad news. Got him into this mess. I don't know much about his mom other than she's apparently sick."

"I can go talk to her. She's probably worried sick."

I see Jax glance at Luke, grim understanding passing between them. I realize with a sick feeling, that may not be the case. I hope this time I'm the one that's right.

"I talked to the guy running Second Street. They've got a bed for him if he needs it," Jax offers. Second Street is the home they found for Mateo after getting him away from his own bad situation. It's a safe place for kids in trouble. And seeing how Mateo is doing, I'm sure it would be a good place for Cory.

"You've been busy," Lucas says, a slight bite to his tone.

Jax sighs again, "We really going to do this now, Luke?"

"When do you suggest we do it?"

Ash gets to her feet and crosses to Lucas, putting a hand on his arm. He releases a heavy breath and immediately relaxes. "Okay, Riley will let Cory's mom know what is happening and test the waters there. I'll go along in case she has any questions about his condition. And if she's been sick, maybe I can find out what's happening there. If she'll be able to take care of him or not."

"I'll call Olivia," Lucas grudgingly offers.

"She's the Children's Advocate that helped with Mateo's case," Jax explains, seeing the look of confusion on my face.

"She can work the system like a pro. And fast. So that should help."

"Good," I say. "That's good."

"Jax, you call Melrose. Sounds like we're going to need all the help we can get. Fuck. Rock." Lucas shakes his head.

LESS THAN AN HOUR LATER, ASH AND I ARE IN FRONT OF CORY'S home. When I checked on him, he was swollen and puffy and still looked like a massive ball of pain. But he was at least awake and alert enough to give us his address. And he seemed genuinely concerned about his mom, which makes me hope she'll be on his side and not just another danger or disappointment.

Taking a deep breath, I ring the doorbell. Almost instantly, the door is yanked open by a flustered woman wearing a Cubs sweat suit. She shrinks when she sees us standing on the other side.

"Can I help you?" She looks wary and distracted.

"Ms. Johnson? I'm Riley Abbott, one of your son Cory's teachers."

She pales. "Did…did something happen to him? He wasn't here when I got up this morning. His bed…." Her voice cracks, and I rush to reassure her.

"He's fine. Well, he's hurt, but he'll be fine. Do you mind if we come in?"

She steps aside and rushes us through the door. "Please. Tell me where he is?"

"Right now, he's at my house," Ash offers. "I'm Ashland Carrington. I'm a doctor at Memorial Hospital."

"A doctor? Where is my son? What is going on? You tell me right now, or I'm going to call the police."

"Please, Ms. Johnson. Let us explain, and then we can take you to him."

"Then explain." She pales again and sways, unsteady on her feet. Ash immediately steps in, guiding her to the couch.

"Ms. Johnson? Can you hear me?" Her eyes are closed, and she's out of breath. "Riley, can you get her a glass of water?"

I nod and rush to the kitchen, grabbing a glass from the dish rack next to the sink. Quickly I scan the room. It's bare and beaten but clean and tidy. Feeling guilty, I open the refrigerator door, sighing in relief when I see all the basics and necessities fresh on the shelves. I hurry back to Ash and Ms. Johnson. She appears to be checking her pulse, and I set the glass of water on the table in front of them.

"Cory mentioned you haven't been feeling well. Do you mind telling me more about it?" Ash asks.

Ms. Johnson waves her hand dismissively. "Never mind about that. Tell me, what's wrong with Cory?"

I sit next to her on the couch. And tell her what I know. Starting with Cory's talent and being a finalist in the contest, Mick threatening me after school, and again later at my apartment, Cory's bruises. Finally, telling her what we know and what we suspect about the underground fighting ring.

By the end, she's got tears in her eyes. Shaking her head, "I told him. Told him Mick was going down a bad path. To focus on school. But the last few months…I just haven't been able to keep up. He told me those bruises were from a fight at school." The tears escape, trailing down her cheeks. "He's okay?"

"He'll be fine," Ash assures her.

"We can take you to him. And then…we have some people you should talk with."

Jax

"So? You want to tell me what's going on?"

"Rock's organizing a fight ring, and he's got Cory fighting. They aren't exactly regulated, as you can see."

Lucas stares at me. "That's all?"

"Mick, Cory's brother, is working for him. With him. I don't know. And he's giving Riley a hard time."

"Mick or Rock?"

"Mick. Although I'm assuming with Rock's say so."

He pulls out a chair and sits across from me. "And you've known this for over a month. When Cory was one of the finalists, you knew he had ties to Rock. And you didn't say anything?"

I lean back in my seat, force myself to control my anger, and not yell at my best friend. "Cory doesn't have ties to him. Mick does. And I was trying to help him out of a bad situation. Like you did with Mateo."

That shuts him up. Momentarily at least. When Lucas first approached me about helping Mateo, one of the kids responsible for me ending up in the hospital for weeks, I was pissed. Betrayed. Eventually, I got it. I got what he was trying to do and why he felt he needed to do it. But it wasn't easy.

Of course, then I met Mateo. And then I really got it. I don't regret fighting for him. I won't regret fighting for Cory. I won't let Rock pull him down. Keep him as long as he did me.

I watch Luke struggle. Of the two of us, he's always had the quicker temper. He's learned to channel it, somewhat control it. Ash has helped. But he still occasionally loses it, especially where his family is concerned.

The Abbotts.

He surges to his feet and starts to pace, but otherwise seems to be holding it together. "And Melrose?"

"I asked him to look into Rock and Mick after Mick showed up at Riley's apartment." He mutters something under his breath, ignoring it, I keep going. "I told him about the ring. But I was trying to keep Cory out of it. He needs something real he can act on. Not just my word."

"Right. So, those bruises seem pretty real. We call him now."

I shove a hand through my hair. "No. It's just Cory's word against Rock's, and you remember how those situations always ended up, right? No one testifies against Rock."

"So, what? He can't hide in my guest room forever."

I swallow. "We do what Ash said. Focus on Cory. Call Olivia. I'll figure out what to do about Rock."

"*We'll* figure out what to do about Rock."

I smirk. "You sound like another Abbott I know."

"Yeah, well. We're the smartest ones. You should listen to us."

"I'll call Melrose."

He nods. "I'll get Olivia over here." He stops his path back and forth through the kitchen and looks at me. "You're an asshole, you know that, right? For not telling me about this."

"Yeah. I know."

"Love you, you stupid fuck."

"Love you too, brother."

He slaps my shoulder and then walks away. I hear him on the phone a minute later. Calling Olivia.

So I call Melrose.

When I give him the run down, he agrees to come over. He sounds annoyed, but Luke says he always kind of sounds like that.

Riley calls just after I hang up.

"Hey, did you find his mom?"

"Yes." I can almost feel the tension in her voice.

"What's wrong, Teach?" I motion at Luke and put Riley on speaker.

"We found her. But then she collapsed when we were leaving. Ash insisted we bring her to the ER to see what's going on."

"Where are you, Riley?" Luke asks.

"At Memorial."

"Okay. Keep us posted on how she's doing. We'll talk to Melrose and Olivia and then check in again, okay?"

"Yes. I'll send you updates when I talk to Ash."

I take her off speaker and walk a few feet away. "Riley? You okay, Teach?"

"Yeah." Her voice is soft. "I'm just worried. Are you okay? How are you and Luke?"

Her concern for me and my best friend makes me smile. "We're solid, Teach. Don't worry."

"Jax...." Her voice trails off, and something about the soft silence makes my stomach clench. This has been happening more and more, a brief and deep space between us filling with words she doesn't say. I'm paralyzed every time, waiting for her to say the words that will force an end to this. An end I'm not ready for, even though I know it has to come.

I see it. When she looks at me. Touches me. It's in the way she flows against me, takes me, falls apart, and comes back together. When no one has ever really loved you, it's obvious when someone finally does. But it wasn't supposed to happen. I was just supposed to be the fun one. The one that got her over her breakup. The one that helped her experiment a little, helped her build her confidence back up. And once she says the words...we'll both have to face it.

I'll have to end it.

"I'll call you later," she says in a rush. "Ash is coming out."

"Stay in touch."

I'm equal parts relieved and disappointed when she hangs up. I exhale in a rush, just as the doorbell rings.

Olivia is here.

CHRIST, I'M EXHAUSTED. I COLLAPSE ONTO MY COUCH THAT NIGHT, resting my head along the back, too tired to even go to bed.

Olivia is a fucking force. She met with Cory and his mother, who was admitted to the hospital overnight for observation and tests. She's running a fever and is likely dehydrated. Olivia got them both to agree to a restraining order against Mick, found a judge willing to sign an emergency order even on a Saturday, and cleared Second Street for Cory to stay until his mom was back on her feet. By late afternoon Cory was moving around well enough to visit his mom and get settled into his temporary home, rooming with Mateo. She was pretty broken up when she saw how battered he was, promising him she would never want that for him. She kicked Mick out months ago when it became obvious he was not only dealing but using. Unfortunately, Cory's had a harder time letting his brother go.

And then she got sick. And the bills started. Cory refused to help Mick sell drugs. He promised his mom. I'm learning Cory is a bit of a momma's boy, and I'm glad she seems worthy of it. But then Mick came up with this other idea to make money. And Cory didn't feel like he could say no.

We didn't make as much progress with Melrose. He's willing to talk to some cops he trusts in vice, but it will take time to build a case, especially if we want it to take down Rock. Which obviously we do. Breaking up a weekend fight here and there won't end the threat to Cory or others. It'll just dip into Rock's profits and likely send him looking for who is to blame.

I feel the couch dip beside me and reach out, pulling Riley into my side. She settles into me with a sigh, soothing me. Deceptively soft and sweet. She's strong where it counts, her head and her heart. Having her steady presence next to me the last twenty-four hours, hell, longer than that, has helped me more than I'm comfortable admitting.

Because she won't always be there.

"Tired?"

I nod. "Yeah. Been a long fucking day." Eyes closed, I just continue holding her. I must doze off because the next thing I know, she's shaking me softly, urging me to my feet.

"Let's go to bed."

Shaking myself loose, I inhale sharply and stretch.

"I gotta hop in the shower." I feel grimy and want to wash this day and all the shit off me before I go to bed.

I press a swift kiss to her lips and head to the bathroom.

I turn the water on full blast, letting the bathroom steam up while I strip. Then I adjust the temperature and step under the spray, groaning when the hot water hits my tense muscles. Closing my eyes, I let the water beat on my face for a second and then turn to wet my hair. I move through the motions, practically a zombie at this point, and finally, crawl into my bed.

Riley's waiting for me, naked between my sheets, and I groan, moving against her soft skin. I lay half over her, nuzzling my face against her boobs. Her nipples pebble immediately, and I brush my lips across first one, then the other.

"Do you want to have sex now?" she asks, and I can hear the teasing smile in her voice.

I press a hot kiss to the skin over her heart before I answer. "Yeah, Teach. I do."

"Thought you were tired?"

"Never too tired for you." It's true, despite the exhaustion heavy in my limbs, I'm already getting hard, rising to the occasion, wanting to lose myself in her. I shift and settle between her thighs, spreading kisses along her neck and collarbone.

She sighs dramatically, "Well, get on with it so we can go to sleep." I feel my smile tugging at my lips, my first smile all day.

Because despite her jab, her busy little hands are smoothing along my abs, one of her legs hitching over my hip and pulling me close. I kiss her, hot and intense, my tongue teasing along hers, and she sighs, soft and sweet this time, melting into me. Fuck, her kisses are so sweet. Her breath hitches, and her hand cups my cheek as she kisses me back.

"Love those hot little kisses," I murmur. She meets my eyes and smiles. I feel a kick in my chest, and my dick pulses against her inner thigh. Feeling the effect she has on me, her smile slips into a naughty grin. One that does nothing to calm my cock down. Riley presses against my shoulders, urging me to my back, and straddles my waist.

She's fucking stunning, my eyes drawn immediately to her rose-tipped tits. My hands soon follow, cupping, caressing, teasing.

"Now, what?" I ask, doing my best to let her lead. Her head falls back as she arches into my touch, her hips moving. I can feel her getting wet, aroused but still languid, still just enjoying. So, I try to do the same and ignore the growing urgency in my dick. My hands trail down her body, squeezing her thighs, cupping her ass.

Finally, I trace my thumb along her sex, pressing briefly against her clit before continuing to explore. Her hands settle on my chest, her head tilting down so she can watch as I play with her. Smirking, I watch her as she breathes in shakily, her hips rolling against me, chasing my fingers. I'm still teasing, not giving her the firm touch she wants.

"Jax," she groans.

I sit up, pulling her tightly against me. "I'm sorry. I'm supposed to be 'getting on with' things, aren't I?"

Her smirk ramps me up even further. "That is what I said, isn't it?"

Then she cups my cheeks, her fingers sliding back into my hair, and she kisses me again. And I know it's too late for me. I feel her wrapped around me, her skin soft and smooth and warm.

Hear her gentle sighs against my ear as she rocks her hips, teasing and tempting me. And I know I'm screwed.

Because nothing will ever feel this good again. Nothing will ever be this same combination of hot and sweet.

Riley twists away, jolting me from my thoughts. But then she's back, smoothing a condom over my aching cock. I groan and let her push me onto my back again.

"Guess I'll just have to take care of things. Since you're so tired tonight," she teases.

Then she lowers herself, taking me inside her. So hot and tight, and I groan again, my hands going to her hips.

"Fuck, you always feel so good."

She spreads her knees, taking me deeper, and I thrust my hips into her. As deep as I can go.

"Jax," she gasps and arches.

"Ride me, Riley. Make us both come."

Her eyes are heavy and hazy with pleasure, and it makes me feel like a fucking god, knowing I'm the one that does that to her.

"Kiss me first," she whispers, so I do. Sitting up so I can reach her lips, I take them in a hungry kiss. She shifts and wraps her legs around my waist, arms at my neck, and keeps me close. Her hips move slowly, still tight against me, as our kisses go on and on.

So sweet. So hot.

Reluctantly, I break the kiss, needing to move.

"Stay," she whispers, her arms and legs tightening around me. "Stay with me."

My chest tightens, breath locking in my lungs. Her stormy gray eyes are open and intense, staring into mine as she moves against me, finding a rhythm, keeping me close. My fingers clutch her hips as I thrust against her, getting desperate. Needing more.

Riley moves one hand down my chest and abs, trailing down until it's near where we're joined, and then she hesitates.

Oh fuck. "Do it, Riley. Show me how you touch yourself. Show me how you make yourself come. So fucking hot."

She does, fingers dipping between her folds, finding her clit, her breath catching on a soft 'Oh!' and she tightens around me.

My eyes are locked on her hand, her sex taking my cock while she plays with herself. Fuck, I'm going to come.

"Riley," I growl. "Are you close, baby?" She whimpers, and I quickly glance up, seeing her eyes clenched tightly shut as she strains against me.

"I love watching you come. So pretty. God, the way you squeeze me so tight."

She snaps with a high-pitched cry, shaking in my arms. I feel her core squeezing and fluttering and grip her hips, raising and lowering her along my cock. I thrust into her, drowning in pleasure.

Drowning in her.

My orgasm crashes into me, my jaw clenching against the pleasure. When I come back to myself, Riley is still wrapped around me, trailing soft kisses along my jaw. I inhale a deep, needed breath while I hold her close. Savoring her nails lightly against my scalp. Her heart slowing against mine.

Nothing will ever feel this good again. Nothing will ever be this hot and sweet. No one will ever be Riley.

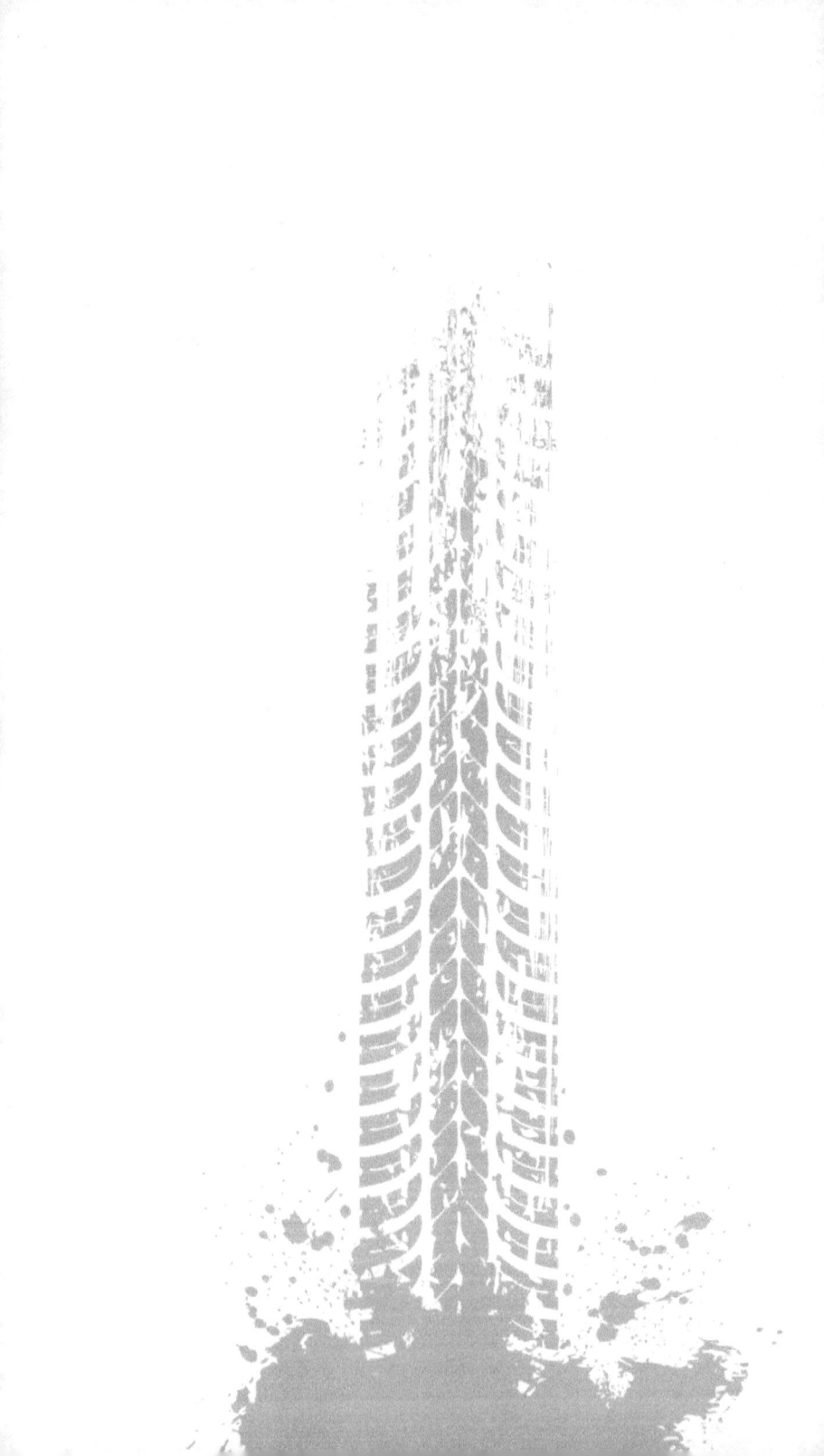

CHAPTER
Twenty-Six

Jax

"Oh my god! It's not that funny!"

Late the next morning, Riley is staring at me with an exasperated look on her face. Her little fists on her hips. Her 'I mean business' stance. Which, unfortunately, just sets me off more. I wipe my eyes, crying, laughing so hard. Something I wouldn't have believed possible after the last few days.

"It is," I disagree, gasping for air. "It's fucking hysterical."

"Jax!" But her lips twitch, revealing she's not really mad. Is, in fact, also trying not to laugh. Although I think she's more entertained by my reaction than anything.

"Say it again."

Riley rolls her eyes, taking a deep breath. "Snollygoster."

And I'm off again, bending over. Laughing harder than I have in ages.

"Well, he kind of is," she mutters. I grab her wrist and pull her into my arms, cuddling into her until the last of her stiffness and annoyance fade away.

"Thanks, Teach. I needed that."

She kind of harumphs but plasters herself against me, tilting her head up, a quiet request for a kiss. I kiss her slowly until I start to chuckle again, breaking us apart. Riley shoves me playfully away.

"Stop!" She's giggling now too.

"Rock is a snollygoster. Wait until I tell Luke."

Snollygoster, I've just learned, is a shrew and evil villainous person. How Riley described Rock.

I mean, she's not wrong. She's just so fucking cute.

My phone vibrates, and I grab it.

"Hey, Mateo. What's up?" I answer.

"Jax?"

"Yeah. What's going on?"

"Uh. Look, I don't want to be a snitch, but…I promised you guys, you know? And I…. It could have been really bad for me. For you. I just -" Shit. Immediately all the good feelings from my morning with Riley are gone, worry crowding them all out. *Cory.*

"Mateo. Spit it out, kid. What's going on?"

I hear him breathe heavily on the other end of the line, still reluctant. "Cory took off after breakfast. And he had a gun. I don't know where he got it or how he got it in, but I know what I saw. He shoved it in his backpack when I came back to the room."

Fucking hell. My heart stops beating for a second, then starts to race. Suddenly I see flashes of the night when I was shot nine months ago. I force myself to take a deep breath and pull it together.

"Jax? You still there?"

"Yeah," I croak out. "I'm here." I clear my throat roughly. "Thanks for calling me, Mateo. You did the right thing. I'll take care of it."

I end the call and brace myself on the counter, still taking deep breaths. Eyes closed. *Get your shit together, Jax.* Breathe. My fists clench.

The scent of vanilla. Soft hands on my face. Warm body next to me.

"Come back to me," Riley's voice finally breaks through the noise in my head. "What happened?"

I push back from the counter and shake myself loose. "Cory bolted. And Mateo thinks he has a gun."

"Oh, my god." Riley's eyes are wide and concerned, her hand covering her mouth. "Where do you think he would go?"

I roll my head, trying to loosen the tension in my neck, and think. "Nowhere good if he has a gun."

"Not home. He knows his mom's not there. I'll call Ash and Olivia in case he shows up at the hospital."

I nod. Good idea.

"I'll head to the diner. Maybe he went back there." But I don't hold out much hope. "Fuck. I should probably let Melrose know." I'm already pulling on my coat.

"Jax." Riley grabs the sides of my coat and moves in close. When I meet her eyes, she says seriously. "Be smart. Please stay safe. You can't help Cory if you're hurt. Promise?"

I rest my forehead against hers, breathing in her sweetness. "I will. I'll stay in touch. Let me know if you hear anything, okay?"

"Of course. Will you kiss me?"

I cup her cheeks in my hands and press a soft kiss to her lips, needing it as much as she seems to. Reluctantly we pull apart, and I head out the door. To search all of Chicago for a fifteen-year-old boy.

Fuck.

I debate taking my bike. I know I can move faster through the city with it. But I have no idea what I'm walking into and what kind of shape Cory will be in. So car it is. I climb in and start driving towards the diner we picked him up on Friday night.

Not there.

I drive by Rock's usual neighborhood haunt, but there's no one around. None of the usual hangers-on. That gives me a bad feeling. If no one is here, where is everyone? I think back to the years I've buried. Tried to move on from, to forget. The full weekend events.

I have to find Cory.

I pull over, park illegally, and put my hazards on.

And then I call Dalvin.

"Jax. What's up, man?"

"I need to know where Rock's running his fights out of. Like now." I don't have time for small talk right now.

Dalvin's silent on the other end of the line. "You know these people, Jax. They don't like surprises."

"Yeah. I know. I know they like watching kids get beaten to shit." Even I can hear the bitterness in my voice. "Can you find me an address or not?"

Silence. Again.

Then. "Let me make a call."

I exhale in relief, scanning the street while I wait. My skin feels hot and tight while I wait impatiently for him to call me back. I text Riley while I wait, just in case, but she's heard nothing.

Finally, my phone lights up with a call from Dalvin. "Anything?" I ask, not even bothering to say hello.

"I don't know what this is, but I don't want any part of it, got me? This is as far as I go."

"Heard." My knee is bouncing, shaking my car. Just give me a direction to go.

Dalvin rattles off an address, tells me it's in the basement. The address is near the edge of the neighborhood. Fewer homes and more empty buildings. But it's not far, which is probably how Cory managed to drag himself to the diner.

He ends the call, and I toss my cell onto the passenger seat, pulling a U-turn.

I drive passed the building first, trying not to look like I'm paying too much attention. Going in is not likely to end well for me. I see no basement windows. No way to try to see if he's in there without revealing myself.

Maybe I should call Luke and Macy. As much as I don't want to drag them into this mess, having them at my back at least increases the chance of us all getting out without major injury. As I'm circling the block, I see it. A flash of red and gray.

Cory.

I jerk my car to the side of the road and jam it into park. And then I chase after him.

I manage to grab his bicep and yank, forcing him into an alley a few doors down from the warehouse. Shit, if I'd been three minutes later.

"What the hell, man? Get off me!" He tries to shrug me off, but he's still slow and injured, and there's no way I'm letting go of him.

"Shut up." I propel him in front of me, far enough I hope we won't be easily noticed from the street, and then shove him into the side of the building.

I hold him against the wall, using my height and weight to my advantage. He struggles but quickly realizes he won't budge me and slumps against the bricks with a scowl.

"Where is it?" I growl. I'm raw with anger and fear and relief.

"Where's what, man? Let me go." He tries to push my arm away, but he's no match for my strength on a good day, and he's still a mess from Friday night.

"The gun, Cory. Where is it?"

"I don't know-"

"Don't fucking lie to me. Mateo saw you with it. Where is it?"

He doesn't answer, his eyes sliding away. I step back, pulling his backpack off his arm. Glaring at him, I mutter, "Don't fucking move, kid." He's still scowling but stays put while I yank the bag open and rifle through it. It takes no time to find it. The gun shoved into a paper bag, resting on the bottom.

Fuck.

I grab it and throw the rest of the bag into his chest.

"What are you thinking? Huh? You gonna go in there and just start shooting, so you don't have to fight again?"

"No! I was just…it was just in case I needed it. He owes me my cut from Friday. You don't know-"

"I do know!" The adrenaline pulses through me. I'm yelling at him even though I don't mean to be. I can't calm my shit down. The terror of what could have happened if I hadn't found him in time…. "I'm one of the *only* people who know!"

I grab a fistful of my hair, turning my back for a second to take a deep breath and get it together. When I turn, facing him again, I'm calmer. "What do you want to do, Cory?"

He kicks his toe against the ground, staring at his feet. Suddenly a choked sob shakes him hard, and his face crumbles as he breaks down. I grab the back of his neck and pull him into me, letting him cry it out.

"Come on, kid. Let me take you home."

He starts panicking, not making sense, still crying. Hospital bills. Rent. I catch something about Rock owing him a hundred bucks.

One hundred dollars.

I picture his bloody face and limp body on Friday night. Look at his bruises and injuries today.

For one hundred dollars.

Fucking hell.

"I've got you. Come on. You don't have to do this."

Cory takes in a shuddering breath. I grip his shoulder and bend my knees until I can look him in the eye. "You'll never have to do this again. Okay?"

He sniffles, hanging his head, and wipes his face.

"Come on."

"Where we going?" he asks quietly.

"Back to my place. We'll figure it out there."

He sniffs again, but when I place a hand on his shoulder and steer him back to the street and my car, he follows.

Riley

FOUND CORY. HEADED HOME.

Oh, thank god. I breathe a sigh of relief when I see Jax's text. I'm full of anxious energy, so I end up puttering around his kitchen, making tea, and ordering a ridiculous amount of Mexican food, unsure what Cory likes. I call Oliva and text Ash, letting them know Cory's okay.

Finally, I hear Jax's keys in the lock, hear the two of them coming inside.

I stand, wringing my hands nervously, and then pull Cory into a careful hug, unable to stop myself. Surprisingly, he lets me.

"There's food on the island. Help yourself."

He nods and shuffles over. I turn my attention to Jax, wrapping my arms around his waist, immensely relieved he's in front of me. In one piece.

"Everything okay?" I whisper, looking up at him.

His eyes are tired, but he nods. "I got to him in time."

I inhale deeply, returning his nod. Reading between the lines, I'm assuming that means he found him before Mick or Rock did.

"The gun?" I ask softly, glancing at Cory over my shoulder. He's at one of the bar stools, cheeks stuffed with bites of tacos.

"Currently locked in my car. I'll give it to Melrose tomorrow."

"Okay." I squeeze him briefly before releasing him, and we join Cory to eat.

I stand opposite Cory on the other side of the island. "I talked to Dr. Carrington a little while ago."

His eyes go wide and fearful. "Is my mom okay?"

"Her fever is down, and they've started her on antibiotics. They think they know what's wrong with her. Which is good. We'll know for sure tomorrow when the tests come back."

"What is it?"

"Dr. Carrington thinks it might be Lyme disease. It sounds scary, but it's most likely treatable. Ash said you can call her tonight if you have questions."

"When will she be able to come home?"

I smile, trying to be reassuring. "We'll know more tomorrow."

"Will they let me go back and stay with Mateo? Until my mom is better?"

I glance at Cory and then at Jax. He sounds so scared.

"Is that where you want to stay? Not going to disappear again?" Jax asks.

Cory shrugs. "It seemed cool, I guess." He looks down at his plate, staring at nothing.

"Then we'll figure it out. I thought tonight you could stay here. Is that okay with you?

He sneaks a quick look at Jax's face. "Yeah. That's okay."

"Good. I'll make up the couch. Tomorrow we'll meet with Olivia. Cool?"

He nods again.

Jax gets Cory a glass of water, and then I follow him into the living area and help him pull out his couch, getting sheets and blankets. We get Cory set up in front of the TV, and then I get all of my stuff together. I don't feel comfortable spending the night with Jax when Cory is in the apartment. Especially with Jax's open-style loft. He walks me to the door.

"You okay going home?"

"Of course. I should go over my lessons for the week anyway."

"Stay safe. Rock and Mick are both still around."

I nod. "Teagan and Ilyssa are keeping Pirate for a few days. Just until...." Until I don't know when I guess. Until things settle down, and I can go back to my nightly walks around the neighborhood without being so scared.

He exhales and relaxes. "That's good. I'll figure this out soon, okay?"

I poke him in the abs. *"We'll* figure it out. You, me, Luke, Melrose. *We'll* figure it out."

His crooked grin flashes, but his eyes are sad. "Yeah, Teach."

He glances over his shoulder, spots Cory absorbed in some action movie, and turns back to me, kissing me slowly. He looks like he wants to say something else, but my phone buzzes, pulling his attention. My Uber is here.

"Let me know when you get home safe, okay?"

"I will. I'll see you tomorrow afternoon?"

He nods. "I'll be there."

We just stand there for another minute, neither wanting to let the other go. My phone buzzes again.

"I should go."

He nods. "Riley...." He swallows but doesn't say anything else.

I stretch up, stealing another kiss. "I'll text you when I get home."

"Call." He gives me his crooked grin. "I want to hear your voice before I go to sleep."

My heart clenches. Sometimes he's just so sweet. It makes me feel so lucky to be in the center of that.

"Okay," I promise and finally walk out the door.

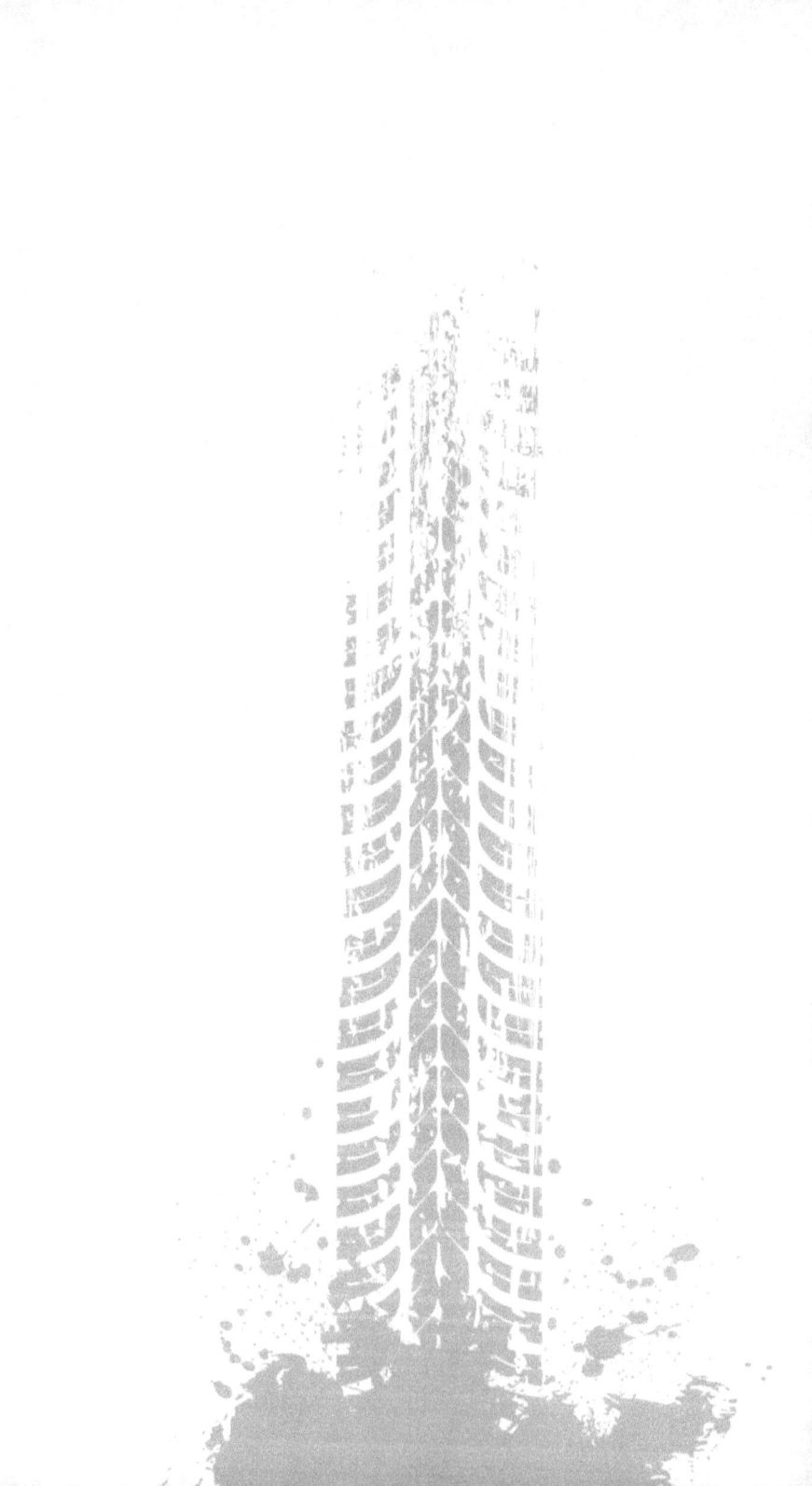

CHAPTER
Twenty-Seven

Jax

But a week later, I, or we, are no closer to a solution.

Ms. Johnson is doing better. Ash was right, and it was Lyme disease which accounted for her sleepiness, pains, fever, and dizziness. The antibiotics seem to have done the trick, although they're still monitoring things to ensure she didn't suffer any long-term effects. So she's home again, although still weak, and Cory moved back yesterday. A judge approved an order of protection, and when Mick didn't show for the hearing, the restraining order was approved.

No one's seen him since the night of Cory's fight.

I should be relieved, but I've got a bad feeling about the whole thing. I'm sure he's either going to show up more violent and desperate than ever, or he's going to show up dead.

I'm not particularly excited about either option.

The police seem fucking worthless in my more frustrated moments, but I also appreciate Melrose's commitment to building a case against Rock specifically. And his willingness to keep Cory out of it until it's absolutely necessary. He's got extra patrols in the neighborhood, keeping an eye on things, but I still don't like it. Any of it.

Today though, we're trying to get things back to normal. And I'm trying to keep a good face on it for the kids and the crowd.

Tattoo Expo. We've got a prime spot right on a corner, able to grab traffic from two directions. Our flash spots are already seventy-five percent filled through the whole weekend, even though it's only Friday. All three finalists took us up on working the booth, coming in after school, and scheduled for several hours over the weekend. Diego is a natural, great with people and sales. Traci and Cory are quiet, for very different reasons, but more than willing to do whatever we ask them to help with.

"Hey, Riley," Macy calls out, and I spin around, spotting her approaching our booth. As usual, just seeing her spreads a gentle warmth through my chest. She's even more tempting in this setting, so prim and clean, just waiting for someone to mess her up. Which will be me in another four hours or so. She's wearing one of her retro-style dresses under an unbuttoned dark green peat coat. The dress is tight at the waist and flares out, ending just below her knees. It's white with a green, orange, yellow, and red pattern. When she gets closer, I realize they're different vegetables. I grin.

"Hey, Teach. How was school?"

She smiles, waving at Cory and Diego before she answers me. "They got here fast," she whispers to me.

I laugh. "Yeah. They were here before four, ready to go. Traci's here too."

"That's sweet. They're so excited."

"Hey, Riley." Luke pops over and offers her a quick hug which makes me smirk.

"How's it going? The booth?"

"Good. Great turnout this year. We're booking up fast."

"That's great!" She smiles widely, seeming genuinely excited for him. For us.

"What's your plan, Teach? Sticking around for a while?"

She glances at her cell, checking the time, before answering. "Just for a little while. And then I'm meeting Teagan for dinner. But I'll be back tomorrow."

"Hi, Ms. Abbott. Hi, Jax." Layla comes dancing up, her uncle a few booths behind her.

"Layla, hi. How are you?" Riley greets her.

"Good! Is Traci here?"

I say hi to Layla and explain Traci will be right back. She's quickly distracted, chatting with Diego, and I watch the man walking behind her.

"Dalvin," I greet, lifting my chin.

"Jax."

We haven't seen or spoken to each other since my frantic phone call demanding an address. He hangs back now, not unfriendly, just keeping his distance. Clearly here for his niece and no other reason. Macy comes over and starts fucking fan-boying all over him, breaking some of the tension.

My next flash appointment shows up and picks one of Cory's designs. I grin and bring him over, introducing him to the guy. Out of the corner of my eye, I see Dalvin studying us closely. Then I see him talking to Layla before wandering down another aisle. I focus on inking Cory's art on my client. A little less than an hour later, I'm finishing up, sending him on his way.

Grabbing some water, I move and stretch, standing near Riley. Cory hands the guy a bag with aftercare information and the free merch we're handing out. He looks…happy. He seems happy for the first time since I've met him.

I feel Riley's eyes on me, and I look down at her, smiling. "What's up, Teach?"

She shakes her head and smiles. "Nothing."

Suddenly self-conscious, I shift from foot to foot. "What?" I laugh, covering up my awkwardness.

Squeezing my hand briefly and then releasing me again, she just shrugs. "You seem…proud of yourself."

I rub the back of my head. She's right. I kind of am. Even though this isn't about me.

"Freudenfreude," she says.

"Is this another snollygoster thing?" I laugh, teasing her.

"Don't start." She rolls her eyes but still has a wide smile on her face. "Freudenfreude. It's the bliss you feel when someone else succeeds, even if you aren't directly involved."

Fredenfreude, I repeat silently. Yeah, I guess so.

"Except, you're kind of involved," she continues. "You helped make this happen."

"Nah, this is all them. And you."

Her phone beeps. "Shoot. I'm late. I have to go." She taps her cell and then looks back up at me.

I dig my keys out of my pocket. "Take my car. It's parked down in the lot. I'll catch a ride with Luke. You can bring it back tomorrow."

"Oh. Okay. Thanks. I'll be here." Turning to everyone else, she yells out a good-bye and waves as a chorus of good-byes returns to her. I tell her how to find my car, and without thinking, I lean down and kiss her. "Have fun with Teagan. Text me when you get there."

Her eyes are wide with surprise, and she nods. "She's…ah… coming over to my place with some takeout."

"Good." That's a relief. I'm trying not to be a smothering asshole, but I still don't like her wandering around alone. I kiss her again, confused by how startled she seems. I watch her walk away and then turn back to find several pairs of eyes staring at me.

Oh shit.

Right.

I see Lucas behind the girls, Layla and Traci, smirking and shaking his head. Macy laughing his ass off while finishing his tattoo. Logan rolling her eyes. Diego and Cory look equally confused and bored.

Layla gives Traci an excited hug. "I told you!" she screeches.

Riley

I'm still in a bit of a fog as I hit the cooler air of the parking garage.

It's the first time he's kissed me in front of his friends. I know they know. It's not like it's a secret. But it's the first time we've acted like a full-fledged couple in front of his friends. I'm trying not to let myself read too much into it, but I want to at the same time. I want to believe it means something.

Oh crap. I wandered right by the aisle Jax said he was parked in, totally in a daze. Focus, Riley. I backtrack, realize I'm on the wrong floor, and head over to the stairs. I shake my head and get orientated, then see his car up ahead.

Suddenly I'm roughly pushed forward and slammed into a car. I feel a heavy body behind me, pressing against me, trapping me against the door. My pulse skyrockets and I scream before a hand is slammed over my mouth.

"You were warned to mind your own business, bitch."

I start frantically grabbing at the hand over my mouth, struggling to breathe. I'm terrified, trying to scream through his grip, knowing I'm not successful.

"Rock doesn't like it when people ask questions. Jax should know better. Interfering in his business. Cost us a fighter. Not okay."

Oh my god. A wave of panic washes through me; I can feel my limbs shaking. I can't let this happen. I can't let this happen for me, to me. I can't let this happen for Jax. I can't leave him to blame himself for…whatever this attack is. This combination of thoughts allows me to calm down enough to remember I have options.

I made sure I would have options.

He pulls us back, his other arm wrapping around my waist as he moves us away from the car. But this gives me an opening, a move Ash has had us practicing repeatedly in our Saturday classes. Instead of leaning back, I fight my instincts and release the hand at my mouth. I use all my strength and adrenaline to bend forward at the waist and turn in one direction, then quickly reverse and use the extra momentum to drive my elbow back and up into his neck.

I hear a grunt, and the arms around me loosen enough for me to twist free. I fall into the car parked next to me and stagger, trying to gain my footing. I can't let him get his hands on me again.

That I am absolutely sure of.

I try to run. He grabs a fistful of my coat, and I stumble forward. My palms hit the parking lot, and I feel the sting but focus on getting my feet back under me. One of my feet manages to connect with some part of the man attacking me, and I'm able to scramble away when he releases me.

"Bitch!" he yells, still so close.

I feel my ankle twist, pain streaking up my leg as I start to run, and it makes me slow and clumsy, but I keep moving forward. Keep moving forward, I tell myself.

"Hey!" I hear a booming voice bounce off the cars around me. I fall, my knee scraping on the cement, causing burning pain to sear along my skin. My ankle is throbbing, but I attempt to scramble to my feet and keep moving. I'm unsteady, though, my ankle protesting every step as I lurch from side to side. I brace myself on the cars, using my arms to try and propel me forward.

I feel him behind me closing in, and it gets harder and harder not to panic. My vision is blurred, and I realize distantly I'm crying, tears in my eyes.

I use needed oxygen to scream again as I feel two hands grabbing my upper arms. I scream louder.

"It's okay. You're okay. Riley? You're okay. Look at me."

Finally, the words break through my panic, and I realize the man who grabbed me is Dalvin, Layla's uncle. She's standing a few feet behind him, her eyes wide and scared.

Gasping for breath, I try to explain. "A man. He grabbed me."

Dalvin's face turns murderous, and he looks over my shoulder, scanning the parking lot.

"I'll go get help!" Layla says and starts to turn back to the exhibition space.

"You stay right here," he barks at her. "You're not leaving my sight. Not when this guy is still out there." Layla swallows and nods, her chin wavering. Dalvin turns back to me, "Your car around here?"

I nod shakily.

"Let's get you both locked inside. Layla, call 911 while we walk over." He helps me to my feet, letting me lean on him when my ankle gives out.

My purse, phone, and the keys are all scattered on the ground near Jax's car. Dalvin unlocks it and helps me lower into the back seat, Layla climbing in the other side. She hands the phone to her uncle so he can talk the operator through how the police can find us. Apparently, they also alerted the security at the exposition center because, moments later, two security guards approach us. Dalvin explains the attacker may still be in the area. Unfortunately, I am absolutely no help, having never gotten a good look at him. All I have is a vague sense of jeans and a navy hoodie. They radio in and have additional security come out to move through the cars, just in case.

I'm holding Layla's hand, trying to keep us both calm. I assure her I'm fine, even though I'm sure it's obvious I am not.

I see a police car pull up, and an officer approach Dalvin before looking at me, sitting in the car.

Suddenly it hits me that speaking to the police could create more problems. The attackers words ring in my ear.

Rock doesn't like people asking questions.

I need to talk to Jax.

CHAPTER
Twenty-Eight

Jax

Riley calling

Confused, she just left the booth a few minutes ago, I apologize to the guy in my chair and accept the call.

"Jax?"

Instantly I'm on alert. That's not Riley. It's Layla's voice on the line, and she sounds upset.

"Layla? What's wrong? Where's Riley?"

"Ms. Abbott told me to call you while she talks to the police and tell you what happened."

I stand abruptly. "The police? Is she okay?"

I cross over to Luke's chair, getting his attention.

"She was attacked-"

"Layla, is she okay?" My voice rises, mirroring my panic. If something's happened to Riley....

"She's okay, I think. But she wants you to come."

"Where are you?" Luke, recognizing something is very wrong, yells for Mace.

Layla tells me they're in the parking lot, and I hang up, assuring her I'll be right there.

"Riley was attacked in the parking lot." I force the words out, my chest and skin feel tight. I need to get to her. See her. Hold her. I need to know she's okay.

"Let's go," Luke doesn't hesitate, having my back.

"Go. Logan and I have things here. Go," Mace assures us, and I see Logan nodding, her eyes concerned.

"Keep us posted when you know more," she says.

Before I can take off, my eyes land on Cory. His face is pale and scared. "Ms. Abbott?" he asks.

"She's okay, Cory. You stay here with Logan and Mateo, okay?"

"But, Mick. What if...?"

Logan steps up, putting her arm around Cory's shoulders. "I've got him," she tells me.

I nod and start running, dodging people all the way through the rows to the entrance. The second I'm out the doors, I can see the blue and red lights flashing across the parking lot, and without hundreds of people milling around, I close the distance in record time. Luke is right behind me, somehow managing to keep up.

Riley's sitting in the back seat of my car, an EMT crouched at her feet, examining her ankle. She glances up, sees me, and struggles to her feet, moving toward me. I plow ahead, grabbing her to me and breathing her in.

"Teach. Are you okay?"

She nods into my chest, but I can feel her shaking against me. I force space between us, just enough to take her all in. Noting the scrapes, the bruises already forming, the tear streaks down her cheeks. The fear and rage, and worry all battle inside me, fighting to take control.

"Ms. Abbott? We need to ask you some questions now." A uniformed police officer approaches.

Her eyes widen in panic, and she pulls me close again. "It was Rock," she whispers so only I can hear. "One of his guys."

Fuck.

Of course, it was. I knew it before she even said it. But having her confirm it…I fight down the rage, knowing we need to keep it together right now.

I nod at her so she knows I heard her and help her sit back down. She's limping.

I look back at Luke. "Call Melrose." He nods and steps aside, pulling out his phone.

I hold her hand as the medic wraps her ankle, and she explains to the cop what had happened, and my rage burns deeper the more she talks. She's smart, though. She answers the questions but doesn't mention Rock by name. Doesn't offer any information that isn't explicitly asked of her.

An endless time later, Melrose shows up and shoos the uniformed cops away.

"Take her home. I'll be in touch. Soon."

"Cory's inside. I'm worried about him and his mom."

Melrose nods thoughtfully. "I'll take him home. Encourage him and his mom to stay with a friend."

"Be persuasive."

He nods, and then he wanders over and huddles with Luke.

I nod, relieved to get her out of here. "Luke!" I call out. He looks over at me. "You good man? I'm taking her home." He nods and waves me out.

I text Logan, let her know Melrose is going to take Cory home.

Dalvin approaches as I get Riley tucked into the car. "How she doing?" I shrug, unable to say the words out loud. "This have anything to do with the favor you asked me for?"

"Unfortunately, yes." My hands fist and I have to fight not to pound it on the roof of the car, knowing that will only startle Riley.

"Call me. If you need any more help with that."

I jerk my head to the side in surprise, taking him in. "You sure?"

"I'm sure." His jaw is tight. "Kids and women. Shit needs to stop."

"Thanks, man."

He nods and walks away.

I walk around to my side of the car and notice a flier on my windshield. Annoyed, I grab it and shove it in my pocket. Then I drive Riley home.

Teagan is at Riley's when we get there. I'd totally forgotten they were supposed to have dinner and a night in together.

I've got one arm around Riley's waist, practically carrying her, so she doesn't put any weight on her sprained ankle.

"What happened?" Teagan demands.

"I was...mugged," Riley improvises, wincing.

"Are you okay?"

"I'm fine." She grimaces again, settling into her couch, and admits, "Well, a little banged up, but I'll be fine."

Pirate comes over and jumps onto the couch next to her. Riley's face lights up, and she starts smothering the little mutt with kisses. "Did you miss me? I missed you," she coos. "Is Aunt Teagan taking good care of you?"

I shake my head, watching them.

"I brought Thai," Teagan offers. "Are you hungry? You should eat something." And without waiting for an answer, Teagan bolts to the kitchen, and a minute later, I hear the microwave.

Riley looks up at me and shrugs, still cuddling with Pirate. "Teagan's not great at sitting still. She's more of a doer."

"Are you hungry?" I ask her.

She shakes her head and presses a hand to her stomach. "No. I'm still too shaky."

"Scared the fuck out of me, Teach." I crouch at her feet, absently scratching Pirate's ears.

"Me too." Her chin trembles, and I can't stop myself. I move onto the couch next to her and pull her into my lap. Pirate woofs at being disturbed and then settles down next to us. Riley wraps her arms around my neck and buries her face in my shoulder, shaking with tears.

"You did good, Teach. Got away. Got help." I have to beat back my fury at thoughts of what could have happened. I see Teagan pop in with a bowl of some kind of rice and curry. She hesitates, then quietly sets the food on the table near us and returns to the kitchen. I sit with Riley, whispering words into her hair until she stills, slumping against my chest.

"Sorry."

I lift her chin and press a kiss to her lips. "You okay?"

She nods. "I need to take a shower."

"You sure? You'll be okay?" She nods again and awkwardly moves off my lap. "Leave the door open, okay? Just in case." Riley gives me a sad smile and squeezes my hand, moving down the hall.

I shove my hand through my hair, feeling helpless and pissed off.

Tonight one of my biggest fears almost came true. And if Riley had been hurt...if she'd been hurt any worse....

Fuck. Enough.

I need to confront Rock.

If Melrose can't do anything yet, then I have to. I won't let Riley get hurt again because of me. Or anyone else I care about.

Teagan pokes her head into the living room and, seeing me alone, walks over. "Is she okay?" she asks roughly.

"She will be. She's tougher than she looks."

She collapses onto the couch.

"Can you stick around tonight? I have to… to take care of some things. I don't want her to be alone."

"Yeah, of course."

"Tell her I'll call her in the morning, okay?"

Teagan nods. "I've got her."

I DRIVE BACK TO MY PLACE ON AUTOPILOT. RUNNING THROUGH ALL the possible scenarios. All the ways this could go. None of them good.

Inside, I throw my keys on the counter, digging in my pockets for my phone. And I find the flier about to toss it as well when I realize it's not just a regular advertisement. It's a piece of notebook paper. I smooth it out.

My heart stops.

Not notebook paper.

Sketch paper.

It's one of Luke's old sketches. It's rough and childish, but I recognize his work. Even from back then.

Fuck.

Rock still has the notebook. He still owns my future.

But now I know. He's got it. And I have to find it.

I walk over to my dresser on autopilot, dread a heavy weight in my stomach. I pull open the top drawer, going through the motions. I promised myself I would never do this again. I would never again be this stupid.

But I see no other way.

I can't let Rock do this. I can't let him threaten my family.

I take out the lock box inside and lift the lid.

Cold metal stares back at me. Cory's gun. I never gave it to Melrose.

I inhale deeply, my breath shuddering through my body. Flashes from last summer come back to me. The split second I saw the gun. Saw the fear in my friend's eyes. The fucking sound, so loud, followed by the searing pain. Angrily, I pound against my dresser. It rattles against the wall. I grab the gun, slamming the drawer shut.

But I just stand there. Staring at it in my hand. Angry and terrified and determined.

Suddenly a hand grips my shoulder, jerking me around and slamming me against the wall.

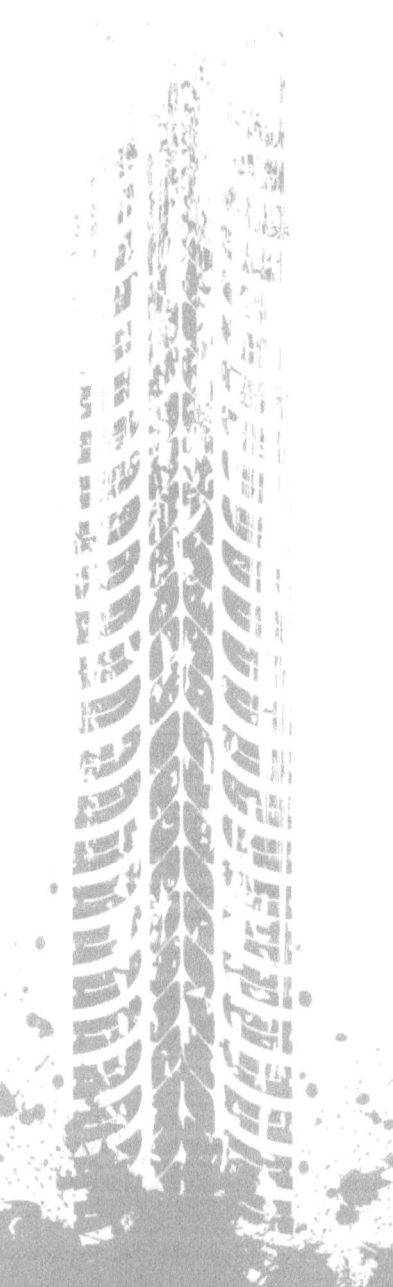

CHAPTER
Twenty-Nine

Riley

I turn off the shower, and my skin immediately pebbles against the cool air. Leaving my door open meant it didn't get all warm and steamy like usual. I shiver and grab a towel, quickly drying off. The scrapes on my knees and palms sting. I root around in my medicine cabinet until I find a bandage large enough for my knee. Then I pull on some leggings and a sweatshirt. Even dressed, I still feel cold. I go back into my room and grab some thick socks.

Then I head back out to the living room, my stomach growling. That's a good sign, I guess. Teagan's curled up on my couch watching a movie, Pirate on her lap. I glance around before asking, "Where's Jax?"

She jumps up when she sees me, rushes over, hugs me, and begins bombarding me with questions. "Are you okay? Do you want me to warm up your food? I'll make some tea. You want tea?"

I shake my head and raise one hand, trying to get her to take a breath. "Where's Jax?" I repeat.

Leading me over to the couch, Teagan explains, "He asked if I could stay. Said he had to take care of something. The police, maybe? I'm not sure."

My stomach sinks. It's possible he was going to see Melrose. But Melrose said they'd talk soon. Soon doesn't mean tonight, right? If he meant tonight, he would have just said tonight. Or later. Not 'soon'.

It's possible he went to see Melrose.

But somehow, I don't think that's where he is.

If that's where he was going, he wouldn't have just absquatulated like this.

> ABSQUATULATE
> Definition: to leave abruptly, without saying goodbye

Frantically, I start looking around, trying to find my phone.

"Riley? What's wrong? You should sit and rest. What do you need?"

"My phone. Have you seen it? Where is it?"

"Your purse is over here." She grabs it off my dining room table and brings it back to me. "Sit," she demands, holding it just out of reach. "You were just mugged. You need to rest."

Impatiently I sit down and hold my hand out for my bag. She gives it to me, joining me on the couch. At first, I can't find it and end up dumping the contents of my purse out onto the coffee table. Finally, I find it in the mess and breath a sigh of relief, calling Jax. Not surprisingly, he doesn't answer. I try again.

Still, it rings until the voicemail picks up.

Jax, what are you doing?

But I know what he's doing. He's trying to take care of it. He's trying to fix it, protect everyone.

He's being Jax.

But in a stupid way. This isn't safe. Rock is dangerous; he proved that once again tonight. And despite all he's told me, I know he hasn't told me everything. There's more he's trying to protect all of us from.

I pick up my phone again.

This time I call Lucas.

Jax

I'M SHOVED AGAINST THE WALL, KNOCKING THE BREATH OUT OF MY chest.

"What the fuck are you doing?"

Lucas is in my face, snarling as he grabs my shirt, fisting it in his hand.

"Me?!" I shake him loose, returning his glare. "What the fuck are *you* doing? Sneaking up and grabbing someone with a gun in his hand?"

He stares at me until I set the gun back on my dresser.

"What the fuck is wrong with you? Why do you even have that?"

I turn away, unable to face him, guilt and shame pressing in on me from every direction. God damn it. I slam my fist down on the top of my dresser. When that doesn't give me enough satisfaction, I unthinkingly punch the wall. The sheetrock collapses, and then I'm swearing as pain splinters through my hand and radiates up my arm. Dammit.

I sense Lucas moving away and hear him in the kitchen. Taking a deep breath, I try to pull myself together and follow him.

He looks at me over his shoulder and shuts the freezer door. Grabbing a towel, he wraps some ice and hands it to me. I wince when I place it on my knuckles.

"You think you broke anything?"

I make a fist and release it a couple times, grimacing through the twinges of pain. "No."

"Sure? I can call Ash to take a look."

I shake my head. Facing Ash right now is low on my to-do list. She'd have questions I'm ashamed to answer. "No. I'll be fine."

Lucas watches me with a steady expression and leans against the kitchen island. He sighs roughly and rubs a hand back and forth over his head.

"So, you gonna tell me what is going on?"

I stare sightlessly at my hand, holding the ice to my skin, silent.

"It's Rock, isn't it? What does he have on you?"

Fuck.

Fuck. Fuck. FUCK.

"You shouldn't be here. You should go." I say numbly.

"That ain't going to happen, brother. You just leave Riley? She and I both know that's not you. She was worried. And so am I. I'm not going anywhere."

I knew that. He won't leave when he knows I'm in trouble. Just like I wouldn't leave him. But before, neither of us had anything to lose. Now....

Fuck. Now… there's so much my shit choices could destroy.

I feel like I'm going to puke. I squeeze my eyes shut for a brief second, inhaling slowly through clenched teeth. Finally, I feel in control enough to move to the couches.

Lucas follows.

I lean forward, holding my hand gingerly, and stare at my feet. I don't want to see the disappointment on my best friend's face.

"It's not what he has on me. On us, brother. It's what he has on both of us."

And, exhausted, I tell him. Everything. I unload it all. The job. The murder. The notebook. The fights. Everything right up until I found those old sketches left on my windshield.

After I've unloaded all my secrets, I finally look up and meet his eyes. He's pissed. But surprisingly, holding it together despite everything I've just dumped on him.

"Come on." Luke abruptly stands and moves to my door. I stare at him blankly for a minute until he looks back. "Let's go." He opens the door.

Wordlessly, I follow him. He climbs into his car, and I slide into the passenger seat. I have no idea where he's taking me. Probably to the boxing gym to beat the shit out of me. Which I deserve.

I don't say anything. I've said everything I have to say. Anything else would just be bullshit justifications. The next words will need to come from him. Silently, he doesn't even have the radio on, we drive through the city, heading towards the Loop.

So, not the gym, then.

Eventually, he parks. I recognize the building across the street immediately.

"No." I guess I will be the next to speak. I shake my head, repeating, "No."

"Shut up. Let's go." He reaches for the door handle.

I grab his forearm, stopping him from leaving the car. "Luke-"

He jerks out of my grasp and turns back to me angrily. "Shut the fuck up. We're doing this."

"I won't let you-"

"You won't *let* me," he explodes. "Are you kidding me?"

He fists his hair in his hands and then shifts in his seat to face me. "Do you think I don't know everything you've done for me? All the times you got in my face, so I didn't do something stupid when I was pissed off? All the times you stepped in front of a fist meant for me? The times you provoked Cliff so you'd get the beating instead of me?

"I *know*, brother. I know everything. Even before all this, I knew what you'd done for me. And I'm not going to just let Rock come back into our lives after fifteen years and destroy everything we've built. No fucking way." He points at the building across the street. "He can help us. And I'm going to ask him. Get out of the car. Let's go."

I move to grab the door handle but still hesitate.

"Jax." He stares at me, waiting for me to face him before continuing. "I love you more than I hate him, brother. This is not a hard choice. And you'd make the same one. You know you would."

I turn away, clenching my jaw against the stinging of my eyes as I stare out the front windshield. He's right. I'd do anything for him. Which is kind of how we got in this fucking situation.

I get out of the car.

Unlike last time we don't have Melrose with his secret club membership card, so we're stopped at the security desk and forced to announce ourselves. Luke gives the guard his name, and we're instructed to wait. A few minutes later, a large man in a suit exits the elevator and approaches us.

"Mr. Abbott is finishing a meeting, but I've been told to have you wait in his office. Please follow me." And he leads us to the elevator and into Ethan Abbott's weird fucking bat cave.

CHAPTER
Thirty

Jax

The entire way up the elevator, I'm second guessing if this is a good idea. Ethan is on rocky footing with Lucas in the best of times, and this is definitely not good times. Not to mention, I'm going to have to admit that my past has put Riley, Ethan's cousin, in danger. He may just tell us to fuck off and deal with it on our own. Or how do we know he won't just take that notebook and turn it right over to the police? He's never seemed particularly thrilled by his discovery of Lucas or the people Luke has brought into his life. Into the Abbott's orbit.

There's a reason these two don't get along.

I'm just about to tell Luke to screw it, we'll deal with this on our own. Get as much help as we can from Melrose. That he doesn't have to ask his cousin, Ethan Abbott, of all people, for a favor. But the elevator doors open, and we're led into a minimalist waiting area, waiting for Ethan.

"Luke-" I start.

Another door opens, and Ethan steps through, looking like a fucking rich tool as always. Fancy suit, shiny shoes, expensive watch, perfectly styled hair. Don't most computer hackers who work for themselves wear sweatpants all day? I'll never get this guy. Although the 41st floor of a skyscraper in downtown Chicago isn't exactly chugging Redbull in your parent's basement. So the stereotype falls apart all over the place.

I'm uncomfortable and fucking nervous.

Ethan's perfectly bland expression takes us both in. "Assuming you're here because my cousin was just 'mugged'?"

News travels fast.

Lucas nods and exhales slowly. "We need your help."

Ethan's eyebrows lift in surprise. "You're asking me for help."

"Don't be a dick about it," Lucas mutters.

"It's my fault," I interject before this gets out of hand. "It's on me. I...."

"Come on back. You can fill me in."

He leads us through a long, narrow, white room filled with only computer equipment and into an actual normal-looking office, complete with a couch and chairs. He waves a hand across the room, silently offering us a seat. Awkwardly, I sit on the edge of the couch.

"So. Tell me."

Where do I even fucking start? I glance at Luke, who chose not to sit but is standing and leaning against the door, arms folded as he glares.

This is going awesome.

"Let me try," Ethan offers. "Here's what I know." He pours himself a whiskey, motions to Luke and me, silently asking us each if we want one. We both decline. Even though I could really use a drink right now. He finally takes a seat.

"Rock Ferrangi."

I wince.

"From what I can tell, he used to run one of the neighborhoods you grew up in. So, I'm guessing there's history there, although I couldn't find anything solid. Mick Johnson, former student of Riley's and the older brother of one of her current students. A student that you, Jax, seem to have taken a particular interest in. Seems Rock and Mick have been dealing, although hard proof is difficult to come by. And Rock has other pursuits. Like illegal fighting and betting. How am I doing so far?"

I nod, gritting my teeth. "Pretty well," I grind out.

"So is it Rock or Mick that doesn't like you and used my cousin to make a point?"

"I'm not on either of their Christmas Card lists, but Rock is in charge."

There's a knock on the door, and Melrose walks in.

"Fuck. Of course," I hear Luke mutter.

"He called when Riley was hurt. He should have contacted me well before today," Ethan explains, ice in his voice.

"I don't work *for* you, Ethan," Melrose says deliberately.

Ethan stands, a flash of anger moving across his face. The first actual emotion I've ever seen out of this guy. "When Abbotts are involved, I am your first call. Always."

"When Abbotts are involved, you're my second call. If necessary."

Ethan opens his mouth as if to respond but then seems to remember he and Melrose aren't alone and pulls himself silently together, and sits back down. "A discussion for another time."

Melrose, clearly more comfortable here, walks over to the bar and pours himself a glass. Then he leans against the desk watching the three of us. "What I miss?"

"Any sign of Mick yet?" I ask.

Melrose shakes his head. "He's totally disappeared. No one's seen him."

"Left town? Hiding? Dead?" Ethan asks.

"He didn't deliver. When you pulled Cory, Rock lost income. Income Mick was responsible for. My guess? We'll find his body eventually. When enough time has passed, it will be hard to link it to Rock, but soon enough, it'll still be a warning to others."

He's a murderer.

"So what do you need, Dylan? To end Rock?" Ethan asks. Demands.

Melrose shrugs. "Witnesses. Evidence. A DA willing to take the case."

"Ian Robertson will take the case."

"If there's enough to make a case, maybe."

"So we get the kid to testify."

"No," I refuse. This is already spinning out of control. But I won't let them put Cory in danger. Any more than he already is.

Because of me.

Ethan sighs. "Then what do you suggest?"

"I can testify. There's no term limits or whatever on murder, right?"

Melrose stiffens. "Statute of limitations? Not on murder, no."

I grab my wallet and pull out the article I've been carrying around for weeks now. About the man from fifteen years ago.

Melrose looks at it, then back at me, handing it to Ethan. "He did this?"

I explain what I know, what I remember from back then.

"Why didn't you come forward before now?"

"Because…." How the fuck do I explain this? I *should* have come forward before now. But I was a kid. Then he was in jail. And then the notebook.

"He was protecting me," Lucas speaks up for the first time. "Stupid fucker thought he was protecting me." And he explains about the notebook, the knife, Rock's lackeys, the page he left for me after Riley's attack. He tells them all of it, everything I told him. But he makes me sound so much better than I deserve.

"So he has an item easily identified as Luke's with the blood of a murder victim smeared on it." Ethan recaps.

I nod.

Ethan shrugs. "Not a problem."

I stiffen, jumping to my feet. "Yes, it's a fucking problem. Luke had nothing to do with Rock. That was always on me. I won't have him linked to a *murder*. Are you fucking kidding?"

Ethan watches me with steady eyes; my outburst doesn't shake him at all.

"It's not enough. That notebook is years old. I doubt Rock has kept it secure; who knows how many sets of fingerprints are on it?" He sips his drink and continues, "For all he could prove, Luke threw it away years ago, and he dug it out of the trash. It's meaningless." He looks at Melrose expectantly.

Melrose shrugs and reluctantly admits, "He's right. It would only matter if someone really wanted to go after Luke, and I can't think of anyone who would. Maybe then. Not now."

"They'd be going after a local hero, not to mention an Abbott. No DA in this town is going to do that without a much better case than this. The word of a convicted dealer and questionable evidence? No. Never happen."

I'm...shook. Stunned. Completely reeling. Slowly I sink back to the couch. Fifteen years, I've been terrified by this hanging over my head, waiting to take me and my best friend down, and they're telling me it's nothing. Dismissed. *Meaningless.*

Holy fuck.

I slump down, holding my head in my hands. Exhausted.

"Rock clearly thinks he has something, though. And I think we can make that work to our advantage."

Forcing myself to focus, I look up. Clearing Luke of the fallout was only one part of the problem. Cory still needs protection from Rock's retribution. Rock still needs to go down. Permanently this time.

"Can we get him for murder?" I ask Melrose. "I want him finished, not something where he can walk in a few years. Nothing will change."

"I can pull the case file. See if we have anything that can be processed. Any fingerprints, DNA, witnesses. At least we'll know if we even have a chance at building a case."

"That could prove Jax was there. Put him on the scene." Luke is tense, clearly not liking this idea. Can't say I do much either.

"Trust me," Melrose responds.

I shift, debating what I'm about to offer. This could potentially also only implicate me. I don't know. I don't know anything for sure, obviously. Except we need to stop Rock.

"What if, um, what if you had the murder weapon?"

Suddenly everyone is staring right at me. With various hard expressions.

"Hypothetically," Melrose stresses. "That could help. Is that a possibility?"

I nod, rubbing my hand over my head. "I stashed it."

"You didn't ditch it that day?" Lucas asks, his voice clearly revealing his disbelief.

Wincing, I admit, "I didn't know what to do back then. And I haven't been back. I don't know if it's still there."

"Where?" Luke asks softly.

I swallow. "I was still at Cliff's," I explain, referring to our old foster placement. "I put it above some pipes and beams in his basement."

"Jesus."

"I'll go by friendly like and see if I can get in. If not...." Melrose looks at Ethan.

"If not, I'll take care of it," he answers.

The two men share a look.

We learned when Tanya kidnapped Ash and Logan that Ethan and his team operate in what some call the gray area. Not exactly entirely legal. Not that we gave a shit then. Or now.

"Can we get him on the fighting? Endangering a minor? Something else just in case we can't find enough on the murder?" Luke asks.

"If we can prove that he's the one running the ring. No one there will testify to it, you know that," Melrose shrugs.

"So what do we do? Cory isn't the only one. Getting him out doesn't solve it."

Ethan, pondering, his fingers tapping on the arm of his chair. "What will solve it...?"

I don't think he expects an answer, he's just processing his own plan, but I respond anyway. "I have an idea about that. I'll have to make a call."

He nods, and I'm kind of shocked when he doesn't demand more information.

"We need to set up surveillance. Where does he live, work, hang out?"

At least I have these answers. "Probably easiest if I show you."

Ethan picks up his phone. "You're up," he says and then hangs up again. Thirty seconds later, a guy I vaguely recognize from the night Ash and Logan were taken walks into the room. It's starting to get crowded in here.

"Nathan, we need a full workup on Rock Ferrangi. Jax will show you where to start."

Nathan nods. "I'll meet you by the elevator in ten minutes." And he's gone again. These guys could be better communicators.

I'll say one thing for Ethan. He moves fast.

He stands, setting down his drink and straightening his suit jacket. "Dylan, you'll stop by Cliff's and pull the evidence from fifteen years ago. Jax, tell him where you stashed the knife. Then go with Nathan so he can get Rock under surveillance sooner rather than later. Let me know if you need anything on the fighting ring. I'll see what I can find on Mick's whereabouts and Rock's business dealings and financials. Look into the victim. See if I can link him to Rock somehow."

I bristle at his tone but bite my tongue. I still need his help, after all.

"I'll go with Jax," Lucas states.

"No," Ethan shoots that down immediately. "If Rock sees you and Jax together in the old neighborhood after everything that's happened, he'll assume Jax told you. If Jax told you, then he might have told others. We need Rock to think that Jax is still alone in this."

Luke looks ready to argue, but I stand, getting his attention. "He's right, Luke. He knows I've never wanted you involved in this. It's better if he thinks he can still use that against me."

With a short nod, Luke concedes. But he doesn't look happy about it.

Melrose takes off, and Luke goes with him. I'll be getting a ride with Nathan.

Before I leave, Ethan stops me, calling my name. It doesn't take long for him to make his point.

"Is there anything else I need to know? Were you involved in this guy's death in any way?"

Tense and fucking ashamed, I snap, "No. I told you what happened. Exactly what happened. I was stupid, not evil."

He nods, seeming satisfied. But then he says, "Until Rock is convicted, you're a target. Don't make Riley one. I'll have one of my security team stay on her. You've done enough."

Gritting my teeth, I nod. His words leave a jagged hole in my chest. But I know he's right.

You've done enough.

I knew it was going to come. The end of us. I know I should have ended it already. I've been greedy and selfish because I wanted her. But I was never her future. I was just for right now. And now is over.

I feel hollow inside, numb, preparing for the conversation I know I'll need to have. Finally.

Riley

IF MY ANKLE WASN'T THROBBING, I'D PROBABLY BE PACING AROUND MY tiny apartment. Instead, I'm sitting on my couch, anxiety eating popcorn to try and deal with all my nervous energy.

I haven't heard from Jax.

Lucas sent me a text, at least, letting me know they were together and both were okay. But I haven't heard from Jax.

I made Teagan go home hours ago. Her particular intensity and energy isn't what I need right now. Although I hadn't fully processed her leaving would mean I would just be anxiously waiting on my own. Alone.

Pirate whines, clearly picking up on my energy but stays curled up on his dog bed in the corner. I'm exhausted, but don't want to go to bed. Going to bed feels like I'm ending the day, and everything just feels too unresolved to end the day.

I nod off, still on my couch, and jerk awake at the sound of my door buzzer. Frantic, I rush over to the door, forgetting for a second about my ankle. I wince at the shooting pain and finish my walk slower and limping.

"Hello?"

"It's me."

I breathe a sigh of relief, hearing Jax's voice on the other end. Finally, knowing for sure he's all right. I buzz him in, waiting at my open door for him to come up the stairs.

"Hi." He looks ragged and worried. Even more tired than I feel.

He gives me a weak grin and says, "Hey, Teach."

I want to throw myself into his arms, launch myself at him and have him catch me, hold me, but something is holding me back. He left after all. Earlier, when things were bad, he left again.

Jax steps inside, and I close the door, things heavy and awkward between us. He stays near the entrance. Doesn't go farther inside to sit down. My stomach sinks. It's like my body knows what's coming before my brain can catch up.

"Are you okay?" I ask softly.

He nods. Then shakes his head. "Not really, no. But for the first time in a long time, I think there's a plan so I can be."

"That's good, Jax." I feel like I might throw up, my stomach is so unhappy and nervous. I force myself to put a normal face on when for some reason, all I want to do is cry.

"How's your ankle? Do you need to sit down?"

"I'm okay." I don't want to sit down. Sitting down feels final. I feel like I have more control standing up, even if I'm a little wobbly. "What can I do? How can I help?"

Jax exhales slowly, his eyes sliding around the room. Anywhere that isn't me. Tears sting my eyes.

Crap.

I don't want to cry. He told me. From the very beginning, he told me what he was capable of. What this could be. It's not his fault I had started to hope we were more.

Not his fault I fell in love with him.

I'm not a forever guy.

We should keep this fun.

And while I know this isn't what he meant at the time, I think it's pretty evident with everything going on right now that this… well, it's gotten far more complicated than 'fun' would imply. This was always supposed to be evanescent. That's all.

EVANESCENT
Definition: something that lasts for a short period
of time

"Jax-" I start.

"Riley-" he says at the same time.

"Go ahead," I tell him. Dreading the next words out of his mouth.

"We've got a plan, okay? We're going after Rock. But," he shifts in front of me, "it could get worse first, you know? And I don't want you caught up in that. Today…."

I know what he's thinking. Today could have been worse. If I hadn't been able to break away. If Dalvin and Layla hadn't been leaving. It could have ended up so much worse than a sprained ankle and some scraped knees.

I want to tell him I can handle it. That I'm strong and capable. That he doesn't need to take care of me.

But…I'm not. I mean, I don't know how to handle men who take money to let kids get beaten bloody. That relish watching people beat each other up until one of them can't leave the ring without help. That attack women in parking lots to send a message. I don't know how to protect myself against someone who will murder people who get in his way.

How does anyone know how to do that?

I press my lips together, stifling the flow of words that want to come out. That will just make this harder for him. For both of us.

"Please be careful. Please…." I trail off, not sure what else to say. Not sure there is anything else I should say.

"I will."

"Will you kiss me?" I whisper.

He cups the back of my neck and pulls me close. His lips brush across my forehead, lingers. Breathing me in. I can't stop the tears now. I don't even try.

"Stay safe, Teach, okay? I promise I'll fix this."

Finally, he steps back, releasing me, and turns away. He hesitates at the door briefly, just long enough to give my battered heart a tiny slice of hope, but then he yanks it open. Shutting it softly but firmly behind him.

I clamp a hand over my mouth, muffling my cry. The tears I've stopped fighting are leaking down my cheeks, and I hobble back to the couch, pulling a blanket over me as I curl up. Pirate comes and nudges my hand, then hops up and settles at my feet.

I'll fix this.

Fix the threat that Rock poses. Fix whatever is going on with Mick.

But I'll have to fix my shattered heart. That one is on me.

CHAPTER

Thirty-One

Jax

A week later, I pound on a rusted steel door. When no one responds, I beat again with my whole forearm. I know I'm late. That was by design.

Eventually, a short guy with a thick neck and thicker arms opens the door. Behind him, I see another collapsible steel door. Rock has always been serious about his security.

"You're lost," he tells me, it's not a question, and attempts to shut the door again.

"I know where I am. I'm here to see Rock."

Ol' Thick Arms pauses and gives me a hard once over. "Name?"

"Jax Hall."

He opens the door wide enough to let me through, glancing around the empty lot behind me. I'm now in a small four-by-six space between the two doors with the less-than-friendly doorman.

"You sure you're here to see Rock? If he doesn't want to see you, it's not going to go well."

"He'll see me," I say grimly.

The guy shrugs and then motions to another through the holes in the second door. He mutters something, likely giving him my message, and sends him on the way.

We wait in the small space. He folds his arms and watches me, not saying a word. It takes an insane amount of willpower to do the same and not start needling him. I don't need any more enemies in this building.

Finally, the second guy returns and nods. My friend Ol' Thick Arms pulls on the collapsible door, pushing until it folds in on itself and motions me through.

I hear the metal scrape closed behind me. I follow the other guy into the dark hallway. As we walk, I start to hear yelling and cheering. The boos and groans. I swear I can hear the flesh hitting flesh, but I know that's impossible. Just my memories playing tricks on me. Turning a corner, we enter a massive room. Part of it is still full of old machinery, but the rest holds an elevated makeshift cage, a good-sized crowd around it.

Taking a deep breath, I steel myself. This is it.

Rock's holding court as usual. The only one with an actual chair to sit in the whole place.

"Jacky!" he calls out, smirking at me.

I grit my teeth at the old nickname. "Rock." I nod.

"What can I do for you?"

Cheers erupt from the crowd behind me. Someone must be bleeding in the ring. I swallow, trying to settle the queasy feeling in my stomach. "Let's talk."

"Talk? Don't you want to watch the fight? I've got a new recruit. Had to replace a recent loss. I think you'll like him. Reminds me a lot of you back in the day."

I stiffen and whirl to face the ring. My hands fist when I see the kid there, arms raised, trying to protect himself from the blows his opponent is raining down. He manages to land a shot on the other guy's ribs and ducks away. My eyes land on Dalvin just outside the ring, in the kid's corner, and I force myself to relax.

Dalvin. He came through.

I hear Rock laughing behind me. "See? Quick. Just like you."

I turn back, staring down at him. "Let's talk," I repeat.

Slowly, Rock stands. I take a few steps away from his minions, creating the illusion of privacy.

"So, talk."

"I told you to stay away."

He shrugs, still with that fucking smirk. "Can't have you messing with my business. Mick owes me money. And Cory was making me money. That's a double hit, Jacky."

Silently, I stare at him. Waiting.

"I was willing to stay away if you did. But you couldn't. Just like when you were a kid. Trying to save everyone else. End up just making things worse."

The accuracy of that statement stings, but I refuse to show it.

"What do you want, Rock?"

"You cost me money. You owe me money."

I roll my eyes. "You and I both know that isn't going to happen. Do you know who that was? The woman your guy jumped? A senator's niece. You really want that kind of heat? You're lucky she didn't give your name to the police. You're welcome for that, by the way."

Rock's smirk just gets bigger. "You think I'm worried about the police? Fuck, there's half a dozen of them in this room right now. You should be more worried about them than I am. You and your friend Luke."

There it is. The opening I need.

I force myself to laugh. "Why? Because you're going to show them some doodles one of your boys made? You think I don't know what Luke's work looks like? That sketchbook is long gone, and we both know it." I step closer, getting in his face. Out of the corner of my eye, I see two of Ol' Thick Arms clones start to move in, on alert.

He lifts his hand, telling them to wait.

"Stay away," I grit out.

His smile is evil. "You pay. I'll stay away."

"Pay you for what? You're fucking crazy."

"You cost me money. And can you imagine how devastating it would be for the city's hometown hero to end up being a murderer? Shit. That notebook evidence gets dropped, the fall out from that," he shrugs, shaking his head. "Maybe I give that to one of the cops here tonight. Start that domino."

"I'm not paying you shit for fake evidence that doesn't exist."

"You know it's not."

"I don't know any such thing. Stay the fuck away from me. Riley. Luke. And from Cory. We don't exist to you anymore." I turn to walk away, my breathing heavy. This is it.

"Fine," he grits out. When I turn back to face him, his eyes are narrowed, a pinched expression on his face. "You need me to prove I'm not fucking around, I'll prove it. Where?"

I name a dive bar on Ashland I used to frequent. It's open until 4am but doesn't usually fill up until the 2am bars close. I haven't been there in a few years now. It's dark and depressing. Unless you're there at 2am drunk after drinking all night. Perfect for this.

"When?" he asks.

I shrug. "You tell me. You're the one that has to produce something that doesn't exist anymore."

He smirks. "Such a cocky little fucker. It'll be fun to knock you back down. Tomorrow night. Midnight."

"Alone," I say. "Just you and me."

"Don't worry, Jacky. I got everything I need."

Back at my bike, I pull on a pair of gloves. "You get all that?" I murmur.

I hear Ethan's voice in my ear. "We got it. Meet you back at the office. Nathan will wait here to make sure no one follows you out."

I nod, swinging my leg over the seat and revving my bike. I take off, letting the wind wash over me. Trying to outrun some of the hold Rock still has on me.

Ethan had given us some of the magical passes Melrose had, so I'm able to get right into the underground garage. While I'm waiting for the others, I call Dalvin.

"Yeah."

"It's me. Your guy okay?"

"He's good. Held back to give them a little show."

I snort. "Tell him thanks. I owe him."

"Already done, man. You good?"

"Getting there. You have any interesting conversations?"

"Yeah. Very enlightening. Don't you worry."

I breathe a sigh of relief. I'm not the only one wearing a wire. "Watch your back. I'll be in touch." We disconnect.

I take a deep breath and press the heels of my hands into my eyes for a minute. Tomorrow night.

Hopefully, this is it. The beginning of the end.

Riley

"WAIT. I'M SORRY. HE JUST *LEFT?* IT'S JUST…*OVER?*"

I'd called an emergency slumber party and invited myself over to Teagan's, tired of sitting in my apartment moping every night. No more wallowing in saudade. I needed to get out among people again.

> SAUDADE
> Definition: a nostalgic longing to be near something or someone that is distant; a love that has been and is lost, but the love remains

I don't even have the excuse of my sprained ankle anymore. It was a minor sprain, and after a few days of staying off it, I'm practically back to normal. Physically anyway.

"Are you okay?" Ilyssa asks, her eyes soft.

I give her and Teagan a wobbly smile. "Not really. But I will be."

"I'm going to kill him," Teagan mutters.

"No. Really. It's not like that. It was just…time, I guess. He's got a lot going on right now."

Teagan snorts and rolls her eyes.

"I'm sorry," Ilyssa says. "It seemed like things were good between you two."

Tears sting my eyes, and I lift my shoulder in a half-hearted shrug, blinking them back. "It was. But…." I make a little noise, not having the words to explain.

"Wait. Does this have something to do with why Ethan and Jax are talking all of a sudden?"

Surprised, I sit up straighter, "What are you talking about?"

Teagan grabs a handful of chocolate-covered peanuts and sits back. "I heard Ethan and Daddy talking. They never pay attention to the little sister. It's like they forget I can hear things."

"Your father and brothers adore you, Teagan, and you know it," Ilyssa says, giving her own eye roll. "You were probably listening at the study door again."

"They don't tell me anything," she grumbles.

"What did you hear?" I demand, trying to get this whole discussion back on track.

"Something about Ethan ordering extra surveillance for Jax. I didn't catch the details. I just figured he had some weird stalker like Lucas last year."

I'm feeling very overwhelmed by this random assortment of facts that my cousin has just thrown at me. "What are you talking about? Surveillance? Ethan?"

Ilyssa looks just as confused as I am. "Ethan works with computers," she states, clearly trying to make the connection.

"That's how it started. Cyber security. 'Cause he's basically been a hacker since he was a teenager. Used to drive me crazy. He would read all my emails and private DMs. Change all my passwords when he was annoyed with me. Shit like that. But he got in trouble once when he was a teenager, and Dad made him tone it down. But computers have always been his thing. Then, like five or six years ago, maybe? He and Dad started having all these very serious closed-door conversations. That's when Ethan launched his security firm. Supposedly still computer stuff, but they do way more. They've even run security at events for my dad and other elected officials. Celebrities. Stuff like that. It's all very hush-hush. No one outside the family knows."

I'm stunned, still processing. "Not everyone *in* the family knows."

"Gotta listen at the right doors." Teagan pops another peanut in her mouth. "His team was the one that found Ash and Logan."

"I thought that was the police?"

She shakes her head. "They came after."

Ilyssa looks pale. My head is swimming.

"So whatever stuff Jax has going on, Ethan's working with him. I don't know if that makes it better or worse," Teagan offers.

I shrug. I'm not sure, either. Although I'm relieved he's not going off on his own, trying to take on Rock and who knows who else. I'm glad he's being smart and trying to be safe. I'm also incredibly annoyed by all these men in my life. These men that supposedly care about me, offering me all of these half-truths.

I may not feel capable of taking on an actual criminal. A murderer. But I am fully capable of handling the truth. All of the truth. I'm smart enough to make my own choices. I'd like to have all the information when I do.

"After you were mugged last week? He's probably got someone on you, too," Teagan says off-handedly. As if it's nothing. To be expected.

"What?" I demand. "What do you mean?"

She stands up and walks over to the window. After a moment, she waves us over. "Yep. See? Him." She points to a black car parked across the street.

"One sec," she bounces away, racing down the hallway to her bedroom. She's back quickly with a pair of binoculars.

"Why do you have binoculars?" Ilyssa asks.

"I tried birdwatching once," she murmurs. Pointing them at the car, she adjusts them, concentrating. "Peter."

She throws open her window and waves, yelling, "Hi, Peter!"

A second later, the car window cracks open, a hand emerges and flicks her off. Teagan laughs and closes the window, returning her attention to us.

"Peter's cool. He's watched me before. And Daddy. He gets family detail a lot."

My hands fly up to massage my temples in disbelief. "Teagan. What is happening? Ethan gave me a bodyguard? Why didn't he say anything?" I have so many other questions, *Ethan even has bodyguards to give out?* but this seems like a good place to start.

324

"Probably because he didn't want you to be uncomfortable. Peter won't get in your way or anything. He'll just make sure no one bothers you." She curls back up on the couch, shockingly calm about this whole thing.

"I didn't realize Ethan's job was…dangerous," Ilyssa says, still pale, still confused. I'm with her.

"He's still mostly behind his computer."

With one last glance out the window, I return to my seat, joining Teagan on the couches. "This is insane. How did my life get so insane?"

"You fell in love with a tatted-up bad boy?"

I grimace. "More like I just found out my cousin is a combination of Tony Stark and Bruce Wayne."

"Please. He can't fly, and his toys aren't nearly as cool. He does have some very good-looking staff, though. Maybe one of them can help you get over he who shall not be named. Not Peter. He's gay. And married."

"Yeah, no." I don't think I'm going to get over Jax by getting under someone else, as they say. That's more Teagan's style than mine. No, I think I'm going to have to just wait this out. Time. And the healthy little ball of anger I'm going to nurse for a while.

At both Ethan and Jax.

Maybe Luke, too, depending on what he knew and when.

Maybe I'll just be angry at men in general for a while.

Rock.

Mick.

Daniel.

The guy from the parking lot.

My eighth-grade history teacher who always seemed surprised when I knew the correct answer.

Screw 'em all.

I grab the wine bottle from the table and tip myself a healthy pour, taking a sip.

"Movie? Riley, you called us together; you pick."

I ponder for a second, feeling out my mood. "Kill Bill?" I offer.

"Chicks with swords. I'm in. Ilyssa?"

"Fine with me."

Teagan searches until she finds what we're looking for and presses play. I settle into her giant couch, sipping my wine, nursing my anger, ignoring my hurt, and focusing on Uma Thurman chasing some good old revenge. She could handle facing a murderer, taking on Rock. But I didn't spend years training to be an assassin. So, there's that.

It's possible the wine is going to my head.

CHAPTER
Thirty-Two

Jax

Ten after midnight. Rock is such a fucking dick. Anything to make me squirm. To give him even an ounce more power. I know he's coming; already on his way. Ethan's had a team on him for a week now. They went in as soon as he left his place, getting more evidence. Rock's just making me wait. Because he can.

Prick.

The bar is mostly empty. Like I said, this place tends to be more popular after the other bars are closed. It's possible it'll get busier after two, but it is a Sunday night. Right now, there's a few guys playing pool, a couple sitting at the bar, and another guy sitting alone at a table up front. I appreciate the anonymity as I sit and wait in a back booth, facing the door, nursing a beer.

Finally, Rock wanders in. He seems to be alone as promised, but I know I have backup waiting outside, so I'm not too worried about it. I just don't want him to know I'm not worried about it.

He stops at the bar and orders a drink. I guess he's planning on sticking around for a while, then. Shit. Or this is just another way for him to make me wait. Try to make me anxious. I school my face. I won't give him the satisfaction. I exhale, deliberately relaxing my muscles, and stretch one arm along the back of the booth, slouching a little. Rock picks up his beer and crosses the room, sliding into the booth across from me.

"Jacky."

I don't say anything. Just wait. He stares back at me, drinking his beer. But he gives first, digging his phone out of his pocket, and pulls up a picture. Then he slides it across the table to me. It's a picture of Luke's sketchbook. Definitely tattered and fifteen years older, but that's it.

It's weird. Seeing it now. Now that I know this thing I'd been so afraid of doesn't matter.

"Believe me now, asshole?"

I shrug. "So you show me a photo. What do you want me to do?"

"Keep him talking, Jax. Nathan's team is in." Ethan's voice in my ear. I exhale slowly and focus on keeping him talking. I'm supposed to be buying them time. See what they can find easily and plant bugs and computer viruses to find the rest. So I need to sit here with Rock. When all I want to do is put as much distance between him and me as quickly as I can.

"You've got a pretty sweet setup these days, don't you? Your own shop, your own show. Oh, sorry, I mean Luke's shop. Luke's show."

I force myself to laugh. "Still with this tired shit? It's boring."

"I feel like I deserve some of that good luck, you know? Considering I kept my mouth shut all those years ago. None of this would have happened without me."

This time I laugh for real. "Are you fucking serious?"

His eyes narrow at me. "I could take everything from you." He sits back, masks his hate with a fake smile. "But I don't want to do that, Jacky. I want you and me to be friends again. Like the old days. Help each other out."

"Is that what you think you were doing back then? Helping me out?"

"You got paid."

I snort. Whatever.

"I gotta say your taste in women has certainly gotten classier. That redhead the type you can land now that you're on TV?"

I battle my instincts, not wanting to show him how much I hate that Riley has any of his attention. Trying to disguise my reaction, I take a drink of the beer still sitting in front of me.

"Heard she was feisty." His grin is vile, makes my skin crawl.

He's fucking dead.

"Listen to me, you stupid fuck. If anything happens to her, I will destroy you piece by piece until there is nothing left. It'll be my purpose in life." So much for not revealing how I feel about Riley.

"The team's set, Jax. Even found the sketchbook he's so proud of. Get out of there quick and quiet."

I don't need to be told twice. I pound the rest of my beer and stand, prepared to leave.

"Stay away from me. Stay away from her. Stay away from Luke. I'm done with this."

He jumps to his feet and fists my coat, jerking me toward him, snarling. "You fucking ungrateful bastard. I gave you a shot."

I bat his hands away, shoving him back. "You *gave* me nothing. I earned everything I got back then. You *used* me. Just like you tried to use Cory."

"Jax. Walk away." Ethan's voice is still in my ear, but I'm too furious to care.

Rock pushes me back, and I let him. I turn away, walking out the back door. We don't need an audience for this. This is between me and Rock. Has been for years.

He follows after me like I knew he would, spewing insults. Trying to get under my skin. The second I step outside the door, he shoves me again from behind, and I stumble a couple steps before regaining my balance.

When I turn to face him, his fist is right there, pain explodes in my cheek, and I'm turned sideways. I shake my head, clearing it, and brace myself for more. He punches me again, this time striking my side. I breathe through the pain and grab his jacket pulling his face right to mine.

"You sure you want to do this? I've never seen you in that ring."

He strikes my side again, in the same spot, and I release him, stepping back.

Fine.

I swing, satisfaction rushing through me when my fist connects with his jaw. But Rock didn't get where he is without knowing how to take a punch and throw some of his own. He comes at me, taking me down at the waist. I fall back into the wall of the building before catching my balance. I get my footing back and throw him away from me. He stumbles and comes back at me, but I duck, and his fist hits the wall behind me. Roaring, he turns on me, but I'm ready now, not just going to take it. I hit him again in the face, then aim for his kidneys.

He grunts but isn't going down easy. I have a vague sense of people yelling at us. Ethan's given up talking me down. There's too much rage and fear, and resentment in my body for me to stop now. I finally manage to get him on the ground and am out of control, throwing punches, unable to keep myself from giving hit after hit. I'm mindless.

Then I just stop. My arm pulled back, ready to land again...I just stop. I'm done. I'm done with all of this.

Exhausted, I get back to my feet, out of breath. My arms are heavy, my side screams, jaw aches. I'm done.

Rock groans and curses at me.

"You taught me well, you sick fuck," I snarl at him. I grab my side and start to walk away.

"Don't move," a firm, steady voice comes from behind me. I risk a glance over my shoulder and sag in relief. A woman's standing there, the one from inside the bar, her gun trained on Rock.

"No need for you, sweetheart. My friend and I were just letting off some steam." Rock pushes off the ground, back to his feet. He's weaving a bit, a fact I take too much satisfaction in.

"I said don't move." She takes three steps closer to him and gives him a vicious downward kick to the knee. He crumbles immediately, howling. My head jerks back, eyes wide. Damn. I know seasoned fighters that wouldn't, couldn't pull off that move. I look at her again, realizing I've seen her before, her wavy blond hair familiar. She was at Ethan's office. The night we found Ash and Logan.

Melrose pulls up, jumping out of his car with a frown on his face. He stops at my side. "You okay?" I've got one hand against my ribs, pressing against the pain, but I'm fine. Will be fine. I nod. He looks at Rock and grimaces. "Christ, you guys require a lot of paperwork."

He pulls out his cuffs and drags Rock to his feet, reciting him his Miranda rights.

"What are you arresting me for, man? He started it. I was just defending myself."

Despite that being provably untrue, Melrose doesn't care. Uniformed police arrive on the scene and put him in a squad car.

"You got it?" I ask.

"I got it."

"And?"

"DNA matches the victim from the scene. Fingerprints match Rock's. We'll have to have our lab verify the results, but…." He shrugs. It's done. Holy shit.

Lucas and Ethan arrive just as I walk over to the squad car. I pull up my own picture, holding it up to the window so he can see it.

"You're not the only one that holds onto stuff," I tell him. It takes a minute before he focuses, and I see recognition narrow his eyes. The knife Melrose managed to recover from Cliff's house. "Oh, and don't worry about that notebook. We returned it to its owner." I jerk my head to the side where Lucas is standing. He raises it, smirking.

Rock's face turns red, and he shakes the back seat with angry screams. "You think you're something special, riding your friend's coattails. You're no different than the guys that hang around me, waiting for a chance to be something. When you all know you're nothing. Or you'd be the one on the throne. The one everyone wants to be."

"Boring," I repeat. And I walk away.

Ethan's standing next to Lucas, his face unreadable.

"We had a plan, Jax. That wasn't the plan. We wanted more time."

I swipe the back of my hand across my mouth, spitting out blood. "Guess I improvised. Sorry."

He stares at me for a second and sighs. "I'll make sure Dylan has what he needs." Then he crosses the parking lot to Melrose.

I steel myself to face Luke. We haven't really talked since this whole thing started. Too focused on just figuring a way out. But now…dealing with his disappointment is all that's left.

"You okay?" he asks. I nod.

"He's wrong, brother. What Rock said. You know that. Right?" I'm startled that's where he goes first.

"You heard that?" I tilt my head at the police car.

"Yeah. I heard."

I shrug, still holding my side. "Think that fucker bruised my ribs."

But Lucas doesn't budge. "Jax. He's wrong. Don't let the shit that fucking asshole spews out mess with your head."

"I'm not," I assure him.

"Or Ethan." He looks over his shoulder and finds his cousin talking to Melrose. "I know he told you to back off. But he doesn't know you. And if you want Riley, if you love her -"

"Of course I fucking love her," I burst out. "She's sweet and smart and funny. She cares about people. She tries so hard at everything and never gives up on anyone because she cares so much. She's shy and clumsy and wears dresses with ridiculous adorable robots on them and has no idea how fucking awesome she is. She's...she's Riley. She's perfect."

I look at my hands, raw and bleeding. With someone else's blood on them. It's repulsive.

"And I'm not going to let all my dark shit poison everything that makes her special."

"Jax."

"It's done, Luke. Leave it."

Riley

LUCAS IS THE ONE WHO TELLS ME. THAT ROCK WAS ARRESTED. THAT Jax is okay. That it's over. Lucas calls me on Monday and tells me that while Jax will be fine, he's a little beaten up and won't be coming to Afternoon with Art. Lucas tells me, not Jax.

I call Ethan, yell at him for not being honest with me, for assigning me a bodyguard without telling me. He apologizes but refuses to call Peter off, arguing that Rock is still a threat until his trial. That he's known for intimidating witnesses, and Ethan wants me protected. I make him promise to offer Cory and his mother the same protection. I tell him I'll cover the cost, but he acts offended and assures me he'll take care of it. I stress the *offer* part. He needs to let them know the situation and make their own choice. Grudgingly, I tell him I love him.

Teagan encourages me to join a dating app. I even let her set up my account on one of them, but I haven't used it yet. I'm not ready.

Life continues.

A few weeks later, I meet my aunt for a late lunch in Evanston. I still miss my parents at times, but I know how lucky I was to have Uncle Theo and Aunt Trish. It's been too long since we've had a chance to catch up, and we spend hours chatting over food and tea. When we finally step outside the restaurant, it's early evening, and I'm startled to realize how light it still is outside. Spring is finally coming. You can feel it in the air too. I drink it in, feeling better than I have in weeks.

She hugs me and makes me promise to come to the house for dinner soon. Then she's off with a kiss and a wave. Smiling, I turn in the opposite direction, heading to my car. Peter discreetly walking behind me.

"Riley!"

I'm deep in thought and stumble when I hear my name called. I look around and then see him.

Oh wow.

It's been so long since I've seen him. He's across the street and glances quickly each way before jogging over. He looks good. Happy. That's good. I'm glad he seems to be doing well.

"Hey. I thought that was you." He smiles at me, and I see a flash of uncertainty in his eyes, unlike him. He's always been among the most self-assured people I've ever met. It's probably one of the things that first attracted me to him all those years ago. When I was unsure, he always knew what he wanted, and it was easy and comforting to just go along. Until it wasn't anymore.

"Daniel. Hi." I nod at Peter, assuring him this is fine.

"How are you?"

"I'm good. You?" This is so weird. A year ago, everyone I knew thought the two of us would get married and spend our lives together, including me. And now we're having awkward, stilted conversations on the sidewalk. Like strangers.

"Great. I got a new job. Promotion."

"Congratulations."

"Let's grab a drink. We should talk."

A flash of annoyance lights my veins. I hated this. In the end, I hated how he always just assumed my answer without asking me. "Do we? About what?"

He looks surprised by my response and, for a second, just blinks at me. "Well, I thought we could talk about us. It's been months, Riles. I miss you."

A laugh escapes before I catch myself. He might mean it after all. Or at least think he does. "Daniel. You can't be serious. After that last weekend, you never even tried to contact me."

"You were so upset. I thought you needed some time."

"And what, now enough time has passed, I should just be over it?"

He shrugs. "Well, no, of course not. I never should have… done…what I did. But can't we at least talk?"

As I stare at him, though, I realize I am. Over it. Over him. And while I've suspected it for a while now, it only proves I didn't love him at the end. We were together out of habit. Discovering his cheating, while painful, was one of the best things that could have happened. Finally, forcing me to acknowledge that marriage to Daniel, a life with Daniel, wasn't what I wanted. We weren't the perfect couple everyone thought we were. That was just a mendacious appearance born out of habit.

MENDACIOUS
Definition: given to deception, false appearance

And now, surviving the last few weeks with a truly broken heart, I know the difference.

"We can talk, Daniel. We can probably even be friends someday. We grew up together, shared so much. But, no, we can't talk about our relationship or getting back together. That's never going to happen."

"Riles-"he tries again.

"I hate it when you call me that. I always have."

He falls silent, surprise on his face. "You never said."

Didn't I? It's possible. It's also possible I did, and he just didn't hear me. It doesn't matter. I'm saying it now.

"It was good to see you, Daniel. I'm glad you're doing well." I pause, thinking about what else I want to say.

Nothing comes to me.

"I'm going to go now," I tell him. And I walk away.

Just like that.

Peter not far behind.

CHAPTER
Thirty-Three

Riley

Even though we've finished our self-defense course, we still continue meeting Ash after her Saturday afternoon class for lunch. It was a relief when Ash and Lucas didn't seem to treat me any differently after Jax and I... stopped being Jax and I. But they haven't. Ash is still friendly and welcoming. Lucas is getting more and more comfortable hanging out with me and with Teagan, frequently giving us both a hard time, teasing, just like he does with Logan. Jax doesn't come, of course. Even when the other members of *Vanished* pop in, Jax never does.

That part sucks.

One afternoon I work up the nerve to ask Lucas about it. About Jax. I know I shouldn't. I'm clearly experiencing a moment of akrasia.

> AKRASIA
>
> Definition: the act of knowing you shouldn't be doing something but doing it anyway

He takes a sip of his water before answering. "He switched up his schedule. Works later on Saturdays now."

"Oh." I don't know what to say to that.

Lucas leans over, bumping my shoulder. "How's Cory doing?"

I smile. "Good. Much better, I think." That's true, at least. He does seem to be doing better, and so is his mom. "He seems less angry. He misses Jax though." Jax has also stopped coming to Afternoon with Art. He's still helping me line up speakers but only communicates through email.

A serious expression falls over Luke's face. "You should tell him that."

Maybe I should.

"I know it's not my business, but I'm sorry about you two. I thought you were good together."

I blink rapidly, hating that still, after all this time, these moments can make me cry. "Thanks," I say, clearing my throat. "I'm just glad everything with Rock worked out. That things are getting back to normal. Have you heard from Melrose? Any updates?"

"Sounds like his lawyer is pushing for a plea deal. Rock claims he can give them information on other crimes. I guess he realized there's no point in holding on to that shit."

Oh no. "Does that mean he'll get out?"

Shaking his head, Luke clarifies, "No. The DA on his case won't let him get off that easy. In addition to the murder charge, they're moving forward on assault, dealing, illegal betting, child endangerment. Dalvin and one of his guys were able to get Rock and some others on video, admitting they knew some of their fighters were underage. And they shared it with Internal Affairs. So they're looking into some of the cops that were there participating. He may get some favors, but he'll definitely be going back to prison."

"Good." I exhale in relief. "That's really good to hear."

"Tell me about it."

"Are they still worried about witness intimidation?" Ethan is. Peter is never far from my side.

Luke shrugs. "It's still a possibility. But Dalvin heard rumblings. Some of Rock's crew got comfortable with him in prison all those years. They didn't exactly like stepping aside again when he got out. He doesn't have the same control he used to have. Melrose thinks it's likely they'll be able to charge him with some other murders. Rivals that disappeared."

Thank god. Maybe it really is over.

"You guys are coming next week, right?" Teagan's question drags us back to the rest of the group. Next Saturday is my family's annual Memorial Day barbecue. My aunt and uncle have been hosting it for years, both for family and for friends and donors. It's become quite a massive affair. Teagan and I have been subtly recruiting Luke and Ash to come for weeks now. Well, I've been subtle. Subtle isn't really Teagan's style.

Ash looks at Luke, a tiny smile playing at her lips. He sighs and runs a hand through his hair, the gesture so reminiscent of Jax I feel a sharp pang in my chest.

"Yes. We're coming. For a little while. And you all better be there to run interference between me and Ethan," he mutters.

"Don't worry. Ethan's always too busy networking to hang out with family. You'll be fine," she assures him, a broad smile on her face. She claps her hands in excitement. "Yay!"

Out of the corner of my eye, I see Ash brush her hand down his back and back up, fingers tangling in his hair briefly before reaching for her glass. His eyes soften as he smiles at her. God, they're so sweet.

"Riley's even bringing a date," Teagan continues.

"Teagan!" I had not decided that for sure.

I hear Ash go 'ooooo' as Teagan looks at me with fake innocence. "What?"

I scowl at her. "Teagan set me up with a guy in her program." I shrug uncomfortably. "He seems nice. I said I *might* invite him."

He is nice. His name is Adrian. He's nice and respectful, and I have fun with him. He took me bowling on our first date, which I thought was kind of perfect. Very low pressure. Especially because he's an awful bowler. On our second date, we went to dinner and a movie. He's nice.

But my heart isn't in it. I'm not ready to date. I planned to explain that to him and ask if he wanted to come to the barbecue as friends. It would be nice to have another friendly face in the crowd.

Ilyssa, I think sensing I'm uncomfortable, deftly changes the subject, asking Ash about her work at the hospital and with her international doctor exchange, helping place doctors at refugee camps around the world. She's been working on expanding the program the whole time we've known her. She and Lucas are going next fall to visit some of the camps. He watches her with pride as she tells us about it.

I want that. What they have.

But I want that, want all of it. I'm not going to settle ever again. So, I'm definitely talking to Adrian. 'Nice' isn't enough.

I deserve more.

Jax

"JAX! GET OUT HERE!" LOGAN YELLS FOR ME FROM THE LOBBY.

I drop the box I'd been carrying, relieved for the distraction. I hate the downtime between appointments. It just gives me time to think. Remember. Dwell.

My therapist encourages me to let my thoughts go down those paths as long as they don't turn too dark. Let myself remember and feel.

Yeah, my therapist. After Rock was arrested, I started having nightmares. Which basically meant I stopped sleeping. It was getting pretty rough for a while until Luke finally called me on it. He made me call and schedule an appointment with Mateo's therapist. Which seemed weird at first. That I would go to the same person someone I knew was going to see. But turns out it's fine.

She thinks it triggered 'buried trauma'. My fight with Rock. Which is why I was having nightmares. Whatever. I'm sleeping again. She's also helping me see I can't blame myself for everything that Rock did. Which is harder to fully believe but I guess I'm working through it.

I stiffen, seeing Riley waiting for me in the lobby. I haven't seen her for nearly two months at this point, and her appearing now, out of nowhere, causes my whole body to tighten in urgency. She's the one thing I've kept off limits. The one topic I refuse to discuss. The only memories I immediately chase away.

"Riley." It's the only word I'm capable of at the moment.

She smiles, but it's sad. It's not her real smile. It's not the smile I love.

"Hi, Jax."

Silence wedges painfully between us. Keeping us apart. Where I insisted we belonged.

Fuck, she looks so pretty. Her dress today has various sea creatures in different shades of green.

"Riley." I stare at her. "Hi, Teach."

Her eyes flicker when I say it, and I feel like an asshole.

"Can...can we talk? For a minute?" She glances at Logan, who is too casually pretending to ignore us while she waits for her next appointment to show up.

That jolts me into action. I shift and tilt my head to the hallway. "Yeah, of course. Come on back." I'm being such a fucking awkward loser. She walks past me and to my station. I leave the curtain open. I don't trust myself if we're actually alone. I still feel like I made the right choice. That doesn't mean it's easy. That I don't miss her.

That seeing her now isn't twisting me up inside and messing with my head.

"Sorry for just showing up like this."

"It's fine. Is everything okay?"

"Oh, yes. Fine. Good. I just wanted to talk to you about the Art program."

I frown. I hate that it seems like I bailed on that. I just felt like it would be…easier…if Riley and I didn't see each other for a little while. I've tried to keep up, help with scheduling guests, checking in with some of the kids over social media, that kind of thing, but I know it's not the same.

"The students miss you." She gets right to the point, making me wonder if she's just as off-balance as I am. And then I realize it doesn't matter. "I just mean," she sighs, tucking her hair nervously behind her ear. "You don't have to stay away because of me. The program is better with you part of it."

I nod. "I'll be there on Monday."

She seems surprised it was that easy. But I was only staying away because I thought she would want me to. If she's okay with me being there, I'll be there.

"Great. Well, then, I guess I'll see you on Monday."

"Okay."

"Okay, well, bye, Jax." She smiles sweetly.

"See you, Teach."

And then she's gone.

CHAPTER
Thirty-Four

Jax

A week later, Lucas ducks his head in while I'm cleaning up my station and holds a six-pack of beer. "C'mon," he calls out.

Surprised to see him, I ask, "Where we going?"

"Roof." He and Ash had gone to an official Abbott family party earlier, but he seems okay. Maybe he needs to talk about it, though.

I shrug and follow him around back to the stairs. We settle into the camping chairs left up there and face the skyline of the Loop. I take the beer bottle he offers and settle back into the chair with a sigh.

I love the beginning of summer. Moments like this, warm air, twilight, city noise and lights beneath us, having a drink with my best friend. Pretty sweet.

Riley would love it up here.

I take a sip of my beer, trying to ignore the sting that thought brings. Monday was a confusing and painful mix of normal and new. Working with Riley again but not being with Riley. It also meant the ban I had on thoughts of her has crumbled completely. Now she's all I can think about.

"I asked Ash to marry me."

Startled, I swallow my beer, and some of it goes the wrong direction, down my windpipe. I cough for a few seconds and then turn to face him. Well, that's a distraction from my memories. "Are you serious?" A wide smile breaks across my face.

"Serious." He's smiling, too, looking a little smug and so fucking happy. "She said yes."

"Holy shit, man." I stand and pull Lucas up, slapping his back in celebration. "Congratulations."

"Thanks." He can't stop smiling as he folds back into the chair. I feel a sharp pang in my chest watching him. Shit. Luke is getting married. Luke is in love.

"We're not really telling people yet. She wants to see her dad next weekend. Tell him in person."

"Oh. Does she know you're telling me?"

He takes a swallow of his beer, then nods. "Yeah."

We fall silent for a bit, both lost in our heads. Lucas shifts, leaning forward, and rests his arms on his splayed knees, his hands still holding his beer between them. "I almost lost her once. Because of my pride. Because of my screwed-up insecurities. Because I was stupid."

I study him in the dimming light, wondering why he's bringing this up now. "You figured it out," I point out.

"You helped." He glances up at me.

"Gonna name your first kid after me?" I joke, trying to lighten his sudden serious mood.

It works. Luke chuckles. "Asshole." And takes another swig of his beer. "You should give Riley a call."

I exhale roughly. Just the mention of her name causing me physical pain. Fuck. Will it ever stop hurting?

"How is she?" The words spill out reluctantly. It's a bad idea to talk about her. Think about her. But I'm also starving for any real news of her. Even though I know I shouldn't. Seeing her in teacher mode isn't the same. Just teases me with pieces of her.

Lucas sits back and stretches his legs out in front of him. "Fine. Well, miserable but pretending to be fine. She even brought a date to the Memorial Day party today."

A date. I feel sick. "Fuck. You're an asshole."

Lucas shrugs then laughs. "You asked."

I focus on my beer, trying to block any thoughts. Unsuccessfully. She's dating.

She's dating?

Of course, she's fucking dating, you asshole. What did you think was going to happen? I down my beer and grab another one.

I hate that she's dating.

I hate that I *know* she's dating.

Except I did know that would happen. Wasn't that the idea all along? That eventually, she'd move on and find someone else. Someone better for her?

I rub a hand over my hair. It's getting long again. I need a haircut.

Shit.

That was the wrong thing to think about. Images of Riley running her fingers through my hair come flooding back. My whole body tenses. So sweet and pretty.

"Guess I deserve that."

Shrugging again, Lucas watches me steadily. "Do you? Deserve what exactly?"

I shake my head. "That's good, I mean. That she's dating."

"You should call her," he repeats.

"Why?" I'm starting to get pissed. "It's not like it's going to be easier for us to break up later."

"So don't break up," Luke states simply.

"Come on, man. Happily Ever After? Me and Riley? Being with me almost got her killed."

"That's bullshit." He sits up straighter, sounding angry. "Cory was her student. That was her world. You didn't bring that to her."

"Rock-"

"Rock would have been there whether you were or not. The fact that you were probably saved both their lives." The fierceness in his tone sets me back for a moment.

Before I can come up with another argument, Ash pops through the stairwell door.

"Hey, Handsome!" she calls out, all smiles.

I watch the tension leave Luke, a contented expression settling over his face as his eyes fall on Ash. "Hey, beautiful. My time up?" He stands up and crosses the roof to give her a kiss hello.

Shit. It hurts to see them together.

"Yep. I came to steal you away."

"Absolutely." He smiles down at her.

I open my arms wide, waiting for her to step into them. "Congrats, Doc," I whisper into her ear when she does.

Glowing, she returns my hug. "Thanks. It's still a little unreal." Her laughter is light and happy.

"So when is the big day gonna be?"

Ash turns back to Lucas, threading their fingers together as she moves to his side. "We haven't gotten that far. I have to tell my dad before anything else."

"We're in no hurry. Now that she's said yes, we can do it whenever she wants," Lucas tells me. She smiles up at him, her eyes shining.

"Shit," I mutter, "you two are the worst."

Ash laughs as Lucas shoves me playfully, and I laugh despite my darker thoughts.

Luke grimaces, then pulls his phone, vibrating, out of his pocket. "Shit. It's Krista. I forgot to call her back earlier. Give me a second?"

"Of course. Take your time," Ash assures him. She settles into the chair he vacated, and I join her as Luke walks across the roof, answering his call.

She props her chin in her palm and starts right in on me.

"You should call Riley."

I grimace. "So I've been told. Recently."

"So? Why don't you?"

I exhale roughly. Why don't I? Honestly, all I can think about right now is her out with other guys. I can't seem to remember any of the reasons why I'm not supposed to call her.

"Jax," Ash says my name softly, waits until I meet her eyes. "Lucas and I, we're really lucky to have you. Logan, Macy, Mateo, Cory, they're all really lucky to have you."

I open my mouth to say something, but she raises her hand, cutting me off. "*Riley* would be really lucky to have you." She smiles softly, her eyes kind of sad. "You're so much more than Luke's best friend. Please know that."

My eyes sting, and I look away. Drink my beer. Clear my throat.

Lucas returns, having finished his call. "Ready?"

Ash nods and stands. I do the same, and she gives me a quick kiss on the cheek before heading to the door.

Lucas and I grasp hands, his other hand squeezing my neck. "Own your shit, brother. But let the rest of that crap go. It's not on you. It never was."

"Now you sound like my therapist," I joke.

"I'm serious. I was worried at first. About the two of you. But I was wrong. She's kinda perfect for you. Don't let other people decide you don't deserve that."

I nod, taking his words in. He slaps me on the chest and releases our handshake, moving to join his soon-to-be wife at the door.

"You coming down?"

"Nah, I think I'll sit for a bit longer. I'll see you tomorrow."

"Later," he calls, giving me a wave.

I sigh, settling back into my chair.

"Oh!" Ash pops her head back out, startling me and causing me to spill some of my beer. "And I happen to know Riley is planning on an evening of Netflix and take-out. In case you decided to *call her*."

I laugh, flipping her off. But she just grins and disappears through the door.

My smile falls as I think about what they both said. Thinking about Riley. Thinking about the last couple of months without her. Thinking more about the months before that. With her. Months ahead. What those could look like.

At least I know she's not out on a date.

Shit.

Riley

COMFY CLOTHES. CHECK. (YOGA SHORTS, NORTHWESTERN sweatshirt, and my favorite bulky socks.)

Chocolate. Check. (Mini KitKats because I feel like torturing myself.)

Salty. Check. (Sea Salt pita chips. My go-to. I'll eat the entire bag and feel no shame.)

Self-Care item. Check. (Face mask and nail polish. We'll see if I actually motivate to do either.)

Movie. Check. (The Thing. Campy horror, no romance.)

Alcohol. Check. (White wine spritzer.)

Apanthropy. Double check.

> APANTHROPY
> Definition: A desire to be alone; a distaste for the company of others

I plop onto my couch with a sigh. I'm such a pathetic mess. Pirate jumps onto my lap, nuzzling around until he gets comfortable and lays down. Absently, I scratch his head and cue up the movie.

Maybe I should move to Antarctica. Bet there aren't any tattoo shops or reality stars there.

Settling into the movie, I munch my snacks and drink my drink and ignore my face mask.

I've just gotten to the part where The Thing busts out of the dog on TV when my doorbell buzzes, making me jump. My wine splashes on my leg and Pirate's head. He whines softly and settles right back down.

"Crap," I mutter, wiping the cool drops off my bare leg. My door buzzes again, causing Pirate to lift his head and woof in a show equal parts protectiveness and annoyance. I scoot out from under him and set my wine glass on the table before heading to the door.

I press the button to speak. "Hello?"

"It's me."

My stomach drops, throat clenching, tears immediately springing to my eyes. It's been two months. Why does it still hurt so much? It didn't hurt this much with Daniel.

You didn't love Daniel, the voice in my head reminds me.

Oh, shut up.

I swallow and blink back my tears, composing myself.

"Jax?"

"Yeah, it's me. Can I come up?"

My chest tightens painfully. I shouldn't let him up. Seeing him will only prolong my 'getting over him' period. One that already seems unbearably lengthy. But I'm also curious, worried, wondering why he's here now after all this time. I debate long enough, I'm not entirely sure he'll still be down there when I finally press the entrance button, unlocking the front door. I open my apartment door a crack for him, and then, because I can't help myself, I rush to the bathroom and try to make myself presentable.

I flip on the light and stare at my reflection. I don't look that bad, I guess. I'm not exactly date ready, but then this isn't a date, is it? I redo my ponytail, fussing for no reason.

There's a soft tap on my door, and the butterflies in my stomach feel like they've been caught in a tornado. Why is he here? I can't do this.

You've got this, Riley. Take a deep breath.

I grip my bathroom sink and do just that. I've got this.

Jax is crouched just inside my front door, rubbing his hand over Pirate's head. Pirate is panting happily, bumping his nose into Jax's leg.

God, he looks good.

Jax looks up, sees me, and smiles crookedly. My chest does that weird and slightly painful tightening and twisting thing again. He gives Pirate one last pat on the head and stands, moving farther into the living room. Moving closer to me. His eyes are inscrutable as they move over me, finally lingering on my bare legs.

"I, uh, I'll just…give me a second to put some pants on." I can feel my cheeks flushing as I scramble to put some distance between us.

"Riley." His voice stops me, freezing me in place before I've gotten more than a few steps away. I feel him coming up behind me. His heat. His scent. Him.

I can't do this. It's breaking my heart all over again. I squeeze my eyes shut, unable to turn around.

His fingertips brush against my shoulder, and I jerk away, afraid I'll shatter into a million pieces if he touches me for real.

"You look pretty."

A sound that's supposed to be a laugh bursts out of me because, no, I do not.

"What are you doing here, Jax?" I steel myself for the sight of him and finally turn back around to face him.

"I heard you were home." He smiles, his eyes crinkling in that way that I love, which only hurts now.

"Please don't do this."

His smile falls, confusion falling across his face. "Do what?"

"Please don't come over here to hook up. I can't do that. Have casual sex with you." I look down, studying my socks, wiggling my toes. I can't have just ex-sex. It would break my heart. But I'm also not confident I could say no to him. I want him too much.

But I want all of him, and that's not what this would be.

"Riley. I would never do that to you."

I shake my head, still not looking up, and my eyes fill with tears again. Despite my attempt to hide it, my voice cracks, giving me away. "Please just go."

"Riley. Please don't cry."

A flash of anger spears through me, and I glare up at him. "I'll cry if I want to! You don't get to decide that!"

He raises his hands in surrender. "You're right. I'm sorry. Can we talk? Will you talk to me?"

I swipe the tears off my cheeks and take a deep breath as I study him thoughtfully. I didn't notice it until now, but he looks... rough. He needs a haircut and a shave, and he doesn't look like he's been sleeping well. A tiny seed of hope blooms; maybe this has been as hard on him as it has been on me.

But I shut that down swiftly. I don't want to see things that aren't there. He ended it.

"Talk about what?"

"Can we sit?" He smiles tentatively and tilts his head to the couch. I shrug and cross to sit down, pulling my blanket back over my lap as some kind of shield. Pirate hops up next to me on the couch and circles twice before plopping down with his head in my lap. Good. He's forcing some distance between Jax and me.

Jax studies Pirate with a half smile and then sits on the far end of the couch, turning slightly so he can face me. I focus on Pirate, scratching his ears.

Now that we're sitting, Jax seems at a loss for words. Stubbornly, I refuse to break the silence. He broke my heart. Is breaking my heart all over again. He wants to talk? Then this is on him.

He runs his hand through his hair nervously. I'm spitefully satisfied he's nervous.

What does he have to feel nervous about?

"Luke said he saw you today."

Oh, HECK, no.

I jump from my seat, disturbing Pirate, who woofs his annoyance and hops down from the couch. Turning angrily to Jax, I blast him with my best angry teacher glare.

"Is that why you're here?!"

His eyes are wide as he looks up at me from his seat. But I'm pissed.

"Luke told you I had a date, so you come over here to, what? Remind me what I'm missing? Tell me you don't want me to be with anyone else? To piss on your territory? I'm not interested, so you can just leave."

CHAPTER
Thirty-Five

Jax

Fuck. I'm losing her.

Again.

She marches across the room to her front door, her tiny little shorts torturing me. I'm an asshole to be noticing her ass at a time like this, but I love her, and I haven't had sex in almost two months.

Also, she's not wrong. I *do* want to remind her what she's missing. What we had. Could hopefully have again. I *don't* want her to be with anyone else. Thinking about it makes me very rage-y. Just like thoughts of other women make me feel gross now. And I *do* kind of want to mark my territory. She's mine, and I'm hers, and I want the whole world to know.

But I think it seems more romantic in my head than in hers.

I stand but make no move to the door. Her angry, tear-filled eyes glare at me from across the room. The pain in those eyes causes my chest to tighten with fear and regret.

"Go."

There's a fist squeezing my throat, and I start to freak out I'm not going to be able to get the words out that will convince her to give me another shot.

I fist my hair and clear my throat, confessing, "I did this all wrong. I'm sorry."

Her expressive eyes flash with indecision, and I risk a few steps closer.

"I didn't come here because I wanted sex tonight. And I didn't come here because I heard you were dating." I thought long and hard about that, and everything Luke and Ash said before I came. I wanted, needed, to be sure this wasn't about my ego. I've put Riley through enough. I won't be that kind of an asshole.

But eventually, when all the people in your life you love and respect tell you you're worth something, that you deserve what you want, that you don't have to be second all the time…eventually even the biggest idiot has to start to wonder if they're right. And, fuck, there's nothing I want more than I want Riley.

"I came because I finally realized that all the other shit I was focused on doesn't matter as much as we do. That shitty things will always happen, but that's life, and it's not my fault. And when shitty things happen, I want to be next to you, figuring it out with you, making it better with you.

"I came because I wanted you. I want you, Riley. And not just for sex tonight. I want everything. Every night."

She doesn't move and, for the first time ever, has a completely blank look on her face I can't read at all.

"You want me." Her voice is flat, disbelieving. Shit, I'm too late. I've hurt her too much.

There's got to be something I can say to convince her.

"I do, Riley. I love you."

Her lips press together firmly for a moment, her eyes again flooding with tears.

No!

"Don't say that," she whispers hoarsely.

"Riley, please." Unable to stand still any longer, I rush to her, cupping her cheeks in my palms.

"You left me. You left." Tears leak down her cheeks, and I have to fight my rising panic so I can focus on what to say.

"I fucked up. I know that. And I am so, so sorry. Don't give up on me."

She squeezes her eyes shut as if she can't stand to look at me.

"I will never leave again. I promise. I will spend every day making sure you have something to smile about. I'll balter with you every morning. I'll freudenfreude," I stumble over the syllables, "with you every day. I love you."

Riley makes this horrible sound, half sob, half laugh but the relief I feel at her tiny smile makes me love it.

"That's not how you use it," she whispers. But she sniffles and smiles.

I use my thumbs to wipe her tears away. Her hands move to my chest, touching me but keeping me at a distance. Fuck, I hope this isn't the last time she touches me.

She watches me silently, her eyes skeptical. Long enough, my skin tightens, and my lungs squeeze. If I can't make her believe me, if she sends me away, I will never get over losing her.

God, I'm such a stupid asshole.

"Every morning?" she finally whispers, and my shoulders sag in relief.

"Every fucking morning," I vow, the vise on my chest easing just a bit.

"Every morning," she repeats. I grin that even now, she won't swear. Shit, I love how adorable she is. "You promise?" she demands.

I nod. "Promise. Whatever it takes, Riley Abbott. I love you."

"You love me," she repeats after me again. Her eyes starting to shine, and I exhale roughly. That's the look I want to see.

Every day for the rest of my life.

"I love you."

A wide smile spreads across her face, and she leans into me.

"I love you, too."

Her words punch me in the chest, grab my heart and twist, but it's a fucking sweet pain. I rest my forehead against hers and just breathe her in.

"Still, huh?"

"Always," she whispers.

I'm not sure how long we stand there, holding each other. Riley is the one that finally breaks the moment.

"Will you kiss me now?"

I laugh, wrapping my arms around her waist and swinging her around. Shit, this woman makes me happy.

I set her on her feet and do what she told me to do. I kiss her.

I brush my lips across hers, gently at first. Getting reacquainted. She sighs and melts into me in that way I love, her lips parting. I don't take advantage of that just yet, teasing her, savoring her with light little kisses.

She makes a slight sound of annoyance in the back of her throat, straining against me. Finally, I give her what she, what we want and deepen the kiss. Our tongues touch, exploring, loving. I'm perfectly happy to do this for hours, ignoring my throbbing dick. He'd like to move things along, but thankfully, he's not in charge. Because despite how badly I want her, sex is not why I came tonight, and while I hope she knows that, I want her to have no doubts.

I reluctantly break our kiss, smiling down into her pretty gray eyes.

"Wanna have sex now?" She grins, waggling her eyebrows ridiculously.

I laugh again and lift her off her feet to press a kiss to the curve of her neck.

"Honestly? I kind of just want to hold you for a while."

She wraps her arms around my neck, her legs around my waist, holding her at eye level. "Aw. You want to cuddle?" she teases.

"I think I need it. I was afraid I'd lost you," I confess.

She presses a sweet kiss to my forehead. Each of my eyelids. A slow brushing across my lips.

My dick is so pissed at me right now.

"Snacks and a movie? I have KitKats," she asks.

"Sounds perfect."

She gives me another quick kiss against my lips and hops down back to her feet. Grabbing my hand, we move back to the couch. I pull her onto my lap, arranging her, so we're both comfortable. Pirate lifts his head from his bed on the other side of the room and barks in approval, settling back down. Even though I've decided to put sex on hold for now, I take advantage of having her within easy touching range. And she's still wearing those impossibly short shorts. I skim my hand along the length of her leg, appreciating her soft skin. Does she actually go to yoga classes in these things? Like, with other people?

Sometimes guys are in those classes, too, right?

I shut down those thoughts before I say something stupid. I'm not looking to mess things up moments after she's agreed to give me another chance.

She's focused on the remote, cueing up the movie.

"What are we watching?"

"*The Thing.*"

"Is that the one with Kurt Russell in it?"

"Mmmhmm."

She restarts the movie from the beginning and settles back into me with a sigh.

She's sound asleep by the final scene, cuddled into my chest.

I fucking love it.

My dick is still super unhappy with me. Having her tight little ass on top of it for the last hour and a half has had the predictable effect of keeping me hard and eager. But this is what we needed. She needed to know I'm here because I care about her, because I want it all. These moments, this normalcy, not just hot sex.

Doing my best not to disturb her, I reach for the remote and turn off the movie. Then I carry her to her bedroom, settling her under the covers. Before I join her, I take Pirate out for a quick walk.

Then I strip down to my boxers and slide into bed beside her, pulling her into my chest. She sniffs and murmurs wordlessly against my skin.

I fall asleep with a smile on my face, confident this is what I want every night for the rest of my life.

Tomorrow I'm going to sex her all day.

Riley

I STRETCH AND SIGH AND SLOWLY COME TO. I'M A LITTLE DISORIENTED, realizing I'm in bed with no memory of getting there. But happily, I burrow into the hard, warm body next to me. I missed this. Missed this sleepy, intimate morning time with Jax.

Jax.

Suddenly, I'm wide awake, springing up to a seated position.

I'm still in my sweatshirt and yoga shorts. Jax is sprawled on my bed, one arm thrown over his face, his chest bare. My eyes take in his muscles and tattoos. I'll never get bored looking at him. Never.

"You didn't wake me up!"

He jerks, his eyes blinking rapidly in confusion. "You apparently don't have that problem," he mutters hoarsely. Lifting his head, he looks around the room before turning his eyes to me. "What's going on?"

"You didn't wake me up," I accuse.

"I thought you could use the sleep. You know, to prepare for today." He leers at me suggestively. All my girly parts start to tingle at that look. Hallelujah. We're so getting it on. "I'm keeping you here all day." He grins.

"But you didn't wake me up *last night*."

"Was I supposed to?" he looks so confused. He shifts, resting both arms behind his head. Showing off his biceps. Momentarily distracting me from, what I consider, my very valid complaint.

"I've heard make-up sex is amazing, and I wanted to have some."

Jax roars with laughter, shaking the bed. He laughs so hard his eyes water. I grab his wrists and straddle him, immensely satisfied when I feel his semi against my thigh.

Satisfied or smug. I'm not sure which applies more in this situation. Whatever.

Still chuckling, he smiles up at me."I promise. I am absolutely sure that you will have plenty of chances in the next sixty years to get pissed at me. I promise you, *we* will eventually have make-up sex."

I lean down, still holding his wrists above his head, and press a lingering kiss to his lips. "You're full of promises these days." I shift, notching his erection against my core, teasing him through the layers of our clothes. "Sixty years, huh?"

He hums in appreciation when I press my lips to the cord of his neck, my tongue slipping out to caress his skin. "Think you can put up with me that long?" he asks.

"I think I'll enjoy trying." I smile down at him, rolling my hips, trapping his erection between us.

"Fuck, Riley." He moves as if to touch me, but I squeeze his wrists and shake my head.

"Stay," I order, and he stills beneath me, his gorgeous crooked smile in place. "You had your chance last night. This morning, I'm in charge."

"Whatever you say, Teach."

I sit up straight, releasing his wrists. "Stay," I remind him. When I trust he isn't going to move, I whip my sweatshirt over my head, revealing my bare skin beneath.

"So pretty, baby." Jax is staring at my breasts, the heat in his eyes causing my nipples to tighten. He groans when he sees his effect on me.

I'm loving it. Loving the way he makes me feel. The way I can make him feel. Loving him. Loving us.

"You are the most beautiful woman I know. And you're mine."

My stomach flips. But I'm not going to let him distract me, and I tell him so. "Don't honeyfuggle me, mister. I'm in charge."

I bounce a little as Jax laughs. "Is that what I'm doing? Honeyfuggle-ing?"

"Yep. Throwing compliments at me to get what you want."

He laughs again. "Believe me, Teach. I'm getting exactly what I want. No complaints here."

I lean down and press a soft, slow kiss to his lips. "That's sweet," I murmur. When I try to sit up, pulling away, he follows me, capturing my lips in a long, searing kiss that steals my breath. Eventually, I press my hand against his chest, urging him back down and breaking our kiss. His eyes spark, that gold ring getting hot, setting off tingles in my core and inner thighs. I'll never understand his effect on me, but I hope we never lose this. This… easy teasing hunger we have. I want his smile to make my stomach flutter when I'm eighty years old.

"I love you," I whisper, and the smile that lights up his face hits my heart. I press my lips to his chest, right over his heart, racing beneath his skin. "You're the best man I know. And you're mine."

"Riley," his voice sounds pained. I don't want him to ever doubt that. Never again.

I shift and shimmy my way down his body, trailing kisses as I go. He's already naked. I lift up so I can yank the sheet off, out from between us, and hum appreciatively when I see his erection spring free. Already hard and reaching for me.

I grip his dick, squeezing lightly, and give the tip a teasing kiss. His hips thrust up, nearly unseating me, and he moans, his breathing getting rough. My tongue traces along the length, still teasing. I feel his hands in my hair, but my mouth is too busy to scold him for moving. Besides, I like that he's losing control.

I peek up his abs finding his eyes hot and heavy on me, watching as I touch him. Keeping our eyes locked, I again kiss the tip of his erection, lingering, my tongue poking out to flutter and tease. He groans loudly, his head tilting back.

"Riley." My name is like an exhale, pleading and demanding at the same time. My core feels heavy with longing, and I'm tingling all over as I finally take him deep, sucking him into my mouth. He groans again, his hands in my hair, urging me on.

He lets me make love to him, using my mouth, giving to him.

"Riley," he grits out, voice rough and sexy with restraint, "I'm going to come. And I want to do that inside you. I want to feel you. Sweet and tight around my cock."

My stomach clenches at his words, wanting the same. Desperately. But I take my time moving up his body, touching, kissing, loving. When I return to his lips, he kisses me fiercely, his hands moving down my body. His fingers slip beneath the waistband of my sleep shorts, and dive down, cupping and squeezing my bare butt.

I gasp into our kiss as he rocks me against him, using his erection to hit just…the…right…spot. "Jax!" Feels so good.

He flips us, so I'm on my back and peels my shorts off, tugging them roughly down my legs. He wastes no time, gives me no torturous lead-up, just buries his mouth against my sex and feasts.

"Oh god, Jax!" Instinctively my hands grip his hair, my back arching, pressing me more firmly into his kiss. His tongue is relentless, fluttering against my clit, licking along my folds. Taking me higher, twisting me tighter. Oh god. And then he slips two fingers inside me, thrusting and caressing, and I'm off. Splintering, exploding, dissolving, and coming back together. I haven't fully recovered when Jax moves smoothly up my body, entering me, joining us in one sure stroke.

I clutch his shoulders, gasping, feeling my stomach and core tightening once again. Working up to another orgasm.

"Damn," he groans into my neck. "You feel so good. God, I missed you."

"Missed you too," I whisper, shifting until I can kiss him. He's pressing into me, his elbows on either side of my head, hips between my thighs as his kiss goes on and on. The urgency of moments ago morphing into this lazy contentment. He flexes his hips languidly, and trails kisses along my jaw, my neck, my ear. I love it. Love him. I let my hands explore, touching his smooth skin and hard muscles. Rediscovering all the places he likes to be touched. What makes his breath catch, makes him groan, his eyes spark with heat.

Eventually, our leisurely exploring isn't enough, and his touches turn more demanding, and I strain against him. His thrusts become more urgent, and I move against him, encouraging him. Wanting him.

I'm so close, on the verge of another beautiful explosion, when he stills.

He pauses, holding himself above me, his breathing harsh. "Look at me, Riley. Look at me."

I open my eyes, looking up into his. The emotion in his gaze makes my breath catch in my chest. If I'd had any doubts about his feelings for me, this moment would have incinerated all of them. He's let all his walls down, revealing everything for me, to me.

"I love you. I'll love you always."

"Jax," I whisper, resting my palm against his cheek. Tears slip from my eyes; I'm so overwhelmed in only good ways. "I love you, too."

"Don't give up on me."

"Never."

He shifts our angle, finding just the right spot, and drives into me. Tipping me over the edge, explosive delicious tingles spreading through me as I cry out. So good. So good. I feel him come right after me, thrusting deep and shouting his release, shuddering in my arms against me.

And then he's sinking into me, his weight warm and soothing as we both catch our breath. Listen to our heartbeats slow.

"Damn, Teach. Every time. Fucking wreck me." He sighs heavily, kisses me sweetly, and rolls to his back. He takes me with him, keeping me close, continuing to touch me softly everywhere he can reach. "Who would have guessed, way back when you walked into my hospital room, that you would be such a sex goddess."

I laugh, snuggling into him. So happy. "Hardly."

He's got a smug smile on his face, eyes closed. "Facts."

I snort but can't help my own little smug smile.

He opens one eye, peeking down at me. "If you don't believe it, I'm happy to spend the entire day proving it to you."

My smile widens. "Prove it to me, Jax."

We spend the rest of the day in bed. Just like he promised.

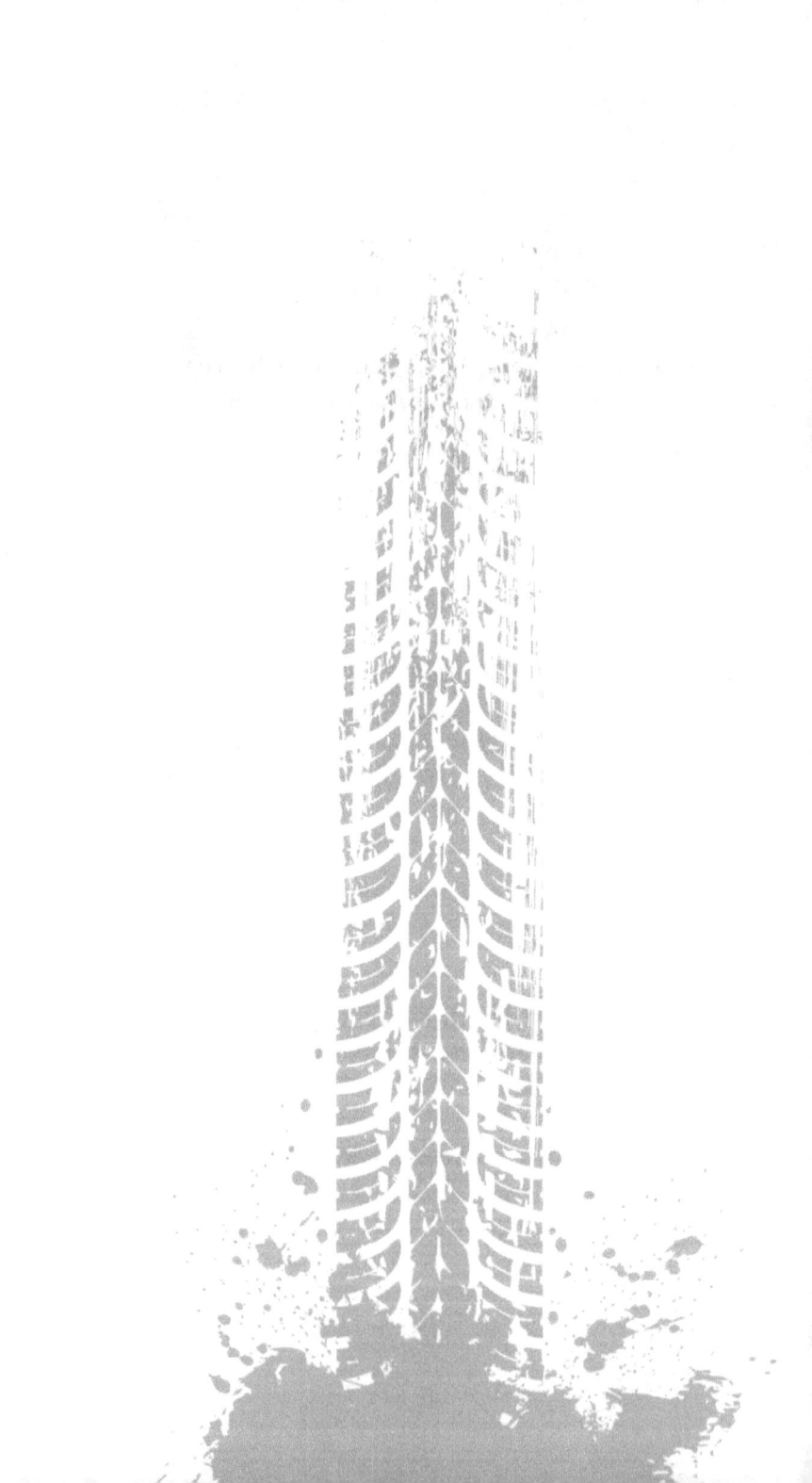

CHAPTER
Thirty-Six

Jax

Something warm and wet nudges my cheek, waking me up the following day. Pulled from sleep, I recognize Pirate's wake-up call. Who needs an alarm clock with this little shit?

I open my eyes, and his cheerful brown ones stare back at me, all up in my business. I groan and shove him off the bed.

"All right, I'm up, you needy prick." He whines at me, pacing along the foot of the bed. "Where's your owner?" I grumble, seeing the bed next to me empty.

"Right here."

I glance over and see Riley standing in the doorway, a small smile on her face. She's back in those short shorts and a loose tank top, her breasts clearly visible, and her hair is a sexy mess. My dick wakes right up, despite the workout we gave it yesterday. Pirate's not the only needy prick in the room, apparently.

"Morning, Teach." My voice is still a little hoarse with sleep, and I see her nipples tighten in reaction. I see it because I can't take my eyes off her tits; they're fucking gorgeous.

She moves forward, crossing over to me, and for the first time, I notice the coffee mugs in her hands. I grab one eagerly.

"You're perfect," I tell her, mumbling into my coffee. She laughs softly and moves between my knees, her fingers going into my hair and lightly scratching my scalp. I close my eyes in pleasure. The hand, not holding my morning caffeine fix, starts exploring the soft skin on the back of her thigh. I take advantage of her skimpy outfit and slip my fingertips into the bottom of her shorts. Finding nothing but skin, I groan, grabbing her bare butt cheek. Her breath hitches, and I bury my face between her boobs, nuzzling into her.

"I came to get you out of bed, not so you could get me back in it."

I groan again and look up at her. "My idea is so much more fun."

She taps my cheek lightly, bending down to give me a quick kiss. "Sorry, stud. But your friends are the ones having the barbecue."

"They're your friends too." It's important she knows that. She's not just an extension of Luke or me or the Abbotts. She's Riley. She's awesome.

Her eyes light up at my words, my reward, another sweet kiss.

"If you want to sleep longer, I can take Pirate out on my own."

"Nope. I'm up. I'm up," I assure her. I turn back to my coffee, gulping it down greedily. I set my empty mug down on her nightstand, taking hers and placing it down as well. I wrap my arms around her and press a kiss to her heart. "This is nice," I tell her.

Riley smiles, "What? Me bringing you coffee?"

"No. Yes. All of it. I like morning with you."

Her eyes soften, melting into me. "Me too," she whispers.

I enjoy holding her for a moment, breathing her in. Finally, I force myself to stand. "All right. Let's do this."

I press a firm kiss to her lips and head for the shower. "Give me ten minutes, and we can go to the dog park."

She follows me. "I'll give you thirty, but you have to share the shower with me…." She whips her tank over her head.

I grin. "I can handle that."

A FEW HOURS LATER, AFTER VISITING THE DOG PARK AND SWINGING BY my place so I could change clothes, we pull up to Macy's.

Pirate is in the back seat, tongue hanging out as he enjoys his outing. I scratch his ears and get him out while Riley locks up her car. I can sense her nerves which I hate, although I think I understand. This is our first 'official' appearance as a couple. Even before, when we would all hang out, it wasn't clear where Riley and I stood. I mean, I think it was clearer to my friends than it was to me. I was such an idiot. I should have known there was more to my feelings for her right from the beginning. I never would have talked to Luke about being with her if all I'd seen us being was some casual fling. I wouldn't have risked it for that.

"You good, Teach?" I ask softly, handing her Pirate's leash.

She smiles up at me and nods.

"The crew's going to be happy to see you," I say, trying to be reassuring.

"They know I'm coming?"

Shit.

I didn't think about that. I mean, Mace's backyard is an open invitation. If anything, they're going to be more excited to see Riley than me, I'm sure. But probably, she would be more comfortable if I'd told everyone ahead of time.

Knowing me as well as she does, I think she can read all my thoughts on my face. She rolls her eyes at me and pokes me in the side. "You're springing me on them?"

"They love you!" I protest. "I think they'd choose you over me in the divorce."

She rolls her eyes again and tells me, "That's never going to happen. I'm never giving up on you. On us."

"I love you, Teach."

"Love you. Let's go. I'm getting hungry."

I reach down and thread our fingers together, turning to Macy's house. "Well, come on then. Let's get you fed."

I squeeze her hand, using my free arm to open the gate to the backyard. Pirate woofs and pulls excitedly against Riley's grip. Once the gate closes behind me, she releases him, letting him run and explore.

Ash looks up from setting the picnic table and spots us crossing the yard. She greets Pirate with some doggy love, then turns her wide smile to us and calls out a welcome.

She hugs Riley warmly and then sends her off to grab a drink from the cooler.

"You called Riley," she whispers, hugging me hello.

I shake my head slightly, admitting, "I *begged* Riley."

She gives me a quick squeeze before releasing me. "Good job, you."

"Yeah." I glance at Riley, standing with Lucas and Mace near the grill, and feel my chest expand. "Best decision ever."

"So, that's it then?"

I turn back, facing Ash. "What do you mean?"

She tilts her head, watching me closely. "You and Riley?"

I nod. "Me and Riley."

Ash makes a face like this is the best news she's ever heard. "Yay!" She tucks into my side and gives me a squeeze. "I'm so happy. Can I tell Lucas? He owes me twenty bucks."

"You bet on my love life?" I can't decide if I'm offended or not. No. I'm pretty sure I am.

What the fuck?

She pauses, I think, sensing my reaction. "Kind of? He bet it would take at least another week for you to convince her to forgive you. But I thought you were ready to be very convincing."

"You guys suck," I mutter.

Riley appears at my side and slips her arm around my waist. I feel better immediately just having her next to me.

"Lucas was kind of pissed I was here," she says softly. I stiffen.

Seriously? What the fuck? Now I'm the one pissed. Seriously pissed.

Riley hands Ash a twenty-dollar bill. "From Luke." She looks up into my face, her eyes teasing. "He said I was too easy on you and should have waited until next week."

I grimace, but my body immediately relaxes. "You asshole!" I yell across the yard. Lucas and Macy burst into laughter.

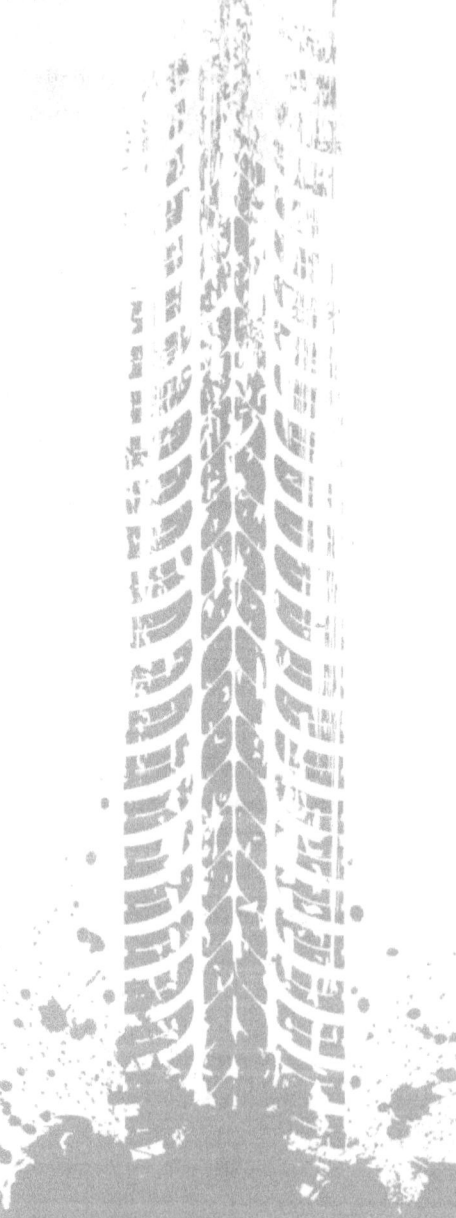

CHAPTER
Thirty-Seven

Riley

"I've got a question," Layla raises her hand at the end of Wednesday's Afternoon with Art. We only have a few sessions left before the summer break. Today we had a set designer for one of the theaters downtown which the students seemed to love. He left a few minutes ago, and now we're just wrapping up.

"Yes, Layla?"

She bites her lip and looks nervously between Jax and me. "Does this mean the two of you are back together again?"

My jaw drops in surprise, and I use all my self-control not to look at Jax standing on the other side of the room. The room is quiet except for a few muffled giggles and whispers.

Jax is the one that finally responds, breaking the silence. "Yeah. It means I stopped being stupid and managed to convince her to forgive me."

Layla turns to glare at Cory. "I told you!" He grins, and cheers erupt from the others, clapping. Someone starts chanting, 'Kiss her! Kiss her! Kiss her!' and soon, the entire class is pounding on their desks, picking up the chant. Jax looks at me and grins.

"Don't even think about it," I mutter and then try to regain control of my classroom. "All right, all right. That's enough! No one is kissing anyone."

Random groans scatter through the mob. I am sure my face is flaming at this point. Luckily it's time to wrap things up. "Okay, you nosy monsters. That's all for today. We'll see everyone next week for our last Monday session." The students grab their books and start moving out the door. I see some of them give Jax high fives or fist bumps as they pass him. I roll my eyes but am fighting a smile.

Cory stops in front of me. "Thanks, Ms. Abbott."

"For what?" I tilt my head to the side, curious.

He shuffles his feet and shrugs. "Everything, I guess. I don't know if I'll see you much over the summer, and I just wanted to say…thanks."

I squeeze his shoulder briefly. "You need anything, you let me know, okay? Anytime."

He nods and heads over to Jax, saying a few words.

"Serious? Woo!" Cory yells, grabbing his head in excitement. "Holy shit! I mean, sorry, Ms. Abbott." He looks at me guiltily.

Jax laughs and hands Cory a card, slapping him on the back. Then he turns to me, his crooked grin on full blast as he walks over.

"What was that about?" I nod after Cory.

"Well, I know he was disappointed Diego got the internship this summer." I make a small sound. Yeah, he had. But he'd taken it well and congratulated Diego. "Well, Dalvin called me the other day and said he needed some help at the gym. Someone to clean up, answer the phones, set up equipment for the classes, that kind of thing, and asked if Cory might be interested."

"Really? That's awesome." Then another thought hits me, and my enthusiasm sinks. "Do you think that's a good place for him? With the fighting and everything?"

Jax nods. "Yeah. I trust Dalvin. He'll teach Cory what he wants to know but won't pressure him into anything. It'll be a good, steady part-time job for him. And if he does want to train with Dalvin, he'll do it the right way, you know?"

I smile and squeeze his hand. "Then I'm happy."

"Anything to make you happy, Teach." He winks at me.

Laughing, I roll my eyes and nudge him toward the door. "Let's get out of here."

We head to my place to walk Pirate and figure out a plan for dinner. He pulls me close as we step inside my apartment, smiling down into my eyes. I am so happy I feel like I'm going to overflow and float away with joy. I can't remember ever feeling like this before. He loves me. He loves me as much as I love him.

It's a little embarrassing how much I smile these days, but I'm too giddy to care.

He rubs his nose against mine and gives me a slow kiss.

I pull back before either of us gets too carried away. I've got a surprise planned. My stomach flutters nervously. Jax makes a sound of displeasure when I end the kiss, but I won't be swayed.

Grinning, I tell him, "Why don't you order us some food. I'm going to change."

"Are you sure you don't need my help?" he smiles lecherously, making me laugh.

"I'm sure. Feed me."

He kisses me, squeezes my butt, and then releases me. I skip back to my bedroom to change. Into my surprise.

"How hungry are you?" he yells a few minutes later. "I'm craving Indian, but it will take at least an hour."

"That's perfect," I shout back.

When I emerge, Jax is relaxing on my couch, focused on his phone.

"Did you order?" I ask, stomach flipping, anticipating his reaction.

"Yep." He glances up, then freezes, eyes hot on my skin.

I'm wearing the blue lingerie I purchased months ago. I'm wearing that for the first time.

And nothing else.

He clears his throat, eyes still burning. "That's new."

I giggle. "Do you like it?" I turn slightly, flashing him my barely-there thong.

"Uh, yeah. I'd say that's an understatement."

Smiling, I stand between his knees, take his phone out of his hand, and place it on the table. Then I put my hands on his shoulders and straddle his lap.

"I hoped you would like it," I whisper.

His hands skim up my bare thighs, and then I feel his fingers digging into the flesh of my naked butt, squeezing, teasing. I shiver with pleasure, sweet tingles building in my core.

"Oh, I like it," he grins. He presses a kiss over my heart, then trails his tongue along the plunging neckline. "Always so soft and sweet, Teach. I fucking love it. Love you."

We kiss slowly, lazily. And then he lifts me abruptly, getting to his feet and carrying me to my bed, where he sets me down and sinks on top of me. Kissing me more. Loving me.

"I've got a word for you," he says to me, pulling away, his trademark sexy crooked grin in place.

I raise my eyebrows in surprise, watching happily as he pulls his shirt off. "Oh yeah?"

"Yep." He settles back into me, pressing against me, rolling his erection into me. I raise my knees, squeezing his hips.

"What is it?" I giggle, thrilled.

"Aeipathy."

"Aeipathy?"

"Mmmhmm. You know what it means?" he murmurs, stringing kisses along my neck.

I do. Of course, I do. Word Nerd, thy name is Riley.

He presses a soft, lingering kiss against my lips.

A fist of emotion grabs my heart and squeezes. I nod, a watery smile on my face.

"This," he says. "Us. Aeipathy."

AEIPATHY
Definition: continued love or passion

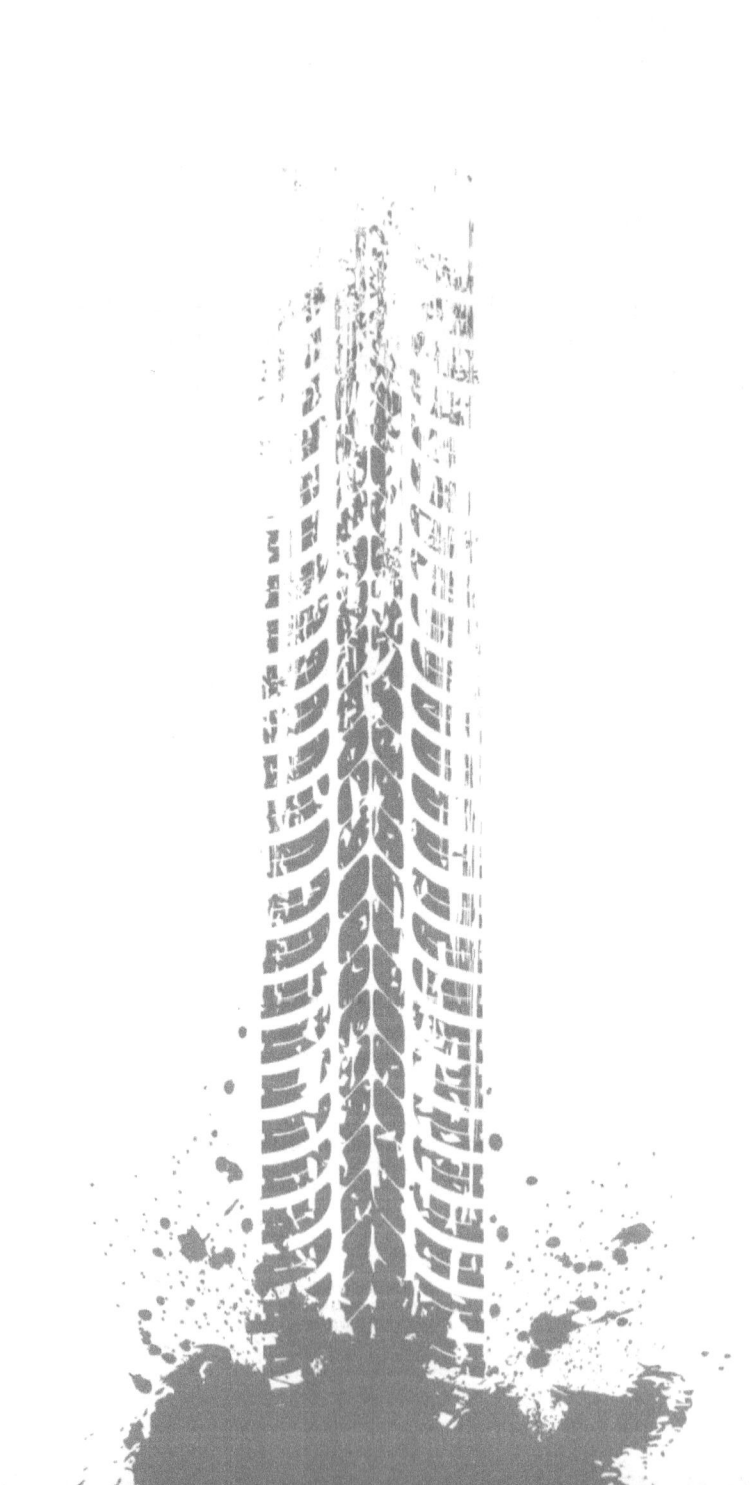

ACKNOWLEDGMENTS

A YEAR AGO TODAY I WAS ON A ROOFTOP WITH SOME AMAZING WOMEN celebrating International Women's Day. We drank and ate and shared. And for the first time, I really committed and vocalized to others that I wanted to write a book. I'd had these characters in my head for so long; this secret dream. And now, I'm writing this for my second book, with more on the way.

It's truly amazing what you can accomplish with a supportive community.

So thank you to all the women that helped this happen. My Fort Girls, my Happy Hour Girls, my mom, my publisher and friend Naja, my RY Girls, my readers. Thank you all for riding this wave with me.

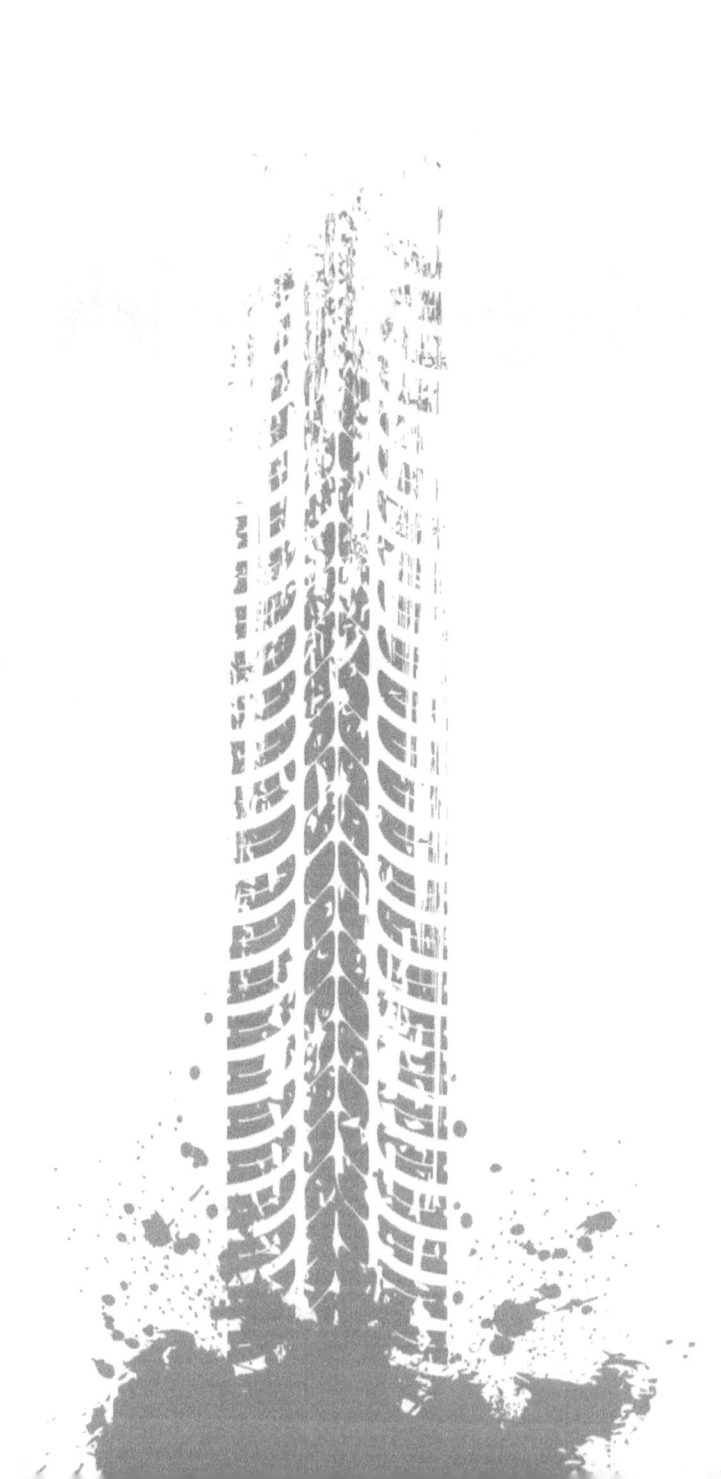

ALSO BY

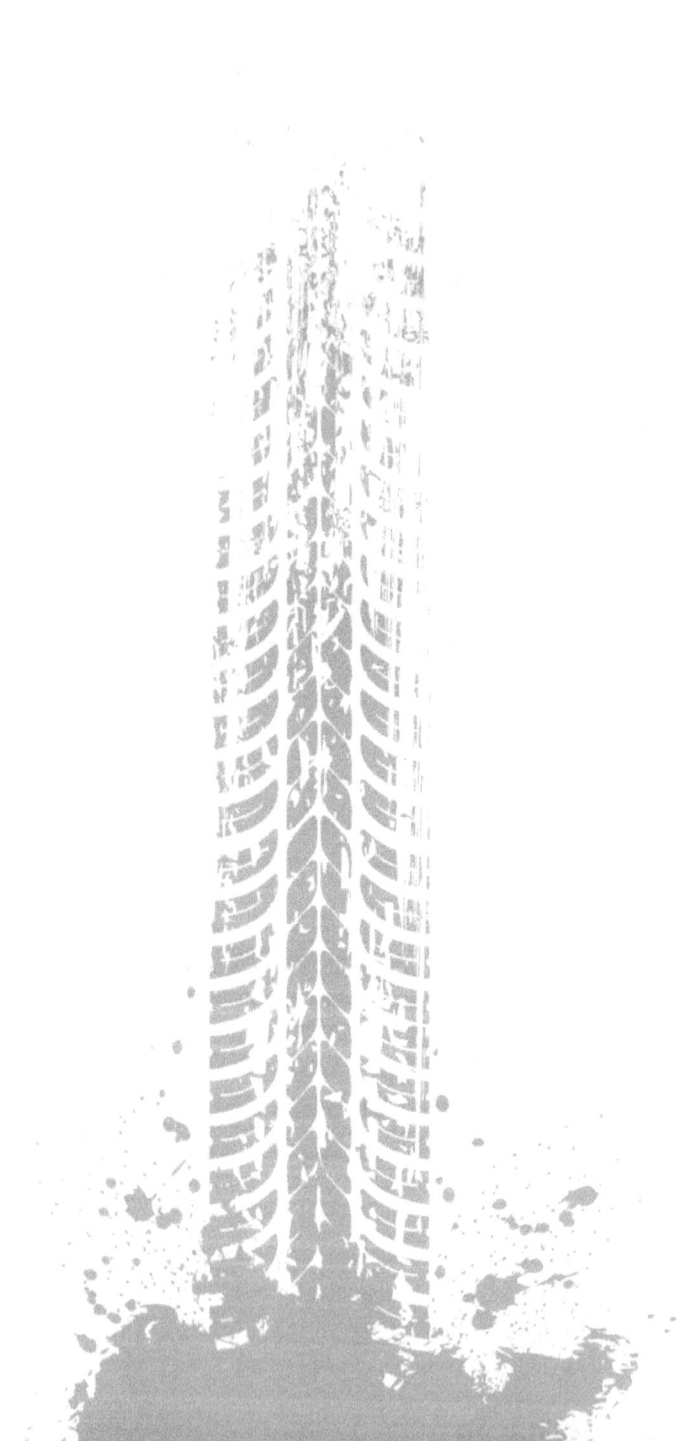

COMING SOON

Book Three–*Tattoo My Soul* follows Logan Dahl, a successful tattoo artist and reality star fighting to be taken seriously in a male-dominated field. When MVP baseball player Connor Thomas enters her life, she can't resist his charm. But as secrets from her past resurface, will she let him in and let him help her heal?

And, in Book Four, *Tattoo My Life*, Macy O'Neill thinks he's found the perfect match in his life, but tragedy turns everything upside down. Hunter has had a crush on Macy for years and can't resist the opportunity for a hot and steamy night together. But as their worlds collide and danger looms, will their passion be enough to save them both?

Don't miss out on The VANISHED Series, filled with steamy romance and heart-pounding suspense. Get the first two books in the series today!

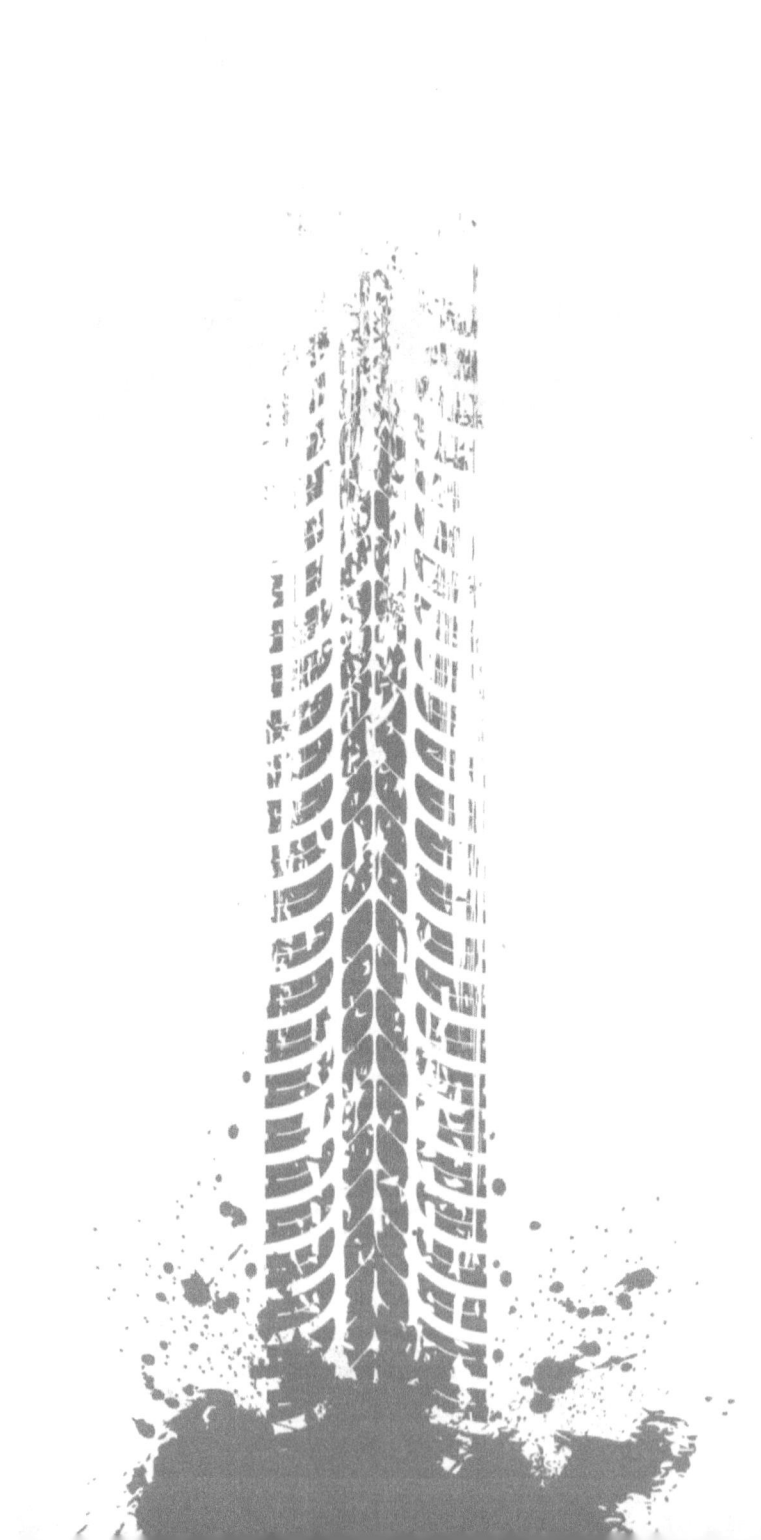

TEASER

Tattoo My Soul

Connor

I can't get into the book I'm reading. I catch myself, realizing I have no idea what has happened on the last three pages. Instead of going back again and re-reading them, I give up and toss it onto the couch next to me. Checking the time, I realize I still have forty minutes before the rest of my teammates are going to arrive.

I have too much adrenaline to sit still, ready to get started. My team has decided to get tattoos, commemorating the end of our Division Championship season. It doesn't help I'm on my own, early for our appointment due to travel schedules and thunderstorms. It didn't make sense to go home when I landed, so I came right to Vanished. Luckily, Lucas Abbott was here early and able to let me in. Otherwise, I would be sitting in my car right now, watching the storm rage.

Shifting forward, I rest my elbows on my knees and grab my phone to scroll through my unanswered texts. I respond to the ones from my brother and mom but ignore several from my ex. I wish Therese would let it go. We've been over for months. During the season, the travel was too much for her, and she found some other guy to spend her nights with. But now that I'm home and have a winning record, she wants to 'work things out'.

I don't.

My thoughts are interrupted when I hear someone yelling, "I'm here! I'm here!" the voice getting closer before the door crashes open, and a rain-drenched blond blur rushes in. Slightly stunned, I watch as she crosses to the lockers on the far wall, stripping off her soaked t-shirt as she goes, revealing a navy bra.

"Uh - Don't mind me."

She whirls at my voice, gripping her vintage band, I can't quite make out which one, shirt to her chest. "What the hell, perv?!"

I raise my hands as if surrendering. "I'm just here waiting for my appointment. Minding my own business. You're the one who ran in and started to get naked."

She glares at me - and it takes all my self-discipline to keep my eyes on her face and not allow them to slip to her hastily covered breasts. She's a mess, soaked to the skin, eye makeup running and smeared, and hair clinging to her cheeks and neck. But she's still gorgeous. I know from the few times I've watched this crew's reality show that this is Logan, currently the only female member of the team, although there are constant rumors that Lucas is looking to add new staff. So far, though, it's remained the core four.

"People usually wait out front. In the waiting area."

I shrug. "Luke told me to wait back here until the rest of the guys arrived."

She rolls her eyes but seems to loosen up a little with this information.

"You mind?" she raises her eyebrows at me and spins one finger in the air.

Belatedly I realize she's telling me to turn around, and I stand to face the wall, my back to her, giving her a tiny bit of privacy. I can't seem to help the grin on my face.

"Crazy storm, huh?" I toss out, then cringe. Am I seriously talking about the weather right now? I clearly need to work on my conversation skills and less on my fielding. But to be fair, most of the women I meet during the season aren't that interested in what I have to say, which is probably why I've been in a bit of a dry spell since Therese.

Logan doesn't respond to my witty repartee, and I shift awkwardly from foot to foot, listening to clothing rustle and things clang against the metal lockers. I'm about to make another effort to break the silence, but I hear the locker slam shut, and almost as quickly as she entered, Logan is rushing back out the door.

Well, that was… interesting.

I manage to wait five minutes before following after her.

I find Logan sitting on a high stool behind the front counter, her knees tucked against the edge and a notepad balanced on her thighs as she sketches away. I lean against the opposite side of the counter, arms resting on the top, and try to engage her in conversation.

"What are you working on?"

"Some designs for a client," she responds without looking up.

"I'm Connor, by the way."

"Welcome to Vanished, Connor. Lucas should be with you in a minute."

Apparently, Logan isn't much for small talk.

Her absorption in her work gives me a chance to study her. She's piled her blond hair into a messy bun on top of her head, the ends still damp. Streaks of blue, her signature look, intermingle with the silver-blond strands. After her quick change in the break room, she is now wearing a black Vanished tank top showing off long-toned arms and a pair of faded jeans with black chuck's. She had also managed to do some repair work on her eye makeup, wiping off the streaks. She looks both punk and artsy.

Before I can think of something else to ask her, the door behind me dings as it's pulled open, and three of my teammates and friends walk in and yell hellos. I lift my chin, acknowledging them but staying next to Logan.

"Hey, man. About ready?" Lucas comes out of the back and slaps me on the shoulder.

"Just about. Last couple should be here soon."

He grins and then heads over to greet the rest of the guys.

"Friends of yours?"

She raises her eyebrows again. I'm beginning to get she does this right before she says something snarky. Surprisingly on her, I'm finding I like snark.

I glance over my shoulder, taking in the others joking around and giving each other a hard time. Turning back, I tell her, "My teammates."

She hums non-committally and returns to drawing in her sketchbook.

I grin. "You...really have no idea who we are, do you?"

Her frustrated sigh is a sure sign I'm annoying her. And that I'm right.

She shakes her head dismissively and shrugs. "Sorry. Should I?"

I tap on the schedule on the screen in front of her. Then I click the mouse, so it's on the correct date.

She rolls her eyes at me before glancing back at the appointment list. I grin at the grimace on her face as she realizes her mistake.

"Well, that explains why Lucas was pissed I was running late," she mutters. I watch as she presses her lips together.

Now I'm starting to feel bad about giving her a hard time. This is her job, after all. And she's clearly had a rough morning considering her arrival.

Then she just shrugs again. "Sorry. Baseball isn't really my thing."

"Fair enough." I chuckle.

She goes back to ignoring me.

I should leave her alone. Go talk shit with the guys while we wait the last few minutes. But there's something about her that both intrigues and amuses me. She's so prickly for no apparent reason. I want to find out why.

"So, am I scheduled with you for the tattoo? I'll have to take my shirt off, so we'll be even."

She rolls her eyes and glances at the computer screen. "You're with Lucas."

"What if I want you to do it?"

"Sorry. Lucas is the boss." Then she hops off the stool and walks away.

I laugh out loud and turn to join the guys.

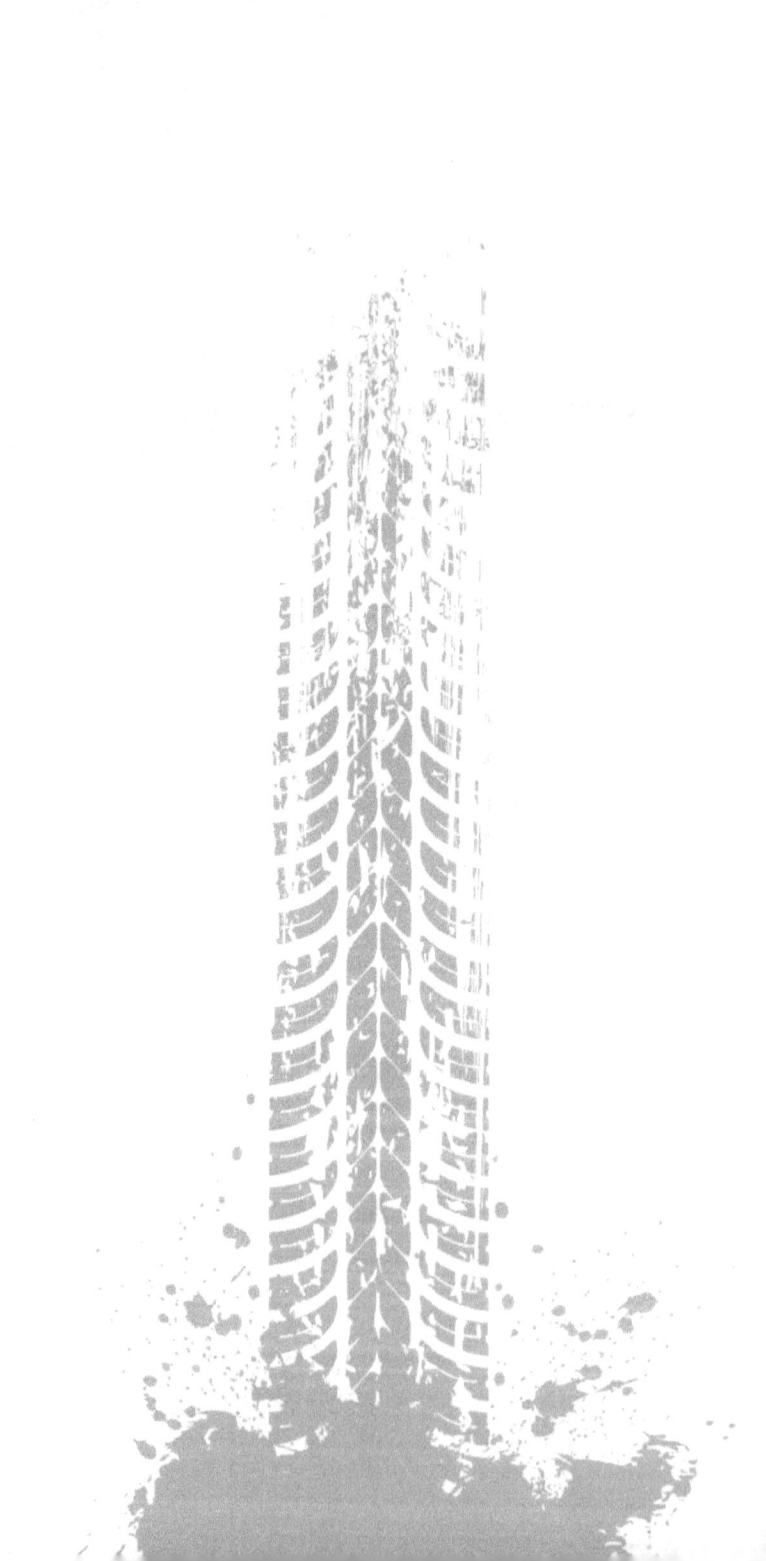